THE EMERALD
TABLET

THE EMERALD TABLET

EVE SIMPSON

Braveship

BOOKS

Aura Libertatis Spirat

THE EMERALD TABLET
Copyright © 2019 by Eve Simpson

Braveship Books
www.braveshipbooks.com
Aura Libertatis Spirat

Book layout by Alexandru Diaconescu
www.steadfast-typesetting.eu

ISBN-13: 978-1-64062-073-5
Printed in the United States of America

For Tom,
Michelle and Johnny

ACKNOWLEDGEMENTS

For their undying patience, steadfastness and candid input, I would like to express my sincere gratitude to my husband Tom and my daughter Michelle. I appreciate Tom's technical expertise, especially on nuclear matters, his willingness to entertain speculative questions and his help in brainstorming what could have happened. The novel came to fruition thanks to Michelle's all out encouragement, dedication and candor as an early reader and front-line editor. I would like to thank my son Jonathan for his artistic contribution and Peter Greene of the Adventure Writer's Competition for his kindness, friendship and creative talent in producing the initial cover artwork. I would also like to express my appreciation to military thriller author, Jeff Edwards, for his invaluable feedback, helpful suggestions, and cover artwork.

CONTENTS

PROLOGUE

331 - 323 B.C.
At the Head of the Persian Gulf

The sky was bathed in an early morning's purplish hue when the silhouette of a solitary horseman materialized at the crest of a distant hill. His sudden appearance was unnerving, like an elusive specter emerging from the shimmering mist of dust trail drifting across the hard-baked earth.

The well-proportioned horseman rode with utmost confidence, his long wavy hair sweeping back in unison with the mane of his powerful black stallion. The sun's glint on his polished bronze breastplate provided the sole clue to his identity. It brandished an intricate carving of the snake-haired gorgon Medusa.

The warrior turned towards the rising sun, surveying the landscape through eerily captivating eyes. His right iris was a scintillating shade of blue; his left was blacker than the night sky. The target in his sight was Charax, the walled Persian fortress on the arid delta below.

"Easy Bucephalas," he whispered. He leaned forward to stroke the powerful steed and gently he ran his hands up the crest of the beast's neck.

He chuckled to himself, recognizing that burning ambition was the impelling motive of his life. What he saw, he had to have. He acknowledged that hubris was frequently at the root of his more audacious actions.

The Persian stronghold was positioned strategically by the edge of a deep-water port at the meeting point of the estuaries of the Tigris in the west, and the Eulaeus and the Pasitigras in the east. The bastion had easy access to the sea and was blessed with a supply of fresh water. It was approachable only by a narrow strip of shore formed from the alluvial deposits brought down by rivers. It was clear to him that whoever controlled Charax would control the trade of the Persian Gulf and the Indian Ocean.

"Shall I organize a scouting party to assess the fortifications?" The question came from a deep baritone voice of the young king's favorite bodyguard. With his ebony hair and cunning olive black eyes, he was as dark as the young king was ruddy and fair.

The king shook his head.

The two men were like brothers. Ptolemy was the son of an adventurer and a cast-off concubine of the former king, Philip of Macedon. Both had been trained in the art of war by Philip's most skilled veterans. They had drilled together in archery, swordplay and horsemanship. As young boys they had liked nothing better than pounding across the turf on the Macedonian plain, riding like the wind and vanquishing imaginary kingdoms. In Greece, they had been tutored by Aristotle in medicine, botany, zoology, politics and philosophy.

At the age of twenty, the handsome royal had inherited Macedonia, a kingdom beleaguered with jealousy and bitter hatred. In the scant number of years since his father's death, driven by ambition, he had proven himself a great leader capable of daring and bold campaigns, skillful military strategy, and distinguished diplomacy.

The young king swept his gaze back to the limestone ridge where his military forces were encamped. He caught sight of the Hetairoi, his cavalry armed with heavy thrusting spears and in the distance, the Pezhetairoi, his infantry. An omnipotent sensation of being in command of a huge military force suddenly filled his veins.

"No, I prefer that just the two of us descend. If my intelligence is accurate, Charax offers more than just potential as an emporium for crucial imports and exports. My source reports it holds not only gold but a priceless talisman from the period before the Great Flood."

The disciplined Macedonian forces had won glory in earlier battles, but not the vast amounts of gold the king had hoped for. The young royal would be the first to admit that his opponent, King Darius of Persia, had been devious when he moved the bulk of his treasury to Charax prior to the last attack.

A grin appeared on Ptolemy's face and he let out a deep laugh. He was unsurprised. The king had an unquenchable thirst for espionage.

The young king gestured to Ptolemy to come alongside, "Draw near to me. What is your assessment?"

Shielding his eyes from the sun's early hour rays, Ptolemy leaned forward and craned his neck towards the fortifications below. "I can discern a single entrance protected by a sentry tower. The Persian palace occupies the northern terrace. It appears to include a royal residence, an assembly hall and a treasury. My guess is that at this hour they shall have posted but one guard."

The young king nodded in agreement. He valued his Ptolemy's input.

"Timing and stealth are critical. We must move quickly while the Persians are still sleeping. The morning mist will provide a degree of cover for scouting. Our mission is to identify a weakness in the fortifications where a breach would be possible. I intend the full military assault to begin just before sunset."

Twenty minutes later, after furtively making their way down the yawning ravine, the pair reached the plain. They quickly dismounted and disappeared into in the wooded area fringing the delta. Melding in to the morning shadows, they furtively crept over to the periphery of the citadel.

A scant distance above the Macedonians the lone Persian guard perched in the tower had his sight locked on the distance. He failed to detect the presence of the intruders who clung to the wall like moss on a tree.

The defensive fortifications surrounding Charax were constructed of sun-dried mud bricks placed on a stone foundation. For an extra measure of security an extensive palisade of wooden stakes had been driven into the brick to create an encircling protective wall of twelve feet around the town.

The two men tiptoed along beneath the lookout, methodically seeking a breach point. Whether by luck or by chance, with a keen eye for reading the terrain Alexander spotted what he was seeking.

"There," Alexander announced, gesturing towards a parched streambed.

The gulch would have swept swollen into the fortress in winter, but during this season it was all but bone dry. The undulation in terrain caused where the stream flowed under the palisade had carved out an opening. It was just sufficient for a man to squeeze beneath the palisade and enter the fortress un-detected.

Ptolemy tilted his head and stared quizzically in the direction his king was pointing. Instantly he grasped the plan and nodded his agreement.

"Our mission here is complete," Alexander hissed.

Within the space of an hour after scouting, Alexander of Macedon stood on the limestone ridge briefing his generals about his plan for an engagement. The cunning assault strategy was a ruse that relied on simplicity and natural curiosity. It exploited the enemy's vulnerability. His genius in unconventional warfare and his insight into human psychology were clearly evident.

At half past three in the afternoon, the Macedonian army descended in procession to the plain from the ridge. On the arid delta, a scant fifty yards from the entry gate to the Persian fortress, the forces drew up into arranged phalanxes.

On signal, the Macedonian infantry wheeled out a colorful military tattoo the likes of which the Persians had never before seen. The infantrymen of the powerful Pezhetairoi marched in tight phalanxes, their formations more than a hundred lines deep. Each soldier shouldered a five-and-a-half meter long sarissa spear equipped with a sharp, leaf-shaped iron head and a bronze butt-spike that could be fixed into the ground to halt charges by enemy soldiers. They stepped in unison and with honed precision each warrior swung a sarissa first to the front, then to the right, then to the left. The steady, synchronized cadence of their movements was commanding. They looked like a single rhythmic body.

From the palisade walls the Persians watched spellbound at the impressive display of coordination by the Macedonian military tattoo. They cheered excitedly when the troops wheeled off in perfect formation into practiced intricate drill patterns.

Their exuberance was cut short. Nothing prepared the Persian onlookers for the orchestration that brought the exhibition to conclusion. In the flash of an eye, the marching units drew up into a formidable wedge-shaped phalanx formation. As if by magic, the Macedonian forces were now in position, a menacing body aimed straight at the gate of Charax.

An inaudible command signaled the Pezhetairoi. In unison, with incredible dexterity and timing, each Macedonian infantryman raised his sarissa skyward. The expanse of long spears turned upward looked like a forest had suddenly sprung from the ground in front of Charax.

The bait set, the trap was sprung. A sudden shrill, visceral *war cry erupted, its wavering pitch resounding from the escarpment,* "Alalala! Alalala!"

The gut-wrenching shout aroused the thumos of the Macedonian forces, igniting their passion and emblazing them with fearlessness. The sound of hooves pounded the air like thunder when the Macedonian military machinery charged towards the barricaded gate. Gone was the quiet plain where the intricate military display occurred. In its place was boiling sea of action.

The barbaric war whoop achieved the desired effect. Caught off guard by the full-blown aggressive assault at their entrance gate, the Persians were oblivious to the infiltration about to take place at the rear of their palisade.

With the diversion underway, Alexander led his unit of mounted special forces on a clandestine mission at the rear of the fortress. According to plan, the Hetairoi dismounted beside the dry streambed, got down on their hands and knees and crawled through the dry riverbed to the breach point. They squeezed commando-style under the palisade, undetected. Once inside they attacked and killed the unsuspecting Persian sentries.

With the main entrance gate of Charax no longer protected, the covert Macedonian unit lifted the huge wooden bar securing the high wooden entrance doors and opened the front gates. Within moments the bloodthirsty Macedonian force spewed through from outside like an unstoppable tide, rampaging and killing the inhabitants. No one was safe from their swords and spears.

The Persians fought back savagely, but they were no match for Alexander's forces. The grueling battle went on for hours with unbelievable ferocity. One by one, Charax's warriors fell in the vicious onslaught that left their streets crimson in torrents of blood.

Darius, the Persian king stood galvanized in horror watching the decimation. The death toll was clearly mounting; the ground was littered with dead and dying. Less than an hour of daylight remained. Darius realized his troops could not hold back the Macedonian army. His men would be lucky if some of them managed to escape. He issued a single guttural command. At the sound of the horn signaling retreat, the Persian warriors abandoned their families and made for the forests in the distance where they could hide and regroup.

By the time the mayhem subsided the sky was awash in rich tie-dyed twilight colors. The mournful sounds of captive women wailing in hopelessness at the loss of their husbands echoed throughout Charax.

Alexander ordered his men to round up all of the survivors. He felt a sense of inner pride and honor at his victory, despite the fact that the Persian king had managed to escape. King Darius had abandoned his royal family; they were now amongst the hostages.

With the flamboyancy for which he was already famous, Alexander of Macedonia made a theatrical display of mounting the flagstone steps to the throne of Persia. At the first landing the high priest bowed to him and in heavily accented Greek, greeted the young king with words that to Alexander sounded like *O pai dios.*

The priest's greeting, which recognized the Macedonian king as part deity, a child of the god Zeus, was like music to his ears. He never paused to consider that the high priest might actually have said *O paidos*, O my child, and had simply mispronounced the Greek.

The priest's phrase played to the young king's narcissism. It was well known that Alexander contended to be semi-divine, the love child of the god Zeus and his mother, Queen Olympias.

Spurred on by the words, with true showmanship Alexander took his place on the opulent carved and gold inlaid Persian throne. Once seated, he proclaimed to all those assembled in the throne room, "History is written by conquerors and I am the conqueror!"

Installed on the Persian throne, beneath a golden canopy in a room filled with golden decorations, Alexander of Macedon looked invincible. He had fulfilled a dream. After four years of brutal conquest, battling Persian armies and sacking cities, he now occupied the Persian throne and at last had a treasury with sufficient gold and silver bullion and minted daric coins to fund his campaign.

True to his diplomatic policy of reconciliation, Alexander treated the vanquished with respect, as free allies. He demonstrated true compassion for the Persian King's elderly mother, wife, and children. He stretched his arms forward to the elderly woman and raised her from the temple floor, addressing her as "mother". He assured the family that Darius was still alive, and that Alexander meant no harm to his royal family. They would be hostages, but their lives would be spared, and they would live comfortably.

There was a definite practicality to the benevolence Alexander showed the Persian royal family. He recognized that he would have a power base by protecting them. The Persians would now see him in a symbolic role, the son and protector of the Persian King's mother.

****

Among those in attendance in the throne room was an incredibly beautiful woman, Barsine, a friend from Alexander's youth. During her childhood her father had sought sanctuary with Philip, the Macedonian king. She had lived the life of a refugee in the Macedonian court. In that period of her life Barsine had been a constant companion of Alexander and his friends. There was not a thing the boys could do that she could not.

There was a time when the young Macedonian king had seemed attracted to Barsine with her exquisite smoky gray eyes and strikingly beautiful facial features, but that was long ago before she was betrothed to some distant royal.

"Barsine!" Alexander thundered, "It's a great pleasure to see you again." He strode over to her and made a public show of taking Barsine's hand.

"It's been a very long time," he said with a wry smile and a melting glow in his eyes. "I've have been wondering what became of you."

Barsine is most definitely a beautiful woman, the young king thought. *Her slim, graceful figure, smooth olive skin, and shimmering dark hair are very appealing.*

Leaning closely to her face, Alexander breathed words into her ear, "Your time amongst the Persians has been invaluable my love."

The throne room held plentiful riches but to Alexander, Barsine, his friend of long ago, was one of the most valuable of all. He was confident that she would help him acquire the sacred treasure hidden within Charax.

****

No one found it unusual that the Macedonian king summoned Barsine to his bed chamber, least of all Ptolemy, for she was a beautiful woman and his friend a conqueror. What the king's bodyguard did not know was that Barsine had long been an undercover emissary for the Macedonians, her marriage to her late husband Memnon of Rhodes, an arranged diplomatic union. She was Alexander's source.

Alexander's eyes traveled over Barsine's firm body, admiring her smooth skin and high cheek bones that set off her smoky gray eyes. His muscles tightened at the sight of her.

She smiled back at the king. She found him particularly handsome with his straight nose, prominent forehead and set lips. She saw the look in his eyes and thought she knew what he was thinking.

"You missed me," she said.

He laughed. Ever the rogue, he leaned forward and drew her towards him, "I did. You are most perceptive. Now do justice to that quality I so admire in you and take me to the treasure."

"You have interesting priorities," Barsine replied coyly.

Later that evening she reached out for his hand and led the way through corridors on a circuitous path beneath Charax. She took him into to the depths of the stronghold, under the inner sanctuary of the temple. The light from the taper she carried wavered, casting dancing shadows on the stone walls.

Alexander followed through the dimly illuminated passageway. In the darkness his senses were heightened. He became hyper-attentive, attune to the visual, auditory, and thermal stimuli. At one point, he could have sworn that he heard an almost inaudible burble, like the sound of running water.

Abruptly Barsine stopped. She pulled Alexander to one side, into a nook in the passage. She placed her finger over his lips.

"Over there," she whispered, pointing past the alcove, towards in a tiny, semi-hidden stream.

Alexander moved in for a closer look at the glowing object. In the dim light the flash of color from a cool green emerald caught his eye. He could discern carved letters on the hard green surface.

"Phoenician, perhaps?" he hypothesized, looking at the writing on the stone.

"From what I have gleaned, it is a gift to man from the Egyptian god Hermes. The talisman is said to represent the sum of all knowledge. It is believed that those who study it acquire the capacity to travel in both heaven and earth," Barsine reported.

"A gift from the god of learning, science, and mathematics," Alexander mused, pondering the possibilities. His heart swelled with excitement at the prospects of studying the tablet.

He had to have it. He reached towards it.

"No! You must not touch it!"

Stunned that Barsine would issue an order to him, her king, Alexander shot her a menacing look.

"The tablet was entrusted to the high priest with the proviso that it must always remain in water." The tone in Barsine's voice expressed alarm.

Alexander's scowl quickly melted. Barsine could be trusted, he acknowledged to himself. She had reacted out of genuine concern.

****

Time marched on. In his search for glory and fame, Alexander led his forces across thousands of miles over deserts, mountains and jungles. His expedition explored and conquered lands that no other Westerner had dared to dream about. By the age of thirty he had amassed an empire that stretched from Greece, across Persia, to northern India. Ambition drove him, but for the sake of his exhausted troops, he made the decision to return home.

News of the homecoming of the Macedonian forces was met with excitement. In the ancient city of Babylon, the inhabitants wanted to pay homage to the charismatic leader whose inexhaustible energy, and courage had earned him the reputation of greatest military leader of all time. They planned a huge celebration and invited envoys from Rome and foreign lands, ambassadors from Africa, and tribal representatives to attend their festivities to honor Alexander the Great.

Alexander was less than excited about the planned festivities for despite the success he had achieved in his expedition, he was overcome with remorse over the extent of losses on the journey back from India. He could not keep himself from thinking about the thousands of men who had been lost when they succumbed to sickness, heatstroke, and thirst.

Trudging westward along the dusty path to the ancient city of Babylon, Alexander's entourage encountered a group of Chaldean priests who had come to impart a dire warning.

"Great leader, it is unsafe for you to venture in to Babylon," cautioned the elderly spokesperson for the Chaldeans. "The oracle at the temple of Bel-Marduk has given prophesy."

"The best prophet is one who guesses well," Alexander laughed with a shrug, quoting from the Greek playwright Euripides.

Like a true leader, he brushed the warning off. He had absolutely no intention of letting his mask down in public. Nonetheless, to the superstitious Macedonian, the prophesy was both disconcerting and dispiriting.

Truth be told, Alexander's self-assured response hid a tsunami of personal feelings. He had seen so many disturbing incidents in the past few weeks that he had honestly began to wonder if he might fall victim to his own credo that it was preferable to live a short life of glory rather than a long one in obscurity.

His dark mood lifted when he drew closer to Charax. The shimmering scene was like a sign from the gods. The long golden rays of the sun cascading down to the water's edge, glistening like a star, elated him.

With his enthusiasm growing, Alexander decreed, "We must commemorate this vision by establishing a new town with a harbor. The point at which the sun's rays transect the shoreline will become a booming international metropolis. The town shall be named Alexandria in Susiana."

Here, on this waterfront, he commissioned to be built yet another city of Alexandria to add to the dozen or so he had already commissioned on his expedition. He issued an order for the lines of the new town, Alexandria in Susiana, to be drawn out immediately. He wanted to define broad streets, a market area, and dockyards. With his characteristic impetuosity, Alexander did not wait for chalk to be delivered. Instead, he seized a sack of barley and with outstretched arms trickled the grain to outline the town.

Suddenly, a murder of crows rose in frenzy from the marshes and headed for the rows of grain that Alexander had just laid out. The sky overhead was filled with so many dark shapes that the bright sunlight dimmed, blotted by a horrific dark cloud. Rhythmic flapping of wings, horrendous squawking and frantic screeching claxoned the pandemonium. Famished black birds zigzagged and dove about, pecking mercilessly at one another in a feeding frenzy. Dead crows fell from the sky like giant pellets of hail in a storm, their carcasses littering the ground.

A flood of negative thoughts raced through Alexander's tormented mind when several of the dark shapes landed at his feet. He wondered if this was a warning. Were the portends of the Chaldeans accurate?

Aristander, the king's his favorite soothsayer, saw his leader's anxiety. He shrewdly offered an alternative interpretation, "The feasting birds are but a divine portent indicating that Alexandria will be prosperous and will nourish the nations of the earth."

Alexander nodded and with growing confidence ordered chalk to be delivered. When it arrived, he renewed his efforts to sketch out the boundaries of the latest Alexandria. In addition to his initial design, he added shrines to commemorate the divine prediction. Mercurial as ever, he hastily rushed off to Charax, before the layout was complete.

In his heart, Alexander was convinced that if he could just hold the talisman he would be closer to the gods. He ignored the welcoming crowd assembled at the gates of Charax. Anxious to find the high priest who was entrusted with the safekeeping of the tablet, he vaulted two steps at a time up the huge stone steps of the palace complex.

It was clear that the high priest had been expecting the returning conqueror. The elderly ecclesiastic materialized from behind the stone columns beside the stairway. He ducked out just long enough to be visible to Alexander. Raising a fingertip and without saying a word the priest beckoned him to follow.

Alexander nodded curtly and immediately obliged. He fell in behind the high priest's rhythmically swaying silk robe and trailed him to the passageway. The two figures filed down the corridor into the dark, dank recesses below the temple.

It was not until Alexander heard the primordial resonance of water flowing deep under the earth that the king knew they had arrived at the location of the ancient tablet.

"Magnificent."

Alexander looked down at the little stream mesmerized by the burning fire he saw in the green crystalline of the tablet. He took a deep calming breath and, forgetting or ignoring Barsine's previous warning, he reached forward to withdraw the sacred tablet from the water.

The elderly priest became distraught. Vehemently shaking his head from side to side in apprehension and tugging at the king's tunic, he called out, "Nah! Nah!"

Alexander took absolutely no notice of the elderly priest's protests. He dragged the Emerald Tablet out from the water and strode purposefully through the corridors to the main temple. He longed to experience the magic and wisdom of the beautiful relic. He was convinced he felt the presence of the gods burning within him.

The magic however did not last. The ill omens predicted by the Chaldean priests persisted. That evening, when Alexander ordered divine sacrifices to be performed to satisfy the gods, one of the animals sacrificed was found to have a malformed liver. It was an ominous sign. A wave of sadness washed over the king. Hastily he left Charax with Barsine at his side and headed for Babylon.

Ptolemy suggested a party in the palace at Babylon to cast off his king's gloominess.

Never one to drink heavily, Alexander surprised his group of friends by downing a huge cup of unmixed wine, in a single gulp. He shrieked in pain when the liquid hit his stomach. It felt like his liver had been pierced by an arrow.

Alexander's friends encouraged him to keep drinking to dull the pain. Stoically, he ignored his aching belly and drank more and more, hoping to dull the ferocity of the pain. He kept drinking well late into the night, until vomiting and suffering from chills, he was led home by his drinking companions.

****

"Ptolemy, please fetch the king's personal physician. I fear for Alexander's health," Barsine ordered. She was distraught by the condition she saw her lover in.

Alexander's health had indeed deteriorated. He lay on his cot in Nebuchad-nezzar's ancient palace in Babylon writhing from severe abdominal pain. He was experiencing extreme thirst, high fever and hallucinations. His feet tingled, and paralysis had set in. Ignoring Barsine's protests he clutched the Emerald Tablet and prayed that the gods would give him the energy to continue his expeditions.

For several days, he attempted to ignore his fever. Despite suffering from extreme headache, burning fever and chills, he insisted on continuing his daily rituals and carrying out his military duties. He was determined to maintain normalcy. He gave orders to his generals concerning preparations for his next expedition.

By the tenth day Alexander's breathing became more and more shallow. He was too weak to utter a word. Rumors began to circulate that he was dead. To dispel the myth of his demise, he ordered that his troops file past. Every soldier walked by his bed and Alexander greeted each with a smile or a nod of his head. His followers were shocked. They could hardly believe that their mighty leader who had outwitted death at every turn on the battlefield was about to pass on.

Bedridden by a raging fever and with his pain growing ever more intense, Alexander ordered Barsine to summon his eldest general to his side. When he arrived, the conqueror removed his royal signet ring and passed it to the general. He asked him to serve as temporary regent.

"Who shall be your successor?" the elderly general asked.

"The strongest," the king answered between spasms of coughing and with those words the 32-year-old conqueror slipped away.

The news of the great king's passing caused Macedonians and natives alike to weep, but not so his generals. They became so caught up in fighting about who should be the new leader, that they unceremoniously left his corpse in a storeroom.

Oddly, when the generals finally held the state funeral, Alexander's body, which ought to have begun to decompose in the scorching Babylonian weather, remained preserved, even after six days in the heat. When the Chaldeans and Egyptians arrived to embalm the king's body, there was no sign of decay.

Throughout the centuries suspicions have abounded about the circumstances of Alexander's death. Did he succumb to disease? Was it Malaria, Typhoid, Smallpox or West Nile contracted from dead birds? Perhaps he was murdered, poisoned by bacterium-ridden water or toxin laced wine? What if the lack of decomposition of his body is proof that the real cause of Alexander the Great's death can be found elsewhere?

Part One

CHAPTER 1

September 2, 1998
New England Coast, USA

A traveler sat alone by a window at a table set for three. He peered out at the world through silver rimless glasses, watching globetrotters from all walks of life scurry along the long corridor to gates, while others consulted monitors to identify the gate for the next leg of their journey.

He might have been an accountant or a financier. In his tailored navy business suit, white shirt and tie, he had the confident manner of a professional accustomed to traveling. At six feet, he was relatively tall with broad shoulders. His conservatively cut wheat colored hair was slightly graying at the temples. Few would have guessed that he was a leading expert in nuclear research.

Dr. Michael Morris had selected this airport restaurant, not for the quality of the food but for its location. It was an easy rendezvous point, a spot where flight crews grabbed a bite before boarding flights to faraway places. The restaurant was one of a popular chain. The meals were passable, and the location offered a good view of the action out on the tarmac.

His cell phone chimed quietly. He looked down at the number calling and his brow furrowed. He flicked the device open and replied, "Yes?"

A tall, fit young man who bore more than a passing resemblance to the traveler waved and approached the table. The university student's tousled wheat colored hair gave him an attractive, casual look.

The elder man was speaking into the phone. He waved at the student, ended the call, and flipped the cell phone shut.

The young man greeted his uncle with undisguised warmth, "How great is it that we're both headed to Switzerland? It's been awhile since I've been back. I hope that call wasn't Maya canceling. I'm looking forward to her joining us for dinner."

"Christopher, that call was indeed from Maya. She sends her apologies. Duty calls; the hospital is short-staffed. She suggested dinner up the coast on our return," Dr. Morris replied.

Disappointment was apparent in his nephew's gray-blue eyes, "I was hoping to talk to her about how my doctoral thesis is moving along. My trip to Macedonia was immensely productive."

A server arrived to take their orders. Neither of the two travelers wanted anything heavy before the flight so they ordered from the sandwich and salad menu.

"So, Uncle Mike, I hear that you're to be the guest speaker at a conference in Geneva. What is your presentation about?"

Dr. Morris' reply was choked out when the sudden unpleasant sound of a restaurant patron reprimanding a server pierced the restaurant drone. The guilty party, a tall bulky business man, with a mix of Greek and Slavic features and a haughty attitude could be heard shouting, "I ordered rare. Do you call this rare, it isn't even pink? Take it back!"

For a few beats a quiet sense of tension descended on the restaurant. Embarrassed for the server, patrons stared for half a moment before quickly glancing away and looking down at their meals.

Dr. Morris took a quick glance in the direction of the fracas. Much to his dismay he recognized the offender. Guardedly he said, "I would have expected better behavior from him, but then again the Macedonian had always been rather full of himself when I've seen and heard him speak at conferences."

Dr. Morris grimaced. *I hope that he is not going to Geneva. His narcissistic approach has a tendency to put a damper on knowledge transfer. He is a formidable scientist, but the way that he puts other conference participants down is unacceptable.*

Christopher wasn't put off by the melee, "I'm anxious to tell you about my expedition. Let's head over to our gate. I can run through the photos with you during our flight."

On the way to their departure gate they walked past a large security poster that reminded travelers of John F. Kennedy airport's strict carry-on bag restrictions. Instinctively, Dr. Morris' right hand reached into his pant pocket and patted a small device. He quickly realized that there was every likelihood that his flash drive would be non-compliant with these new security restrictions.

"For backup, I put my presentation speech and notes for the conference on my flash drive. It's a new device, a present that your mother gave me. I realize now that having it with me is possibly not the best plan," he said pulling a red Swiss Army knife from his pant pocket.

"Oh, I've got one just like that. Mom gave it to me to remind me of my Swiss connection," Christopher retrieved a matching red knife from his backpack.

"Well, that poster warns that this airport has recently implemented new security measures. Pocket knives are specifically cited as articles no longer accepted in carry-on. Our dual function devices, Swiss pocket knife and flash drive, will probably be considered weapons," his facial expression revealed how he felt about the restriction.

Christopher was quick to find a solution, "Look, there's a US Post office over there. Let's mail the flash drives to ourselves rather than have them taken from us. It will only take a couple of minutes and then we shouldn't lose them."

"Excellent idea," Dr. Morris replied.

After mailing their pocket knives the two men proceeded along the moving escalator to the long security lines shielding entry to the departure gates. Like their fellow passengers, they performed the customary drill, removing shoes and belt and placing them in the gray storage bins with their laptops, cell phones, loose change and watches. Without the USB knives Dr. Morris and his nephew easily passed through security.

At gate B-18 they found seats by the large windows overlooking the tarmac. From this vantage point they could see air traffic taking off and landing. Flight 111 was in front of them being refueled and taking on food and drink. Below, on the tarmac in the aircraft service area the ground crew was starting to load luggage onto the McDonnell Douglas MD-11.

Christopher watched the ground action with interest. His curiosity was piqued by a member of the ground crew carrying a pack. He saw the man move stealthily under the belly of the plane. His fluid movements were in contrast to those of the other ground crew whose actions appeared more stop-start and defined. Christopher lost sight of what he mentally termed "the odd one" when the crewmember moved around behind the giant wheels of the plane.

While his nephew was eyeing the outside action, Dr. Morris, a self-acknowledged people watcher, had been panning the waiting area. The New York–Geneva flight was nicknamed the "UN shuttle" because it frequently transported staff between United Nations headquarters on the two continents. He recognized several of the passengers, made eye contact with them and gave a nod of acknowledgement.

Seated alone, by the far window, was a nuclear physicist known for his genius, love of music, and talent. In another row Dr. Morris spotted a renowned scientist, famous for his work on using radiation to treat brain cancer. Farther along, closer to the departure desk, he saw a former toxicologist who had pioneered lead poisoning research at an Ohio Medical School.

When the boarding was announced the experienced travelers dutifully queued in the last line in which they would ever need to wait. When their row numbers were called, all 215 travelers dutifully filed past the Swiss Cabin Crew, dressed impeccably in their navy blue uniforms accented with deep blue scarves.

CHAPTER 2

The late summer evening was calm and warm, perfect weather for a transatlantic flight. In the cockpit the crew settled in for what they hoped would be an uneventful flight to Geneva.

By any standard the flight crew was experienced. The captain, who was just shy of his fiftieth birthday, was a tall Swiss with a substantial moustache, a veteran pilot and a seasoned flight instructor. He was looking forward to spending the weekend with his children. His quiet spoken copilot, in his mid-thirties, was also a seasoned pilot, with 2,100 flying hours under his belt. The younger pilot had joined the airline a good twenty years after the captain and had been flying this particular jetliner for just under a year. They worked well as a team and enjoyed flying together. On this flight they had decided that the younger pilot would fly the plane for the majority of the flight home.

While the copilot prepared for the flight, the captain reviewed the flight manifest with interest. The document showed that the plane was headed to Cointrin International Airport in Geneva and on it would be 229 passengers, 14 crewmembers and a number of treasures. The captain's attention was piqued when he read that the cargo section would hold a crate holding a piece of art valued at $1.5 million, called Le Peintre by the famed Spanish master Pablo Picasso. In addition, in amongst the plane's general cargo of textiles and computer and automotive parts would be a strongbox holding 4.8 kilograms of banknotes, one kilogram of diamonds, two kilograms of watches and 4.8 kilograms of other jewelry.

A cabin crew of a dozen looked after the passengers while the aircrew communicated with the air traffic control tower and prepared for flight with documents supplied by flight dispatchers. The pilot and copilot concluded their risk analysis and calculated the amount of fuel they required.

During the initial climb after takeoff, the deck angle ranged from 12 to 20 degrees while the jetliner climbed to flight level. The intent was to fly at 33,000 feet for most of the transatlantic trip.

The muffled drone of the three Pratt and Whitney engines proclaimed that the plane had reached flying altitude. A flight attendant announced that electronics could be used in the cabin, only when sending and receiving functions were disabled.

****

"I'm anxious to hear more about your research expedition in Macedonia, Christopher," Dr. Morris said, turning to look at his nephew.

"Uncle Mike, it's quite the story. For my doctorate I wanted to follow-up on leads I had uncovered about Alexander the Great, so I traveled to Egypt, Macedonia and Greece."

"Much has been written about Alexander's expedition from Macedonia to Egypt and Asia and his death," Dr. Morris commented.

"Yes, but in contrast there is little clear evidence about his tomb and the fate of his remains," Christopher replied.

Dr. Morris could literally feel his nephew's enthusiasm for his research.

Christopher's face fairly beamed, "Alexander's death in 323 BC in Babylon, is well documented. It's also shrouded in mystery. The Greek historian Plutarch reported that even after the King's body had lain in a coffin for six days it was not subject to decay and didn't even have the slightest discoloration. Some say that this was proof of his divine ancestry."

"Interesting. That's unusual," Dr. Morris said, intrigued.

"To this day the whereabouts of Alexander's final resting place has perplexed scholars. In 1977 a discovery of three royal tombs was made in a mound at Vergine Macedonia, by Professor Andronikos. One of the tombs had been pillaged but the other two were lucky enough to have escaped damage. In Tomb II held the skeletal remains of a male. It has long been theorized that this was the tomb of King Phillip II. In Athens I met an ex-military man, a researcher, who felt that it was not King Philip who is buried there. Instead, he is convinced that the tomb is the final resting place of Alexander the Great. He asked me to help him prove this, so I accompanied him to the site."

"So, why does the military man think it might be Alexander?" Dr. Morris asked.

"His conjecture rests on artifacts found in the tomb. Here, let me show you my slides."

Christopher opened his laptop and pulled up a file.

"Amongst the artifacts is a gold-plated collar decorated with rosettes. See those four big circles? One has a young man riding a horse, holding his right hand high and clutching what looks to be a wreath. That's Alexander on his favorite mount, Bucephalus. Then, on the bas-relief of the collar you can see two little images of the head of a clean-shaven young man with a well-formed mouth with full lips, and a noble nose, who very strongly resembles Alexander the Great."

"But you don't think its Alexander's tomb?" Dr. Morris asked.

"I'm not convinced. However, I found something there that really interested me, and it led me on another trajectory. There was a frieze painted over the entranceway in the tomb. That painting bears quite a resemblance to the famous mosaic that was uncovered in Italy, during the excavations at Pompeii."

"How can that be? Isn't the one in Pompeii Roman?" Dr. Morris queried.

"Yes, it is. That's why it piqued my curiosity. The artwork was from different centuries. I saw something special in the frieze. I knew I had to compare it to the mosaic in Pompeii. I took photos of the Macedonian frieze in the tomb and I went off to Italy to compare it with the mosaic in the National Archaeological Museum in Naples, Italy, where artifacts from the catastrophic eruption of Mount Vesuvius in 79 AD are displayed. Watch, I'll bring them up on the screen so you can see," the youthful academic searched through his computer files, came across the images and opened them for his uncle.

Indeed, the pieces of artwork really did seem quite similar despite the differences in their vintage. The principle dissimilarity Dr. Morris noted was in the palate of colors selected.

"The Macedonian frieze is far more than what meets the eye. It led me on adventure of sorts, into the mountains of Macedonia."

"A Macedonian frieze led you on an adventure?"

"Well yes, the frieze along with some research about the artist who painted it sent me trekking. I became interested in a particular mosaic of Alexander that was commissioned by Olympias, Alexander's mother, following the death of her son. See this photo of it," Christopher said gesturing to a new image on the screen.

Dr. Morris looked down at the image on the laptop. The mosaic in the photo was bordered by a gold colored fret. Inside the fret was yet another close up scene of Alexander in battle riding a magnificent steed.

"So, what is special about this particular mosaic?" Dr. Morris asked.

"It holds the key to finding a long-lost relic from Alexander's time. The artifact was once housed in the Great Library in Alexandria. Ancient Alexandria has long since disappeared and no one seems to know what became of the relic. Several expeditions have attempted to find it but up until now there hasn't been any trace."

Dr. Morris looked at him incredulously.

"Until now. So, you think you know where to find it?"

Christopher nodded.

"That's spectacular! Your mother will be excited about your findings. She has really made some significant academic contributions to historical and archeological research. Her work is second to none. You're definitely cut from the same stone. Pardon my pun," Dr. Morris chuckled.

"Definitely, I want to discuss the find with her. That's part of the reason for my trip to Switzerland. My advisor at Columbia suggested that my mother might have some background research that would have a bearing on how I proceed. Mom's also had dealings with the Ministry of Antiquities." He sighed. "You have to admit that it is rather disconcerting when your mother is so well known in the academic world."

"That she is," he said thinking of his sister-in-law Hélène. She always seemed so formidable. He admired Professor Jullian even if she was prim, academic, and driven. He understood why her marriage to his easygoing twin brother, Matthew, had ended. His brother had lost out to her career.

"My goodness but you have been having an exciting time."

Just when Dr. Morris was about to question Christopher about the unusual artifact he had found, a flight announcement from the captain interrupted their discussion. The seatbelt light came on and passengers were requested to return to their seats and ensure that their tray tables were in the upright position.

CHAPTER 3

回回回回回回回回回回回回回回回回

Two hours into the transatlantic flight there was trouble in the cockpit.

"What's that smell?" asked the captain, sniffing an acrid and not easily identifiable odor. His mustache crinkled, "It sure smells unpleasant."

"It could be coming from the air conditioning system. Maybe someone left the meals in heating too long and they have burnt. Ask them to close the vent and see if that improves things," suggested the copilot who was at the controls.

"Would the Purser please close the vent to the cockpit?"

Initially the smell seemed to subside, but within a few minutes it returned with a vengeance. Trails of gray smoke began to appear. The captain quickly ran through the emergency checklist for air conditioning smoke.

"Call it through! The smoke must be coming from a fire in the air conditioning system," the captain ordered.

Running his fingers through his dark curly hair, the copilot followed the command. He calmly radioed through a distress call to the air traffic control center handling transatlantic aircraft departing North American airspace.

"PAN! PAN! PAN! We have smoke in the cockpit. Request diversion to Logan Airport in Boston!"

A Canadian air traffic controller was quick to reply, "Logan is 300 nautical miles. Suggest a vector to Halifax Airport, just 66 nautical miles from your current location. You'll be off the coast in about 15 miles and then you'll be within 35 to 40 miles of the airport if you must get there quickly."

Moments later the copilot radioed "We are declaring an emergency at time zero one two four."

Halifax Airport was an unknown to both Swiss pilots, but it made sense to head there. It had the distinct advantage of being closer, though the pilots would need landing charts. The captain asked the chief flight attendant to bring the charts forward and to announce the diversion to the passengers.

The cockpit filled with thick caustic smelling smoke. To avoid inhalation the pilots donned their oxygen masks. The copilot-initiated procedures to divert towards the Canadian airport.

"We'll need to jettison fuel. The jet is too high and heavy to make a direct approach on the Halifax runway," the copilot announced to the air traffic controller.

"I recommend we dump the fuel here and now and head directly to the airport to land," the captain said, revealing his concern that heading over to the sea would waste precious minutes.

"Swissair One Eleven, you're cleared to ten thousand feet," a Canadian controller radioed.

"So, we can go lower and use a steep approach for an emergency landing," the copilot.

"No, don't, it is better not to descend too quickly," the captain said firmly.

"Okay, you are my superior, I've slowed the jet's rate of descent to 3,100 feet per minute from 4,000 feet per minute," the copilot said.

The crackle of flames was clearly audible behind the firewall. If action were not taken immediately to quench the fire, the firewall was not likely to last long enough to matter. The atmosphere was electric.

"What is your preference for jettisoning fuel?" the copilot asked, his tone showing deference to his superior.

"Don't bother me! I'm going through the checklist," the captain responded brusquely, his respiration rapidly increasing to 25 breaths per minute.

In contrast, the copilot's breathing rate was a moderate 11 breaths per minute. The younger man at the controls could generally handle whatever was thrown at him, without any increase to his stress level.

Back in the dimly lit belly of the aircraft the oxygen masks dropped automatically. Passengers fumbled to place the air masks over their faces, following instructions from the cabin crew. The air felt thick with anxiety; breathing was labored. The victims braced themselves against the seats in front of them.

The incessant drone of the aircraft amplified the stress. Soft crying sounds were abbreviated by whimpering. Repetitious prayers rose from the seats. Stoically the group of seasoned travelers put their trust in God and the skills of the highly trained Swiss pilots who had made it home so many times before.

Dr. Morris reached over for his nephew's hand and took it in his, "No need to worry. These Swiss pilots are some of the best in the world. They are highly trained. They'll get us through this."

In the cockpit the drama grew more tense. When to jettison fuel was the question. Should they discard fuel immediately or wait awhile. Jettisoned fuel might splatter people and property below, but if the smoke got too thick the pilot would be able to land more quickly without its weight.

"Are you able to take a turn back to the south, or do you want to stay closer to the airport?" the Canadian controller asked. He knew it would be environmentally safer to turn back and dump over the sea, but the decision was up to the pilots.

"OK, we have the go-ahead for a left or right turn toward the south to dump," the copilot replied.

"Bear left, south towards the sea. I'll advise you when you're over the water. It should be shortly."

"Roger," the copilot replied calmly.

Below the aircraft impenetrable gray fog rolled in. Visibility became poorer and poorer. The crackling and spitting of flames intensified. Inside the cabin waves of dark smoke billowed in. Suddenly none of the gauges and indicators supplied readings.

In an even tone, the copilot alerted the air traffic controller that the plane had just descended 7,000 feet in ten seconds, "We must fly the plane manually now. We have lost all instrumentation. We are heavy and declaring emergency."

"Roger. You are cleared to start the fuel dump," the controller replied.

"Roger. We have commenced dumping. We must land immediately," the copilot warned.

In the tower the air traffic controller sat grim-faced on the edge of his seat and listened helplessly. He heard the noise of what he assumed was the captain leaving his seat.

"I'm going to try and extinguish the flames. Ease up on the throttle. Keep a comfortable distance between the underbelly and the Atlantic!" the captain ordered over the crackling sounds of flames licking at the back of his seat.

The fire propagated. A blaze shot out from all of the combustible materials. The foam, the plastic clips securing bundles of wires, and the acoustical insulation all acted like kindling stoking the fire.

The air traffic controller thought he heard the sound of the fire extinguisher being unlatched, followed by the hiss of foam being sprayed on surfaces in the cockpit.

Tiny beads of sweat rolled from the copilot's brow. He devoted his full concentration to the risky job of flying the crippled plane. Cruising at such low altitude along an unfamiliar coastline was challenging. Great wisps of fog floated past the windscreen blocking his sight path and smoke kept creeping in at the edges of his oxygen mask. Undaunted, he kept his eyes glued straight ahead.

Through the fog the copilot sensed and almost felt the great swells, trough following crest in an endless roll. Lives depended on his skill as a pilot. Just one twitch from a wily air current and a wing tip might hit the crest of a wave and propel the plane to summersault into oblivion.

Flying low, the copilot knew he must jettison fuel but retain enough to make it to Halifax. He shut down engine two and reduced the speed to barely 350 mph. Shrouds of melted ceiling began to fall all around him. He ignored the searing pain when a scorching piece dropped onto his skin. He did his utmost to try and fly the plane without instrument power. Then, when it seemed the situation could not get much worse, a blast ripped through the cockpit.

The captain, who was still at the rear of the cockpit fighting flames, was thrust into the air by the blast. His body catapulted into the copilot's back then it hurdled towards the windscreen.

A wingtip dipped and collided with the crest of a wave. In the tiny community of Blandford on the South Shore of Nova Scotia, a deep rumble resonated ominously through the buildings before a violent bang like an abbreviated clap of thunder rocked the shoreline. The force of the impact sprayed debris over two kilometers.

Part Two

ISOTOPE CRISIS

CHAPTER 4

The Present Day
Upper Ottawa Valley
Canada

Maya knew that not just anyone would have been granted access to this site, let alone this private office, but she was no stranger here. Her eyes swept out over the forested campus to the towering granite cliffs encircling it. Once this landscape had echoed with the robust songs of coureurs des bois, fur traders, loggers, woodsmen, and native peoples paddling and trekking through the dense mixed wood forest. She contemplated how things had changed with time.

The nuclear site neatly tucked away on the Ottawa River, in the Laurentian Hills, two hours from the capital, was where the worst nuclear leak in Canadian history occurred. Rated at Level 5 on the International Nuclear and Radiological Event Scale, the leak was on par with the Three Mile Island incident in Pennsylvania. Until quite recently this site with its red brick laboratory buildings had produced the majority of the world's supply of critical medical isotopes used in diagnosis and treatment of life-threatening diseases, like cancer.

One might have assumed Maya was a researcher. She was clad in a white lab coat that hid her hourglass figure. Her shoulder length, lush black dark hair tumbled in gentle curls framing her attractive Latina features and creamy bronze complexion. Despite the garb, she wasn't there as a researcher. She was on campus to gather up the books and mementos that had belonged to her recently deceased Uncle Matthew. It was little enough she could do for the man who had provided her with ample family support after her only parent, his twin brother, had perished on a flight to Switzerland so many years before.

That's the last box.

She felt a tear begin to well in the corner of her dark almond shaped eyes. She tried to force her thoughts away from visions of the plane tragedy at Peggy's

Cove. She thought back to the times, after her mother's death, when she had been allowed to visit her father in this very building and do her homework in his office. Those days seemed so far away. Now her dad and his twin brother, both nuclear scientists who had worked at Chalk River, had passed on.

Her uncle's recent death by cardiac arrest had been totally unexpected. His passing had caused Maya to reassess her situation. Since her father's death she had been working as a medical doctor in New York. Now, she was back in Canada primarily because her uncle had bequeathed her his home in Ottawa. His gift had led her to the giant step of applying for a position in pediatrics at an Ottawa hospital. She had been offered a position, but the administrative process of an American trained doctor coming to Canada would not be quick. She was left with time on her hands.

Maya let out a deep sigh. Her gaze shifted from the packed cardboard boxes to the glass partition that separated her uncle's office from the corridor. She couldn't help but notice a handsome stranger in his early thirties go whizzing by with such speed that his lab coat unfurled like a fluttering flag.

Their eyes met. He smiled a contagious smile and gave her a nod.

I wonder why he's in such a great hurry?

Maya wished he had stopped. She would not have minded talking with someone her age, at least for a moment or two, to help lift her spirits. So far, the only people she had spoken with were all bookish older gentlemen that worked in adjacent offices, researchers who had known her uncle well and were also experiencing his loss.

****

Marc McLaren, the young man in the lab coat, was late for an agreed-upon pick-up time with his chum and working associate. Normally he was quite punctual, but he had been delayed by a meeting that went longer than anticipated. He was concerned about whether he and his chum would have sufficient time for some rock climbing before driving back to Ottawa. He had been looking forward to the outing; climbing would be a welcome diversion after this stage of his work.

McLaren's tanned face and sun streaked chestnut hair confirmed that he spent a great deal of time outdoors. At six feet three inches, he had an athletic build with broad shoulders and muscles developed by alpine ski racing and climbing. To his friends he was an adventurer and a jack of all trades. His employer called him his 'go-to' man. He was employed by CANDO, Canadians Assisting Nuclear Dilemmas Oversees, a non-governmental association that helped a variety of international bodies in finding solutions to nuclear problems. It was with CANDO that he had acquired the international reputation of first-class nuclear engineer.

McLaren had recently been called in for vessel inspection at Chalk River. Now, he was anxious to get out into the sunshine to clear his head and exchange the metallic smell that had assailed his nostrils during his work and replace it with the fresh smell of the outdoors. His inspection of the vessel had detected no changes in the vessel wall, no detectable corrosion and no problems on the welds. It was an excellent sign for the integrity of the aging nuclear reactor. He would be able to report positively on the outcome of his inspection when he gave his report in Europe.

It was a relief. The poor old reactor had been the subject of much bad press in recent years when shutdowns resulted in a worldwide shortage of radioactive isotopes. For five decades, the aging reactor had chugged along with the only update a vessel replacement. A shutdown in 2006 had precipitated a shortage of medical isotopes. That was the beginning. When the reactor suddenly shutdown in 2009, due to a power outage, a heavy water leak was discovered. The problem was the result of corrosion on the outside base of one of the reactor's vessels. The telltale sign of pin holes revealed the presence of corrosion on the inner walls; corrosion that some scientists had predicted was now quite visible. There was no alternative but to undergo a lengthy shut down for maintenance. That's when worldwide attention became riveted on the aging nuclear reactor.

It had taken more than fifteen months of repair activities before the reactor was finally restarted. During that time another aging nuclear reactor in the Netherlands went down. With only five old large nuclear reactors in the world to make medical isotopes and two shut down, an international crisis in supply of medical isotopes developed.

That crisis sparked concern in the International Nuclear Safety Agency. Added to this initial concern was the failure of the cooling pumps at the reactor in Fukushima *Daiichi* where an earthquake and tsunami had resulted in a catastrophe at the nuclear site. Now, regular monitoring of the reactor was a must. CANDO had been brought on board to for an overall assessment of progress. McLaren was the lead on this project and would be reporting in Geneva.

****

Sam Sorrento ran his fingers through his kinky black hair, mulling over thoughts about the heightened security measures now in place at Chalk River. He viewed the changes as a travesty. At the first gate the officers had taken his beloved camera, 'Maggie', complete with her long telephoto lens, and they had confiscated his cell phone. By chance today he was not armed. That was lucky for Sam because the guards would have relieved him of his weapon and that would have necessitated a ream of paperwork.

Sam had chosen to wait at the second gate. If he had wanted to enter the laboratory his CANDO credentials would have been sufficient, but he felt no need. He knew his buddy Marc McLaren would be out shortly.

Sam's choice of wheels for the climbing outing today, a Jeep Grand Cherokee SRT8, was well suited to him. Like Sam, the Jeep was black and could never be considered slow or reserved. It was a rock crusher that could bob and weave with finesse, rather like Sam did on an alpine slalom course. The Jeep was the love of his life. He'd kept it longer than any girlfriend he'd ever had.

Sam looked down at his wristwatch. He mentally checked the load of gear he had brought for rappelling and smiled. Security had not removed it from his Jeep. He considered that oversight an error on their part. He was ex-military and that kind of experience had taught him plenty. He would not have let anyone onto the nuclear site with this gear.

Half a second later Sam glanced up and caught sight of his buddy bounding down the stairs two at a time. He flashed a grin that showed teeth so white and perfect that one might have mistaken them for veneers.

"Thanks for the lift, Sam." McLaren jumped into the Jeep.

"No problemo," Sam replied jovially.

A lengthy lineup at the main gate meant that the duo lost precious time while retrieving their belongings. Sam was relieved to get 'Maggie' back in his hands. She was one of the tools of his trade. Even while on the CANDO payroll he often freelanced as a landscape photographer. His artistic expression was highly praised in cultural circles. Few realized that his creative gift was often a cover. Today, however, Maggie accompanied him for artistic fun. While they were rappelling, he hoped to grab some panoramic shots of the Ottawa River Valley. The outing would be a quick break before McLaren and Sam set off for

Geneva where McLaren would report to INSA on progress at the Chalk River site.

****

"Let's move it out. We only have so much daylight." McLaren was eager to take advantage of the warm early spring day.

In contrast to the traffic at the main gate the main highway back to Ottawa was deserted. Sam booted out the V-8 hemi in the direction of the cliff side viewpoint he had spotted earlier. He'd identified that it had potential for both rappelling and capturing dramatic shots of the river.

Sam hugged the corners making his way eastward along Highway 17. In less than eight minutes he pulled over and parked the Jeep deep at the back of a lay-by lined with scrub pine. With Maggie slung over his shoulder he walked over to the railing where the land dropped away. He climbed over and panned the blue vista to take a full series of shots leaving his buddy to remove climbing gear from the Jeep.

Shielding his eyes from the sun, McLaren gazed at the view, taking in the surroundings and anticipating the rappelling route they would take. There was still some ice and snow left on the rock cropping that would add to the pleasure. His vantage point afforded a deep appreciation of the height of the escarpment. Below the valley lay spread out, a reminder of how ten thousand years ago the weight of the glaciers depressed the land and allowed the salt water of the Great Champlain Sea to extend up into the valley. When the ancient glaciers receded, they carved out the Ottawa River.

A searing screech of tires suddenly shattered the peaceful serenity of the forested hills. McLaren and Sam pivoted in unison in the direction of the sound to see the drama folding. Unwittingly the pair had become witnesses to an unnerving game of cat and mouse.

A black SUV was toying in the most aggressive manner with a helpless Honda Civic. Repeatedly the macho American vehicle nudged the small Japanese car from the rear, letting it get ahead and then rushing at from behind.

Eyes glued on the highway in front of her, the young woman at the wheel of the silver Honda tried desperately to accelerate and outrun the black Suburban, but the powerful SUV kept pummeling her car. She fought desperately to retain control, gripping the steering wheel with all her might. She was so intently focused on the asphalt ahead that she failed to notice her attacker barreling down on her for one last vicious attack.

The bang which resounded when the SUV slammed full force into the Honda was brutally loud. The assault hit the rear of the Japanese vehicle, smashing through the passenger side tail lights, and crumpling the tailgate. The savage blow shoved the car sideways on a leftward trajectory into the oncoming lane. At that instant the lane was clear. A collision with the guardrail protecting the far lane from the escarpment seemed imminent, but before reaching the metal guard the Honda's tires hit the shoulder.

The change in road surface from hard pavement to lose gravel jolted the vehicle in another direction. Spinning at an awkward angle tail-on and then head-on, the car twirled until it hit the rock cropping abutting the east lane. The little car did not stop there. Like a rubber ducky thrown by a toddler, it flew back, end over end across the road until it hit the flimsy guardrail.

The impact sheared off the protective metal rail and thrust the railing down the embankment. With nothing to restrain it, the Honda careened over the edge of the escarpment, dropping like a rollercoaster down the steep shale slope. One minute the silver car was on the highway and the next minute it was gone. All that remained was a shadow from the black SUV, speeding off, never stopping to see the damage it had inflicted.

Sam, who had been capturing the deadly game on camera, quickly turned his telephoto lens towards the predator and snapped a shot of the license plate.

McLaren sprinted along the gravel shoulder that ran along the edge of the escarpment. He punched 911 into his cell while he ran but his call did not go through. There were no cell towers. He stared over the edge and scanned the area at the point where the Honda had disappeared. Below he could just make out its silvery shape teetering in a tangle of tree branches.

By some miracle, the car had come to rest wedged in the upper branches of an old oak. Tires spinning, it dangled in the light breeze. Steam spewed from its engine and drifted slowly to the top of the escarpment.

McLaren's mind went into overdrive, "Sam! Bring the Jeep over here. There's no time to lose. We'll need to do a hasty rappel to get down to the car!"

Sam knew exactly what McLaren had in mind. He fully accepted that McLaren was the kind of guy who took on the toughest challenges, often putting the himself and Sam, in danger to help a stranger. For his part, Sam had total confidence that each situation warranted the risk.

Sam quickly pulled the Jeep over to the edge and lined it up so that the recovery point on the right side of the front bumper would be a secure anchor point.

Without wasting a second, McLaren grabbed the gear from the Jeep and made the attachments to the Jeep's tow hook. From the pile of climbing equipment, he chose a favorite pair of goatskin transition gloves that would provide him with the dexterity he'd need in the operation ahead. He took a spare length of single static climbing rope and secured it to his waistband. He stood at the lip of the escarpment prepared to make his descent.

"On rappel!"

"Belayer," Sam replied, confirming that he was ready and paying attention.

McLaren placed the climbing rope across his back and positioned himself slightly sideways from the Jeep's anchor point. Methodically, using his left hand to guide him, he walked sideways down the rock while letting the rope go through his gloved hands and across his back. He quickly established his rhythm. His movements were, catlike, smooth and fluid, all signs of an experienced climber.

The valley was ominously quiet except for the soft rustling sound of withered oak leaves that had neglected to fall during the autumn or winter. A cold dampness wafted up from the rock face where remnants of winter ice still clung. The limestone surface was scratchy and rough and furnished adequate friction for the rock shoes McLaren had on.

McLaren saw the vehicle perched precariously 70 feet below the roadway. The car's descent into oblivion had been halted when it became snarled in the hefty upper reaches of an old oak tree. The branches had caused the vehicle to decelerate when it dropped. They had been an effective brake and had cushioned the blow.

When McLaren drew closer he noticed that the driver's door was pushed in. The glass in the driver's side window was completely gone and the engine compartment was pointing downward. The Honda looked for all the world like a grand scale teeter totter see-sawing at knife point.

A low-pitched sound drew his attention. He quickly brought his brake hand forward and locked the climbing rope so that he could move in towards it. Tree branches blocked his way, hindering his view. Carefully he pried them back so that he could peek through the driver's window. He could not get in close to the window because placing any extra weight on the branches was likely to set the Honda tumbling.

"Hi there. Are you all right?"

Another soft sound of distress was the only reply. On instinct, McLaren reached as far as he could through the broken glass to gently touch the victim's shoulder.

"Hello there," he said in a clam reassuring voice.

The victim, a dark haired young woman turned her head in the direction of the voice. Her eyes fluttered open. She thought she saw a tanned face with a strong jaw line.

With gentleness and a smile that could bolster courage even in the roughest predicament McLaren asked, "What's your name?"

She replied in a faltering voice, "Maya, Maya Morris."

Her attractive oval face was marred by blood from a wound on her right temple. Her brown eyes glistened with tears that ran down her smooth cheeks.

"I'm Marc McLaren. I saw the accident. My buddy and I would like to try to get you out of there. First, I'll need to ask you some questions. Are you okay with that?"

Maya did her best to attempt regain her composure. When she nodded, she grimaced. The movement had increased her level of pain.

"Maya, please try not to move," McLaren advised.

Maya quickly noted that this man was no stranger to victim assessment. His very presence helped put her somewhat at ease. Through a pulsating headache, she responded with precise medical terminology to the series of questions McLaren posed in his primary victim assessment.

McLaren quickly identified that the victim had suffered a head injury. He observed that there were no identifiable symptoms of a spinal injury accompanying the head wound. Her responses and choice of words caught him a little off guard. She responded using precise medical terminology.

Maya let her eyes drift over the face of her rescuer while he posed questions. He was certainly handsome. His face was tanned, with well-defined cheekbones and an aquiline nose. His wavy, chestnut hair was combed back, except for an unruly lock that tumbled forward. When he reached up to tuck it out of his field of vision, she noticed his eyes. They were a scintillating shade of deep cobalt blue, a shade that made her heart beat just a little bit faster.

McLaren turned his head skyward and signaled to Sam to attach his climbing rope to the alternate D ring and make his descent. Moments later Sam was by his side.

"Heck of a place to land!" Sam said.

"Maya has suffered a head wound. She needs to get to a hospital. I'm thinking we could deploy the penetrating chair that you use for taking photos while climbing. If we attach it to the winch line hook on the Jeep, then we could lift her into it once we extract her."

Sam surveyed the scene and noted the precarious situation of the car. "There's a chance we'll destabilize it when we try to get her out."

"Excellent observation! The driver's door is so badly pushed in that it's not worth trying to get it open. Just pulling it open might create an overturning moment. I suggest we brace the car to the upper branches before we try and get her out. I'll need you to get underneath it and tie off carefully to the thickest branches," McLaren replied.

Sam flashed a pearly white grin, "Why does your plan not surprise me?" He was all too familiar with the stunts his buddy could and would do for others.

It might have seemed crazy, but Sam accepted the risk. Perhaps it was because he became accustomed to danger when he was a Special Forces officer. Then there was the fact that they had a shared history. McLaren had been at his side during a number of military operations. He had the utmost confidence in his friend's ingenuity and ability.

"The passenger window will serve as our extraction route," McLaren said decisively.

Sam simply nodded.

The two men carefully inched forward. The Honda teetered above while they ducked underneath it and secured it to the thickest branches. They had not quite finished tying off the suspension struts when they heard a telltale cracking sound.

Sam heard the ominous sound of branches breaking. He felt his gut tighten.

****

McLaren grinned when thankfully nothing gave way.

Sam winked and finished fastening his final knot, "Okay, that ought to hold it while I get the chair. Give me a second. I'll be right back."

Leaving McLaren teetering on the end of his climbing rope, Sam pulled back up the escarpment. He lost little time making the ascent up to the Jeep where he quickly lowered the penetrating chair and rappelled back down to the tied-off wreck. His movements demonstrated the lightness of a skilled climber.

"We'll need to move simultaneously to keep things balanced. Sam, I need you to take the driver's side and reach in and unlock the passenger side while I work from passenger side."

"Got it!" Sam nodded. He moved closer to the driver's door.

"Excuse me miss," Sam said on approaching the door.

Inside the Honda Maya drifted in and out of consciousness, lapsing between fragmented dreams which intertwined with reality. Groggily she looked to her left and was shocked to perceive a dark-skinned arm reaching in through the smashed window to the power window switch. She turned her gaze upward from the arm searching for a face. The eyes that greeted her gaze were so blue they looked like sapphires burning bright. Her would-be rescuer was now a handsome African American whose movie star good looks were set off by remarkable eyes.

How can that be? Am I dreaming? The man I just spoke to was white.

"Hi, I'm Sam Sorrento. Earlier you met my buddy McLaren, over there. We've worked out a plan to get you out of here. If you're okay with it miss, McLaren intends to pull you towards the passenger side and take you out of the car through the window. To do that I'm here to help you get your legs out from under the steering wheel and around the stick shift."

Maya's brain registered that the quiet voice addressing her emanated from a rugged face framed by a rebellious cloud of ebony curls.

Sam's gaze met Maya's, "Can you work with me on this?"

She saw his bright blue eyes smiling and encouraging her spirit. She pushed herself to reply, "Yes, I'll try."

"Good. I'm going to reach in now to unlatch your seatbelt. Are you okay to lean towards the passenger side?" Sam asked.

Maya looked puzzled.

"We can't risk trying to open the door with those branches in the way," Sam explained.

Maya murmured, "Okay."

From the other side of the car McLaren called out, "Sam, I'll need you to maneuver Maya's legs over the gear shift. When I get her out I'm going to want to place her right in the penetrating chair, just in case things begin to shift."

Maya turned her head to the right at the sound of the second voice.

Oh! It makes sense now. There are two of them.

McLaren gave Maya a reassuring smile.

"Ready Maya? I'm going to drag you towards me," McLaren announced. Gingerly he began to pull gently on Maya's arms and shoulders. He sincerely hoped that he was not hurting her.

"Excuse my touch, but I have to reposition you," Sam said with respect.

Sam did his best to gently move Maya so that McLaren could get her out. There were some tense moments, like when an almost imperceptible crack heralded an ear-splitting snap.

"Careful!" McLaren shouted.

The ominous sound sent a tingle up Sam's back. He responded, "Ma mama didn't raise no dummy!"

Another ear-splitting snap was the precursor to a severe jolt.

Sam experienced a sudden weightless feeling in the pit of his stomach. The sensation was akin to riding in an elevator while it dropped downwards in a free fall to the next storey. The jolt repositioned the car. It took on a defiant slant, like the angle of a diver about to execute a high dive. Sam's heart beat a tick or two faster. There was nothing to do but anticipate the plunge. He glanced over at his buddy to see how he was faring.

McLaren clenched his pearly whites and sucked in his breath, waiting. He noted that a trickle of gasoline was dripping slowly from the smashed tank. With a gnawing sense of dread McLaren recognized that the risk level in moving Maya had increased a notch or two.

****

"Mighty close!" Sam's crooked grin showed his relief that the ropes were still holding. For a brief instant, he had wondered if the jig was up.

"Let's hope there isn't an encore. I'm not ready for a wild ride." McLaren calmly renewed his efforts to painstakingly pull Maya out of the window.

Despite some tense moments, with his friend's capable assistance, the balancing act of Sam and McLaren met with a degree of success. They had Maya out of the vehicle.

Once out, McLaren secured her into the penetrating chair and jerry-rigged support to prevent her head and spine from twisting. After assuring himself that Maya was well positioned for the ride up the escarpment, he motioned to Sam that he was ready to leave the branch he was perched on.

For the sake of balance, it was imperative that the two climbers abandon the branches they were on at the same moment. On McLaren's signal, in unison they pushed off.

Without waiting a second, Sam used his long legs to swiftly scramble back up to the Jeep and initiate the process of hauling up the penetrating chair.

Their luck didn't last. Just as the chair carrying Maya neared the upper ledge, the pulley rope snagged on a rock ledge and the ascent halted abruptly.

Realizing that a delicate adjustment would be needed to realign the rope, McLaren called up to Sam, "Stop!"

Sam instantly complied. A second later he was horrified by a noise that could only herald imminent disaster. The implacable force of gravity was winning out, suctioning the wreck into the abyss.

Reacting to the ominous snapping sounds, Sam shouted with a composure that masked his anxiety, "Brace yourself. I recommend that you hang on for dear life!" The grin that he usually wore in challenging times faded to an expression frozen like granite.

The branches of the old oak could no longer take the strain. The climbing rope lashed to counterbalance the vehicle's weight tensed, foolishly fighting back against the insurrection. With agonizing slowness, the Honda tipped forward and suddenly, like Houdini, it broke free of its bonds and hurled headlong down the escarpment.

Hunched over the rope at the top of the escarpment, Sam gazed unblinkingly at the scene playing out below.

During its descent the Honda rolled over and over again. Each rotation of the car was marked by a Satanic flash of silver glinting skyward. The noise of the car tumbling reverberated like vicious claps of thunder. The Honda thrashed about, pummeling trees and scrub on the way to the valley floor. A bone-jarring bang announced that it had reached its destination and within seconds a plume of dark smoke billowed upwards. Bright flames engulfed the wreck and the acrid smell of charred debris contaminated the fresh spring air.

CHAPTER 5

Twinkling lights spread out like fairy dust scattered over the city as Sam propelled the Jeep down the steep hill on the highway at the western outskirts of Ottawa. The top arc of the sun had just disappeared, leaving a deep blue sky. McLaren rode shotgun and Maya rested on the seat behind Sam. The threesome rode in silence taking in the tranquil twilight view that was a stark contrast to their adrenaline-charged excitement earlier in the day.

The tension of the previous few hours dissipated once Maya's head injuries had been assessed and the lacerations to her scalp treated at the hospital. The injury had been diagnosed as a Grade I cerebral concussion and the examining physician had prescribed rest and plenty of sleep. He had warned that it was essential for Maya to be wakened several times during the first night following the trauma. It was crucial that she be monitored for dizziness, slurred speech and a number of other symptoms which would call for a return to hospital.

Since Maya had no family in Ottawa, McLaren had extended an invitation to her to stay at his home. He assured Maya she would have female company since his younger sister Danielle was staying with him. They would to take turns awakening Maya. It was the only way Maya was permitted the speedy discharge from the rural hospital where she had been taken following the accident.

Reluctant to place any further burden on her rescuers, but not wanting the alternative of remaining in hospital to be regularly wakened, Maya accepted McLaren's offer. Now, after having filed a police report, they were on the way to Maya's home in Ottawa where she would pick up an overnight bag and some toiletries.

"How are you doing back there?" McLaren asked while sliding his Oakley sunglasses with a one-handed motion to the top of his head and turning his head to face Maya.

"Feeling much better, thank you," Maya responded. She tilted her head slightly to one side and pushed a strand of dark hair back behind an ear with her fingers, "I really appreciate what you two have done for me."

McLaren seemed genuinely flummoxed about how to respond. He simply nodded.

Eastbound traffic was moderately light into town compared to the steady stream of commuters heading west after work. Sam took the Parkdale exit from the Queensway and drove south towards a picturesque tree-lined area of older, upscale homes not far from the Experimental Farm. He whistled when he pulled into the laneway of a classic three storey Tudor home.

"Beautiful home."

"The house used to belong to my Uncle Matt. When you stopped to help me, I was returning home from clearing out his personal items from his office at the Chalk River reactor site. You see, my uncle died unexpectedly quite recently and left his home to me."

"Sorry for your loss," Sam said with respect.

"Uncle Matt knew that I had always loved the house. When I was a child it was my home away from home on summer vacations. With its front and back stairways to the upper stories and many nooks and crannies the house was a child's dream for hide and seek on a rainy day. I used to play with my cousin Chris all the time. He and I were the same age."

"He didn't leave the house to your cousin?" McLaren asked.

"No." Maya replied with an audible sigh. "Chris died in a plane crash about the time I was doing my residency in the US. It was hard on everyone. My dad died on the same flight. "

"Oh! I'm so sorry Maya," McLaren reached over and gently touched her hand.

"It was a long time ago. My mom had already passed so I was very much alone. Uncle Matt took me under his wing. The crash was particularly hard on him. You see, my dad was his twin. He lost his son and his brother and by then he was no longer living with my aunt. While I was never a replacement for his son, my uncle very much treated me as his daughter, thus, the house. When Uncle Matt bequeathed his home to me I was working in the States. I thought it was a sign that should return home to Canada and practice medicine here. So, I applied for a vacancy at the Children's Hospital. I've got a provisional job offer. I just need my security clearance. They say that that might take up to six weeks or longer."

Sam and McLaren followed Maya up the steps to the front door. To their surprise there was no need for Maya to unlock the big wooden door. When she turned the knob, the heavy door opened.

"That's strange. I always lock it." She gave the door a gentle push and reached to her left to hunt for the light switch.

"Maya is anything out of place?" McLaren asked. His suspicions were aroused.

Maya walked from room to room inspecting. In one of the bedrooms she stopped and fingered two items sitting adjacent to each other on a dresser. The little sigh that she let out when she touched them was audible. It was obvious that they held some special meaning to her and that she was in some way relieved to see them. One was a small cameo picture frame that opened to reveal the photo of a handsome young man. The other was a small red Swiss Army knife.

"It doesn't look like anything has been disturbed, but it is strange that the computer is on in the office. I wouldn't leave it on and I had no real need to use it because I have my tablet. I can't say for sure that I didn't leave it on though, because with that bump on my head my memory is a trifle fuzzy. Please make yourselves comfortable. I'll just be a few minutes while I gather up some things in an overnight bag."

McLaren gave Sam a sideways glance that his chum immediately interpreted correctly. After Maya left the room he whispered, "Take a look around the back. Don't show any sign of concern. Maya has been through enough today. My bet is that there is more to today's events than meets the eye. If someone was in here, then it is a good thing that she is coming back with us."

"I agree." Sam replied.

McLaren felt uneasy. What were the odds that these incidents were unrelated?

"We need to find out what's going on. How about you use your contacts for information about the plate number of the SUV that ran her off the road?" McLaren's concern was evident.

Sam smiled fox like and murmured, "Way ahead of you."

****

It was dark when Sam navigated the convoluted network of Ottawa roads to the bridge traversing the Ottawa River and reached the Quebec highway that snaked its way up the back country to McLaren's lakeside home. The last stretch was a narrow tree-lined lane that ended at a contemporary cedar home set in a forest clearing. Artistic perimeter lighting illuminated the chalet's elegant and clean lines.

McLaren opened the rear passenger door and helped Maya out of the Jeep. He took her hand and they navigated the snow-covered path up to the house. When they reached the porch steps they found them ice-covered and slippery.

"Danny still hasn't found the snow shovel," Sam chuckled.

"Nor has she located the bag of rock salt for the steps," McLaren shook his head.

McLaren had barely placed his hand on the doorknob when the wooden door flew open revealing an attractive brunette.

"Marc, did you remember to bring wine?"

The woman at the door bore a striking resemblance to McLaren. She was tall and like her brother had high cheek bones, and an aquiline nose. Her long wavy chestnut hair was tied back into a ponytail. Her skin was tanned and smooth with just a hint of a goggle tan. Though casually dressed in worn jeans and a matching blue gingham shirt that accentuated her striking cobalt blue eyes, there was no hiding her killer body.

"No, but I brought a new friend," he responded with a mischievous grin.

Facing Maya, McLaren made the introductions, "Maya, I would like you to meet my sister Danielle. Most of us call her Danny."

"Oh, hello. It's great to meet you. Please come ahead in."

Danny threw Sam a questioning look hoping he might explain the arrival of this newcomers.

Sam shrugged and smiled at Danny.

McLaren led the way into a large room that took advantage of its sweeping lakeside vista. The elegant post and beam home with its vaulted ceilings made a strong architectural statement. It was modern, open and designed for easy livability. The outside deck was lit, and a wall of glass seemed to bring the entire outdoors inside. A wood fire burning in the tall flagstone fireplace added to the coziness.

"I wondered when you'd get back. I have supper all set."

Maya felt at ease in these surroundings. She enjoyed the dinner which was a casual affair with everyone helping get the meal to the table and clean up. The main course was Spaghetti Alla Capresetti and it was accompanied by a garden salad and homemade bread. She found the conversation pleasant. She was drawn to Danny's quick intelligence and wit.

When the topic of how Sam and McLaren had met Maya came up, McLaren replied that they had found Maya hanging around on the way back from the nuclear site. On hearing this explanation, Danny cocked her head to one side and gave her older brother a long stare in disbelief. From her expression, it was clear that she didn't think much of his response and wanted more information. To further tease his sister, he did not offer any explanation.

Danny continued efforts to press for details, but McLaren was not forthcoming.

Sam was amused. He was accustomed to the playful banter between the two siblings.

Maya, on the other hand, felt that Danny should hear how Sam and McLaren had come to her rescue. She retold the tale complete with details of the danger the two friends had placed themselves in during the rescue operation.

As the story unfolded, Danny leaned in closer to her brother, so close in fact that her head almost touched his shoulder. It was clear that she was proud that her big brother and his chum had come to Maya's aid.

"Sounds like you were lucky that these two scallywags came along?" Danny said.

"Scallywags? Why do you call them that? They risked their lives to get me out of that car."

"Well, these two are infamous for getting into and out of high risk, precarious situations. The term "scallywags" dates back to their high school days when they were roommates at a private high school in Upper New York State. The school was devoted to winter sports. The boys were alpine ski racers and pranksters. Marc was one of the few Canadians at the school and although Sam is American, he took a shine to his Canuck roommate," Danny said, grinning at Sam.

Sam threw up his hands. "My mom's from Nova Scotia, what can I say?" he replied, implying that he'd felt a duty to befriend the Canuck because his own heritage.

"The boys competed against each other on the ski slopes, on wrestling mats and academically. They were inseparable and mischievous. They got into so many scrapes that everyone at the school referred to them affectionately as the scallywags," Danny said with a smile.

"Dan's just jealous. She didn't have the chance to attend school in Lake Placid with us. Her mom and dad wisely thought that she might get up to the same high jinks that her brother often found himself in. They were probably correct to make this assumption. The end result was that she attended high school in Canada, even though she was an elite alpine racer in her own right. Dan went to secondary school in Ottawa and raced on the Quebec circuit. After university, she became a biochemist. Now she does freelance work for CANDO, the same firm that we work for, but she is usually stationed out in British Columbia. We often get to work together. This upcoming week the three of us are off to Geneva where McLaren will present his findings on the reactor leak. After that meeting, we'll be off on a little ski holiday in Zermatt before the next assignment," Sam said smiling at Danny and giving her ponytail a tug.

"Zermatt is heavenly. When I was a teenager, I skied there with my cousin Chris. His mom, my aunt, is a professor of archeology at a university in Switzerland. We used to visit her and when we did we always took to the slopes at Zermatt," Maya said. She thought back to the good times she'd spent with her family, her uncle and her cousin. Sadly, those days were gone. Only her aunt remained, and she was living far away in Switzerland.

"The aunt that you are referring to, would she be the wife of the man who left you his home?" Sam asked, trying to put the genealogy together.

"Yes. Uncle Matt and Tante Hélène were each devoted to their work. She was an academic in Europe and he was a nuclear scientist in Canada. They couldn't make a go of a "long distance marriage" so they divorced. The split occurred before the plane crash killed my dad and my cousin. I haven't visited my aunt in years, but we keep in touch," Maya said. She felt the sad memories well up and unconsciously lowered her head.

McLaren realized that the subject was painful and in a quick side step he re-diverted the conversation.

The evening flew by. It had been a long time since Maya had been in such a relaxed familial setting. She quite enjoyed the fireside conversation and company. She felt comfortable with McLaren's easygoing sister. She found her vivacious, with a humorous outlook on life.

"Look, you should be with family after what you have been through. Here's my suggestion. Since you won't be working at the hospital for the next few weeks, why not come with us to Switzerland? You could visit with your aunt while we're at meetings in Geneva and then if you're feeling up to it, you could come skiing with us at Zermatt!" Danny suggested. It was obvious that she was keen to have Maya come along on their trip to Switzerland.

Maya was totally surprised by Danny's enthusiastic invitation. She thanked her and said that she would need to sleep on it. She had to admit that the invitation held a lot of appeal, but she wasn't normally one to jump into anything.

Frankly, from a medical standpoint, going skiing right after a head injury wouldn't be the best idea, but the opportunity to visit Tante Hélène in Switzerland would be great. I guess that in about a week I might be able to take to the slopes, Maya thought to herself.

It came as no surprise to Sam that Danny invited Maya to Switzerland. He well knew that his friend's sister was always a catalyst for action. He looked across the room at McLaren. He wondered if the smile he saw on McLaren face might just hold a trace of apprehension.

CHAPTER 6

The train descended into a Swiss town nestled in a sheltered bay on the largest, deepest, and bluest of all the Swiss Lakes. The near-tropical color of the lake combined with the mild winters by the lake long ago earned it the title of "Swiss Riviera".

Maya gazed out the window of the train at the steeply terraced vineyards, rows of pines, cypresses and palm trees sketched against the breathtaking backdrop of snow-covered alps. She reflected that it was natural that her aunt had chosen to pursue her academic career from this lakefront town. It was well served by impeccable Swiss railways and elegant antique ferries that plied the croissant-shaped lake.

After making arrangements for her skis and bags to be delivered to her aunt's home, Maya strolled along the flower-bordered promenade that skirted Lake Geneva all the way to the Castle of Chillon, made famous by the poet Lord Byron. It was not long before Maya spotted the familiar stone manor house where her aunt, the renowned historian and expert in classical archeology, lived.

The elegant home sat on a promontory in the hills overlooking the town of Montreux. Gazing up at it, Maya considered that it was much like her aunt. It had a serious, no-nonsense, aristocratic demeanor, yet it was graced with warmth and broad perspective. Maya admired the timeless beauty of the manor with its stone balconies and terraces that afforded panoramic views of the shoreline and the snow-capped alps.

The elderly housekeeper who answered the doorbell gave Maya a warm welcome. Claire had been in her aunt's employ for as long as Maya could remember. She led Maya to a sitting room with a spectacular view of the lake, where sitting erect, reading in the sunlight passing through the leaded windows was Tante Hélène.

The historian cut a striking figure, tall and businesslike prim in a gray tailored suit. Her silver-gray hair was pulled back in a chignon, and a single strand of pearls encircled her neck. She peered over her oval rimless glasses at her visitor. On recognizing her niece, she smiled and rose from her comfortable forest-green brocaded seat.

Tante Hélène greeted Maya warmly. She leaned her face forward into Maya's and touched Maya's left cheek and then the right while making a kissing sound in the customary French greeting of faire la bise. Then she enveloped Maya in a hug and wiped a moist tear from her intelligent gray eyes. It was obvious that she was glad to see her niece. "Maya, it's been so long. I'm so glad you have made the trek across the pond. Do come in. We must have tea."

Ah yes, tea. One always has tea with Tante Hélène. Maya remembered.

Maya wondered what her aunt's university students would think if they saw that tear in Tante Hélène's eye. Her dear aunt, the highly-esteemed professor of Classical Archaeology and History, was renowned for her "stiff upper lip" and rather formal approach. All the same, Maya knew she had a soft side. She loved her dearly and had fond memories of times spent with her.

Maya dug into her purse to retrieve gifts for her aunt.

"At the house in Ottawa I saw these two treasures and I immediately thought of you, so I brought them along for you," she stretched out her arm to pass the gifts to her aunt. "The cameo has a lovely photo of Christopher and I think the Swiss Army knife contains some of his work for his thesis."

"How very thoughtful of you, my dear." Tante Hélène smiled. She examined the gifts, turning them over with the long slender fingers of her graceful hands.

"I remember the day I bought those red Swiss Army knife flash drives for the two academics in my life, your dad and my son. I thought that they each might enjoy a souvenir of Switzerland. Your dad was such a strong presence in Christopher's life after my divorce. He was so involved in nuclear research that he was able to help Christopher understand how important my research was to me and how driven I was to return to Montreux to pursue it once he no longer needed a mom at home. It wasn't that I no longer loved his father; rather, I felt driven to pursue my academic work."

"Dad loved Chris as if he were his own son. In fact, he was more like a brother to me than a cousin. We had great times together, especially when both families would get together at the house in Ottawa. I loved it when you came back to Canada for the summer and our family came from British Columbia for a visit at uncle's home."

"Yes, and it was wonderful for me to spend time with your mother. Our friendship went back a long way, back as far as the archeological dig in Mexico when we met those handsome twin boys. Oh, so long-ago Maya. So much sadness has happened since then. It sends a shiver up my spine to think that the four of them have passed on. But look, I still have you in my life, my best friend's daughter, my very own niece. I am so glad that you decided to pay me a visit."

Maya smiled. She was glad that she had decided to make the trip. *The visit will be good for both of us.*

"This is quite a coincidence. I haven't thought of the two matching knives in years. Did you know your father mailed his Swiss Army Knife to me just prior to the crash? It seems he had neglected to pack the knife in his checked baggage. At the last minute, he remembered that he could not clear airport security with a little knife in his pocket, so he decided to mail it here. I am quite sure that I have his knife in the study. Let me just take a look."

Maya followed her aunt up a narrow flight of stairs which appeared to lead to the roof. The stairwell opened instead, onto a comfortable garret-like room in the highest reaches of a tower. Tante Helen's study was quite a contrast to the tidy sitting room. A tall arched window allowed natural light to flow into a paneled room that would best be described as an impressive library. Ceiling to floor book shelves were crowded with rare books and a vast collection of maps. A rolling ladder gave easy access to even the nethermost shelves. Two matching mahogany desks sat in juxtaposition. On one desk an old-fashioned stained-glass lamp shed light on pages of notes strewn over books which that were heaped on maps that dangled over the desk. On the other desk two ultra modern computer screens were linked to state-of-the-art computing equipment. It was an office where old research methods abutted new.

Tante Hélène opened the drawer of the desk where the monitors sat and retrieved a Swiss Army Knife that was identical to the one that Maya had just given her aunt. "You should have this," the professor said. She passed the red flash drive to Maya.

Maya smiled.

"I took a look through it briefly. I recall that it was filled with data and equations, something to do with production of radioactive isotopes. It contains a copy of a presentation that your father intended to present in Geneva at that Nuclear Conference he was slated to attend."

Looking off into the distance her aunt asked, "Did you take a peek at what is on Christopher's flash drive?"

Maya simply nodded.

"Christopher was on that flight with your dad because he wanted to share with me his research on Alexander the Great. At the time, he was working on his doctoral dissertation. I was certain that his Advisor at university would have provided every bit of advice that he needed, but I was happy that he was coming to me as an expert in the field. He said he had made a very important find. I was really looking forward to discussing his academic work. Then with that terrible crash, I assumed all his research work was lost."

"I had a brief look at it Tante Hélène. That's why I wanted to bring the flash-drive to you. I think that Christopher was on to something, something right up your alley."

At that very moment Claire arrived with tea.

CHAPTER 7

McLaren put the pedal to the metal in his rental BMW M6 on the motorway and marveled at the Swiss road engineering. The German vehicle he had selected was a balance of luxury features and sports car performance. It was targeted at high end consumers seeking performance as well as practical space for sports equipment, like as the skis it now transported.

Yes. This is the right stretch of motorway to put the M6 through the paces. McLaren smiled. He relished the speed and acknowledged that the vehicle was indeed living up to its reputation.

Out of nowhere, the heavy back-beat guitar rhythm of Bachman Turner Overdrive's "Taking Care of Business" thrummed. The distinctive ringtone signaled a call from McLaren's boss, Dr. Patrick Shearwater, head of CANDO.

McLaren picked up the call using the BMW's hands-free communication system. He'd been expecting a call from his boss. No doubt Patrick would be looking for an update on the previous day's meeting at the International Nuclear Safety Agency.

"Yo, Patrick, how are things in Ottawa?"

Never one to waste time with pleasantries, Dr. Shearwater got right to the point, "More importantly, how did the meeting in Geneva go?"

"The three days were long, but I'd have to say that overall the meeting went quite well. Everyone was glad to hear that there was good progress in bringing the Chalk River reactor on line again to help with the international isotope shortage. The NRU shutdown has been hard on everyone."

"Yes, it's good to know that our antique is up and running again, but there is very little in the way of backup and that need must be addressed. I'm trying to work on that, but our PM seems set on another agenda." Dr. Shearwater was never one to mince words.

"With the Geneva meeting behind us, my team and I are planning on taking a couple days of R and R. We're heading over to Zermatt to ski. After that Sam will be doing a scenic photo shoot, in Pompeii, Italy, for one of the travel magazines he freelances with. My plan is to stay on this side of the Atlantic while he does that, provided you don't need me. I'll just be a call away if something comes up."

McLaren knew that it was always practical to remind his boss about his comings and goings. Despite being flexible with his employees, particularly when they put in long hours, Dr. Shearwater nonetheless expected them to always be ready to swing into action at the drop of a hat.

"You have my clearance. Please maintain regular contact with my office while you are on the continent."

The call terminated just as McLaren reached the outskirts of Montreux. Traffic was unexpectedly light. In a few minutes, he was on the tree-lined cobblestone lane that lead up to the manor house, where Maya's aunt lived. The wrought-iron drive-way gate stood open. On the elegant covered porch he could see Maya's ski gear and luggage ready for the trip to Zermatt.

The front door opened, and Maya and her aunt stepped out. Maya saw the car pulling in and waved.

When Maya introduced McLaren to Dr. Jullian, he was immediately struck by the professor's air of confidence. There was a stately elegance about her. Clearly here was a woman who was accustomed to being in charge.

Professor Jullian's intense gray eyes gave McLaren the assessing once-over of a professor, as if evaluating what he had to contribute. Her jowls and lower lip formed an arc when she stared at him.

It had been a long time since McLaren had experienced the stare of parental assessment that came when a young man arrived at the home of a date, but sure enough that was how he felt at that moment, self-conscious.

He was surprised that it was her voice which unnerved him the most. The professor plied him with a multitude of questions about his work and the reactor shutdown. Her pointed queries often approached a level that necessitated that he skirt a security issue or two.

McLaren judged that he must have passed the test when her manner became more engaging. Nonetheless he was thankful that Maya had her ski gear ready so that they could make a quick escape.

Maya gave her aunt a hug and promised to return before departing for Canada.

McLaren gave Dr. Jullian a disarming smile, shook hands with her and said that he hoped he that they would be able to talk in more depth on a subsequent visit. Then he loaded Maya's luggage and skis into the vehicle and opened the passenger door for Maya. He was anxious to get on the road to join Danny and Sam in Zermatt.

Maya cheerily talked about her visit with her aunt while they sped along the motorway towards Täsch, the connecting point for the local train into Zermatt. She enthusiastically related that during her stay in Montreux, she and her aunt had taken the opportunity to examine the contents of her cousin's Swiss Army knife flash drive which she had deliberately brought from Ottawa for her aunt.

"From the moment Tante Hélène began to read Chris's notes she realized why he had wanted to discuss his doctoral research with her. It appears that Chris made a remarkable archeological find. It would have sent jolts through the academic archeological community, but it would have been controversial," Maya said.

"What did he find that would have been that contentious?" McLaren asked.

His question went unanswered because just at that moment McLaren and Maya heard a train whistle blow.

"Oh boy! The shuttle train's already in the station. We'll need to hurry to get our tickets and get on board." McLaren pulled the BMW into Täsch, the last rail station before car-free Zermatt. He parked the car in the lot adjacent to the little station house, grabbed the luggage and ran with Maya to the ticket kiosk.

"Great timing," Maya smiled.

"Maybe not. You might need to bat your eyelashes at the station clerk if he's Swiss officious and he says that we're too late," he replied with a grin.

****

The ride on the narrow-gauge track into the picture postcard village of Zermatt took McLaren and Maya deep into the center of a remote valley in one of the highest Alp mountain ranges. Their destination was a quaint little village that lay nestled between steeply scarped mountains. The lower slopes were dotted with rustic chalet style homes, inns and hotels perched amongst the forest trees. High in the azure sky above the village, the spire of the huge, gracefully chiseled pyramid of the Matterhorn towered. At 14,690 feet, it is one of the highest peaks in the Alps. With its iconic shape and solitary stance, the Matterhorn is the epitome of a mountain.

The air was fresh, the sounds almost hollow. There were no gasoline powered cars. Almost everyone, locals and visitors alike, was on foot happily bustling about along Zermatt's narrow main street which was lined with shops, cozy restaurants and hotels. Horse-drawn carriages tinkling with bells and micro electric cars carried travelers to their "Old World style" hotels along the cobblestone main street. Alpine charm was everywhere.

Danny and Sam were waiting at the Zermatt train station. It had been easy to persuade their hotelier to lend them his electric taxi to pick up their friends. On more than one occasion he had played host to this group of friends. He had been a world class ski racer in his time and had since become a hotelier.

"Wait until you see our ski apartment. It's at the far end of the village near the ski lift. It has a glass elevator, a spa and a pool that has a chandelier made of ski medals. You'll love it. You and I share a lovely room with a balcony that has a terrific view of the Matterhorn. Let's drop off your things and then we can go down to the village before dinner. The boys can meet us down there. It's great that you decided to come along with us," Danny's exuberance, effusive personality and mile-a-minute delivery made it more than obvious that she was glad to have Maya along.

****

After exploring the village Danny and Maya met Sam and McLaren for dinner at Chez Gaby's. It was a good location, tucked neatly on a side street, half way between the rail station and their apartment. The exterior of the rustic restaurant resembled many of the other chalet-styled buildings in the village. It was weathered, rustic, and unpretentious, a welcoming haunt for locals after a day on the slopes.

The menu was simple but delightful with soup, salad, a mixed grill of beef and veal followed by sorbet. The foursome sat around a large circular table facing an open fire pit enjoying their meal. Danny wanted Maya to tell the story of her cousin Christopher's interest in Alexander the Great.

"You had me intrigued when you said that his find would send jolts through the archeological community," Sam said.

Maya found she had a captive audience. Her eyes lit up as she told the story of the discussion she had had with Tante Hélène about her cousin Christopher's interest in Alexander the Great. She was surprised by the number of questions posed. She wished she had answers.

"One of the photos on my cousin's flash drive was of a mosaic unearthed at the dig at Pompeii. My aunt said that it's now on display at the museum in Naples," Maya said.

McLaren glanced over at Danny and saw the wheels turning in her head.

"I'd love to uncover more about your cousin's find. Look, Sam's headed to Pompeii to do a photo shoot for an archeological magazine after our ski break. Pompeii is so close to Naples. Why don't you and I tag along with Sam and while he's at work we could take a look at the display at the museum in Naples?" Danny suggested with obvious delight.

Danny's invitation came as no surprise to McLaren. His sister could be counted on to be enthusiastic and eager. Her suggestion was made with Danny's characteristic impetuosity and it set off his inner alarm bell. He'd learned the hard way that his sister's spontaneity could lead to trouble.

CHAPTER 8

Dr. Patrick Shearwater contemplated the setting of the bi-lateral meeting between the two North American giants. The distinctive room with its high ceiling and elaborate molding held such history that it was impossible not to be awestruck. The architectural features of the Oval Office were reminiscent of baroque, neoclassical, and Georgian traditions. The three large south-facing windows behind the president's famous Resolute desk, the imposing fireplace crowned with a portrait of George Washington, the bronze sculptures of horses by Frederic Remington and the large grandfather clock standing in the northeast corner of the room ticking off minutes of time, all contributed to the sense of prestige and power.

The head of CANDO could readily see why the press found the American President a remarkable divergence from his predecessor. The former president had a natural way about him that put everyone at ease, while the current US leader, an older mogul, exhibited alpha tendencies aimed at reminding everyone around that he was not the kind of guy you push around. In contrast Dr. Shearwater noted that most political leaders from around the world found themselves powerless to the handsome Canadian Prime Minister's charms.

Dr. Shearwater's presence at the in-camera bilateral had been at the specific request of the President. He was the head of CANDO; his input on nuclear matters was often sought out. He observed with trepidation that the American Secretary of State Nathan Rothberg had also been summoned.

After formalities and introductions, the President got right down to business, "Jared, I gauge our meeting today as an opportunity to reaffirm America's tough stand on trade with US allies."

The US leader was known to disagree with his predecessor's approach to trade deals and had spoken out on his long-standing view that Washington was being exploited by existing trade agreements. He had unilaterally increased tariffs without congressional approval, citing national security needs.

"Whether you like it or not, certain political leaders are the ones who must step to the forefront and dictate what must be done because there is a world out there to be run," the President proclaimed.

"Mr. President, I'm all ears, go on," his Canadian counterpart said.

"Canada is to blame for creating a world-wide shortage of medical isotopes. You had no strategic measures in place to replace the aging Chalk River reactor. The thing's well over fifty years old. I know you gave incentives to find other ways to produce isotopes with cyclotrons, but those methods will never produce anywhere near what is needed. Face it, it would take more money than your country can throw at it to regain the edge Canada once had in medical radioisotopes.

The shutdown has had dire consequences in the US and abroad. America has turned elsewhere to address our supply needs and we've found suppliers. Our new suppliers are using LEU, low enriched Uranium, in South Africa and Argentina and Macedonia is using Thallium.

For years, because Canada has been our close neighbor supplying America with the majority of radioisotopes used in medical diagnostic and therapeutic procedures, our nation has given Canada an exemption. In the past 20 years or so, America has shipped over 500 kg of enriched Uranium to Canada, so that you can produce the products and then send them back to us. I'd like to remind you however, that for decades the US has sought to phase out the use of highly enriched Uranium. Our Energy Department's Reduced Enrichment for Research and Test Reactors program has literally converted dozens of reactors around the world from highly enriched to low enriched.

With true candor the Prime Minister replied, "I take it then that the incentives that your government offered for using LEU-based medical isotopes in the US have paid off? The $163 million put aside to foster LEU-based production and the cost-sharing to encourage and subsidize construction of facilities that do not use LEU to produce Molybdenum-99 have had a positive impact then?"

Ignoring the question, the President continued, "Look, building nuclear bombs and medical treatments for cancer are not unrelated pursuits. They can both start with highly enriched Uranium. While America has been sending weapons-grade Uranium to Canada for years, at the same time we have tried to wean other foreigners off using HEU. HEU frankly needs no further enrichment to make an atomic bomb. There is an inherent risk in using highly enriched Uranium in the production of Molybdenum-99."

The Canadian PM spoke up, "Mr. President, Canada ships America raw product and America trucks HEU into Canada accompanied by military convoy. We take extreme measures to ensure its security. Canada does not enrich Uranium even though we are the leading producer of Uranium and we have that expertise. We have always realized that it would be viewed as an act of aggression if we did."

Looking steely eyed the President affirmed, "Bluntly put, while America needs a reliable commercial supply network of medical isotopes to meet our current and longer-term needs, I am not happy providing an exemption to Canada to use HEU."

The Head of CANDO saw the nod from the Canadian leader, indicating that the PM wanted his nuclear expert to enter the discussion.

"Mr. President, using low enriched Uranium results in huge volumes of liquid waste which is fissile and highly radioactive. Two to five more times the amount of Uranium must be irradiated to yield the same amount of Molybdenum 99. Canada uses enriched Uranium because it reduces waste upstream by a factor of five. So far no country has developed a large scale commercial process for handling the waste if LEU is used. It is a huge problem."

"I hear what you are saying, but for the sake of security, that arrangement is over," the President announced.

The silence in the room was palpable. It was like an intuitive boundary that suggested countless possibilities and unpredictable scenarios.

Demonstrating a whimsy so characteristic of his presidency, the American head of state shot ahead. "Now, on to another pressing matter, one somewhat closely related. It's the reason why I specifically requested that Dr. Shearwater be present."

The President looked Dr.Shearwater in the eye and said, "Doctor, during the isotope shortage we have experienced a problem with medical isotopes shipped into America. We have been using a patchwork of supply networks from around the world to address our needs during the shortage. There has only been a trickle of products from Canada. Our concern is the ever-increasing incidence of death following the administration of the radioisotopes in parts of Europe."

The President lowered his eyebrows and narrowed his eyes, "Suspicions are that this could amount to bioterrorism by radiological means."

The American, with his mop of comb-over hair, looked as if he were an actor on stage. He used exaggerated lip movements and odd hand movements to accentuate his point, "In America, we do not want to raise the level of apprehension because there is enough hype with the shortage. Suffice it say we are extremely concerned. I want CANDO to identify the source of the problem and help ensure that the radioactive products we are using are safe."

The Canadian Prime Minister was experiencing firsthand the capricious nature of the American President. It was a further example of POTUS being rude and self-serving, more attuned to his own needs than the concerns of others. The PM knew too well that the American President could be disparaging. Despite this, the PM followed his own mantra — in the face of ignorance, one should choose reason. Canada would demonstrate leadership and investigate the problem with the radioactive products to save lives, even if this undertaking might return to haunt the PM.

Looking over at Dr. Shearwater to gauge his buy-in, the PM responded, "CANDO will look into this situation."

"Yes, for sure, precisely," the President smirked. "Thank you and Dr. Shearwater, Nathan here will arrange for you to have a briefing regarding the situation and the steps that are underway. We want you to have the latest information with which to update your team."

The President reached forward in an open manner to shake hands with his Canadian visitors, clearly indicating that the bi-lateral was over.

CHAPTER 9

Maya just couldn't sleep. She reached over to the bedside table and from her purse removed the Swiss Army flash drive which her aunt had given her. She sat on the edge of the bed for a brief moment contemplating her next move. Then she stood up and took a deep breath before tip-toeing out to the living room.

She was dying to see what was on her father's flash drive, but she hadn't had time to take a peek because of all the excitement of examining her cousin's flash drive with her aunt. She reached for her laptop and plugged in the little red knife. Not unexpectedly, there were numerous folders; most were filled with chemical equations. Anxious to see the paper that he would have presented had his ill-fated plane not crashed into the sea, she searched through and located a PowerPoint presentation, labeled 'Nuclear Conference in Geneva'.

"So, you're an insomniac too?" McLaren asked. He had wandered in wearing comfy plaid pajamas and a t-shirt that accentuated his broad shouldered, athletic build.

His voice startled Maya. She had been so thoroughly absorbed in the computer file that she had not heard his footsteps.

"Oh my gosh, no. I just seem to have a lot on my mind," she blurted, trying not to focus on his chest. "Did I wake you?"

"I'm a light sleeper," McLaren smiled. It was a smile that drew her in and captured her like a charm. "What's so engaging that you are looking at it in the wee hours?"

"It's my dad's presentation. Tante Hélène said she gave my father a flash drive that was identical to the Swiss Army knife flash drive that I found at my uncle's in Ottawa. Dad had sent it from the airport to her home in Switzerland, with a note saying that it was a backup of the presentation he was going to deliver at the conference in Geneva."

McLaren shook his head and with common sense and kindness suggested, "A word to the wise, screen time at this hour will only keep you up longer. At least, that's my experience. Let me make you some warm milk and we'll toast our holiday and then maybe you'll be able to get some shut eye." With that he opened the kitchen cupboards, reached for two mugs and went about preparing the beverage.

Passing the warm cup to her he asked, "May I take a look?" In leaning over to view Maya's computer monitor, he caught the scent of her dark curls. He found it delightful, like almond cookies.

He sat down beside her on the couch and with their heads side by side they scrolled through her father's presentation.

McLaren was truly impressed by what he saw. Well before it became a hot issue, Maya's father had examined a sore point in the nuclear industry. The material on the flash drive was so incredibly timely that McLaren wondered why he had never heard about this research. His own career was in nuclear engineering and yet he had never come across an approach of this type.

"Wow Maya, your dad's work is brilliant! His presentation shows that he'd arrived at a cost-effective method of producing isotopes with low enriched Uranium. If he'd had a chance to present his findings in Geneva, there could have been huge changes in production of medical isotopes. With his approach, the concerns that the Americans have over having high enriched Uranium in use outside of their borders would be quelled."

In response to Maya's questioning look, McLaren gave a quick explanation, "The US government is bent on phasing out the use of HEU in research reactors. It was banned in most American civilian reactors about twenty years ago. You see, highly enriched Uranium U235, is also known as weapons-grade Uranium. It's the only grade of Uranium from which it is possible to directly produce a nuclear bomb."

Maya nodded, she understood only too well.

"The Americans fear that any stockpile of HEU is a potential source of atomic bombs. The more radical US politicians fear that Canada might build bombs and the less radical fear that there might be thefts by terrorists. Quite frankly, they've let Canada go on using HEU in reactor-produced isotopes purely out of need. In reality however, the ability to treat a disease such as thyroid cancer would all but disappear if we couldn't use HEU."

"Why don't we just use low enriched Uranium?"

"Frankly, I believe Canada hasn't headed in that direction, despite US efforts to encourage the use of LEU and other proliferation-resistant technologies and fuels, because with LEU there's about five times the liquid fissile waste and beyond that it has to be irradiated so much more to yield the same amount of moly 99. Canada looks at this strategically and we would not want to face that waste problem."

"It sounds complex."

"That it is. Instead of moving to the next generation of reactors that would use low enriched Uranium, Canada spent money on the flawed MAPLE reactors. The very name, MAPLE —Multipurpose Applied Physics Lattice Experiment, attests to the fact that they were an experiment. It proved to be one that didn't work. The feds scuttled MAPLE when it became clear that it was over-budget, over-designed, and filled with inherent technical problems and economic impediments. The shutdowns of our infamous, aging NRU reactor have brought it all to a head. After fifty years that old reactor was bound to start having problems."

"I thought I'd heard that some countries had stepped up to help during the isotope shortage?"

"Yes, several have. In fact, two countries have started to use LEU for production, South Africa and Argentina. South Africa has already shipped its first batch of LEU produced medical isotopes approved for patient use to the USA. The catch is that these countries are really just making small amounts and is anyone really looking at the problem of the waste?"

She let out a low sigh.

McLaren looked down at the computer screen, "Maya, your dad was definitely on to something for large scale production using LEU, while addressing the waste dilemma. What a blow to the nuclear world that he died in that crash before he had a chance to present this. The approach he put forward is truly innovative. It's so much more on target than the solutions being developed with the funds the feds announced."

Maya looked inquiringly, and McLaren responded, "The feds offered incentives for collaborative efforts amongst academic, private and public-sector partners to develop alternatives for producing isotopes, using linear accelerators and cyclotrons. While outstanding work is being done across Canada on this topic, the amount that can be produced is on a small scale, and just won't meet the demand. In contrast, the potential of your dad's work is mind-boggling."

Maya shivered. McLaren pulled a woolly throw off the sofa and wrapped it around her.

She sipped her warm milk and looked at McLaren's cobalt eyes, "I wonder what became of his actual research?"

CHAPTER 10

The peak of the Kleine Matterhorn came nearer and nearer but it was impossible to see where the aerial cable car would stop. There was no lift station in sight. Passengers stoically stared at the narrow valley floor miles below while the cabin floated effortlessly towards the summit. Suddenly, forty-five minutes after pulling away from the gondola station in Zermatt, the cable car quietly bumped into a landing port cut into the steep rock on the north side of the mountain and its payload of alpine skiers spewed out.

The view was stupendous. Maya looked down from the highest ski station in Europe and imagined the daredevil construction that had gone into it. She offloaded with her friends and walked through the 100-yard tunnel that led to the ski runs. At this altitude, the air was thin, and Maya found it surprisingly difficult to carry her equipment. When she emerged from the tunnel onto the Matterhorn Glacier Paradise ski area the view took her breath away. While the snow-capped mountain panorama of the highest peaks of France, Switzerland, and Italy was truly magnificent, it was the iconic spire of the Matterhorn soaring into the heavens which captivated her. She understood why many consider this view to be the single most breathtaking in skiing.

McLaren looked over at his three fellow skiers and grinned. He gazed up at the cerulean blue sky above them and announced, "You couldn't ask for more. It's how I imagine arriving in heaven. We're lucky today; sometimes it can be a bit cold and windy up here."

"The air is thin, but I'm sure I'll be accustomed in no time." Maya exited the tunnel and set down her skis.

"The runs down are not difficult. It's intermediate bliss," Danny reported.

"Just one warning before we begin. Don't ski off-piste. Stay on the groomed trail between the orange markers. We don't want to lose anyone. The stories of crevasses swallowing up skiers are painfully true," came a dire warning from Sam. The next moment he hopped into his bindings and set off down the slope with Danny striving to overtake him.

McLaren watched amused at the competitive nature of his sister and Sam. Turning to Maya he grinned, "Come on. We don't want to be left behind."

Ski conditions were fantastic. Under the quintessential spire of the Matterhorn, the foursome spent the better part of the morning schussing down corduroy slopes and chatting on the lifts on the way back up. Just after noon they stopped on a terrace to grab a bite and sit on deck chairs in the warmth of the sun in sight of a panorama of snow-covered Italian, French and Swiss alps.

The idyllic peace was short-lived, shattered the minute McLaren's cell phone pounded out the backbeat of 'Taking Care of Business'. McLaren's carefree expression evaporated on hearing the caller's narrative. The plan for the day had to change.

"Sorry, duty calls. I intend to make it back up for a run or two before closing time. I'll text you on my way up. Sam, take good care of the ladies. Gotta run."

In what seemed an instant to his friends, McLaren was a just a speck moving across the white expanse.

****

McLaren sped down the mountainside in a racer's tuck, seriously hoping the ski patrol would not see him and chastise him. He didn't have time for that. He was determined to complete his work and then catch the lift back up in time for a few runs before the lifts closed.

He thanked his lucky stars that their apartment was on-piste. Leaving his skis and poles in the ski rack at the entrance, he opened the glass front door and bolted up the back stairway two steps at a time in his ski boots. When he rounded the corner on the last set of stairs he glanced up and a sixth sense indicated something was amiss. He reached out for the doorknob and it turned.

That's odd, I locked it when we left.

McLaren cautiously opened the door, reached in and switched on the lights. The dining room chairs which had been precisely lined up with the table after breakfast were pushed aside at odd angles, and two had been knocked over. The sofa had been moved and the cushions cut open. Someone had been in a great hurry looking for something. Thankfully McLaren had remembered to lock his computer in the safe before heading out on the slopes.

What would they have been searching for? The information Patrick requested for the Geneva Conference was important, but it would be in the public domain in the next day or so, so it would not have warranted a search of this kind.

The apartment appeared deserted, but McLaren had that strange feeling that he wasn't alone. He moved cautiously through the room. Out of the corner of his eye, an almost imperceptible movement behind the drapes caught his attention. He swept his gaze over the drapery, anticipating. The barest rustle alerted McLaren's instincts.

There it is again.

McLaren frowned. Firm resolve was evident in the set of his jaw. It was not in his nature to back away from any danger.

Suddenly, a figure burst forward from behind the drapery. The intruder had the physique of a heavyweight boxer. He had dark skin, was a shade over six feet tall, and weighed at least 200 pounds. His dark eyes bore an aggressive look. The right side of his wide, high round cheek boned face was marred by a scar that was visible through his heavy beard stubble.

The intruder never hesitated a second before he struck.

McLaren dodged the straight left jab with lightning speed. The intended blow went over his right shoulder. In a counter-move McLaren quickly shifted his body weight onto his rear supporting foot and swung his right fist horizontally at his opponent's head. The unorthodox move went over the intruder's extended lead and made a hard connection.

The blow caught the intruder on his cheekbone. Stunned, he dizzily staggered back into a half open patio door. Receiving such an offensive response was like a wake-up call for him. He suddenly remembered that he had come equipped with a more lethal weapon. Slyly he extended his brown tattooed arm down beneath his left pant leg to unsheathe a tactical knife from its leather scabbard.

Alarm bells rang in McLaren's head. He had a scary thought that this might not end well. He knew from hard experience that knife fighting is callous, uncaring, and fast. In his high school years in the US, he had witnessed the same move pulled in a street fight in Albany. Only speed, linear movement and visuals could help him avoid being cut. He drew a deep breath and with breakneck speed, charged at the intruder like a raging bull before his adversary could wield the knife.

The intruder was ill-prepared for the offensive attack. The force of McLaren's charge propelled the interloper backwards and out the patio door where he tripped on the doorsill and lost his balance. The knife clattered to the floor.

A malicious gleam of anger flared in the intruder's coal black eyes. His lip curled in an animal sneer. Undeterred, he pulled himself to his feet and started towards McLaren. In an instant, he thought better of it, when his brain registered that McLaren now held the Ka-Bar, like a pro, and was brazenly waving it at him. The intruder's wide nostrils flared in contempt. He grasped that he no longer had the upper hand. Retreat would be his best option.

Furtively glancing over the deck rail, the assailant gauged the drop below. He stared at McLaren contemplatively in Machiavellian guile. Swiftly, in a single move, he placed the palm of his right hand on the rail and vaulted his long muscular legs and torso over the deck rail. He landed on the path below with all the agility of an athlete and sprinted towards a crowd of skiers making their way towards the ski lift.

McLaren didn't waste a second. In his ski boots, he clomped down the stairs in pursuit. At the entranceway he glanced to the left and right and just caught sight of the black man cutting through a queue of brightly clad skiers and boarders who were about to board the gondola up the mountain.

McLaren took chase; he dashed along the cobblestone path leading up to the ski lift. Passing the ski rack where he had left his equipment, he grabbed his skis and poles.

Ahead, up at the entrance to the cable car station, the lift attendant was motioning to a group of waiting skiers that it was their turn to board. On cue, a red gondola swept in and took on waiting passengers. The doors slid shut and the red gondola lifted off with the unsavory man on board.

McLaren's thoughts were on Maya's safety. There had just been too many unnerving incidents, particularly were she was involved.

McLaren saw a blue gondola pulling in to take on the next load of skiers. He knew that he didn't have time to wait his turn. He looked down at the cumbersome ski boots he was wearing and shrugged. Ignoring the distain of skiers in the queue, he muscled his way through the line up to the take off point; however, despite his mad dash he failed to reach it before the door slammed shut and the blue gondola left the departure station.

Because every moment counted McLaren made a desperate move. Oblivious to the drop off below him, he ran forward and bounded in a death-defying leap, from the gondola departure deck towards the rear of the blue gondola which was just beginning its ascent. In an adrenaline rush he propelled his body airborne. His heart beat faster, increasing the blood flow to his body and muscles. He extended his left arm fully, attempting to reach the outside frame of the blue gondola, all the while juggling his skis and poles over his right shoulder.

Later he could admit to himself that the clunk of his ski boot announcing he had made it and actually landed on the maintenance ladder attached to the rear of the blue gondola cabin, was reassuring. He hadn't made a leap like that since high school when he and his chums had gone roof jumping in Lake Placid.

Below him, the crowd of waiting skiers gasped in unison. The lift attendant shouted, but to no avail. The blue gondola was already on the way up the mountain with a skier hanging precariously by one arm on the rear of the gondola.

The screams from the onlookers at the lift take-off were muffled both by the eerie swirl of the wind across the mountain and the sound of McLaren's heart pounding in his ears. He sensed his heavy ski boots threatening to pull him downward when first the gondola passed over the flat traverse and then ascended higher to clear a ridge.

The wind tore at him. Below the drop was so far down that McLaren didn't care to estimate it. He craned his head and body to create some form of counterbalance against the gravitational pull. With a series of tricky maneuvers McLaren managed to pull himself onto the roof of the gondola and attempt to access the emergency roof hatch.

I don't think I would want to do this maneuver every day.

He managed to get the hatch opened and stuck his head through into the seating area of the gondola. He nodded to one of the male skiers on board and the gentleman kindly reached up to receive his skis when McLaren lowered them into the cabin. A moment later he dropped down through the hatch and took his place amongst the passengers. No one on board batted an eyelash.

Ah, the reserve of the Swiss. No one wants to start a conversation with a stranger even if it isn't commonplace to board a gondola from the roof hatch, McLaren thought, sitting and holding his ski equipment just like any other passenger.

Before long the gondola arrived at Furi station. McLaren looked around, but he didn't see his quarry at the arrival point. He estimated that he must have headed further up the mountain. He boarded a large cable car for the next leg up to Trockener Steg, in pursuit.

Once aboard the larger cable car, McLaren reached for his cell phone, verified that he had a tower and placed a call to Sam to arrange a meeting point on a terrace further up the mountain. He took the opportunity to update Sam on his altercation with the intruder and alerted him to the prospect that the inter-loper might be out to harm Maya.

On reaching Trockener Steg, McLaren made his way across the terrace to the pizzeria. At this time of day, the eatery was almost empty, so it was easy to spot his friends. He saw them relaxing in the sun, admiring the unforgettable view of the famous Matterhorn, crowned with snow and sunlight. He greeted them with a wave.

Sam had been careful in selecting the meeting point. Anyone would have to be bold or crazy to go after Maya in such a public location. It might have been a lovely spot to linger for the afternoon if it weren't for the fact that they needed to get Maya off the mountain, to a safer location.

McLaren filled Danny and Maya in on the scene back in the apartment in Zermatt, "I'm uneasy with what has happened. Clearly, it would be unwise for Maya to return to Zermatt. Sam and I have a ski chum who has a chalet in Cervinia, the village on Italian side of the mountain. Sam has contacted him so that we can get a key for his place."

"What do you make of this?" Danny asked.

"I'm not quite sure yet. It may something have to do with Maya's accident and the intrusion into her home in Ottawa. It's damned unlikely but the guy who ran Maya off the road may have followed her to Switzerland. When I got down to our apartment, it was apparent that someone had given it quite a toss. It will be a whole lot safer if we get Maya away from the apartment in Zermatt and down into Italy."

Danny was about to try and put the best face on the situation by extolling the benefits of seeing the Italian side of the mountain, but her words were short by a loud snap and a bullet whizzing overhead.

The bartender screamed. The air was electric.

"Everyone get down!" McLaren shouted.

It was difficult to ascertain from which direction the shot came. The noise actually sounded like it was coming from every direction.

"He's using a suppressor," Sam shouted. He shoved Danny and Maya to the floor and knocked the table over to give them some cover.

"He's masked his position. The ambient noise from the lift makes it almost impossible to pinpoint the location of the shooter," McLaren said.

"Not much accuracy on that first shot but he'll get zeroed in now," Sam announced.

The words were barely out of Sam's mouth when a second shot whizzed by shattering a bottle on a shelf over the bar. The lone bartender screamed again and ran for the exit behind the bar.

"Okay I've got his position. Black ski suit, about 300 meters out. Quickly, everyone move for cover behind the bar," McLaren ordered.

"Cover behind the bar? Who are you kidding? The shooter just hit a bottle on the shelf behind the bar. Do you have a plan, big brother? No random musings, please. I need to know the plan. I don't like being shot at!" barked Danny.

Quick as a flash McLaren spit it out, "Okay, here's my plan. Get behind the bar. We'll split up. Sam and the ladies will take the two old-fashioned lifts up to Plateau Rosa. To conceal your exit, I'll instigate a diversion. When I say go, keep your head down and make your way out the doorway at the back of the bar. Grab your skis and ski down to the T-bar. It's a lot harder to hit a moving target."

Sam nodded, and crouching low led them behind the bar.

"If you three make it in time before the lift closes, you can ride down on the Italian side into the village below. If the lift is closed, you'll have to ski Ventina Route 7 down into Cervinia. The cruiser down will take a good twenty minutes from the crest. Don't dawdle though because if the clouds come in then the light will be poor, and it will be hard to ski the cat trail."

"Where will you be?" Maya asked.

"I'm going to try and run interference with this guy. Hopefully that will buy you some time. Don't worry about your things down in Zermatt. Provided you've got your ID with you, you're okay. You'll be safer in Italy. I'll look after dealing with the Swiss authorities and I'll get your bags over to you in Cervinia."

"Don't forget my toothbrush," Danny chastised.

"Sam, before you go, hand me your bandana. I need a drink, something with a high proof. How about that Bacardi 151 on the shelf behind you?"

"Guys, we're being shot at. Now is totally not the time to be having a drink even if we are holed up behind a bar," Danny reprimanded.

"It's okay. I see where our fearless leader is going with this. But, hey, I'm not sacrificing my favorite bandana," Sam protested.

"Okay then, pass the rum and a cloth napkin and a couple of those storm matches they use to light the tea light candles."

"What are you up to?" Danny asked.

"The rum's for an incendiary. I'm going to toss a Molotov cocktail at this guy to give you guys some cover. And, just for you Sam, I'll use a cloth napkin and save your favorite bandana. Everybody, when you see the burst of flame, get out of here. Grab your skis and get down to the old lift."

Sam handed McLaren the bottle of Bacardi 151 and a cloth napkin. McLaren soaked the napkin in the rum and while it was soaking, used a small knife to pry off the stainless-steel flame arrester crimped to the neck of the bottle.

"This stuff should be the ticket. It is so potent that the manufacturer supplies a flame arrestor to prevent the rum from igniting, just in case the bartender ignores the warnings," McLaren announced while stuffing the rum-soaked napkin into the neck of the bottle.

Using strips torn from a cloth napkin McLaren attached storm matches to either side of the bottle of rum. He carefully aligned the matches so that they extended well above the neck of the bottle. Then, using a lighter that he found on a shelf under the bar, he ignited the matches. He stood up quickly and with the arm of a seasoned quarterback, tossed the improvised incendiary weapon towards the shooter.

McLaren's throw was perfect. The Bacardi bottle with its flaming wick sailed through the air until it fell to the icy ground and smashed. Immediately yellow-orange flames erupted, and the fire began consuming the potent liquid spewing from the bottle.

"Go, go, go! Ladies, no lollygagging. We don't want to be questioned by the Swiss authorities," Sam said tilting his head in the direction of the security officials.

"See you in Italy. Take care," McLaren replied.

A plume of dark smoke billowed up and the blaze intensified. The shooter's dark eyes darted probing through the fire. The situation was impossible. There was no way he could get a clear line of sight on his target. The flames grew in ferocity. Within moments a huge orange fireball erupted. The force lifted the shooter and then slammed him towards the ground. Brilliant orange flames danced around him, singeing his short woolly black hair and eyebrows. The interloper scrambled to his feet and filled his lungs in a frantic gulp. He cursed under his breath; he had missed his chance.

Anxious screams of onlookers triggered a new concern. The infamous Swiss security personnel would be on the scene in no time. It would be foolish to be caught with the weapon. Ignoring the pain, the shooter rubbed his eyes and groped through the smoke over to the terrace, seeking a place to hide his gun. His assignment down in the village of Zermatt had been thwarted and now this fiasco. It might damage his reputation and have consequences with his employer.

Barely two hundred feet away, McLaren scoured the crowd in vain searching for the figure in the black ski suit. He prayed that the same billowing smoke that made it hard to find the shooter would make it easier for Sam and the ladies to get to their skis and schuss down to the lift undetected.

The light wind that had been blowing earlier in the day was now gusting up to 35 and 45 miles per hour, whipping up powder into little ground blizzards. McLaren looked skyward and saw ominous storm clouds rolling in.

Mountain weather was apt to change rapidly. Sometimes early afternoon could be sunny and bright and then a slight wind would come up and a thick cloud cover would descend, making skiing hazardous. McLaren realized that if the current cloud cover were to become really heavy, his friends would encounter white-out conditions en route to Italy. He hoped they would move quickly.

Common sense dictated that he ought to make his way off the mountain, but McLaren was anxious to find the shooter. Like a cinematographer panning a scene for a motion picture, he swept his focus across the ski runs. Just over the rise, on the stark white snow that seemed even whiter against the steel gray clouds, McLaren caught sight of the dark outline of a tall skier moving quickly towards the ski rack.

McLaren's experience in counter-insurgency and peace-keeping kicked in. He had spent enough time in the forces assessing covert adversarial intents to realize that the skier he saw had the movement signature, the same distinctive movement traits and gait displayed by the intruder. He didn't waste a second contemplating. Amid swirling eddies of snow, McLaren jumped into his skis and poled off onto the steep slope in pursuit of the schussing dark outline.

Chapter 11

The traffic jam of skiers was horrendous at the entry point to the two, long T-bars which provide skiers passage from Trockner Steg up to the terminal point. At Testa Grigia, the hub where skiers decide whether to ski back into Switzerland or cross the border and ski down into Italy, Sam and Maya paired up and entered the queue while Danny got into the singles line.

When it came time to mount the T-bar, Sam turned to Maya and smiled "Ready to roll?"

"With pleasure," Maya replied. She looked over at Danny who was still waiting in the singles line and gave her a thumb up sign.

The long wait in the singles line gave Danny the opportunity to peruse the endless stream of skiers who were boarding the lift. After what seemed an eternity the lift attendant finally paired her with another single.

"Thank you, signor," her new companion replied to the lift attendant when he got on the T-bar.

The pair rode up in silence, their legs balanced on their skis, absorbing the changes in terrain while the lift carried them upwards.

Danny smiled over at her companion. He was just a touch taller than Danny. His dark curly hair jutting out from under his helmet and the Briko goggles, led her to surmise that her companion might be Italian. His face structure was sharply cut and deeply tanned. She guessed he might be in his early thirties.

They had only just begun the trek up the mountain when the T-bar came to an abrupt stop. At first Danny assumed that someone must have fallen either getting on or off the lift. When the T-bar didn't move for upwards of fifteen minutes she began to think that something wasn't right. During the wait the spring-loaded mechanism on the T-bar slackened and it became more difficult to hang on. Danny tried shifting her weight from foot to foot to relieve the

pressure on her ski boots. She tensed wondering whether the delay had something to do with the shooter. She told herself that she was just being paranoid,
that the T-bar would start moving again soon. She turned around to see if she
could spot a problem below and saw several skiers hopping off the lift and skiing down the mountain. Other skiers apparently showed no optimism that the
T-bar would restart.

She turned to her companion who appeared quite relaxed and asked, "Does
this happen often?"

"Which, the clouds rolling in, or the lift stopping?" her companion asked
grinning at Danny. His smile revealed perfectly white teeth that contrasted
with his deeply sun-tanned face.

Danny liked his genial smile. He didn't seem at all perturbed by the hold
up. His off-handed reply gave her a sense of relief. It felt good because being
stuck on the lift with a grump would not have been her cup of tea.

"Yes, both unfortunately. The lift is old and there are other ways up so the
Swiss and the Italians do not see it as a priority to repair this old lift. When
sufficient skiers give up and get off then the load will be light enough. It usually
starts up again. Be prepared for the jerk when we finally get started."

"So, you ride this lift frequently?" Danny asked.

"Yes, I ride it often to get back to Cervinia. I prefer to ski the Swiss side,
but my lodgings are on the Italian side. Allow me to introduce myself. I am
Francesco Veroli, art restorer by trade."

"I'm Danny McLaren, Canadian skier on vacation. Nice to make your ac-
quaintance."

Several minutes later Danny felt the jolt of the old T-bar when it started up.
She turned to Francesco and said, "You were right."

Despite the introductions, they rode along in silence. Visibility became
poorer and poorer. The spire of the Matterhorn disappeared into the clouds.
Danny wondered how Maya and Sam were faring up ahead.

Did they manage to get off this lift and onto the next T-bar before the lift
stopped? How far up ahead are they?

"We'll be getting off momentarily. We'll have to hurry to catch the next lift
before it is closed for the day," Francesco said.

Through the dense mist up ahead, Danny could just make out the form of
the hut that sheltered the attendant for the next T-bar. There was no sign of
her friends. They must have already boarded. Surely, they were further up the

mountain riding towards the gondola that would take them down into Cervinia. She would have to make good time on the next lift or she would be too late for the gondola and that would mean that she would have to ski down into Italy.

The wind and snow blew at their faces as Danny and Francesco skied off the T-bar and proceeded over to the next lift. They could hear sound of the T-bar running, but when they got closer they saw that the gate was closed barring access to the upper lift. Francesco headed over to speak to the lift attendant. Danny could see him pointing up the slope at the lift, his arms gesturing wildly. She guessed from the expression on his face, after he spoke with the attendant, that he was frustrated.

"He says it is closed for the day. There is no way we can go up the lift now."

Her arms crossed in a defiant stance, Danny retorted, "That's what he thinks!"

Frankly, she didn't have time for this. She had to get to the top and find her friends before the last gondola downloaded. She turned abruptly and made her way across the deep snow over to the far side of the hut, where the attendant's view was partially obscured. She released her bindings and tossed her skis and poles over the wooden fence. Guessing what she was up to, Francesco was quick to hurry over to the fence. Before he could say anything, Danny vaulted over the fence and clamped on her skis on the other side. It was obvious that she intended to be on that lift and a closed gate was not going to stop her.

"Bella, not without me!" In an unexpected move, Francesco tossed his skis over the barrier and leapt over. Within a moment he was alongside Danny and together they grabbed the next available T-bar.

"I see you are a lady who does not let something as trivial as a closed gate stand in your way. I like that. The attendant however will not," Francesco tossed his curly head back and chuckled at Danny.

Indeed, the attendant was not happy with their maneuver. Stunned at the sight of the pair on the lift, the little man yelled after them waving his arms like a madman. There really wasn't much he could do. He dared not stop the lift. Much further ahead on the lift was a ski class taught by an influential ski instructor. There would certainly be trouble for him from administration if that ski class were delayed in their efforts to make the last gondola into Italy.

The snow swirled, and the wind buffeted the pair during the ride up the T-bar. Very soon the lift attendant was completely out of sight. Danny found that on this portion of the ride up the mountain Francesco was more talkative. Perhaps all it took to get him started was to hop a fence after a pretty girl.

"You seem very intent on getting up to the top of the mountain. Are you hoping to get the gondola into Italy?"

"My friends are up ahead, and I would like to catch up with them."

"I prefer to ski the Ventina run. My place is on the far side of the village, so it is far easier to ski home than get off the gondola and walk in ski boots across the village," Francesco admitted.

All the way up Danny wished the T-bar would move more quickly but she found the conversation with Francesco pleasant and it helped to pass the time. She learned that Francesco was an Italian and an avid skier from Caramanico Terme, in the Abruzzo region of central Italy, where his family roots went back for centuries. He had studied to be an artist and now worked for the national museums doing restorative work, primarily on paintings.

By the time they reached their destination neither of them felt like strangers. They dismounted the lift in almost whiteout conditions. Francesco wished Danny a friendly goodbye and headed off in the direction of the infamous Red 7 Ventina down into Cervinia.

Danny made her way over to the gondola station in the blowing snow and howling wind. She wasn't thrilled when she found that the lift was closed, and no one was around. This time even jumping a fence wouldn't help. She tried to reach Sam by cell, but there were no cell towers. There was no alternative but to ski down into Cervinia. She clenched her jaw, annoyed that she had missed the opportunity of skiing down with Francesco. He knew the run well and in this weather his familiarity with the piste would have been helpful. Besides, he had been good company.

She looked at the map of the ski runs that was posted on the wall of the lift office. She was looking for the Ventina, the classic 12 km run down to the village. Normally it would have been a picturesque run with glorious scenery, but with all the blowing snow and darkness setting in, even the markers were going to be very hard to see. Francesco had warned that up here you had to be careful and stay within the colored markers on each side of the run to avoid drop-offs. She'd need to focus and manage her speed, so she could see the markers and avoid any hazards.

CHAPTER 12

McLaren bounded up the steps to the apartment, trying to shake off his suspicion that there was more to the shooting up on the mountain than met the eye. The modern building combined the old school ski chalet feeling with a contemporary atmosphere. Clad in wood siding, it had lots of glass and the apartments all had breathtaking views of the Matterhorn.

It's a shame that the dust-up I had with the intruder messed up our unit.

He knew he should not focus on that now; he had to get through to his boss. Shearwater would be wondering why it was taking him so long to forward the slides. McLaren pictured his boss in his office overlooking the Ottawa River. He would be pacing by now.

Shearwater had been somewhat of a mentor for McLaren, both at university and during his stint in the military. He had a brilliant mind, was respected by the military and bureaucrats alike for his integrity and was feared by some for his bluntness. Dr. Patrick Shearwater had made a point of supporting McLaren's career and recruiting him into CANDO.

"Yo, Patrick, sorry for the delay in getting back to you."

"I take it you and Sam have been enjoying the skiing and getting an alpine glow?"

"The skiing's been great, sir. However, if you are referring to the cocktail alpine glow sir, the answer is no, that is not the reason for my delay. It was Molotov cocktails with Bacardi 151."

Unperturbed by his protégé's response, Dr. Shearwater replied, "Fair enough. What's been happening?"

McLaren related the series of events, including the invasion of the ski apartment, and the gunshots on the mountain that gave rise to the Molotov cocktail.

"Do you have any idea about who this guy is or what he wants?" Dr. Shear-water asked.

"None," McLaren replied. "My feeling is that it must have something to do with the research work that Maya's uncle was doing up at Chalk River. Her car was run off the road on the way back from the nuclear site after she cleaned out her uncle's office. Then her uncle's home in Ottawa was broken into and now this."

"Interesting sequence of events."

"Sam had his camera with him when we saw the accident on Highway 17. He got a shot of the plate and gave it to the authorities. He tapped into his network and found that the SUV that ran Maya off the road was a rental taken out with a stolen credit card. He got a description of the guy who rented it. I'd say that it matches the description of the intruder I encountered in the apartment earlier today."

"Interesting that there has been trouble on both continents. Where are Sam and Danny now?"

"Sam has taken the ladies to a friend's place on the Italian side, in Cervinia. Our thinking was that Maya might be further out of his reach across the border."

"Be careful."

Dr. Shearwater was all too familiar with the escapades the boys could get into. He trusted them implicitly and at the same time was quite justifiably con-cerned for the reputation of CANDO.

"Keep me posted. Do try and keep the CANDO name out of your adven-tures."

"Will do. So, on a different topic, I just emailed the slides you requested."

"Yes, I see them, thanks. Now there is a new urgency in the isotope shortage and that leads me to your next assignment. I'd like you to head an investigation for the European Medicines Network which monitors the safety of medicines through a pharmacovigilance network. The Americans have requested our help. An investigation was begun by the Greek National Center for Nuclear Scientific Research. The US feels that CANDO should take the lead and thoroughly look into the situation. The Head of the Greek Center is an old friend of mine and he is pleased to have help from CANDO."

"Isn't it a little unusual for us to lead a European project of this nature?"

"The Americans are anxious to have an international lead. The President feels that we can help get the work out from under the quagmire that it has fallen into. High rates of mortality are cause for serious alarm. The worry is that it could amount to bioterrorism by radiological means. My friend in Athens knows they need quick action and they want to keep a low profile on the investigation. Our Agency has expertise in all things nuclear and has a reputation for diplomacy and international peace-keeping," Dr. Shearwater said.

McLaren remembered being introduced to the Head of the Greek National Center for Nuclear Scientific Research at a nuclear meeting quite a number of years back. He conjured up an image of this scientific guru discussing the predicament with Shearwater. It must be pretty serious to be keeping it under wrap. One might have expected this state of affairs to have been discussed at his recent meeting at INSA in Geneva, but it wasn't. The fact that the President of the USA reached out directly to Dr. Patrick Shearwater at CANDO was curious. Why hadn't he taken the problem through diplomatic channels rather than contact the Canadians?

"McLaren, I need you to put your ski trip on hold and report back to Geneva for a full briefing."

****

"Yo, McLaren, is Danny with you?"

McLaren heard his buddy's question and immediately felt a pang of worry. It was getting dark. Where was his sister? Why wasn't she with Sam?

"Danny was supposed to go with you and Maya over to Italy. Didn't she take the lift with you?" McLaren asked.

"No. The three of us headed to the T-bar. Maya and I loaded together, but Danny went into the singles line. We kept going up, caught the second T-bar and then got the last gondola down into Italy. There was no sign of her at the top. We waited as long as we could, but the lift was closing, so we headed down. I thought that if Danny got to the top and the gondola was closed, then she'd just ski down the Red Ventina run. But, that was a couple of hours ago and there's been no call from her. I heard there was some kind of trouble that delayed one of the T-bars. We weren't delayed, but maybe Danny was. I just thought she might have missed the second T-bar and decided to ski back to Zermatt."

"She's not with me," McLaren stated flatly.

Sam could tell by the curt reply that his buddy was worried, "Oh, she'll turn up shortly on one side of the mountain or the other. She's a determined lady and a strong skier," Sam replied.

"Don't alert the ski rescue yet, because she'll be madder than all get out that we didn't trust her abilities," McLaren cautioned. He hoped he was making the right call.

"I hope you're right. It is cold up on the mountain, but she hasn't been out of sight for long," Sam agreed.

"It's good that you called. We have to cut short our ski vacation. Shearwater wants us to help with an impending crisis linked to the isotope shortage. Since Chalk River went off-line, there has been a noticeable increase in mortality rates with the isotope products now being used in Europe. I'm headed to Geneva for a briefing. I'll let you know the specifics of our assignment as soon as I get more information. I recommend that if you want to get your photo shoot at Pompeii completed for the travel magazine, you go directly there and get started. I'll meet you at Pompeii after my briefing. But, I want to know where Danny is before we go anywhere. Hopefully she'll call. Let me know the moment you hear from her."

****

The train sped south past small farms with varying crops and green rolling hills, occasionally topped by the ruins of an old abbey or monastery. While Sam was off in the next rail car speaking with McLaren on his cell phone, Maya and Danny were passing the time chatting and enjoying the scenery during the train trip to Naples.

"We were a little worried when you didn't arrive at the apartment in Cervinia until late, yesterday," Maya said.

"Ah, no need to worry. I always turn up, just like a bad penny," Danny replied with a smile. Her vivacious personality shone through. "It was quite the run down the mountain though. The clouds were so low and the mist so thick that I could hardly see at times. I was lucky to have someone with me who knew the piste. Imagine my surprise when I found Francesco waiting for me at the top of the Ventina run. I really thought that I would be on my own after I discovered that the gondola had closed." As usual the words fairly toppled out of her mouth.

"Well, I was concerned, even if Sam seemed to take it in stride. It was indeed fortunate that you met Francesco on the T-bar. It's nice to know that when we feared you were missing you were just having après-ski drinks with him. He seems like a kind soul, what with waiting for you at the top of the run because he thought the lift might have closed early, and ensuring you had company on the run down. It was also very nice of him to drive the three of us to Genoa this morning." Maya said.

"Yes, getting a lift out of Cervinia and down to where we could get a train made it much easier. The ride to Genoa was a bonus," Danny replied.

"Sam seems anxious to get going on his photo shoot at Pompeii," Maya probed.

"Yes. He loves taking photos and he's quite good at it," Danny replied. "Sam's photos will be published in an upscale travel magazine next month so he's on a tight deadline."

"Where did he take training in photography?" Maya asked.

"US military," Danny answered. "After high school in Lake Placid, Sam attended West Pointe Military Academy. I used to go and watch his ski races when he was on their team. After graduation, he made a somewhat unprecedented move to Special Forces. You'd be surprised how often Special Forces need a photographer. Nowadays he tends to be more artsy with his shots. He's quite into archeological photography and his photos are frequently published in travel magazines," Danny said.

"And, your brother?" Maya asked.

"After high school in the US, Marc attended Royal Military College in Canada and got his degree in engineering. He was on RMC's ski team, when they had one. He did a stint in the military and was a member of Joint Task Force 2 before he decided to go to grad school for nuclear engineering. The guys remained friends through university and during their time in the military. They even managed to get a couple of tours of duty together. They had both seen quite a bit of action by the time Dr. Shearwater recruited my brother for his trouble shooting nuclear group. Soon after, Sam was also invited to join CANDO," Danny explained. "What about you Maya?"

"Shortly after my mom died, my dad was offered a job in Washington and off he went. I didn't want to be far away from him, so, I applied to med school at Johns Hopkins in Maryland and was accepted. I did my residency in the US. That's why it's taking a little longer for me to get cleared to work at the Children's Hospital in Ottawa. My mom and Tante Hélène, my aunt who I went to visit in Montreux, were very close friends. They met when they were archeology students and married the twins, my dad and my uncle Matt." Maya replied.

"So that's where you came by the interest in archeology?"

"Yes. I'm thrilled that we are going to see the Alexander Mosaic in the museum at Naples. Truth be told, I'd love to follow the trail of my cousin's research on Alexander the Great. I am sure my aunt would find it fascinating and would provide me with advice," Maya said.

"You've got a bit of time between jobs. I'd say the timing couldn't be better. Why don't you do some follow-up on his work?" Danny genuinely encouraged.

****

While he walked along Geneva's famous lakeside promenade, a fine mist from Jet d'Eau drizzled over McLaren. He gazed admiringly at the tall column of water that soared into the sky against the backdrop of the Alps and the Jura mountains. Though he looked for all the world like a tourist, McLaren's eyes probed the environs for lurking danger. The recent incidents had awakened a new sense of caution in him.

The café up ahead, by the wooden bridge, was the rendezvous point for his briefing. He walked through the arched doorway of the quiet café and headed out onto the sunlit terrace. Seated at a table in a corner he found Dr. Patrick Shearwater, head of CANDO, and Dr. Dimitrios Souflias, Director General of the Greek Center for Nuclear Scientific Research.

The Greek immediately rose to greet McLaren. In his well-cut suit, Dr. Souflias had a sophisticated air about him. He was in his mid-fifties, had an olive complexion, a slight physique, and somewhat longish receding thick curly gray hair.

Dr. Shearwater greeted his protégé warmly with a pat on the back. Tall and lanky with a shock of salt and pepper hair, in his navy-blue blazer and gray flannels, he appeared every bit the university professor that he once had been.

"Thank you for agreeing to forego your ski trip and meet here to discuss our predicament," Dr. Souflias said.

"Gentlemen, I must say you have raised my curiosity," McLaren replied.

Dr. Souflias spoke in a measured tone, "We have a bit of a dilemma. I asked Patrick for CANDO's assistance because the risk is great across the nations, not just in our part of Europe, and it is growing."

McLaren nodded, "So tell me about what has happened that has raised concerns to this level."

The Director General proceeded to explain, "During the worldwide isotope shortage, we have sought suppliers from all over the world. It has been an excellent opportunity for smaller suppliers to acquire a market share where once they had little chance. We have undertaken qualitative monitoring to compare results from radioactive isotopes produced and shipped from Southeast Europe, including Greece and Macedonia. Sadly, there has been a higher than usual incidence of death following injection from products from this region."

"I have been given to understand that those results have not been released for general consumption. Given the world-wide shortage, we do not want to alarm the public, nor curb any isotope production, but something is very wrong. There are some who are worried that it might be bioterrorism by radiological means," Dr. Shearwater added.

Dr. Souflias continued, "The International Nuclear Safety Agency initially asked our Center to look into this, but the Americans felt that there was greater wisdom in having CANDO undertake this work. For one thing, the investigation needs to be more at arm's length than we can do. As you know, there have been tensions in this area and there have been some technological breakthroughs in isotope production methods. It might look like we are trying to undermine the effort of smaller scale producers in the region."

McLaren stroked his chin and bluntly asked, "Do you suspect foul play?"

Dr. Souflias replied, "In reality we do not know what to suspect."

"Do I understand correctly that so far you have been able to keep this secret out of the press?" McLaren asked.

Dr. Souflias looked directly at McLaren and replied with surprising honesty, "Yes, we have kept a lid on it. It was a necessity. It is bad enough that there is a world-wide shortage of isotopes. If it gets out that the isotopes that are available are causing deaths, fear will be rampant. We need CANDO to quickly find out what is causing the increase in death following administration of radioactive medical isotopes in Europe and in America. This is no small problem. The labs and research capabilities of the Center for Nuclear Scientific Research in Athens will be at your disposal. We need your help." Concern was clearly evident in his dark eyes.

"My team will give it our best shot," McLaren replied looking over at his boss and giving a quick nod.

Direct and to the point as usual, Dr. Shearwater announced, "Your assignment is to assemble your team and head to Athens where you will identify the specific source or sources of the problematic isotopes and set out a plan to remedy the situation."

"Dr. Shearwater informed me that your team is now at Pompeii in Italy. You'll find a flight ticket to *Capodichino Airport in Naples* in this envelope. It will be the quickest way to reach your team. I will arrange to have a motor launch sent to the Amalfi coast. The launch will take you and your team to an overnight ferry en route for Athens. Once you arrive, the Nuclear Superintendent will bring you up to speed on the details of what the investigation has found to date," the Greek Director General said, handing McLaren a brown envelope with his ticket and details of the itinerary.

Though the meeting was over, McLaren's intuition told him that they were deliberately omitting something from the briefing. He put his trust in his boss and hoped that sometime soon he'd share the information with him. McLaren shook hands with both men and left the café.

****

"Dimitrios, I'm really not comfortable keeping him in the dark. He's a man to be trusted," Dr. Shearwater said.

"I fully realize that you put your trust in him, but the stakes are too high. We are in no position to divulge more to him," Dr. Souflias replied.

Dr. Shearwater's eyes pursued McLaren while he walked back along the promenade. His gaze followed him until he was out of sight.

CHAPTER 13

Maya was in awe when they approached the pink facade of the National Archae-ological Museum of Naples. Originally a cavalry barracks and later home to the University of Naples, the museum was founded by the Bourbon King Charles VII in the late 18th century as a place to house the rich collection of antiquities he had inherited from his mother, Elisabetta Farnese. Now it is considered one of Italy's top archeology museums, hosting extensive collections of Greek and Roman antiquities.

Maya and Danny passed through security and proceeded to the office of the Curator Antonio Del Falco. Maya had been granted a meeting with him thanks to her aunt's connections and Danny was with her for moral support.

"Che piacere vederti! Welcome," said the impeccably dressed, silver-gray haired gentleman who greeted them. "Maya, how lovely to meet you." In his *elegant, dark gray Italian business suit, crisp white shirt and tie of muted tones,* Curator Antonio Del Falco *cut quite a stylish figure.*

"The professoressa has told me the purpose of your visit. Christopher was a wonderful young man. We had many delightful conversations. I am so sorry that he was taken in his youth. I must say that he impressed me. He had a basic goodness about him. It was some years ago, but I still miss his youthful enthusiasm."

Del Falco's rapid-fire bilingual conversation surprised Maya. She found his smile infectious and she could not help but smile back.

"Buongiorno! I would like to introduce to my traveling companion, Danielle McLaren," Maya said.

"Molto lieto di conoscerla," Danny said, extending her hand to the curator.

The meeting was short, but productive. Anxious to learn more about her cousin's research, Maya posed many questions. She confirmed what she had learned. Christopher had come to the museum frequently and was particularly interested in the Alexander mosaic.

The Curator explained that the large mosaic was discovered during the excavation of Pompeii in 1831. It was originally on the floor in Pompeii's most luxurious residence, the House of Faun. For reasons of preservation the mosaic was removed from Pompeii in 1843 and placed on a wall in the museum.

"The artwork is composed of countless tiny colored tiles and dates from circa 100 B.C. It is an unusually large and detailed work for a private residence. Scholars have hypothesized that the mosaic is a copy of an ancient Greek painting which has been lost," the Curator explained.

Maya eyed him with an intensity that would have made others uncomfortable, "Why do you suppose Christopher came to see this mosaic so often?"

Antonio Del Falco paused for a moment before replying. He looked into Maya's doe-brown eyes as if he were considering his response, "I always thought that young Christopher was intent on studying the mosaic, not just for its beauty, but because he felt that it might hold some important clue for his research into Alexander the Great."

Maya nodded.

The Curator Del Falco gestured towards an ornate staircase, "Enough background. Allow me to take you up to the Alexander mosaic. It is up on the mezzanine level, beside our wonderful collection of coins and medals from antiquity."

Musical notes cut the silence of the museum hall. Antonio Del Falco reached down into his tailored suit coat pocket to retrieve his phone. He glanced at the message and his expression changed.

"I am so sorry. I must return to my office. Circumstances have arisen, and I regret that I can no longer give you my guided tour. The mosaics are just down this hall. Please visit them and the other artifacts in our museum. Drop by my office before you leave and if you have any further questions, I will try and answer them. Please, enjoy our museum, ladies," the Curator said, leaning forward with a dramatic bow.

He headed in the opposite direction of the grand stairway but after a few steps he turned back to face the women with a reminder, "Per favore ricorda, it is forbidden to use a flash camera in the museum."

Danny smiled back at him and Maya nodded.

Wasting not a moment Maya and Danny went off in search of the Alexander mosaic. In truth they could not have possibly missed it. Affixed to a wall, not on the floor like it had been found in Pompeii, there it was, all 19 feet by 10 feet of it.

"Oh my gosh, it's huge!" Danny said in awe, staring up at it.

The battle scene the mosaic depicted was intricate. The artist's use of repeated diagonal spears, clashing metal, and crowding of men and horses evoked the din and slaughter of battle. Alexander the Great of Macedonia, in his full battle regalia, was depicted charging bare-headed into the midst of battle on his famous horse, Bucephalus. The Persian King Darius was portrayed in a chariot, and his face bore a worried look. He appeared to be commanding his frightened charioteer to flee the battle.

"Wow! Look at the detail on Alexander's armor. You can see Medusa the Gorgon depicted on his breastplate. Look at the features on her face. She looks truly dreadful with her hair of venomous snakes. You can see why the Greeks believed that anyone who looked directly at Medusa would be turned to stone," Maya said.

"The mosaic must have held some special significance for your cousin," Danny said, taking a furtive glance over her shoulder. Registering that there was no one in sight, she took out her cell phone and started to capture the mosaic in a series of photos.

"Danny, what are you doing? The Curator told us no photos," Maya admonished.

"No, we were told no flash camera. I didn't use a flash, and this is a cell phone, not a camera. What are your aunt's coordinates? We should email her these photos, so she can help us find out why your cousin was interested in it," Danny said.

"You are so into this, aren't you?" Maya smiled and provided Tante Hélène's email address. She wouldn't have dared take the photos, but she knew her aunt would like to see photos of the mosaic that her son had visited so many times.

After pondering the mysteries of the mosaic, they wondered through the museum. A little over an hour after the Curator had rushed off, Maya and Danny ducked their heads into his office to say goodbye. He was not there. His secretary passed along his regrets at not being able to talk with them further. He had been called away unexpectedly.

The women exited the museum and headed down a quiet alley. Maya suggested that they grab some lunch at a nearby osteria before taking the local train up to Pompeii to rendezvous with Sam.

"Great idea. I'm starved. Looking at antiquities sure builds up a girl's appetite."

The calm of the warm sunlit day was suddenly broken by an obnoxious roar. A revving noise reverberated off the stone walls of the narrow cobblestone alley.

"Look out!" Danny's warning was barely audible over the two-stroke engine noise of a Vespa flying past them.

In a split second the olive-skinned teen riding pillion reached out to grab Maya's purse from her shoulder, while simultaneously giving her a big shove intended to knock her to the ground.

Maya hung onto her purse for all she was worth. The force of the blow knocked her off her feet and she tumbled to the cobblestones. In an instant, she was being dragged along by the Vespa.

"Maya, let go! It's not worth it!" Danny screamed.

Danny was afraid that Maya might be run over by a passing vehicle. She ran after the little moped. A second later the Scippatori felt the impact of her vengeance. In that moment, when the Vespa struggled under the burden of Maya's drag weight, Danny slammed her leg into the back of the pillion rider, with a powerful judo kick.

Danny's reaction was so quick that she had clearly not thought things out. Suddenly, she was aware that she had placed Maya in a precarious position. "Oh, no!"

The force of the blow unbalanced the bike. The Vespa tipped like it was going over, but somehow the teen at the controls managed to recover.

Lady Luck was with Maya. The leather strap on her purse could not withstand the tension and one end snapped. Scrapped and bruised, Maya was left on the cobblestones with her purse in her arms, staring back at the little Vespa speeding away.

"Good god Maya, you are a lady with guts! Are you all right?" Danny asked.

"I'm fine," Maya responded. She opened her purse, grabbed a tissue and dabbed it on her bloodied elbow. "I had no intension of losing my passport. It would have been such a hassle."

"You could have broken your arm or worse. Those Scippatori are everywhere in Naples," Danny said.

"Scippatori?" Maya gave Danny a questioning look.

"That's the term for the scooter riding bandits that steal purses from walking tourists. I guess we'll have to keep a closer look out for them."

"You mean it happens so often they have a name for them? Good grief!" Maya exclaimed.

****

After consuming a quick lunch, Danny and Maya made their way to the Stazione Centrale, Napoli Garibaldi train station. They shouldered their way through the chaotic crowd to board the dingy, graffiti covered train and wedged themselves in beside commuters and local students for the half-hour milk run. From this departure point, the tracks that serve the Circumvesuvian line head directly for the Pompeii Scavi station directly across the street from the entrance to the archeological site of Pompeii.

The train was not air-conditioned. That didn't seem to bother the locals, but the North Americans found it hot and stuffy sitting on the hard-wooden seats, lurching and swaying while the train passed through villages and tunnels. Despite enjoying the scenic beauty of the Bay of Naples and the views of Mount Vesuvius, the women were decidedly uncomfortable. They were ever so relieved to get off at the Pompei Scavi station.

"Come on. Let's purchase our entrance tickets to the archeological site and see what's left of Pompeii after the devastating volcanic eruption of 79 AD," Danny said enthusiastically.

"As anxious as I am to see the place where the Alexander mosaic was discovered, I have to tell you that I'm going to need a lemon soda before I get started. It's hot!" Maya replied with a smile.

CHAPTER 14

Maya and Danny trudged towards Porta Marina along the long stone ramp that sloped decidedly upwards to the two imposing archways that greeted visitors to the ancient Roman town. When life had thrived in Pompeii, pedestrians headed through the left arch while mules and carts carrying salt and fish from the sea passed through the significantly taller right-hand arch.

Maya paused at the top for a moment to look around. The sun was warm on her back. She found the juxtaposition shocking — the permanence, craft and symmetry of the Roman stonework — the ephemerality of their existence. Life for these Romans was snuffed out on the fateful day when the mountain they worshipped as a divinity unleashed its fury and hurled rocks and burning pumice on the ancient cosmopolitan center.

Danny checked her watch while she stood waiting. "Come on, let's find Sam."

"They say that the Vesuvius's eruption was multi-phased. During the initial explosion, a column of ash and pumice ranging between 15 and 30 kilometers high, rained on Pompeii. The plume of ash was driven by super-heated steam created when magma came in contact with groundwater which had seeped into deep faults. Residents of Pompeii were exterminated by exposure to the extreme heat and the layers of ash which fell preserved what lay beneath for thousands of years," Maya reported what her aunt had said about the archaeological site.

They meandered along the uneven cobblestone path and soon found themselves in the Forum, Pompeii's central piazza and center of power. The threatening shape of Mount Vesuvius loomed menacingly in the distance beyond the monuments.

"Did Sam give any indication of where we might find him?" Maya asked.

Danny shook her head, "Not really."

They searched the Forum for Sam and within a few minutes Danny spotted him, tripod and camera in hand.

Sam always found archeological sites interesting, however to him Pompeii belayed comparison. His photographic interest was geocultural. Pompeii offered an unparalleled view into Roman life, capturing the scene of August 24th AD 79, when unsuspecting residents were buried under 30 feet of hot volcanic ash. On this assignment his goal was to capture the feeling Pompeii evokes about nature's awful embrace.

Sam's artistic work was in demand. His compositional tactics contributed astonishing glimpses of the world. At this moment, in his viewfinder was the magnificent Temple of Apollo, glistening as the sun's afternoon rays radiated from the bronze statues of Apollo and Diana. When he adjusted his tripod to achieve the optimum angle to capture the repetition and interplay of light on the slender columns by the altar, he glanced up and saw Danny waving.

"You're here! Isn't this place superb? I can't believe my luck with the weather and the scarcity of tourists," a broad smile crossed Sam's full lips. He gave a happy wink to Danny.

Danny smiled, "Last time we were here it poured. What a contrast it is today."

Sam laughed, "Pompeii is the essence of photography. Like photography it records a moment out of time and alters life by holding it still."

Very insightful, Sam. Maya thought, seeing Sam in a new light.

"I'll be about another half hour or so. McLaren said he would meet us here. Why don't you two go ahead and have a good look around? Maya, you'll love Pompeii. It's like a time warp back into the Roman era. Many of the buildings are still intact. You'll get a fine taste of how life was in Roman times." Sam said.

"I'm anxious to see the House of Faun, where the Alexander mosaic was found," Maya said.

****

Guided by a map of the site Maya and Danny set out towards the Via della Fortuna. They followed an ancient lane that was rutted with a couple of centuries of cart traffic. Deep depressions in the paving stones bore vivid testimony to ancient traffic patterns. In some spots the path was just wide enough for pedestrian traffic, while other parts were built using solid Roman road engineering with a route designed to take two carts at a time.

Along the streets, houses seemed to range from modest dwellings to magnificent villas embellished with frescoes and mosaics, enclosing inner courtyards with swimming pools, gardens and fountains, featuring central heating and other amenities. They passed public baths with remnants of hot and cold running water, heated floors, dressing rooms and saunas. They peeked into homes and explored stores, cafes, and workshops, wandering in search of the Casa del Fauno.

Maya had to admit that she was totally unprepared for the House of Faun.

Named in honor of the bronze statue of a dancing faun found at the villa, and dating back to the 2nd century BC, the Casa del Fauno was one of Pompeii's most palatial private residences. Its sheer size was amazing. The villa took up a full city block. It was shaped in the form of a parallelogram following the contour of the surrounding streets which had not been laid out on a square grid.

Inside the residence the women found the temperature much cooler. It was a definite respite from the heat that radiated off the street outside.

The rooms of the private residence were primarily rectangular in shape, except for the end rooms which were irregularly shaped and followed the parallelogram perimeter. The volcanic eruption had been devastating, heaping layers and layers of ash over the villa. By some miracle the home's various artworks, including the famous Alexander mosaic, had survived.

Maya had read that in 1830, a German archeologist discovered the famous artistic floor mosaic in the exedra, a small sitting room positioned between two porticoed gardens. A dozen or so years later the mosaic was moved to the museum in Naples. A replica rumored to have been created from over 2 million pieces of variegated marble now replaced the original Alexander mosaic.

Danny stared at the skillfully crafted reproduction and asked, "Why do you suppose Christopher was interested in the mosaic?"

"I only wish I knew," Maya replied.

****

"Buonasera, you are in a good spot here to see the tourists passing, no? Have you by chance seen two young English speaking North American ladies? They both have dark hair. One is tall, the other smaller and darker. I come from the Museo in Naples with a package for the small one," an older male voice said in heavily accented English.

Sam looked up from his viewfinder to see where the gravelly voice was emanating from. He peered down from the ruin where he was perched taking photos. Below him stood a short, gray-haired, balding Italian in a security guard's uniform. Behind him Sam was surprised to see the tall figure of his buddy, McLaren. In an instant, his mind went from considering whether the guard was going to scold him and tell him to get down off the ruins, to wondering why his friend was with the guard.

"Sam, have the girls arrived yet? Marcello here has something for Maya."

Sam smiled and nodded while giving McLaren an open-eyed inquiring look. The intense sapphire blue color of Sam's eyes contrasted sharply against his mahogany skin, "Yes, they are on the site. Actually, I can offer a plausible guess about where you might find them," he said, before jumping down off the ruin.

"Good. Marcello is from the Museum of Naples. Maya and Danny were there earlier today and must have left something. He was sent on a mission by his curator to deliver an envelope to Maya. As luck would have it, I met him on the way into the site. He guessed that I was a North American and asked for my help. If you've finished your work for the day, perhaps we could walk with him to find the girls?"

"Grazie per il vostro aiuto. Antonio Del Falco, my Curator of Museo at Naples asked that I hand deliver this to Dr. Maya," he said waving a large manila envelope bearing the insignia of the Archaeological Museum of Naples.

Curious about the envelope, Sam replied. "No problem. I can wrap this up now and come with you."

From his hip pocket Sam pulled a map of the archeological site and passed it to McLaren, "Danny and Maya have probably reached the House of Faun by now. That's where they were headed."

****

Less than a quarter of a mile behind them, outside the Porta Marina, a swarthy male got out of a black sedan. He strode up the ramp to Pompeii and pulled out his cell phone. He examined the video footage that had been sent to him and paused the video to enlarge a still. The somewhat blurry enlargement showed two female faces, one his target, a petite, luscious dark-haired, dark-eyed woman of mestizo descent, the other her companion, a taller Caucasian looker with long chestnut colored hair.

As usual his employer had given Alketas short notice of his assignment. He was provided with a description and told that his prey would be at the Museum of Naples in the morning. Time had been tight, so he had hired from the Camorra, but his plan had failed when the reckless teen missed his chance while playing the scippatori game. He had been blatantly displeased when Giuseppe reported to him that the woman had managed to escape.

Now on the scene himself, he dared not miss this time or for sure there would be consequences from his employer. He thought of the old guy who had engaged his services. He seemed to have eyes everywhere. He had given Alketas another chance at completing the assignment and sent a car and driver to take him to Pompeii. He wondered how his employer could know so much about where the woman could be. He would not be comfortable if someone were keeping track of him like that.

He turned his attention to the map of Pompeii. The archeological site might appear to be extensive, with plenty of hiding places, but the walls and designated exits confined the space and made it an easy killing ground. He'd get the job done and get out. He turned his head back towards the black Mercedes. The thick polycarbonate window made it impossible for him to see the driver assigned to ensure that he would get the job done.

****

"The old villa is still welcoming visitors," McLaren said with a wry smile. It was just like him to comment on the entrance threshold with the traditional welcoming inscription, HAVE, carved into the doorsill of the Casa del Fauno..

"Dan are you in here?" McLaren's voice echoed eerily against the stone walls.

Sam gave a slight shrug, "Let's take a look around."

Further inside the Roman residence, Danny was proceeding towards her brother's voice. She ducked around corners in the impressively large villa hoping to find him.

"Beautiful isn't it?" Danny said, greeting the arrivals with a warm smile. She wondered who the older man in the uniform was.

"Dan, this is Marcello. He's come all the way from Naples with a package for Maya," McLaren said returning his sister's smile.

Her face lit up. "Maya's in the exedra studying a mosaic. I'll get her."

Without another word she was off. In no time, she returned with Maya and introductions were repeated.

"Dr. Maya, I have an envelope here for you from my director, Antonio Del Falco," the elderly messenger said in halting English. He leaned forward to extend to Maya a manila envelope. The envelop bore the insignia of the Archaeological Museum of Naples.

Crack! The moment was shattered by the sound of a single bullet whizzing by.

"Everyone down!" McLaren yelled.

The elderly man's face contorted in pain. He stumbled to the travertine floor. Blood trickled from the corners of his mouth.

Three more bullets whizzed by. One shot hit the right side of an altar table beside Maya. She felt stone splinters pelt her arm.

Maya dropped to her knees and crawled towards the motionless messenger. She was all too aware that he needed more medical attention that she could possibly provide. His eyes were lifeless. The bullet was imbedded in his back.

Marcello's mission to bring the package to Maya had come at a high price. At a later time, Maya would relate that the incident happened so quickly. In his act of leaning forward, the elderly Museum security guard had saved her life.

"Stay down!" McLaren's mind was churning. A second of silence passed before he spoke.

"Remember the Alamo!"

Sam's eyebrows rose. The lexicon quickly percolated through. "You think he'll take the bait?"

McLaren simply nodded.

It was an unusual signal, but it might just work. "Okay, Santa Anna!" Sam replied.

Danny didn't have a clue about the plan that had just been hatched. She watched Sam carefully extend the slim legs of his camera tripod and wondered what he was up to. She tilted her head in quandary when Sam removed his black t-shirt and tied it to the clips at the feet of his tripod. It looked for all the world like a black flag.

****

McLaren silently made his way down the passage towards the Tetrastyle Atrium. He'd been intrigued on seeing from the outside that this portion of the residence had its own street entrance. Now he hoped to use the exit to take out the shooter.

"What the…" he muttered when he turned a corner. This was not exactly what he was hoping to find.

A good portion now lay in rubble. The inner exit to the street was blocked by debris. The atrium had been a casualty of Allied bombing during the forties, but the destruction hadn't been noticeable from the exterior of the residence.

McLaren shook off his annoyance and looked around to reconsider his options. He patted his leg, touching the souvenir that he'd acquired in the apartment in Zermatt. Even without that street exit, there was a good chance he could still accomplish his goal. The solution was to a perch atop the stone walls.

With gritty determination McLaren slid through a narrow opening between columns and climbed through debris to reach the outer wall. He fingered the old masonry in the courtyard wall searching for a handhold to mount the ancient stone walls. Using arm strength, he hoisted himself up to the top. While he gripped the stone, dangling by his arms, his feet groped the crumpling stonework for a toe-hold.

Another high-pitched metallic crack rang out. It sounded like someone hitting a hammer against a thick sheet of metal. The pitch indicated that the shooter was within close range.

McLaren cautiously peered over the wall.

"Come on, Sam. Now's the time."

General Santa Anna was infamous for the black flag at the ruthless battle of the Alamo. Today the plan was for Sam to wave a black flag out the door to draw the shooter out and give McLaren a clear target.

Keeping his body flat against the wall and hanging on with his left arm, McLaren reached his right arm down to the sheath attached to his leg. He needed the knife that was secured to his right leg under his pants.

Suddenly, below in the street a piece of black cloth unfurled at the entrance doorway of the House of Faun. As if on cue, the shooter emerged from where he was hiding onto the cobblestone lane.

McLaren straightened up and aimed the knife with precision honed from experience. In one fluid and powerful movement he optimized release angle and throwing force to maximize power and distance. The blade made exactly one half turn in the air before it delivered a sudden and unexpected blow.

The walloping impact from the Ka-Bar forced the shooter to release his grip on the gun. His weapon toppled to the cobblestone with a heavy thunk. The action was so rapid that there wasn't a chance for the shooter to fire his gun.

The hitman yelped in pain; his left hand shot up to his wounded right shoulder. Unflinching, he attempted to apply pressure to stem the tide of blood oozing where the knife's sharp point had pierced his olive skin. Realizing he needed quick medical attention, he turned on his heel and ran, disappearing like a dark ninja into the maze of shadows in the narrow Roman lanes of Pompeii.

CHAPTER 15

"You sure gain respect for the Italian engineers who built this road when you take these curves," Sam said. He deftly maneuvered the rented Lancia through the switchbacks. There was no doubt that he was enjoying the drive.

The scenery whizzed by in streaks like strobe lights on a dance floor. Intermittently Maya caught a glimpse of a sandy cove in the bay below and the sparkle of sunlight off the azure blue Mediterranean. The blur of pastel colors on cantilevered roofs of villas and terraced hotels clinging to steep hills above the Gulf of Salerno looked like brush strokes on an abstract painting.

The Amalfi Coast was breathtaking, but this wild ride put a new spin on it. Maya heard the Lancia's engine roar when Sam downshifted to make the corner of a tight hairpin. The shear drop-off on the right shoulder terrified her; it must have been at least 500 feet.

Sam took the curve at double any sane speed. The tires screeched in protest as the vehicle lost traction.

Maya felt like her stomach was in her mouth. She gripped the armrest; her knuckles whitened. The memory of her Civic going over the embankment was all to fresh.

"Up like a rocket ship, down like a roller coaster, back like a loop-the-loop, and around like a merry-go-round," Danny happily sang the lyrics of a popular sixties sound.

Good grief. Danny likes driving with Sam on this insane road. Maya thought to herself.

Sam floored the accelerator on the straights and zipped through several switchbacks. He glanced in the rear-view mirror. A black Mercedes following kept pace.

"We've got a tail."

McLaren nodded, "Yes, the Mercedes has been behind us for quite some time, even though we've taken a convoluted route. Danny, can you make out the plate?"

"The road's too twisty. It's hard to get it in the view finder," Danny replied aiming a telephoto lens out the back window of the car.

Sam rounded a blind hairpin. In a split second, a huge tour bus dominated the scene and was bearing down on the Lancia.

"Lookout!" Maya screamed.

The deep guttural sound of a vehicle horn announced that the bus driver thought he was boss.

There was to be no mediation in this dispute. As if he was sparring, Sam pounded on the Lancia's klaxon. The horn unexpectedly emitted the merry sound of trumpet notes.

"That's sure to tell him who's boss!" Danny giggled.

Amidst the melee of blaring horns and screeching tires, Sam wrestled with the steering wheel. He swerved to avoid imminent collision and managed to remain in control while riding the narrow stretch of shoulder separating the touring bus from a stone wall enclosing a farmer's field. Somehow, he squeezed the Lancia through the tight opening. The only casualty was the passenger side mirror which let out a scraping sound when it bounced off the stone wall.

Maya saw the bus driver gesture wildly with his arms and heard him yell 'Stronzo' out the bus window.

Sam flashed a one finger salute to express his thanks and say goodbye.

Moments later the black Mercedes that was following Sam rounded the curve and encountered the tour bus. A squeal of tires, followed by a loud sound reminiscent of nails scraping on a chalkboard, announced that the sedan had sideswiped the farmer's stone wall. A second later, a loud bang proclaimed the failure of the German vehicle to negotiate the narrow space between the tour bus and the stone wall.

"That was close! Let's hear it for our Lancia!" Danny shouted.

Sam focused on the road ahead. He stomped on the accelerator until the transmission whined, indicating that it was time to shift again. Barreling into the next set of curves he shifted down to third.

"Impressive driving, Sam!" McLaren said.

"What can I say? It's in the blood. My grandmother was Italian, and Italians are about getting where they want to go as quickly as possible despite the obstacles."

Sam's light mood did nothing to alleviate the anxiety Maya felt. She sat in the backseat stunned, clutching the manila envelope and staring out the car window, thoroughly shaken by everything that had taken place.

This can't be happening.

She had followed orders in Pompeii. It seemed like she had no choice. McLaren was vehement that they had to get out of there. There was no time to waste. He had a boat waiting on the coast to take them to Greece where there was some kind of emergency that required his team.

I was the intended victim. McLaren was correct that nothing further could be done for the guard. He was dead. But, leaving his body was not what I would have done. What kind of mess have I gotten myself into by traveling with these new-found friends?

Maya had difficulty coping with the notion that the elderly messenger was dead, his life taken while handing her the envelope that she now held in her hands. While anxious to see its contents, she had been unable to open it. She reminded herself that Sam had stopped at a pay phone so that she could call the Curator of the Museum. She'd been in tears when she told him of the messenger's death. McLaren had also spoken with the Curator and made one additional call. When he completed the call, he had told Maya that all of the details had been taken care of.

Maya's negative reverie was interrupted by McLaren's blunt assessment of their predicament.

"That encounter put a bit of space between us and the Mercedes, but I'm sure that we haven't seen the last of him. We need to lose him. There's a medieval village up ahead. Sam, once you reach it hang a right into one of the narrow side streets. My hope is that he'll be so anxious to catch up with us that he won't notice that we've left the main road," McLaren ordered.

Sam kept the pedal to the metal until he reached the outskirts of medieval Ravello. When he saw the village coming up he decreased his speed. He crawled past the stone buildings then made a slow right turn into a lane that was so narrow that the Lancia could barely fit through. He stopped a few feet short of the end of the lane just before it opened into a small open square.

Some minutes later, while peering out the rear window, Maya caught a glimpse of the battered black Mercedes speeding by the opening of the narrow street.

"I think that this would be a good time to take a hike and see the scenery," McLaren announced. "Pull up to the square and we'll leave the car here. There's a walking trail that goes down to the coast from Ravello through the village of Scala down to Amalfi."

****

"Hope you're wearing your walking shoes," McLaren laughed.

The town of Ravello was geared to pedestrians, with steps and ramps designed to assist the walkers. It sat high on the hills above the Tyrrhenian Sea by Italy's Amalfi Coast. McLaren knew instinctively that by melding into the group of tourists ambling about they would be less conspicuous. While walking past the local tourist office, he picked up a hiking map for directions to the ancient path that led towards Amalfi.

Maya was thankful to be out of the car. The feel of solid ground under her feet helped relieve her motion-sickness. She had had no desire to be shoved off the road again and that seemed to be the intent of the black Mercedes.

The sun-drenched path took the foursome past a terraced village that hung suspended like an eagle's nest above the dizzying landscape of the Mediterranean. The sun began to set, and a spreading panorama of pinks and mauve clouds lit up the sky. The temperature dropped slightly while they trekked though the shade of old stone churches and houses trudging down steps and more steps cut into the cliffside. They soon arrived at the sleepy village of Scala where gnarled locals set about early evening chores. Far below in the twilight, the lights of Amalfi began to glow like fireflies.

"I didn't think I'd miss riding in the car," Maya laughed. The muscles in her calves ached from the cornucopia of stairs she'd descended.

Within half an hour on the steep path the foursome reached the outskirts of Amalfi, where they followed the coast road towards the sea-front.

"We'll get a lift by launch to a ferry headed to Athens this evening," McLaren said. He scanned the wharf of the Amalfi Marina. The dock was almost completely deserted.

"What are on earth is that car doing here?" Danny asked.

Down the street, across from the hotel, a large black Mercedes sedan marred by a long crease along its side panel was parked. No driver was visible.

"There's only one reason I can think of," Sam said.

"How could he have known we were headed to Amalfi? We could easily have been going to Positano."

McLaren knew that he wouldn't relax until they were safely on board the ferry. He needed to assure himself that they hadn't been followed. He turned his gaze to the wharf and looked for the launch.

Chapter 16

The Tyrrhenian sea was as calm as a summer lake when the Italian ferry made its long journey to mainland Greece. Nautical dusk had crept in. Stars, like Sirius and bright planets like Venus began to appear in the deep purple, indigo sky. Along the shoreline lights twinkled against the evening panorama of sunset and moonrise.

Maya leaned against a rail of the ferryboat and looked out at the intoxicating view. She ran her fingers through her dark hair and closed her eyes for a moment. The night crossing was just what she needed, a peaceful idyll after the day's upsetting events.

"Aren't you ever going to open it?" Danny asked.

"Yes, now is a good time," Maya sighed. Carefully, she slit open the end of the manila envelope with her dad's Swiss Army knife.

"What's inside?" Danny asked eagerly.

Maya looked into the envelope. Inside was an 8 by 10 glossy photograph of the famous mosaic of Alexander's victory over Darius. There was also a note from the Curator of the Museum in Naples. The note was written in a beautiful script.

"What does it say?" Danny moved in closer to Maya so that she could have a better look.

"The Curator suggests that I contact a former military man in Athens. He has provided his coordinates. He says that this retired Greek general accompanied Christopher to the museum in Naples on several occasions to examine the mosaic. It seems that the General had undertaken some research of his own on Alexander the Great. There's a chance that he might have further insight into my cousin's work."

"Why wouldn't the Curator just have told you about this chap in Athens?" Danny asked.

"For that matter, why would he send someone down to Pompeii to give me a note with the photo? The old man was killed giving me the photo. It was a senseless loss of life," Maya said sadly.

"Maya, I hate to break it to you kid, but that shot was meant for you. That little man saved your life."

"Why would someone shoot at me?"

"Likely for the same reason they tried to shoot at you up on the ski run. Look at it this way, Marcelo died passing you a clue to information you might not otherwise have be able to access. Now you have a lead."

Maya looked out to sea. She refused to give in to her emotions. Just when she was beginning to wonder how long she could keep things bottled up inside she saw the reassuring sight of McLaren and Sam approaching.

Danny took their arrival as an apt moment to quiz her brother on the upcoming mission, "By the way big brother, you haven't said too much about why we are off to Greece?"

"I'm sorry for telling you so little on the way out of Pompeii and down to the coast. We were a trifle busy, so it wasn't the appropriate time. Now that we are underway I'll fill you in. Maya, I am trusting you not to say a word to anyone about what you are about to hear," McLaren said.

Sam and Danny looked at McLaren.

"I met with Dr. Shearwater in Geneva. He's assigned our team to a priority health emergency. The fact is that the American President and the European Medicines Network have asked that CANDO lead an investigation. The media have not made a hay day of it yet, but there have been a significant number of deaths which have been linked to the use of medical isotopes in Greece and in southern and eastern Europe. Our team is tasked with heading the investigation. We'll be headquartered in Athens and will work out of the Greek National Center for Nuclear Scientific Research. This ferry will dock in Piraeus in the morning. The usual hotel is booked for us in Athens. If you have questions, ask away, if not I suggest you grab some shut-eye while you can."

Maya was surprised that Sam and Danny turned in without asking a single question.

"See you down in our cabin," Danny said, leaving Maya with her brother.

"Maya, I realize this is a bit awkward. I am sure you were not expecting to zip down to the Amalfi coast and then be ferried off to Athens. Truth be told, I feel better that you are with us because something is going on. There is real evidence that you are in danger, but there is no time to get to the root of that with this assignment. We'd all feel a bit more secure if you would stay and work with us. Someone wants you out of the way, so we'll take you out of the way," McLaren offered.

The moon cast a silvery swathe across the sea like a pathway to follow. Maya looked down at the bioluminescent wake behind the ferry then up to the handsome face smiling at her and nodded. In the rapture of the moonlight, their eyes shared a moment.

Yes, Maya felt safer with McLaren, but what in the world was going on? *What are the odds?*

It seemed an unusual coincidence that the Curator had suggested to Maya that for more information on her cousin's research she should contact a military man in Athens, the same city that McLaren and his team were headed for. Was it a coincidence or synchronicity?

****

The ferry docked in the busy port of Piraeus early the next morning. The foursome caught a cab into downtown Athens. Their destination was a hotel in the old quarter of the bustling city.

"We've stayed here before. You'll love it. It's a respectable place, within walking distance of historical sites, great restaurants and the flea markets. In one direction, you have modern Athens and in the other, the Plaka. And, best of all there is a rooftop terrace with a lovely view of the Acropolis. You have to see it at night. The Parthenon is lit up and it's awesome." The sentences tumbled out of Danny's mouth.

"Maya, the reservations show the ladies sharing a room. Are you okay with that?" McLaren asked.

"Sure, no problem," Maya replied.

Once in their hotel, the foursome squeezed into a tiny elevator, about the size of an American refrigerator. It looked as if it had not been updated since the seventies. It had old style mechanical buttons and an open cage with a continuous view of the shaft. Sam pressed the button for the third floor. It plodded and grumbled its way along.

"They don't seem to post the weight limit for this thing," Sam said twisting his head to see around Danny and get a better view of the elevator registration glued to the mirror.

"It will be Greek to you!" Danny said laughing.

Undeterred, Sam continued reading. Amidst the Greek lettering on the elevator certificate he recognized the numerical value 150. That had to be 150 kilograms or 300 pounds.

"The recommended weight load is two persons. We've overloaded this elevator," Sam reported matter-of-factly.

"Well, we'll soon be off," Danny replied.

The elevator came to a stop at the third floor. The bell did not ring, and the door did not open.

Sam reached a long arm over to press the door open button. Nothing happened. He squeezed by Danny and pushed on the door in a further attempt to open it. Once again, nothing happened. He put considerable weight into another try. The elevator door rebuffed his attempt at brute force.

"What do you think?" Sam asked. His question was directed at McLaren.

McLaren squeezed forward to examine the doorframe.

"The cabin appears to be sagging. It's not in alignment with the door," McLaren said giving a clinical assessment.

Danny reached in and pressed the emergency button. Nothing happened. She repeated the action and there was still no response.

McLaren glanced up at the ceiling where one normally would find an escape hatch. There was none.

Maya was feeling the heat of four bodies pressed into a tiny space. It wasn't that she was claustrophobic, but the situation just wasn't comforting. With all that had happened she was beginning to feel that she led a jinxed life.

"Well, we aren't going to suffocate because there is air movement around this cage," Danny said. "Try your cell. Call the front desk," Danny ordered.

McLaren reached for his cell, looked at the screen and shook his head. There was no reception.

Danny tried shouting into the shaft hoping that someone would hear. No one appeared.

"What if we try to redistribute our weight?" McLaren suggested. He waved Danny and Maya over to the back-right corner.

"Maybe some heavy weight will help," Sam jumped towards the back corner and landed with a heavy thump.

The elevator groaned and shifted slightly but the cage was still, and the door did not release.

"Statistically speaking, for the billions of elevator rides that take place each year, there are extremely few cases of people being trapped and dying," Danny announced.

"That's good news for us?" McLaren bantered back at Danny.

Danny rolled her eyes.

"Can you make out what's holding it?" McLaren asked. He trusted Sam's mechanical genius and correctly assumed that Sam knew what he was doing.

Sam realized that shifting the weight had done some good, but not enough. He ran his eyes up and down the opening and nodded. He could just make out something in the space between the door and the cabin. It was the mechanism that normally triggered the door to release and open, but in this case, it was still caught so the door was locked in place. He pointed so that McLaren could see the offending device in the top right-hand corner of their floor landing.

McLaren stuck his head closer to get a better view.

"You are right about alignment causing a problem," Sam said crouching down. "I think there's a way, if I just…"

Beads of perspiration appeared on Sam's forehead. He began pushing the bottom right hand corner of the metal door.

"Come on baby," Sam willed.

He hoped that he could exert sufficient pressure. His goal was to apply force at the base of the door, to leverage pressure on the upper corner. He anticipated that this counterforce would trigger the offending mechanism to open.

Sam's jiggery-pokery worked. A moment later the door opened.

"Piece of cake!" Sam announced.

"About time," Danny sniped. She catapulted out of the claustrophobic space.

Just like that, the incident was over. The foursome walked away from the cage and down the hallway to their rooms.

Danny and Maya's room seemed quiet and spacious after the confined space. Danny kicked off her shoes, opened the small hotel refrigerator, selected a Greek ION chocolate almond bar and took a bite.

"Would you like a bite?" Danny's infectious smile gave every indication that the candy bar was delicious.

Maya smiled and shook her head. She sat down on the bed.

"Weren't you worried in there?" Maya asked. It appeared to her that Danny had not been shaken by the experience, but she had.

"Heavens no. I knew that with those two engineers on board we'd get out of there. Besides, I came prepared," Danny smiled. She rummaged through her purse until she found a small gift bag, "I want you to have this. I saw it and immediately thought of you. I hope you'll wear it."

Maya opened the gift bag. Inside was a wrist bracelet set with an eye shaped black and blue stone.

"It's called an Evil Eye. The energy emitted by the amulet is believed to ward off evil influences and bad luck. The blue center charm is a Nazar. It's a symbol synonymous with protection against malicious intentions in many countries like Greece and Turkey and even Brazil."

Maya was obviously surprised by the gift. She looked down and studied the blue charm that radiated concentric circles in shades of white, light blue and black. Had it worked in the elevator?

"You're so thoughtful. I *definitely could use some help in warding off malicious intentions.*"

CHAPTER 17

The hypnotic rhythm of bouzouki and guitar music floated over the red-tiled roofs. The music seemed to be serenading Maya. She wandered along the narrow cobblestone street and found herself very much enjoying the rose-tinted warmth of the afternoon sun and soft music of the Plaka. Her outing took her past souvenir shops and whitewashed Greek tavernas where old Athenians came to drink Retsina on the cool terraces hidden between shops and restaurants.

How extraordinary, I didn't expect to be here in Athens following up on Christopher's research.

Dressed in a light-yellow sun dress, appropriate for the late afternoon sunshine, Maya had taken her bearings from Syntagma Square, and headed for a destination in the Plaka. She walked along the wide pedestrian street named Ermou, watching for the small back street where she hoped to find the General. She was glad that she had picked up a map from the concierge at the hotel.

Where in the world is Kydatheneon Street?

The street address was located in a trendy tourist quarter inhabited since antiquity. It lay at the base of the northern and eastern slopes of the Acropolis, in the shadow of the Parthenon. In this neighbourhood, the streets were a labyrinth of neoclassical architecture. The quarter had the quaint atmosphere of a village within the bustling a city of Athens.

Maya had planned out her day. After her companions had gone to work she made contact with the Brigadier General. She had taken the morning to familiarize herself with the files her aunt had sent to her from the nonencrypted material on her cousin's Swiss Army knife flash drive. Now, she was on her way deep into the Plaka to meet the man who the Curator in Naples said was familiar with her cousin's studies.

She walked up the steps from the south slope of Acropolis to reach Anafi-
otica, with its tiny winding streets and small whitewashed houses all built with
the Cyclades island architecture. She felt like she was on a Greek island. She
glanced to her left at a bougainvillea clad home and realized she had reached
her destination. She rang the doorbell.

The older bespectacled gentleman who answered the door looked up and
down the street before he invited her in. He was tall and thin to the point of
gaunt. His skin was deeply tanned by many years of exposure to the sun and
the wiry steel gray hair on the top of his head had begun to recede. His dark
suit was pressed to a level that would pass military inspection.

"Please won't you come in," he said shaking hands with Maya. His voice
was raspy.

"Thank you for seeing me on such short notice, sir," Maya smiled and tried
to make eye contact. It was difficult because of the Brigadier's thick yellow
tinted horn-rimmed glasses. She wondered if he had glaucoma.

"I am so sorry for your loss. Christopher was a brilliant young man. I enjoyed his intellect. I miss his company."

"When I called, I mentioned that the Curator at the Museum of Naples, Mr.
Del Falco, suggested that I contact you."

"Yes, I accompanied Christopher on more than one occasion to Naples."

Maya tilted her head in curiosity. The General took this as a sign that he
should recount how he came to be friends with Christopher.

"While working on his doctorate, Christopher contacted me regarding a
treatise I wrote about the provenance of treasures uncovered in a Macedonian tomb. I had put forward viable evidence of the burial place of Alexander
the Great and his wife, but my writings have proven to be rather controversial.
Christopher asked if he might visit the tomb with me. Initially I thought he
was interested in pursuing this subject line for his doctoral studies; however, it
turned out he was more eager to do his own original work."

"What was his line of study?" Maya asked.

"He was fascinated by a painting on an ancient frieze in the tomb. The artwork had been done in buon fresco, a style where the pigments are plastered
into the wall. Interestingly this artistic technique rendered it quite durable," he
said and began to cough.

His coughing spell persisted. He tried to continue the conversation using
shorter sentences, panting and emphasizing his words.

"Christopher recognized the battle scene. It is the same battle scene depicted in a Roman mosaic uncovered in Pompeii. He was intrigued. It was the same scene, centuries apart–"

Another coughing spell erupted. His speaking became more labored.

"We became friends. I traveled with him to Naples to see the 'Alexander at the Battle of Issus' mosaic. He hoped that having an older, published researcher with him might help him obtain permission to take photographs of the artwork."

He paused to take a breath.

"Did you obtain permission?" Maya asked.

"Yes" he replied. His eyes were now watery from coughing.

Maya could see that the conversation was taking a lot out of the older man.

"Christopher thought it significant that the hues were different. I felt that perhaps the frieze might have become discolored with age, but Christopher believed it was intentional," the Brigadier paused and took a deep breath.

"Intentional?"

"He was convinced the frieze was a cipher that would lead him to one of the most important relics of all time.

"What was the artifact?"

He did not answer immediately. He seemed to be considering whether to divulge a secret, "Let me show you."

With obvious effort, the Brigadier got up and slowly moved over to his bookshelves. From high on the shelves he removed a thick volume and opened it to a page, "Christopher wanted to find this."

The exertion caused by taking the book down from the higher shelf brought on an extreme round of coughing. Tears welled up in the old man's eyes.

Maya led him to a chair and helped him sit down. She offered to get him a glass of water, but he declined.

He fumbled with the book and opened it to a photographic plate. She drew closer, so she could have a better look.

"He believed the frieze painting could lead him to this," another coughing spell interrupted his words.

Maya drew a deep breath and stared at the photographic plate, "What does it mean?"

"I have notes from our days together. I have never shared them with anyone. He would want you to have them." Another violent fit of coughing overcame him.

"These days I find conversing very tiring. It will take time to locate them." He tried to catch his breath.

"If you would come back another day, I would have them for you. Please, I must conclude our meeting today."

It was evident that the visit had clearly exhausted him. Maya thanked him and set an appointment for the following day.

****

The lights were just coming on in the Plaka. The warm colors and ambience of the old quarter at dusk seemed festive. Like a moth attracted to light, Maya was drawn into the older part of the Plaka. Suddenly it dawned on her that she might have wandered too far. The narrow streets began to have less illumination and were less frequented by tourists. She turned to retrace her steps.

Venturing this way would be best done with a companion. It's looking a trifle sketchy down this way.

Maya pulled out her cell phone and dialed Switzerland.

"Hello Tante Hélène. I'm calling to give you an update. I've just met with the Greek Brigadier General who accompanied Christopher to Naples. He said Christopher was interested in the Alexander mosaic from Pompeii because it was similar, yet different from a frieze he had seen in a tomb. That would be the tomb the Brigadier wrote about. It seems Christopher was convinced the artwork would lead him to a precious artifact."

"Really?"

"I think that there are photos of the artwork and the artifact amongst the notes that are on Christopher's USB stick that I gave you. Could you give them a more in-depth look?"

"Is there something specific I should be looking for?"

Maya was so engrossed in her conversation with her aunt that she failed to sense any motion behind her.

A tall man dressed all in black, sprung out from a dark alleyway. He grabbed Maya's arms in a secure lock behind her back and quickly pressed a rag against her mouth and nose.

Maya struggled against the dark-skinned assailant. Fear surged through her veins.

At the other end of the phone Maya's aunt heard the sounds of a scuffle.

"Maya! Maya! Are you there?" Tante Hélène asked helplessly.

Maya's heart fluttered in her chest. Alarm bells rang in her head. She recognized the ether-like odor and slightly sweet taste of chloroform. She felt a burning sensation in her mouth and nose. She knew from her medical training that a too high dose of this potent anesthetic could easily kill her. It would slowly depress her central nervous system.

Despite the odds Maya quickly assessed that her best chance was to feign going limp before she began to feel too woozy. She hoped her attacker would assume she was out cold, release his hold and remove the rag before it was too late.

The ploy worked. He loosened his grip a fraction.

Maya felt a red-hot sear of pain. The outer nerve endings of her skin burned like she was experiencing a thousand skin-peeling scrapes on grainy pavement. It was hell. She knew that she had to stifle her scream.

The assailant dragged her body across the rough cobblestones into the alleyway. In this lonely place she succumbed to the distorted hollowness that announced the chloroform was winning out.

Her aggressor looked down smugly at Maya's prostrate body. His black eyes glared triumphantly like those of a sport hunter who had bagged an exotic animal. He picked up his trophy and effortlessly carried her through the doorway of a derelict building. When he crossed the threshold Maya's cell phone slipped unnoticed from her grasp. It landed in a recess between the doorway and the cobblestone lane.

****

Less than four miles away from the Plaka, the President of the Center for Nuclear Scientific Research was about to introduce Marc McLaren to a group of carefully selected experts from the European Medicines Network. The assembly was an interesting collection of medical minds and representatives from a number of European countries.

"I am honored to introduce to you a Canadian whom many of you may know for his efforts helping the nuclear industry. Marc McLaren has been selected to lead the Task Force investigating unexpected deaths associated with the use of medical isotopes in this area of Europe."

McLaren's youthful appearance belied his depth of experience. However, when he stood erect at the podium, it was evident that Marc McLaren was no stranger to public speaking.

"During the worldwide isotope shortage, new suppliers have been encouraged from all over the world. The shortage has been an opportunity for smaller suppliers to acquire a market share. Now, random monitoring has indicated that radioactive isotopes produced and shipped from Southeast Europe, including Greece and Macedonia have seen a much higher than usual incidence of death."

McLaren paused before continuing.

"CANDO has been asked to lead a Task Force aimed at uncovering the reason behind the exponential increase in deaths following administration of radioactive medical isotopes in this area of Europe. The stakes are quite high. There are concerns that the problem may spread further, even as far as America. If it were to get out that some of the isotopes may have resulted in death, fear would be rampant. It could be cataclysmic. For this reason, we ask that you respect the need for secrecy. Once we have a better understanding of the situation and can plan out a solution the embargo will be lifted."

McLaren looked down at the assembly and saw heads nod. Apparently, they understood the need for silence. It would not be good if the media got wind of this.

"Our Task Force will be divided into three teams, each with a different focus. Data is now being fed to a computer base in Canada to examine the geospatial incidence of the deaths to pinpoint areas of increased occurrence. This information will be available shortly. It will furnish data on to the specific locales where the death rates have risen. A team will take that data and determine which isotope production facilities regularly shipped, in the past three months, to those areas where there has been a higher incidence of mortality."

McLaren took a sip of water and continued, "A second team will examine the areas of high incidence to ascertain what, if anything is different about the radioactive isotope used there. Could there be something different in their makeup? Production facilities have been requested to prepare samples for the reviewing team for testing purposes. The third team will examine symptoms and cause of death using autopsy records with a geo-spatial alignment. This information should help identify if there are common causes of death from certain shipments."

****

"She's still not picking up!" Danny's tone indicated annoyance. "She said that she planned to do some reading today. I had no idea that she'd leave the hotel before I got back."

A moment later, while they were walking along Adrianou Street towards the restaurant where they planned to meet McLaren, Danny's phone chimed.

"Is that her?" Sam asked expectantly.

Danny shook her head. The number displayed on her screen was not one she recognized. From the country code digits, she guessed the call originated in Switzerland.

"Hello?"

"Danny, this is Professor Hélène Jullian, Maya's aunt. I am sorry to intrude. I did not know where else to turn. Maya left your number with me. Would you know how I might reach my niece?"

"I'm trying to reach her myself."

"Oh dear, I fear Maya may be in some kind of trouble. I've contacted the police in Athens, but they contend that a dropped call is not sufficient cause for alarm."

"What happened that gave you cause for alarm?"

Professor Jullian related the unsettling end to her phone call with Maya.

"I looked up the Brigadier's coordinates and attempted to call him but there was no answer. I called the police in Athens. Maya is by no means a missing person given their criteria. They said that there might have been trouble on the line or she may have gone shopping and now her phone is in a dead zone. I know what I heard, and I am concerned. Please, can you help?" She sounded anxious.

"Professor, I'm sure there is no cause to worry. Can you give me the Brigadier's number? I'll see what I can do and get back to you with news. Is this the best number to reach you at?"

Concern was evident on Danny's face. After all the scrapes Maya had been through she hoped that this was just a false alarm. She related the substance of Tante Hélène's call to Sam.

"Look, I'll see if I can initiate a trace on Maya's cell. This isn't North America, so I don't know my chances of success, but I'll give it a try," Sam offered.

"Well, another idea is for us to use my laptop."

"And, why would we do that?"

"Maya's wearing a bracelet that I gave her. It's a little artistic gismo I dreamed up. I thought that since she has been in such difficult situations recently that it might be helpful to know where she is, particularly since I knew she would be on her own in Athens while we were working."

"Does Maya know the bracelet is a tracking device?" Sam raised his eyebrows.

"No. I saw no reason to tell her," she replied nonchalantly.

"Danny, I believe that your older brother would consider that unethical," Sam chuckled.

Sam could just imagine McLaren's reaction. He was sure his buddy would have scolded Danny about the intrusive bracelet. Nonetheless, perhaps it was an idea that had merit given the current circumstances. The woman seemed prone to getting get herself into unusually dangerous situations.

"Danny, you're incorrigible. On the other hand, being practical, how does your device work?"

"I'll need to open my laptop to show you."

Sam smiled. He had to admit that Danny was tech savvy. *A tracking bracelet. What would she come up with next?*

They reached the restaurant. After ordering refreshments, Danny pulled her laptop from the briefcase she was carrying. She opened an icon and a map of Athens appeared. A tiny red light peeped on a far corner of the map.

"It looks like she's way out beyond the airport," Sam said in an alarmed voice.

The red light appeared to be moving out over the sea.

"What's the range on the transmitter?"

CHAPTER 18

The effects of the drug had begun to wear off. Maya's world was blurry, and her body felt ponderous. The sensation was like that of a swimmer thrust under by a breaking wave, struggling through the churning water to reach the surface.

"Ah, you're awake, my dear."

A bulbous nose stared down at Maya, just inches from her face. It reminded her of the nose of the Mayan rain god Chac.

Maya's thoughts transported her back in time to when she was little girl accompanying her mother on one of the professor's archeological explorations in Mexico. They were at Kabáh in front of an unusual stone mosaic at the Palace of the Masks. It was decorated with four hundred plus views of the long-nosed Mayan rain god Chac.

Maya couldn't fathom why the ancients had wanted to repeat such a scary countenance over and over again. For the longest time, the monstrous masks had troubled her. At one time, she thought that she had set aside that childhood fear, but when she blinked her eyes open she found that the Mayan deity had returned. The grotesque face looking down at her was none other than the Mayan god Chac. She would recognize those large round eyes and that proboscis-like nose anywhere.

Maya clamped her eyes shut. Through her closed eyelids she had her own personal fireworks display of shimmering zig-zag lines and flashes of light. She felt like she was floating. When she pried open her eyelids, Chac was gone.

Oh my, what has happened to me? Think girl, think.

She forced her aching mind to recall how she had gotten here. In her fog, she remembered meeting with the elderly Brigadier in the Plaka. She dug deeper into her memory and recalled a cell phone conversation with her aunt. Everything after that was fuzzy. Somewhere though she had a vague recollection of flying over the sea.

She inhaled a deep breath forcing more oxygen into her lungs. The softness under her outstretched body indicated that she was lying on a bed. She attempted to thrust herself up upright. She swung her legs over the side of the bed and got to her feet. The room began to swirl. She reached out to a dresser for support. The feeling subsided.

Maya tried to walk, and the dizzy sensation returned. It came in waves. There was a horrible taste in her mouth. She glanced at the reflection in the mirror over the bedroom dresser. The face that greeted her was that of a woman with unkempt dark hair, large dark circles under her sunken brown eyes and skin that appeared ghostly pale.

Is that me? I'm a mess. I need to get cleaned up.

Maya staggered to the bathroom. She bent over the marble countertop and turned on the ornate tap. She splashed cold water on her face and instantly felt relief. She leaned her head over and took a drink from the running stream of tap water. The moisture felt good on her dry throat.

I must be dehydrated.

She looked down at what had been a pretty dress. Now it was rumpled and dirty.

She sighed. Water helped. She felt a trifle more alert. She padded back into the bedroom and looked around.

She tried the door handle. It was locked. She moved over to the windows and pushed back the elegant drapes. The long windows were barred and firmly affixed in an open position that allowed air in but did not in any way facilitate escape. She noted that the room was a storey above the lawn that stretched outside. She saw the undulating surf roll endlessly beyond the cliffs in the distance.

Sudden hammering at the door jarred her.

A uniformed guard stuck his head in and announced in a thick Slavic accent, "Doctor, your host demands your presence for dinner. You will find appropriate dress in the closet. Get ready now. I will escort you to the dining room in fifteen minutes."

Who is it that commands me to dress for dinner?

While she didn't like the thought of being ordered about, she was intrigued. She was anxious to know what was going on. Going to dinner might provide an opportunity to find out why she was here.

Curious, she made her way over to the closet door and turned the crystal doorknob. Inside she was amazed to find a rack full of women's clothing. She selected a dinner sheath in her size and tried it on. She went to the washroom and tried her best to tidy up her appearance.

In fifteen minutes, the husky guard returned and with gun drawn escorted her along a carpeted hallway and downstairs to the dining room.

What kind of deviant has a dinner guest brought to the table at gunpoint?

****

The grand staircase was classic, set off with ornate carved wood paneling. It wasn't the sumptuousness of the stairway that caught Maya's eye though, it was the trio of black and white etchings at the entry to the dining room that grabbed her attention. Her brown eyes brightened with curiosity.

The center etching was larger and featured an ancient tablet carved with writing in bas relief. Flanking it on the left was an etching of the tablet set in a rocky outcropping by a stream. On the right side was a sketch of an exquisite ancient temple. Sunlight streamed through its slender columns giving it an almost mystical look.

The three images burnt into her memory. They reminded her of the pictures she had seen in the book which the Brigadier had taken down from the shelf. She forced her eyes away from the etchings and focused on her host in the dining room.

Pace yourself. Count your blessings. You're still alive.

Maya took a deep breath and exhaled slowly and quietly. Most of the drug had worn off but she still noticed a slight residual effect. Instinctively she knew that with more oxygen she'd be in better shape to make an assessment of her captor.

Her host rose to greet her. His very bearing announced he was accustomed to having people obey him. He was in his late sixties or at the most, early seventies. He was husky and tall. He would not have been considered bulky because he carried his weight well. His skin was a light olive color. His ancestors appeared to have been a mix of Greek and Slavic; he had a thick big-boned structure like a Slav and a face that was round and wide. His eyes looked like they were ensnared in deep pockets of flesh. His clean-shaven countenance and shiny bald head did nothing to offset his bulbous nose.

Maya found him intimidating. The hard set of his pale eyes and his thick lipped mouth which opened to reveal a golden glint were ample proof that this was the entity that had leaned over Maya conjuring up her dreadful childhood nightmares.

"I'm glad you could join me, my dear," said her host, extending his muscular hand to her.

Refusing to accept his extended hand, Maya snapped her reply with no civility.

"As if I had a choice. Surely you could have extended a dinner invitation without the use of force. Why did you abduct me? Where am I?"

Maya's dark eyes shone in defiance. She felt the adrenaline rush that accompanied her anger.

"You are definitely a chip off the old block," the well-dressed Slav responded with a smile that revealed a gold-capped tooth. "You are on an island."

"Why did you abduct me?" Maya could hear her heart pounding in her ears, but she convinced herself that by displaying utmost confidence she'd have a half a chance to unnerve him.

The haughtiness with which he expressed his next phrase led her to believe her tactic was not working.

"You must not be so agitated my dear."

Maya glowered at him, her face transfixed with rage.

"At my order, you have been flown to this island. Now, having provided you with this information, I have questions for you. If you cooperate I could give you some freedom on the island. And, if you don't, well you will see firsthand my innovative methods of torture. It's as simple as that. First off, where is the research paper?"

Maya struggled to make sense of the situation. *I'm a chip off the old block. Does that mean he knows my father? Why would he take me to an island? He wants to know the whereabouts of a paper. Whose paper?*

"What about what I want?" Maya asked eyeing her host in a confrontational manner.

"My dear, you must see that you are not in any position to make demands. Answer my questions now before you try my patience. Remember there is always the potential for you to arrive at a similar fate to your father."

Maya's steely gaze hid the shock she experienced on hearing his words. Inwardly she seethed but anger would not help her make heads or tails of the situation. Her father had died years ago in a terrible plane crash. The investigation following the crash had identified a wiring problem as the cause. She tried to fathom what could this monster be talking about.

"Young woman, I want to know the whereabouts of the formula. Answer me."

"Normal dinner conversation does not comprise orders and demands," Maya said with petulance.

"What position are you in to tempt fate? A few drops from a syringe and your heart will take on a different beat and you will die like your father," the monster threatened.

"My father died in a plane crash. He did not die of a heart attack," Maya retorted.

A miniscule change in his facial expression indicated to Maya that this reply had elicited emotion in her captor. *He seems nonplussed by what I've said?*

"No. He died of a heart attack and you have his papers. You went to Chalk River to get them."

"You are misinformed. I went to clear out personal belongings. I did not have access to research papers," Maya snapped.

Maya's mind fought to sort out what she'd heard. *Did this maniac think that her uncle was her father? What research formula was this madman looking for? Did her uncle have a research formula that had gotten him killed?*

The only formula that Maya was aware of was the one on her father's flash drive.

It was obvious that her captor was unaccustomed to having a woman speak back to him. Stunned by her assertive behavior, he took less than a second to make his decision.

"You lie. I have had enough of your mulish behavior. Guard, take her back to her room. Make certain to lock the door," he angrily rose from the table, knocking over his wine glass, turned on his heel and left.

Maya's jaw dropped. She stared at his broad back storming from the room.

My uncle's heart attack was drug induced. This monster had something to do with it.

CHAPTER 19

"You'd better have good reason to take me away from my lucrative business of taking tourists over the islands," snapped the pilot at the controls of the Robinson R44 helicopter.

"Well Pescatori, you'd better give me the scenic tour my travel agent recommended," Sam quipped back.

With his bushy salt and pepper handlebar moustache, traditional Greek fisherman's cap adorned by braided band trim and brass anchor buttons and his gold cross necklace, the pilot looked like a fisherman who made a wrong turn and ended up at the airport instead of at his fishing boat.

Truth be told, Pescatori had spent a good part of his working life in the American navy. He was one of that special breed who knew his way around any type of equipment, whether it operated in the air, on land, or in the sea. A few years back, after a stellar naval career, instead of heading off to Tarpon Springs, Florida, where he had grown up, he had retired and settled in his wife's homeland, Greece.

"Just sit back and let Island Hoppers give a customized tour, with all the rocks, islands and water your vision can absorb," Pescatori replied over the noise of the main rotor winding to a high pitch.

"Thanks for your help," Sam said before he briefed his old naval buddy on Maya's disappearance.

The Robinson climbed and banked to head over the Aegean Sea, flying straight as a die under Pescatori's experienced, firm hand. Skimming over the open water, soon what had been a speck on the horizon grew larger and finally became a rocky island cresting out of the turquoise water.

"The coordinates where you lost the signal from the tracking device came from that private island. It's known to be owned by a wealthy businessman who values his privacy," Pescatori said, pointing to the island.

"Acknowledged. It would be best not to in get too close. Just give me a regular tour, perhaps with a gentle sweep to take a closer look. This flight is more for reconnaissance, to get the lay of the land."

Approaching the island, Pescatori gradually increased the chopper's altitude. When he got close enough, he banked left to make a counter-clockwise circuit of the grassy island's tabletop perimeter.

"Owned by a wealthy businessman you say?" Danny's familiar voice broke in. She was back at the hangar listening in on their flight. She'd been tracking the signal from Maya's bracelet until the moment the signal was lost.

"I'll contact Lazer back home and ask him to look into the proprietorship of the island. It might be prudent to know a bit more about the owner."

"Good idea," Sam replied, staring through low power binoculars and attempting to take in every detail of the island.

"On the north side I can see a heliport. On the south side, well removed from the noise of the heliport, I can see a large villa type residence with multiple porches and decks. Along the shoreline in between the two is a docking area capable of handling sizable watercraft. I see a yacht and two small vessels," Sam reported.

"Can you make out the name of the yacht?" Danny inquired.

"Negative. My view is impeded."

Sam nodded to the right in the direction of a sandy cove beneath a rock outcropping. If the tide was right, it might offer an approach from the water, "Shall we take a quick look?"

Pescatori followed Sam's nod and aimed the chopper in that direction.

"Got enough?" Pescatori had no desire to linger and raise suspicions.

"Give me two seconds," Sam was eyeing at a spot above the docking area where he saw a smaller building that repeated the architectural lines of the residence. The building appeared to have been built to house security personnel.

Before he had a chance to reply, out of the corner of his eye, Pescatori detected a flash of fire. In an evasive move calculated to save lives, instinctively the veteran pilot pressed hard on the left foot pedal and threw his chopper into a half-spin. The blade frequency changed; the rotor whined in protest.

Suddenly, the brutal hail-like sound of bullets battered the chopper. The sound almost obliterated the thumping of the chopper blades. The offensive shattered the Robinson's instrument panel rendering it useless.

"Told you they liked their privacy!" Pescatori bellowed. He reefed on the throttle for maximum thrust, determined to get clear of the gunfire.

Sam refrained from dishing out a comeback. Right now, it was all in Pescatori's hands. On the ground, he saw two men in Russian tactical camo with their automatic rifles trained on the helicopter.

Seconds later there was another ugly barrage of fire. The helicopter made a sickening lurch.

"Not good. Hit on the hydraulic lines!" Pescatori announced.

The chopper began to buck. The engine belched smoke, but the rotor chugged on, coughing and gasping. Foul blue smoke seeped into the cockpit.

"We're losing height!" Pescatori's mouth clamped in a determined smile.

"Next island's not that far," Sam called out after a quick glance through his binoculars.

"Be prepared to ditch. If you're a religious sort, now would be the time for a prayer."

Pescatori used all his strength to control the stick that was now shaking like a jackhammer tearing up a concrete street. The turbine wailed like a banshee.

Through the blue smoke Sam could just see a shoreline ahead. It was excruciatingly close.

The wounded chopper lurched ahead.

"As long as the turbine's squealing we've got a chance."

Years in the military had given Pescatori great reflexes for emergencies. Where another pilot might have panicked, Pescatori kept his cool. He pulled for all he was worth on the collective lever. He instinctively prepared to raise the nose before power to the rotors was lost. When it came time, he wanted the tail rotor to be the first section to slice into the Aegean to slow his chopper's trajectory. That way he calculated there'd be a moment before the water enveloped the cockpit. He touched his gold cross. Their fate wasn't just in his hands.

CHAPTER 20

There was a saffron hue over the Gatineau Hills that made it look like the entire landscape had been painted in gold when the sun dropped from view. Lazer Kadinsky leaned back on his chair and stared thoughtfully out the window from his computer station on the sixth floor of CANDO's office building in Ottawa's west end. Briefly he admired the purple hills that rose beyond the river. Early evening was the period during the day when he particularly enjoyed being at the office. The light was perfect, and the building was quiet except for the soft hum of computer hardware.

The lean, shaggy-haired computer whiz kid looked more like a rock-musician than a computer guru. He wore black horn-rimmed glasses that matched his dark hair, was happiest barefoot, or at least in sandals and preferred funky t-shirts and skinny jeans to dress pants, shirt and tie, although he always had a plaid sports jacket at the ready to wear for meetings with executives from outside the Agency.

Lazer had been invited to join the CANDO team five years previously, right after graduate school. He had never regretted the decision. The job suited him. He free-handed the Agency's extensive computer network, which contained a vast array of material on nuclear science, biology, medicine, physics, and surprisingly archeology and history. He was a first-rate researcher with the knowhow and equipment to access a multitude of sources, from national and international government files to private information sources. No data was inaccessible with his skill set, even if it was thought to be buried in secure classified files. He performed a pivotal role for the group of young professionals who made up the CANDO team. His boss, Dr. Shearwater gave him free rein and an ample budget and left the operation of the Agency's extensive computer network and digital library to the maestro.

The sharp ring of an office telephone pierced Lazer's tranquility. He leaned over to check the caller ID. Recognizing the number, he immediately picked up the receiver, "Fire away, Dan."

"So, McLaren's tied up in a meeting and Sam is off flying with an old navy buddy. I was in touch with him, but I can't seem to raise him now. Do you suppose you could take a look at some satellite images and see if you can pinpoint the helicopter the guys were flying in?"

"Danny, there's a bit more to this than you are sharing. What's behind this inquiry? First you wanted to know the ownership of an island in the Aegean and now this request."

Lazer noted that this new request was beyond the usual type he received from Danny, "What's happened?"

"That's just it, I don't know what happened. One minute Sam was sharing info with me while he was flying with Pescatori. The next thing I knew there was a really loud noise and then no further contact."

"Not to worry, I'm on it," Lazer flexed his fingers over the keyboard. "I'll tap into the geospatial lab. Using SAW we'll have up to the moment 3-D imagery with superb resolution."

"SAW's new to me. What is it?"

"It's an acronym for See Anywhere Worldwide. It is just what we need for taking a look around."

"Thank you."

"By the way, the island you asked about earlier, is owned by a wealthy Russian, Vladimir Janovic. For your edification, foreign ownership of Greek islands was entirely prohibited until 2003; however, since that time purchasing an island in Greece has become relatively straightforward. Regardless of nationality, anyone can be a property owner. Not too much is known about Vladimir. He made his money in petrological and mineralogical research and has no known ties to the Russian mafia. He's a guy with money and a low profile."

"Did you find anything unusual about him?"

"Not really, but he does own a sailing yacht notably named after the Greek Goddess Galena who personified calm seas. It's an interesting choice of names for a Russian who has made his fortune in ores. Just to give you some background, the Roman naturalist, Pliny, used the Latin word galena to describe lead ore. Galena is the primary ore mineral of lead; it was mined for its lead content since 3000 BC. It's one of the most abundant and widely distributed sulfide minerals."

"So, an interesting play on words."

"The Galena is homeported on a Greek Island not far from Athens."

CHAPTER 21

The predawn wind was sluggish, hindering progress, but when the light crimson rays of the sun began to melt into the sky, the air picked up and the kaiki cut through the water, clipping along at a steady six knots. Like the other classic fishing craft from the village, Ari's wooden boat was painted white, trimmed topside with chromatic colors and rigged for sail.

McLaren sat in the prow watching. The sea was so calm that in the water he could see the reflection of the white hull and the veil of clouds above. The salt tang of the sea breeze was a pleasant contrast to the steamy acridity of Athens. A moment like this made him understand the lure of fishing as a way of life. He appreciated why Greek families cherished the old boats and kept them in the family.

On returning from his late evening meeting at the Institute, Danny had informed McLaren that Sam had taken off with his old naval buddy, Pescatori, in search of Maya and that she had lost contact with Sam. In her update she mentioned that she had reached out to Lazer, in Canada, for assistance in locating the chopper. Lazer had used all the satellite computing resources he could muster and painstakingly searched to pinpoint the area off the Greek mainland where the helicopter had gone down.

McLaren knew immediately that he was in need of a boat. He had reached out to someone he knew would help. Now, on board the small fishing vessel he was certain he'd made the right choice. He looked over at Pescatori's brother-in-law, Ari, unfolding the chart on his lap so he could plot their position. The Greek fisherman had been more than willing to help. In no time at all Ari had stocked the boat with water, food and supplies and secured the special diving equipment McLaren had requested.

"How long before we get there?" McLaren looked back at the shoreline bleeding away.

"Depends on whether we catch a tailwind," the handsome Greek fisherman replied with a smile.

Some minutes later there was an audible snap when the white canvas caught the wind and billowed out. McLaren thought he sensed the bow lift slightly. The boat took on speed.

"There, just what we need," Ari said. He reached up and tugged on his woolen fisherman's cap. Almost simultaneously his sinewy arms adjusted the tiller, while the wind pushed them more rapidly over the waves.

The rhythmical sway and flow of the waves was mind clearing. They traveled in silence for quite some time across the shimmering sea.

McLaren scanned the horizon through binoculars. Bright shards of light bounced from the sea forcing him to blink rapidly to force away temporary blindness. In the moment preceding his visual difficulties McLaren caught sight of a tiny island. When his sight returned it was almost too late for the occupants of the kaiki.

"Starboard! Debris!" McLaren shouted. Between rolling waves, he had just caught sight of three helicopter rotor blades poking out from the sea.

Ari reefed on the tiller and swerved dramatically to narrowly miss the wreckage. A white-foamed ripple of spray splashed over McLaren who was leaning on the bow rail.

"Good timing, Ari."

"Not to worry, it might bob wildly but a Greek kaiki is virtually unsinkable," Ari grinned.

"Do you see the haze by the shoreline?" McLaren pointed in the direction of a misty spot on the island.

Shielding his eyes from the sun, Ari stared over the surface of the water towards the low-lying island.

"It looks like smoke from a fire. I'll bring us in closer, but you're best to use the dinghy to go ashore."

McLaren climbed into the dinghy. The little boat rocked precariously in the swells. He rowed towards the rocky shoreline where anorexic pines struggled to survive. He could see two figures waving their arms.

"Sam, Pescatori! Are you two okay?"

Sam scrambled over to the water's edge, eager to greet McLaren. His sapphire blue eyes twinkled. He beamed a bright white smile at his friend.

"Yah, we're fine. The chopper's not, but we're fine." His dark skin did a good job of hiding the scrapes on his cheeks and the gash on his temple.

"What happened to your forehead?"

"Nothing too serious. I didn't get my head out of the way fast enough. The glass shattered when we hit the surf."

"Good to see you again McLaren. Do you want a Fix Hellas or perhaps some Retsina?" Pescatori nonchalantly got up from a helicopter seat and leaned over to open a cooler. There was a length of bloodstained bandage covering his left arm.

"We weren't sure how long it would take you to get here, so Sam got the seats out of the chopper and the cooler, and we lit a fire, so we'd be more comfortable. Is that my sister's husband's fishing boat out there? He'll want a beer. I didn't know you'd enlist his support."

"I am definitely glad that you didn't lose your gusto for living nor your beer or Retsina in the crash. Damn shame about your chopper, Pescatori," McLaren said shaking his head in disbelief. It was just like old times.

"So, what happened to your arm?"

"Grazed by a bullet. Could have been worse. Lucky to get out of there and almost make it here. All those years in the military and I never lost a chopper like this," Pescatori replied, looking somewhat sheepish.

Luck and skilled flying had been on their side. Neither of them had incurred a major injury from the shooting nor the crash and sinking. The chopper had gone down relatively close to shore on a rock ledge in the sea. During the impact, the fuselage door had sheared off leaving the two occupants with an easy escape route. While the helicopter was rapidly filling with water Sam had released his own seat belt and Pescatori's and he had helped his friend get out the opening and up to the surface. Pescatori was a strong swimmer even with his injured arm but Sam had made sure that Pescatori was safely ashore before swimming back to the chopper for supplies.

****

"Are you sure you're game for this?" McLaren asked Sam.

"It's not like I'm going to sit here on this fishing boat while you are on that island setting off explosions. Just because I've been shot at and the chopper I was riding in fell out of the sky, doesn't mean there is any reason to leave me behind," Sam feigned looking hurt.

The kaiki was anchored about a half a mile off the island. Ari had invited some of the locals to fish in the area with him. A few extra boats fishing in the area around the island would provide a measure of cover for the mission.

"You boys better not be long. Remember, security on the island is tight. Even with the other fishing boats around these guys will get suspicious," Pescatori warned.

"We don't plan on being gone long," McLaren said. He stuck the regulator between his teeth and rolled his wetsuit clad body backwards off the gunwale into the Aegean.

Sam was quick to follow.

Pescatori watched the trail of air bubbles. The navy man knew that it was not a good time of day for the men to do this. The sun was high in the ski and the sky so blue that it all but matched the color of the sea. McLaren had been adamant though. He feared for Maya's safety each moment she was gone.

In a watertight container, Sam carried the explosives and weapons Ari's friends had furnished. McLaren carried a spare tank and fins for Maya, if they found her.

Based on all the evidence Maya had been taken here. This conclusion had been reached using Lazer's satellite imaging and intelligence acquired during Sam's reconnaissance. McLaren proposed that they use the diving gear and explosives that Ari's friends had supplied. They would swim under water to a secluded rock faced cove on the island and hide the tanks in an area that appeared not to be well covered by security. Sam would set off an explosive diversion and draw the guards away from the estate so that McLaren could search the villa for Maya.

Visibility in the water was good. There was a clear view to the rocky bottom. McLaren and Sam kicked their fins in unison. When they were teens they had learned to dive in Lake Placid, New York, when the high school they were attending offered a spring credit for scuba diving. From that time on, diving had become a pastime that they loved and one which had been behind Sam's decision to join the US Navy. He'd become a Navy Seal and worked alongside good buddies like Pescatori.

The divers made their way towards a rocky outcropping. This position offered some degree of shelter from the island above them. Once on shore they slipped out of their wetsuits and stuffed them along with their tanks, into an overhead crevasse. They donned their cross-trainers and set off climbing up towards the table top surface of the island.

At the top of the rock face they peered beyond to assess the lay of the land. Immediately ahead they saw large fields of brightly blooming poppies, each rimmed with a long line of bushes and almond trees in blossom. The trees had obviously been planted to thwart the wind. A narrow dirt road wound between the rows of trees that bordered the fields. Off in the distance, about a half a mile ahead, was a large Mediterranean style villa and a number of smaller out buildings. Palm trees and cypresses graced the entrance to the estate. On one side, not far from the villa was a cove with a beach. In the opposite direction, just about out of sight, was long dock where a small a yacht and two speedboats were berthed. The heliport was nowhere in sight, but McLaren and Sam knew from the satellite photos that it was located on the north side of the island.

"Lazer provided a headcount based on the satellite images, but at the time of the photo the yacht wasn't in berth," McLaren said.

"I'm okay with his estimate. Your mission, if you so chose, is to go get the girl," said Sam light heartedly. "Me, I'll create a diversion at the boat dock that should draw everyone away from the villa. That ought to give you some time to look for her."

"Promise me your nefarious action will not be out of proportion," McLaren requested.

"When I have ever done anything like that?" Sam grinned.

"What about guards at the dock? Do you want me to give you a hand with them first?" McLaren asked.

"I think I'm okay. I have my taser and fireworks and I have my trusty roll of duct tape to disable the guards. Give me about 12 minutes lead time," Sam said.

"Red Green would be so proud," McLaren chuckled. "Let's get started. I'll meet you back at the rock face once I've got Maya. Radio silence for the entire operation, unless something goes disastrously wrong."

Each of the two men went their separate way.

CHAPTER 22

A few drops from a syringe and your heart will take on a different beat and you will die like your father.

Maya repeated the phrase to herself.

Why on earth would someone kill my father or my uncle and then kidnap me?

In her frustration she cursed in Spanish, her mother's native tongue.

She was geared up and scared. Her dad had died in a plane crash off the Atlantic coast. She had seen the death certificate declaring that his twin, her dear Uncle Matthew, had died of a heart attack at Chalk River. With this revelation from her captor, it appeared that the heart attack her uncle suffered was induced.

He wants a formula and he thinks that I have it.

Puzzled, she struggled to put the pieces together. Her captor seemed to think that her uncle was her father. The twins had both worked in the nuclear industry. Her father had been the more academic of the two. He had been en route to a European conference to present his research findings when his flight went down. From what she knew, her uncle's career had been more operational. Uncle Matthew had been the one who was more hands on, always tinkering with mechanical equipment and making time to play with the children.

This guy thinks my uncle was my father. And, he thinks I know where the formula is.

Maya thought of the Swiss Army Knife, her dad's paper for the conference years ago and the formula that his paper contained. It hardly seemed worth getting killed for. On the other hand, even if she had it offered it up, she did not believe for a second that he would have any qualms about disposing of her.

He's killed before. He basically admitted that he had taken steps to bring about uncle's heart attack.

Maya was more than intimidated. She was scared.

****

With care honed from experience, Sam checked for and eliminated surveillance. Sometime since the fateful helicopter ride when Sam had seen the vessel through his binoculars, the white and blue yacht that was berthed on the island had departed. Now all that remained were two small runabouts tied at the dock. The area might have looked deserted, but Sam knew it was unlikely that he was alone.

In the area north of the dock, Sam put his martial arts training into use. He quickly put two sentries to the ground, removed their weapons, zip-tied their wrists and ankles and gagged them with duct tape before dragging them into the wooded area. He wanted them out of the way of the blast. His mission was a diversion, not a killing spree.

With the guards removed he methodically placed an explosive charge in one of the two small runabouts. The blast would provide a distraction. The islanders would be kept busy extinguishing the flames and Sam and McLaren could get down to business.

An unexpected, swoosh sound pierced the quiet. He swiveled his head towards the danger. He saw an electric vehicle approaching on the roadway.

Was I caught on video surveillance? What condition changed to require another vehicle to come this way?

Sam had not foreseen that anyone would arrive at this juncture. His first thought was to mitigate the mayhem that would be caused if the vehicle drove any closer to the blast area.

I've got to set off the explosives now or there will be serious injuries if that vehicle gets any closer. Timing is critical.

Sam took a deep breath, lit a road flare and, with the skill of a major league ballplayer, drilled a pitch into the runabout at the dock. He quickly sprinted for cover in the nearby wooded area. From his sheltered position, he shifted his gaze towards the two occupants in the approaching vehicle. He sighted through his scope and suspended the crosshairs over one of the rear tires of the approaching golf cart. He made the shot.

They ought to thank me for this.

He had to stop them from getting into the blast zone. Sam knew from experience that it would take but a moment for the fuse to fully ignite and then the boat would be engulfed in flames. The raw boom of thunderous explosions would announce that the flare had touched off the diesel on board. The resulting fireworks would generate a tremendous release of raw energy in the form of bright light and heat.

Sam's shot hit the rear tire in the nick of time. The little cart swerved out of control, tipped and landed on its side well out of the way of the explosive range. The two occupants were thrown from the vehicle onto the ground just as the anticipated series of explosions took place.

****

In the sultry heat, McLaren hugged the line of trees for cover and shade while making his way across the island towards the villa. Drawing closer to his destination, he stopped. He positioned himself in the foliage, so he could study the building and look out for sentries.

The villa was two storied. The upper level had two large outdoor terraces. Each had a shady pergola that covered a seating area. The upper windows were barred. One of the far windows was slightly ajar. He estimated that the open window was positioned near the far end of a hall.

The clanging sound of a screen door closing caught his attention. He froze in position. Seconds ticked off. Through the green foliage McLaren saw two men in fatigues exit the side door of the building adjacent to the villa. Each carried a machine pistol in a sling. They walked toward the front of the villa where two golf carts sat parked in the lane. They got in one and drove off.

McLaren looked down at his watch. It was almost show time.

The golf cart was almost out of clear sight, when the first thunderous explosion rocked the silence. Even in the broad daylight McLaren could see the orange fireball. It sent smudges and swirls of smoke eddying through the sky.

Without warning, two more armed guards bolted out of the small building and sprinted to the remaining golf cart.

From another direction, McLaren heard the heavy sound of thumping feet on the wooden floor of the verandah that encircled the villa. He turned his head and saw a bulky figure, dressed in a smoking jacket, stomp down the timber stairway and lumber towards the guards.

McLaren could not hear the man's exchange with the guards, but it was obvious from his overbearing gestures that the heavy-set male in the smoking jacket was in charge.

The two men squeezed to make room for their employer in the cart and the trio in the vehicle took off with a whirr. The humming noise produced by the electric golf cart dissipated when the vehicle vanished into the smoke along the tree-lined lane.

McLaren waited a few seconds to make sure that they were well on their way. He scouted and disconnected the feeds on surveillance cameras. Assured that his entry would not be caught on camera, he strode across the manicured lawn and up onto the front porch. For a brief second he paused and listened. Confident that he did not hear sounds from inside, he quietly opened the leaded glass front door.

****

No expense had been spared on this island retreat. The villa was sumptuous. A cascading Italian Borghese blown glass chandelier hung above the hexagonal entrance hall in front of the ornate semi-circular stairway.

McLaren glanced to his left and to his right patiently listening before tip-toeing up the beautifully honed Dionysos white marble stairs.

If Maya is here, my best guess is that she is in the back bedrooms or in the basement.

The open window on the second floor had been his clue to search the upper storey first. McLaren crept down the long marble tiled hallway and another round of loud detonations exploded in the distance. The thunderous noise masked the slight squeak that his cross trainers made.

McLaren was alert to the possibility that the house was occupied. He moved stealthily, listening, observing and searching for hidden details and clues.

Suddenly, McLaren saw a door near the end of the hall begin to open. Thinking quickly, he tried the closest door handle and ducked into a room. It was vacant. He held his breath. He pressed his ear against the door to listen and heard the sound of heels on the tile floor.

There must be someone else in the villa.

He listened intently a moment or two longer. When he felt certain the footsteps were out of earshot he peered out and looked around. No one was in sight. Encouraged, he tip-toed down the hall to the end door. He reached out for the handle, turned it and found the door locked. He put his weight into the door. It didn't budge.

****

Sam heard the rhythmical thumping sound of chopper blades minutes after the orange fireball rose from first blast. Seconds later, he heard the swoosh of another electric vehicle approaching quickly. He saw the driver and passengers gesturing wildly. He heard them shouting. The newcomers drew up beside the overturned golf cart.

It was time for Sam to leave.

****

Alone in the bedroom inside the villa, Maya heard the door handle rattle. She stared at the knob, anticipating. The ominous sound of the door being forced open sent her pulse racing at Olympic speed.

This is it. Maya thought, steeling herself for what was to come.

Her eyes blazed like living coals; her lips pursed in readiness to spit venom. She swallowed nervously, curled her delicate fingers tightly around the shaft of her makeshift weapon and waited.

The door opened a fraction.

"Back off!" she barked.

Maya raised her right arm above her head. She viciously lunged forward to thrust the rapier slim weapon she had concocted. The strike was full force with every intent to maim.

The tall intruder managed to sidestep the quick and dirty blow. Using his height to full advantage, he overpowered Maya and forced the weapon out of her hand.

Horrified, Maya felt him pull her body snug against his. She kicked and squirmed like a caged animal.

She was infuriated at herself. *I should have anticipated lightning reflexes.*

A large hand clamped over her mouth, effectively silencing her scream. A jaw touched her hair. Warm lips brushed her ear.

Unnerved, Maya squirmed, bit one of the intruder's fingers covering her mouth and pummeled his ribs. She wriggled and contorted her slim body so she could pull away.

"Maya, calm down, it's me, McLaren. I'm here to help, not hurt you. Please stop struggling and for God's sake don't scream. I don't want anyone to hear us. Understand?"

Maya had difficulty making sense of the words she heard, however she quickly processed that this was a familiar voice. When she saw the cobalt blue eyes, a sharp tremor ran through her frame.

"Maya are you okay?"

She drew a breath and nodded. Shaking, she threw her arms around his chest and hung on tightly, so he couldn't see the moisture welling up in her eyes.

"How in the world did you get here?"

"Luck, just luck," he whispered. He felt an overwhelming sense of relief and hugged her a full ten seconds before pulling back.

"Maya, I'll be the first to admit that's quite the weapon. I'll bet the toilet isn't working very well right now," he said grinning. He recognized that her weapon of choice had been fashioned from the metal float assembly of a toilet tank.

"No, it's not working now," Maya said. She looked down uncomfortably at the floor where her stiletto style knife had fallen. Her nervousness dissolved and she smiled.

"Ready to get out of here? Sam's waiting."

Without waiting for her reply, McLaren opened the door just wide enough for a peek. His raised his finger to his lips, grabbed Maya's hand and shepherded her out of the villa.

"Wait, I have to go back!"

McLaren could feel Maya's weight pulling at his arm, slowing the progress of getting to cover in the woods, "Maya, there's no going back. There isn't time."

"I have to go back! I saw a trio of etchings. I'm positive that they depicted a tablet like the one in the illustration the Brigadier showed me. He said Christopher was looking for a tablet. Maybe there's a connection. Please, I must go back. I have to get photos."

He hadn't heard of Maya's visit to the Brigadier, but he saw the intensity in her eyes. He realized that nothing he could say would deter her.

"I'll probably regret this, but look, let me get you to Sam. I promise I'll go back and take the photos. For now, just hurry. There are woods up ahead. We need cover."

There was no obvious path. Maya struggled to keep pace with McLaren while he shoved the brambles aside. Exhausted from her ordeal, she caught her foot, tripped and tumbled in a tangle of undergrowth.

McLaren turned around at the sound of the snap. He reached out just in time to save her fall, but not quickly enough to save her ankle.

Maya winced in pain.

Feeling badly that his attempt at speed had caused her to get hurt, McLaren leaned over and kissed her forehead. Looking into her velvet doe-like eyes, he thought to himself how lovely she was. He pulled her close to him and kissed her lips, long, soft, and tenderly.

"Now's not the time for that, folks," Sam admonished.

Caught up by the tumble, McLaren had failed to see Sam's stealthy approach. He cracked a grin at Sam, "I wasn't expecting you."

"I can see that! Better get moving."

Embarrassed, Maya pulled away from McLaren. She tried to put some weight on her injured ankle. A jolt of pain made her wince.

McLaren gently tucked an arm around her waist, "Lean on me for support," he said.

Sam looked at the pair and shook his head. *Twitterpated fools. The injured ankle is not going to make the swim out to the boat easy for Maya.*

"I suggest an alternative plan," Sam announced. "A helicopter landed about the time I set off the explosives. I know that the pilot and passenger headed in the direction of the fire. I strongly recommend that we borrow their chopper. It will make life easier."

"Well, sounds like a plan," McLaren said. "One little catch, I promised Maya some souvenir photos and now that you're here I'd like to run back for them."

"Not a good idea," Sam said firmly. He looked McLaren straight in the eye and shook his head, "We really shouldn't hang around." His look made it clear he was against the change of plan.

"I promised. Look, I'll run back. I won't take long. Let's say you offer Maya a piggyback to the chopper and I'll meet you there. Give me ten minutes. If I'm not back, lift off. Just get Maya to safety. If I hear the chopper, I'll know to swim back to the boat. You didn't suggest this alternate because you blew up our tanks during your firework display, did you?"

Sam grinned. His pearly white teeth sparkled against his dark skin and his blue eyes twinkled mischievously.

"No, I did not destroy our air reserve. The tanks should be safe and sound exactly where we left them. For god's sake, be quick."

"The trio of etchings is on the wall in the dining room. Thank you," Maya stretched up on her tippy toes and demurely planted a kiss firmly on McLaren's cheek.

Sam rolled his eyes and muttered under his breath. "Women."

****

McLaren realized full well that returning was not a good idea, but he never reneged on a promise.

The etchings must be really important to Maya if she would risk going back for photos.

For safekeeping, during his sprint back to the villa, he kept to the wooded area that lined the roadway. Conditions were warm. He was thankful for the light ocean breeze. He scanned the grounds to see if anyone was around. Nagging in his memory was the sound of the pair of heels clacking on the tile. He had no idea to whom they belonged, but he sincerely hoped that this time he would not meet anyone.

He crept over to the outside stairway and up and across the verandah. He pushed the ornately carved door open and looked inside.

During his previous entry he had headed directly up the marble stairway. This time he stayed on the main floor and tip-toed towards the dining room. He listened carefully, realizing that there might be kitchen help still around. When he heard nothing he cautiously moved on until he located the dining room.

The trio of etchings were featured on one expanse of wall. They were indeed exquisite. He took out his cell phone and snapped several photos. He intended to take took a quick look around on his way out, but the sound of booted feet coming up the verandah stairs cut the idea short.

He quickly sprinted up the marble stairway and stopped outside a door. He stood for a brief moment and listened. When he heard nothing, he turned the ornate handle, opened the door a crack and crossed the threshold.

McLaren wasn't prepared for what he found.

CHAPTER 23

"Place your weapon and cell phone down on the desk and raise your hands above your head, if you want to live to see another day," a sultry voice, tinged with sensuality and barely contained violence commanded.

Tall, lanky, and in her thirties, the seductress was obviously accustomed to taking command. Her racked Glock 26 revolver was pointed at McLaren. Her wavy auburn hair was pulled up into a casual yet elegant updo that added height to her bombshell looks. Her formfitting long black sheath, slit to her thigh, accentuated her curvature.

McLaren studied her with detached curiosity. From her accent, he surmised that she was American, likely from the wealthy Atlantic seaboard. The decided lack of nervousness she exhibited, and her defiant stance indicated to McLaren that she knew how to handle herself.

She had wide-set feline green eyes which radiated a striking personal confidence. She left little doubt that she would carry out her threat.

Her choice of weapon is interesting. The polymer-frame and magazine body render it virtually invisible to metal detectors in airports. That would make it handy for an American abroad.

McLaren presumed she was waiting for him to display some degree of anxiety. He failed to oblige.

She stared back and repeated her command.

"Who are you? What are you doing here?" her husky tone was demanding.

"Nice to meet you, too," McLaren said trying to bring some decorum to the situation.

She laughed. Her laugh had a rich tone, but it was far from friendly.

McLaren took a step forward and stopped.

Immediately, a flash of concern registered on her face, "I will carry out my threat!" The muscles in her trigger hand flexed tightly, "That's far enough. You get one chance to explain."

McLaren smiled disarmingly, "If intimidation is your game plan, I hope you have a better one."

Because the ploy was meant to cultivate underappreciation, his next move had to be fast. With the agility and speed of a ninja, he swung an outstretched leg at the woman's wrist. His lightning move caught her off-guard and knocked the weapon from her grasp.

She didn't see it coming. Pain shot through her wrist. Her eyes burned like a tiger. Instantly she pivoted her body sideways, chambered up, tightly tucking her knee into her chest to pump out explosively towards McLaren's groin. It was a wicked show of force.

Experience was on his side. His well-trained eyes discerned her kick at inception and identified the strike commitment. He timed his response, countering at the critical moment. Using his surprisingly long reach he grabbed her extended leg with his hand and forced the seductress off balance until she toppled backward.

McLaren reached out and caught her midfall before her auburn hair hit the floor. He whipped her arms behind her back and held her down with a force meant to keep her in line but not break any of her lovely bone structure.

She sucked in her breath and hissed, "Let go of me!"

In that split-second McLaren realized that his hold was insufficient to restrain her. She twisted her lithe body like a circus contortionist and broke free with a back jump. When she landed a diminutive gun appeared from nowhere.

How could anyone conceal a weapon with that slinky dress? Oh McLaren, you've underestimated her!

Taking no chances, McLaren grabbed his pistol from his waistband and pointed it at the red head before she had a chance to get a shot off.

Undeterred, legs apart, she stood in front of him in a defiant stance pointing her SwissMiniGun directly at him. The lethal replica of a Colt Python was so tiny it would have made a derringer look like a Desert Eagle.

They stared at each other, guns drawn, for what seemed to McLaren an interminable time. They might have remained at this impasse, if McLaren hadn't resorted to humor.

"That's your weapon of choice?" he inquired with an eyebrow arched.

McLaren wondered whether she actually had a sense of humor, but continued nonetheless with the age old pick-up line, "Haven't I met you before?"

It wasn't just a canned ice breaker, it was the truth. McLaren remembered seeing her in the company of the Macedonian delegate at the Research Center.

Recognition dawned in her bright green eyes, "Land sakes, you're the nuclear expert from Canada. My, you do get around. I can't say that it is a pleasure to see you again."

McLaren grinned slyly, "I see that you came prepared. I wouldn't have expected a woman who accompanies a delegation representative to be such rough stuff."

Best guess is she's an operative, CIA, Interpol, whatever. I wonder what in the world is she doing here?

She found the intensity of his magnetic blue eyes riveted on her disarming. She stared back at McLaren sizing him up.

"I strongly doubt that you are going to shoot me, and I am sure you would prefer that I don't shoot you, so why don't you just answer my questions and we'll resolve this impasse."

"Seems like an idea," McLaren replied. He felt a sense of relief that his attempt at humor seemed to have mitigated the stalemate. He really hoped his curiosity wasn't overriding his judgment.

"I'll ask the questions," she snapped. "What are you doing on this estate?"

"I simply came to pick up a friend," McLaren smiled. "My turn now. Who are you and what are you doing on this estate where a woman is being held against her will?"

"That's two questions. I was on the estate when that little Latina arrived. I had no part in her getting here," she replied, purposely skipping over her identity.

"Really?" the inquiring tilt of his head revealed that he doubted the truthfulness of her response.

"Why did you feel that it was necessary to make such a grand entry with explosions?"

"Explosions? I wasn't involved in setting off explosives."

"So you say," her green eyes revealed that she didn't give much credulity to his reply.

"Why was the woman brought to this island?"

"I repeat, I had nothing to do with that woman coming here."

McLaren's skepticism was evident. He smiled and started to say something but before he got it out she posed her next question.

"At what stage is the isotope investigation?"

McLaren forcefully masked his surprise, "Normally my response would be reserved for a conference representative, but in this case, with a gun pointed at me, I will share with you the news that we have concluded geostatistical work and identified the area of Europe where there has been an increased incidence of death after the use of isotopes," McLaren replied. It was more information that he might normally share but he hoped that he'd get something back in return.

"When will you have the information on the shipments?" she asked.

"It isn't your turn; however, I'll answer. We are now investigating the origins of shipments to these areas."

"And, you will have that information when?"

"An estimate would be within twenty-four hours. Why do you want to know?"

She ignored his question.

He stared at her intently before he posed his next question, "What is your relationship with Janovic?"

McLaren could see her try to hide her surprise, but the ever so tiny change in the micro-expressions of her beautiful face gave away her astonishment that McLaren knew who owned the island.

"Good grief, you are aware of who owns this island and you still chose to storm onto it and blow things up! Are you crazy?"

"I did not blow anything up. Once again, you haven't replied to my question. Your Russian friend, why did he kidnap the woman and bring her to this island?"

She shook her head, "To my knowledge, he had nothing to do with her being on this island."

Without letting McLaren take his turn, she asked another question, "Are you aware of any other methods of producing radioactive medical isotopes without the use of highly enriched Uranium?"

McLaren tried not to show that he was nonplussed by her question, "Several countries have studies underway and two in particular, including South Africa and Argentina have started to produce with low enriched Uranium. They are producing just small amounts."

"What do you know about a Canadian formula to do this?"

"Not using neutrons? Well, a taskforce in British Columbia is working on using a unique photo-fission accelerator technique."

The exchange was cut short. The sound of heavy footsteps reverberated off the marble floor out in the hallway. Someone was headed in their direction.

In that split-second the redhead made her decision.

"This exchange is over. Now you had better get the hell out of here before security finds you," she motioned towards a French door that opened onto a second storey terrace.

The woman's unexpected behavior left McLaren wondering, "Who are you? Why do you want this information?"

"Shove off! Leave, before I change my mind and sound the alarm."

"Nice talking to you," McLaren cracked a half smile and tipped his hand to his head in an old-fashioned gesture of acknowledgement. He was certain he detected the faint hint of a stifled grin on the redhead's impassive face.

He exited the room by French doors which opened onto an airy terrace on the upper level. Outside, a rhythmic thrum that was anything but music to his ears, caught his attention. He shook his head and climbed climb down the bougainvillea trellis to the ground while the sound faded.

So much for the helicopter — I guess I've missed my ride.

CHAPTER 24

Professor Hélène Jullian sat erect at the mahogany writing desk in the garret-like room that served as her office. She spoke into the receiver of the vintage black rotary phone, while gazing out the tall arched window at the beauty of Lake Geneva. Absent-mindedly she twirled the coiled telephone cord around a finger.

"I am so relieved to hear your voice and know that you are safe! That nice young man put himself in a dangerous position by going back to get photographs of the etchings for you."

Attempting to avoid discussing her recent misadventure, Maya asked "What did you find?"

"Christopher's Swiss Army knife memory stick holds files that are encrypted. I have not yet been able to open them. As you mentioned, it also holds photos in non-encrypted files. I do believe that you may be correct that the subject matter in the photos taken of the etchings on the island closely resembles pictures on the memory stick."

"Were you able to identify the artifact?"

"I believe so. I would augur an opinion that it is the Emerald Table."

"The Brigadier said that Christopher had made it his quest to find the artifact. What can you tell me about it?"

"Scholars have suggested that the Emerald Tablet dates back to around 3,000 BC, when the Phoenicians settled on the Syrian coast. The author of the tablet is reputed to be Agathodaimon who was the great Thoth, the Egyptian god of science and mathematics. He is said to have been responsible for teaching men how to interpret things, arrange their speech in logical patterns, and write down their thoughts using hieroglyphics. He appears to have represented the ultimate archetype of the Word of God."

"So, the Tablet has Egyptian roots?" Maya asked.

"Yes. Thoth, who is also known as the First Hermes, is said to have set out to preserve the ancient wisdom by inscribing two great pillars and hiding sacred objects and scrolls inside them before the Great Flood. Ancient texts reveal that Thoth inscribed the Emerald Tablet and hid it in a pillar at Hermopolis before the great deluge."

"Go on. I'm intrigued."

"*In Iamblichus: On the Mysteries,* Thomas Taylor, who was the first transla-tor of Plato into English, quoted an ancient author who said that the Pillars of Hermes dated to before the Great Flood. Other Roman and Greek historians also describe the mysterious pillars."

"What's its connection with Alexander the Great?" Maya asked.

"During his conquest from Babylonia to India, Alexander the Great is re-puted to have found the Emerald Tablet in a temple sometime around 331 BC. Alexander was interested in antiquities. In fact, he built the great library at Alexandria primarily to house and study Thothian materials. In Alexandria, he assembled a panel of priests and scholars to prepare Greek translations of many sacred artifacts he had acquired during his travels."

"Are there descriptions of it?"

"Yes, the Emerald Tablet was described as a mysterious stone or crystal-like tablet resembling melted glass that had been cast and hardened into a mould. Some authors say it had the appearance of an emerald. On its surface, a text was written in bas relief characters. In itself, this was unusual because the writ-ing was not carved into the stone. A translation of the text passage revealed a cryptic epitome of the alchemical opus, revealing the secret of primordial sub-stances and transmutations."

"Do you have more?"

"Yes, a scribe named Manetho worked on it in Alexandria. He wrote that the writing was over 9,000 years old and that it contained the sum of all knowl-edge. Sadly, none of Manetho's writing survived the burning of the great library of Alexandria, but some of his letters to Ptolemy II did survive."

"The sum of all knowledge on one tablet. That is something."

"It seems the Tablet disappeared from Alexandria. The legend goes that, around 32 AD outside the city of Tyana, a young boy named Balinas found it in a cave in Cappadocia. Balinas was a precocious child. He copied the writings on the tablet and studied them to expand his knowledge. He even sought out teachers in Hermetic philosophy. On reaching adulthood, he assumed the name

Apollonius of Tyana, moved to Alexandria and became renowned for his magical powers and healing capabilities. History shows that he wrote a number of books, traveled extensively and inspired many with his wisdom. Sadly, not one of the books written by Apollonius remains. He was a contemporary of Christ and his works were destroyed by Christian zealots. The Tablet appears to have gone missing sometime after 70 AD."

Professor Jullian took a deep breath before continuing, "The earliest surviving translation of the Emerald Tablet is in the Arabic Book of Balinas, circa 650 AD. Several Arabic translations reached Europe with the Moorish invasion of Spain in 771 AD. An Arabic text produced around 800 AD by the alchemist Jabir Hayyan cites Apollonius as the source. The first Latin translation appeared around 1140 AD in a book by Johannes Hispalenis. Later, in the mid 1200s Albertus Magnus issued a translation that spread like wildfire. In fact, most medieval alchemists hung a copy of the Tablet on their laboratory wall and constantly referred to the secret formula it contained."

"Secret formula and all, it sounds like an unusual Tablet. I can see why Christopher would have been interested in it."

"Well, as for the whereabouts of the Emerald Tablet, there are a few indications that it was buried for safekeeping in a vault on the Giza plateau around 400 AD, but no trace has ever been found. However, several expeditions have been undertaken to search for it," Professor Jullian reported.

"The Brigadier said that Christopher was convinced that he had found a cipher map. With his interest in the Tablet, do you suppose he thought he might have found a map that would lead him to the Tablet?" Maya asked excitedly.

"That could be. It may well be that Christopher was on that fateful flight to Switzerland because he planned to have a tête-à-tête with me about a change in direction of his doctorial research. I will know more once I get into his encrypted files," Professor Jullian said.

The professor turned her head to gaze at the cameo picture of her son. She was grateful to Maya for having brought it from Canada to Switzerland.

CHAPTER 25

"Speak of the devil. Where have you been?"

"Sailing on the Aegean, with Pescatori and his brother-in law, Ari," McLaren chuckled.

The cell phone connection was weak at best, but McLaren felt he needed to give Danny an update.

"That was quite a daring move you made, going back to take photos of the etchings for Maya."

McLaren ignored Danny's reproach, "I heard from Sam that they made it off the island in one piece. By the way, I've asked him to use his sources and look into an unusual woman I had the chance to meet on the island."

"Another woman? Don't you have your hands full with Maya?" Danny teased.

McLaren disregarded her remark. His tone became very businesslike, "I would like to hear about the status on the isotope project?"

"Yes, sir," Danny replied imitating his business-like style. "The intrepid Lazar has been busy with his computer in Canada. He sent us the results of his geospatial analysis. It's ready for your review. I looked it over and identified the primary source of supply to the areas with high incidence of death following administration of the isotopes. The shipments were primarily from a company called MNOP, Macedonian Nuclear Official Products."

"So, we have two parts of the equation. Has there been any news about the exact cause of the deaths? We'll need to have that. With that piece, we'll be better positioned to see what might have been happening during the production runs that could have caused specific types of deaths," McLaren said.

"We haven't had a lot of cooperation in obtaining cause of death data. I think that we'll need to garner some support to get more intelligence. There's a meeting tomorrow of the European Medicines Network that you'll be expected to speak at. It will give you an opportunity to exert some influence and hopefully get us more data on cause of death. I'll give you a briefing when you get to the hotel."

"I'll be there within the hour."

"Oh, by the way, the President of the Institute has also announced that there will be a formal dinner on Lycabetus Hill tomorrow night. It's being held in honor of the co-participation of the various states working on the isotope problem."

"I take it attendance is obligatory?"

Danny could almost feel his sense of annoyance. She knew McLaren preferred the rugged outdoor life to networking at formal dinner affairs. He would attend, and no one would be any the wiser of his preference. She, on the other hand, was looking forward to the formal dinner.

"Your presence at the gala is not optional. This is Greek hospitality. It will be fun. I've asked Sam to be my dinner date. I'll bet Maya would be your dinner companion. We could double date. Want me to ask her?"

"Dan, some things I can do myself," McLaren replied tersely.

****

The small auditorium was once again filled with experts from the European Medicines Network. When McLaren stepped on the stage, he received a round of applause.

"Ladies and gentlemen," he began. His voice was moderated and his stance confident. "Thank you for taking time out of your busy schedule."

Using a tiny remote held in his left hand, McLaren called up a series of slides and quickly got down to business. He brought energy to the presentation.

"To answer your question, there are three key phases to our search approach. The first stage has been completed. We have completed a geo-spatial analysis of the data on deaths following use of the isotope. This analysis indicated that the majority of deaths following the administration of the isotope were in and around Greece and Macedonia and the Balkan Peninsula. A small number of deaths have been reported in the United States. The second phase of our work involved identifying shipment suppliers to those areas. This phase has been completed."

THE EMERALD TABLET 149

McLaren paused and took a sip of water. His open and approachable manner concealed the fact that he was holding back on them. A production facility in Macedonia, one with an excellent reputation, had been identified as the primary source of supply for shipments in which isotope usage resulted in higher than usual numbers of deaths. He was reluctant to announce this fact until the team had more detailed information.

"The third phase is proving to be more challenging due to concerns over patient privacy. While medical authorities have been approached and requested to release information about the cause of death, to date this has been extremely slow because most are reluctant to supply it. I now seek your help in obtaining this data. Our research team requires this information to ascertain whether there is any commonality in the cause of death."

Abruptly, a muscularly built representative in his late sixties rose from his chair. At six feet tall, with a large head of wavy silver hair, he was imposing. He stood there with his legs apart in a confrontational, almost belligerent pose. He had obviously come prepared to throw his weight around.

"I do not see why we have any need of an investigation, particularly one conducted by Canadians. It is through lack of strategic planning that the Canadians have brought about a world-wide isotope shortage. Now a Task Force from this same country is trying to tell us that our isotope production, which is helping to address the shortage, is causing increased deaths. This Task Force is a waste of time and money. We should put a halt to this needless investigation and spend our scarce research dollars on finding other methods of assessment and treatment. The number of deaths is not a cause for alarm because these patients are the victims of cancer. If the individual hospitals are themselves not alarmed, why should the Medicines Network be alarmed?"

In the room filled with representatives of different temperaments, philosophies, and European personalities, the representative's comments ignited discussion. The viewpoints of representatives were wildly divergent. Some were adamant that they wanted to halt production at the isotope plants in question.

The President of the Greek Institute was dogmatic that the investigation was well underway and would not be halted.

McLaren's talent for negotiation, diplomacy and compromise was put to the test. The passionate interchanges amongst foreign colleagues created the type of engagement that McLaren knew was needed. If he handled it correctly, he was confident that he could achieve full blown commitment.

In the audience Danny watched her older brother use his charisma and sense of humor to help diffuse the difficult state of affairs. It was remarkable how his persuasive talents helped focus attention on key points and motivate the group to work together. She was impressed.

McLaren walked over to the edge of the stage and surveyed the group, "My friends, it is impossible to overstate the need to get at the root of this isotope problem. Many lives are at stake. Can we work together on this problem? Can our Task Force count on you?"

The vote taken at the conclusion of the discussion was just about unanimous. It was agreed that there was value in the Task Force investigation and that it should continue. To speed comparative analysis of symptoms and cause of death, primarily data from incidents in Greece and Macedonia would be used, although other countries were also welcome to submit their data.

CHAPTER 26

A small yellow vehicle cab peeled out from the curb and merged into chaotic Athenian traffic. While vying for lane space with cars, buses, people, bicycles and other obstacles on piste, the driver whipped through the throngs at upwards of 80 miles an hour. He careened down back streets and commandeered bus lanes trailing a cloud of black smoke.

With his eyes glued ahead, the cabbie narrowly missed sideswiping a tourist bus that was crawling along. Moments later he fearlessly charged past cyclists with less than 5 inches to spare. His four nervous North American passengers gripped the door handles firmly. They rode in tense silence, catching glimpses of cyclists faces frozen in terror when the cab brushed past.

Sam, sitting shot-gun, seemed to be enjoying the white-knuckle ride. His enthusiasm dwindled measurably when, with less than an inch to spare, an oncoming car suddenly darted out in front of the cab.

He braced his wrists against the dash expecting an imminent crash and lamented, "I should've worn my helmet!"

Above the roar of the engine, the screech of brakes and the honking of horns, Danny ignored the mayhem and played tour guide.

"Myth has it that Lycabettus Hill was created when the goddess Athena removed a piece of Mount Pendeli to increase the height of her temple on the Acropolis. While she was enroute, two blackbirds brought her bad news. She was so thrown off balance by their disturbing tidings that she dropped the rock she was carrying before she made it to the Acropolis. The name of the hill reflects a popular belief that it was once inhabited by wolves, since in Greek lykos means wolf."

When the cab arrived at the popular tourist attraction, Sam hopped out of the front seat and in a ceremonial gesture knelt down in his tuxedo and kissed the ground. Danny giggled, Maya looked on astonished, and McLaren paid the taxi fare.

The foursome took the funicular to the top of Lycabettus Hill. While riding up through the pine trees covering the base towards the twin peaks some 1,000 feet above Athens, Sam leaned over and whispered in Danny's ear "I'm walking back, how about you, babe?"

Danny grinned and nodded her agreement.

The memorable taxi ride was soon forgotten, pushed into the recesses of memory by a priceless panorama. From atop Lycabettus Hill, Athens dazzled like jewels. The vista extended from Mount Parnes in the north, to the port of Piraeus in the west and over to the Saronic Gulf. Half way to the sea, on the Acropolis, the illuminated Parthenon shone in shimmering shades of silver and gold, like a crown above the city.

The evening was an extravagant affair. Diplomats dressed in evening wear mingled, glass in hand with pre-dinner drinks. A sumptuous meal ensued with the ubiquitous bread and olive oil, and black olives at the table. At each table a bucket of chilled bottled water and a pleasing Greek rosé rested on ice.

The ladies chose local lobster served over tagliatelle and the gentlemen opted for grouper with risotto and a lemon sauce. Dessert consisted of a selection of tarts along with a digestif of Metaxa.

Once the lavish dinner and speeches were over, the strains of music began. Sam winked at Danny and asked her to dance. She smiled in response and got up to join him on the dance floor.

Maya looked on enviously while Danny danced elegantly, looking radiant in her white Grecian style gown.

"That boy's got rhythm. He loves to dance," McLaren smiled, watching Sam dancing with his sister.

McLaren, in contrast did not go up to the dance floor. He remained seated at the banquet table in conversation with Maya and a Serbian delegate and his wife.

During the next set Sam returned to the table and asked Maya to join him on the floor. Danny reached out for her brother's hand and led him to the dance floor.

As McLaren floated across the dance floor with his sister he was surprised to catch sight of an auburn-haired beauty. Her vivid head was conspicuous amongst the dull tints of the other dancers.

I would recognize that body and those green eyes anywhere.

An impulse of curiosity made him announce to his sister, "Excuse me Dan, there is someone I just have to dance with." Abruptly, he abandoned his sister.

If Danny was surprised or irritated, she didn't show it.

McLaren walked over to the Macedonian representative who had confronted him in the afternoon session and tapped his shoulder.

The older representative quickly realized that McLaren was requesting a dance with his partner. He bowed to his auburn-haired companion, giving McLaren permission to take her across the dance floor.

"We appear to move in the same circles. I'm so glad to have this opportunity to hold you in my arms again. The ambiance here is much more pleasant, don't you find?" McLaren's unswerving cobalt blue eyes twinkled with mirth.

McLaren's new dance partner's beautiful porcelain complexion remained frozen, but her green eyes smoldered. When she finally spoke, her sultry voice made it clear that she had no idea what McLaren was talking about. Her polite stiffness did nothing to deter McLaren.

Maya returned to the table and joined Danny in watching the dancers. Both women looked on inquiringly at McLaren and the elegant, auburn-haired woman in a formfitting laurel green dress.

Danny couldn't help but notice the intensity in her brother's eyes when McLaren drifted effortlessly across the floor with the stunning woman in his arms. She was annoyed that she couldn't guess the connection. She couldn't ask Sam because he was over at the bar getting drinks. She felt obliged to take matters into her own hands.

Two can play this game.

"Excuse me," Danny abruptly rose from the table and went over to where the woman's original partner, the Macedonian, was seated.

Smiling and speaking directly to the fashionably dressed gentleman with the silver hair, Danny asked, "Might I have this dance?"

The Macedonian graciously accepted. He stood up, bowed to her, took her hand and led her to the dance floor.

Danny was surprised to find that despite their age difference, conversing with him was quite easy. She inquired about his accent, indicating that she thought she caught a trace of American mid-west.

The Macedonian chuckled and quickly replied that he had attended Missouri University and subsequently did research in the US, so he might well have acquired a mid-west accent.

Danny found the man charming but by no means handsome. His natural presence and confidence set him apart, despite his less than glamorous wide forehead, and broad nose. She thought that his stylish silver hair was his best feature.

When the music ended the Macedonian invited Danny to accompany him for a walk on the terrace. He continued the conversation against the backdrop of the Athenian city lights.

"What you can see of the Parthenon, over there, is the ruined shell of a temple. It stood the test of time from the Ottoman Empire until 1687 when a group of Venetian holy warriors led a siege on the Acropolis. Sadly, the Turks were using the Parthenon to store gunpowder, and when a Venetian cannonball hit the barrels, half the temple was blown away, along with all that was inside," the Macedonian said.

"How did you know I was interested in ruins?" Danny asked.

"I have always been fascinated with the beauty of the ruins of antiquity. There is so much one can learn from the ancients. But enough about me, what are you doing in this part of the world?"

Danny explained that she was part of a Canadian Task Force working in Athens.

"A number of years ago I worked in Canada, at the nuclear installation at Chalk River. My work there instilled in me a desire to help create a nuclear isotope facility in my own country. When I returned to my homeland I set up my facility. It is one of the few of this type in the world. It is a precious resource for Macedonia," he said with passion.

Danny found herself quite taken with him. He was charming. In his expensive Italian suit, he cut an elegant figure. She liked the fact that he was interesting, a man of strong character, and one with vision.

She wasn't surprised when the Macedonian asked her whether she would be going out to Greek and Macedonian production facilities during the investigation. She acknowledged that she would be undertaking visits of this type.

"If my facility is one of the ones that are selected for observation and you happen to be the task force member charged with the inspection, I would be honored to personally show you around," he said. He reached into his suit pocket to pull out his business card. His hand lingered on Danny's when he presented it to her.

Looking down and reading his card, Danny smiled and replied, "Thank you for your kind offer, Aleksander Petkovski."

Then, unexpectedly, the Macedonian said, "If you will excuse me, I should return to my companion."

****

Following an enjoyable evening the foursome descended Lycabettus Hill by fu-nicular only to see cabs and limousines lined-up, waiting for the guests. True to his word, Sam walked back to the hotel and Danny accompanied him. McLaren and Maya chose to wait for a cab.

McLaren immediately got back to the task of reviewing data from the iso-tope investigation. Maya opted to get some shut eye.

When Sam returned he was anxious to give McLaren an update. Danny was curious, so she joined them in her brother's room.

"Do you have anything on the wealthy Russian recluse who owns the is-land?" McLaren asked. "I'd hazard a guess that the bald guy with bulbous nose on the island wasn't the Russian who owns the island."

"What makes you think that? Who was he then?" Danny asked.

"I still don't know," Sam replied.

"Did you get a description of him from Maya? Sam, you could do a sketch and we could send it off to Lazer," Danny said enthusiastically.

"If you are thinking that he might be able to use facial recognition software on my sketch, then you have a tremendous belief in my drawing skills," Sam chuckled.

"The sooner we know who her abductor was, the better. What have you got so far?" McLaren said.

"Aside from owning a Greek island and a yacht, Vladimir Jankovic is good buddies with the Macedonian Aleksander Petkovski. He's the same Macedon-ian who expressed concerns about the Canadian Taskforce. They both went to university in Macedonia and both majored in Engineering. Jankovic has a financial interest in the Macedonian's isotope plant," Sam reported.

"Tell me about the Macedonian delegate, other than the fact that Danny chose him to be her dancer partner this evening?" McLaren gave an inquiring look at his sister.

Danny shrugged.

"My sources say that the Macedonian, Aleksander Petkovski, is well known in the American medical radiopharmaceutical business. He did his Master's degree and Doctorate at the University of Missouri," Sam said.

"Interesting. That's the location of the University of Missouri Research Reactor (MURR), a 10-megawatt facility. It's the most powerful research reactor available on American campuses," McLaren said.

"Petkovski also worked at the Chalk River nuclear plant in Canada for a couple of years in the late nineties. He is quite familiar with how Canada makes medical isotopes," Sam said.

"Quite the background. Do you have more?" McLaren asked.

"Yes. His facility in Macedonia does not use highly enriched Uranium, which is a plus for his relationship with the Americans who are definitely not keen on Canada using highly enriched Uranium to produce medical isotopes. Aleksander Petkovski is known to have a working relationship with lobby groups in the USA that are trying to stop the shipment of HEU out of the USA in favor of the USA producing their own radioisotopes and gaining control over that market. You know from what you've seen in the meetings at the Institute that he's a heavy weight in this part of the world regarding nuclear medicine. He's respected, ambitious and greatly committed to his homeland, Macedonia," Sam reported.

Danny smiled. She was pleased that she had uncovered similar information while dancing with the Macedonian.

"He's invited me to go out and visit his facility," Danny announced.

"I don't trust him," McLaren said.

"You wouldn't be basing your opinion on the fact that he had a pretty redhead on his arm at the dinner this evening? You seemed to take quite a shine to her. Would that have anything to do with your lack of trust?" Danny teasingly asked.

He ignored his sister's comment. "Sam, what do you have on the woman? I swear that she's the same woman I encountered on the island."

"Uhh," Danny tried ineffectively to stifle a hiccup that would reveal her surprise.

Rolling his eyes, Sam continued, "Ah, the seductive siren. Like you suspected, she's CIA. She goes by the name Sacha Cazan. It was really difficult to find out much about her, there were so many roadblocks. It seems clear that she's working undercover. What I don't know is whether she is looking into the Macedonian, Aleksander Petkovski or whether she is keeping tabs on the Russian, Jankovic. Clearly, my fellow Americans were reluctant to give me much. They were concerned about blowing her cover. I'm looking at it from another angle now. My contacts were really firm that we are to do nothing that would endanger her assignment."

CHAPTER 27

Too wound up for sleep and anxious to discuss Christopher's archeological work, early Sunday morning Maya took to the internet for a webcam chat with her aunt while Danny slept.

"It's like puzzle pieces. We just need to find a way to put the clues together and then we'll have the big picture," Maya said to the digital image of Professor Jullian, seated at her antique desk in her garret-like office in Switzerland.

"I'd say that Christopher became engrossed in the Emerald Tablet when he realized the importance of the lost treasure. It would have been quite a credit for him to have been the archeologist who found it," Professor Jullian said.

"Well, let's lay out what it is that we know, for sure, or almost for sure."

"First, the Curator of the Museum in Naples thought that it was so important for you to meet with the Brigadier General who was familiar with Christopher's work. He also thought you should have a photo of the mosaic uncovered at Pompeii. It is significant that he sent a messenger with these items to the ruins of Pompeii," Professor Jullian said.

"Oh, Tante Hélène that was an awful experience. It really seems that the messenger got a bullet that was intended for me. The old man died instantly. There was nothing I could do to save him. While I realize that McLaren and his team were on a mission and could not afford to get involved with the Italian Police and all, I am more than a bit worried because we just left the scene of a homicide. Sam said that it would all be taken care of. I made the call to Curator Dalfalco. He was naturally stunned at the news. McLaren spoke to him at length." Maya said.

"Maya don't dwell on it. You'll be having nightmares again. Look, Marc McLaren told me that arrangements were made with the Curator to keep CANDO out of it. The messenger's family will be very well taken care of. Don't worry.

The Museum of Naples and an unidentified Canadian benefactor will help them out behind the scenes. There will be funding to help his grandchildren attend university and his family will not want for anything. Take your mind off it by turning your focus to the archeological clues," Professor Jullian advised.

"That's easy advice for you to give. I'm a doctor. I try to help save lives."

"What else have you got, Maya?" her aunt asked tersely.

"Before I was abducted in the Plaka, I learned from the elderly Greek Brigadier that Christopher had consulted him about a tomb in which the Brigadier had found a number of Macedonian artifacts. The Brigadier had published a series of articles. He believed his find dated back to the time of Alexander the Great. Christopher became friends with the Brigadier and asked if he could accompany the older gentleman to the site. The Brigadier is of the opinion that the tomb may hold the remains of Alexander the Great. However, from what I understand, academics say the tombs in that area date back to royalty who predeceased Alexander," Maya said.

"Continue, please," Professor Jullian said in the tone reserved for speaking to her students.

"The Brigadier mentioned that while at the tomb Christopher became fascinated by a fresco painting on a frieze. Christopher recognized that the frieze depicted the same subject matter as the famous Alexander mosaic discovered in the ruins of Pompeii. At a later time, Christopher asked the Brigadier to accompany him on a visit to the Museum of Naples where the Alexander Mosaic from Pompeii is on display," Maya said.

"That explains Christopher's visit to Naples," Professor Jullian said.

"While I was at the Brigadier's home, he showed me a photo plate in an old book. He said that Christopher wanted to find the artifact in the photo. I had hoped to learn more, but the Brigadier found conversing strenuous and suggested that I return another day. I've tried to set an appointment for a return visit, but the old gentleman is quite ill and is not receiving visitors," Maya reported.

"I also made some progress. Thanks to the help of Danny's friend Lazer, the computer whiz in Ottawa, I was able to access Christopher's encrypted notes on the Swiss Army memory stick," Professor Jullian said.

"Wow."

"I've had an opportunity to review the photos and now the encrypted notes on the flash drive and I have to say that there is good reason to think, like the

Brigadier did, that the tomb in the photos dates back to the time of Alexander the Great."

"What makes you say that?" Maya asked.

"It's the roof structure that is significant. The fact that the tomb was built using a curved ceiling called a barrel-vault is important. Archeologists have identified the earliest recorded barrel vault in Greece dates back to the late 320s BC, which is the time of Alexander the Great. The technique was introduced in Greece from the Near East by Alexander's architects. The Brigadier may have been on to something when he thought it was a possibility that the ancients might have wanted to place Alexander's remains in that area. That said, more recent analysis has shown that the remains are not those of Alexander," Professor Jullian said.

"Tell me about the photos on the flash drive?"

"The photos were indeed interesting. Christopher had set up four folders of photos. The first folder had photos that appear to have been taken at the tomb the Brigadier found. Another folder contained a series of artwork and these all had a similar subject matter, namely Alexander at Issus. Yet another folder contained photos of a rather unique temple with slender columns. There was also a folder with a series of photos on the Emerald Tablet."

"Very interesting. What do make of the photos?"

"A photo of a frieze appeared early in the photo sequence. The photo identification shows that it was from the tomb which the Brigadier found. Christopher also had photos of what I am now almost positive is the famous Alexander floor mosaic that was unearthed at Pompeii. These may have been ones that he had been given permission to take at the Museum in Naples. There were also photos of another mosaic, one with a fret or interlocking motif around it. In this mosaic, the subject matter was more focused on Alexander and his horse Bucephalus."

"The Brigadier said Christopher was really interested in a frieze painting found in the tomb. The elderly gentleman said Christopher thought it was a cipher," Maya said.

"The frieze, a cipher? Interesting," Dr. Jullian said.

Maya could almost see the wheels turning in the professor's mind.

"It is remarkable that the painting on the frieze found in the tomb the Brigadier discovered was so similar to the Roman mosaic found in the House of Faun in Pompeii. The Roman Historian Pliny the Elder, who died near Pompeii, during the eruption of Mount Vesuvius in 79 AD, wrote that the mosaic in Pompeii was a copy of a painting by Apelles, a renowned painter and contemporary of Alexander the Great. It's said that Alexander so liked one of the drawings Apelles created for him, that the Macedonian leader gave the painter one of his own concubines whom the artist had admired," Professor Jullian said.

"Wouldn't it have been unusual to give an artist a concubine?"

"Yes, but Alexander could be quite generous," the professor replied.

"I read somewhere that Ptolemy stole Alexander's body after he died."

"Yes. Ptolemy Lagos was one of Alexander's most trusted generals and was among his seven personal somatophylakes or bodyguards. Ptolemy was a few years older than Alexander and had been his closest friend since childhood. He was reputed to have hijacked Alexander's embalmed corpse in 323 BC, while it was on its way back to Aigai, the old Macedonian capital. History shows that Ptolemy took his remains to Alexandria where he had them displayed in a glass sarcophagus."

"Why would he have taken Alexander's remains to Alexandria?"

"For power is the quick answer. Aristander, Alexander's favorite soothsayer prophesized that the country in which the body of Alexander the Great was buried would be the most prosperous in the world. It would have been quite natural for Ptolemy to want to take his friend's body back to Egypt. It was a power base with excellent resources. When the generals divided Alexander's empire, following his death, Ptolemy became the general in charge of troops in Egypt. He was made satrap of Egypt first under Alexander's half brother and then under Alexander IV. Ptolemy was ambitious. By 305 BC he had become King of Egypt, taking the title Ptolemy I Soter, meaning savior, and founding the Ptolemaic dynasty."

"Well Ptolemy definitely had power."

"It would be undoubtedly a unique exception to tradition if Alexander's bones remained in a foreign land, like Egypt. The ancient Macedonians are reported to have twice tried unsuccessfully to take back Alexander's corpse. There is strong evidence that later they were successful in recovering their king's corpse and replacing it with an effigy. Reportedly, an effigy of Alexander the Great was buried in Alexandria and that is the one the Roman Emperors saw when they visited his grave. On the other hand, the armors of Alexander the Great, which according to the ancient historiographers, were placed on the hearse in Babylon, were never mentioned to have been found in Egypt," Professor Jullian said.

"What did you find about the smaller mosaic that has a fret border?"

"Sorry, so far I have found absolutely nothing on that particular mosaic."

"You've read Chris's notes and seen the photos. Did he believe that the armor in the tomb might have belonged to Alexander?"

"Yes, they could well have been part of his armor."

"Do you think that Christopher thought the Brigadier had found Alexander the Great's final resting place?"

"I think Christopher found enough evidence that made him wonder whether the Brigadier might have located Alexander's tomb. That would have been a very controversial find."

"Did you have time to look at the photos that McLaren took for me when I was on the island? When I saw the etchings, I was almost certain they resembled the artifact pictured in the book that the Brigadier had shown me. That's why I asked McLaren to take photos of them."

"Hm," Professor Jullian was reluctant to comment. She had almost lost her niece on that island.

"Do you think Christopher's photos of the Tablet are copied from the book the Brigadier showed me, or his own shots?"

The professor's reply was deadpan, "I don't know. I didn't see the book."

"I realize that."

"As I mentioned after your misadventure, the Tablet was believed to be a sacred gift from the Egyptian God of Science, Thoth, who wanted to preserve ancient wisdom. Alexander the Great is reputed to have come across it after a battle during his conquest. He recognized its significance and ordered that it be taken to Alexandria and translated. Its message was passed down through the ages. Alchemists believed that it revealed the secret of transmutations and called it a secret formula. Its whereabouts have long remained a mystery."

"Secret formula?"

"Yes, let me show you a copy of a 17th century translation done by Isaac Newton."

Professor Jullian tried to adjust the webcam camera so that her niece could view the text.

Tis true without lying, certain & most true.
That which is below is like that which is above & that which is above
is like that which is below to do the miracles of one only thing

And as all things have been & arose from one by the mediation of one:
so all things have their birth from this one thing by adaptation.
The Sun is its father, the moon its mother, the wind hath carried it in
its belly, the earth is its nurse.
The father of all perfection in the whole world is here.
Its force or power is entire if it be converted into earth.
Separate thou the earth from the fire, the subtle from the gross sweetly
with great industry.
It ascends from the earth to the heaven & again it descends to the earth
& receives the force of things superior & inferior.
By this means you shall have the glory of the whole world & thereby
all obscurity shall fly from you.
Its force is above all force. For it vanquishes every subtle thing & pen-
etrates every solid thing.
So was the world created.
From this are & do come admirable adaptations whereof the means (or
process) is here in this. Hence, I am called Hermes Trismegist, having the
three parts of the philosophy of the whole world
That which I have said of the operation of the Sun is accomplished &
ended.

Maya was not sure what to make of the translation, so she tried another angle.

"But where does the frieze in the tomb fit in?"

"On the memory stick the frieze lies in numerical sequence with other photos taken of the inside of the tomb and prior to the sequence of photos of the Emerald Tablet."

"Uh," Maya wasn't looking for an answer about the precise numerical location of the photo. She was anxious to know the why of it all. She tried reposing her question, "Tante Hélène, I wasn't asking about numerical sequence, I meant how it fits into the overall scheme?"

"Ah, but the numerical sequence on the memory stick provides us with a clue. Think about it."

Maya felt like she was a student in one of her aunt's university classes. She pulled out the photo of the Alexander mosaic from Naples and a copy of the photo of the frieze and stared at them. They were similar, yet different.

"Do you give up?" Professor Jullian asked.

The situation felt like being on the hot seat. Though she loved and admired her aunt, Maya wondered whether Professor Jullian's university students ever found her teaching style somewhat frustrating.

"The sequence is important. I think initially Christopher intended to put forward conclusive proof of Alexander the Great's final resting place for the topic of his doctoral dissertation; however, he saw that the Brigadier's writings had proven extremely controversial. He decided to research a related topic but one not nearly so contentious. Remember he wanted to complete his doctorate, not be mired down by controversy. So, he chose to pursue a tangent. The photo sequence shows that he became interested in the frieze in the tomb and subsequently the Emerald Tablet," Professor Jullian suggested.

"I don't see the significance of the numerical sequence. I do however see a common denominator between the photos of the ancient frieze and the Roman mosaic from Pompeii. It's the subject matter. They both portray the visual of Alexander in battle. What could it mean?"

"At Issus Alexander used a very unusual tactical maneuver. Employing the element of surprise, he appeared before Darius unexpectedly which caused the Persians to flee in panic. The artist caught the human dimension of battle. His representation of Alexander illustrates both his honor and sympathy to his opponent Darius. Following the battle, it was recorded that Alexander treated his prisoners with a level of care and regard which Persians had never encountered. So, the mosaic in effect reconstructs Alexander's superiority and one might say the typology of his victory."

Maya smiled, "Tante Hélène, I didn't mean what does the work of art portray. I was actually asking the significance of Christopher's interest in the two pieces of artwork."

"Good question, Maya," her aunt replied. It was the reply she gave to her students when she wanted them to use their deductive reasoning.

"Christopher must have found the connection. They both display the visual of Alexander in battle and the golden artifacts. Look at how they make use of strong diagonal lines. The midpoint is dominated by intersecting diagonals of the Persian speared by Alexander and the Persian restraining the rearing horse. Then there are the other sets of intersecting diagonals created by the figures of Darius and his charioteer and by Alexander and the wounded Persian. The lances in the background have a diagonal motif. Even the twisted tree limbs in the background continue the sense of diagonal."

"There must be something we are missing."

"Yes, and then there is the question of the cipher that the Brigadier said Christopher had found," Maya said.

"I refuse to be stymied on that one. I'll go over his notes another time to see if I missed something."

CHAPTER 28

The din of morning traffic in the narrow streets around Syntagma Square made it hard to concentrate. McLaren walked over to the open hotel window and closed it. Behind him, at the table Sam, Danny, and Maya were engrossed in a map of Greece, Macedonia, and the Balkan Peninsula. On the map clusters of multicolored dots pinpointed data sets and exposed the extent of the growing isotope problem.

"I asked Lazer to use the data we had and plot the incidence of death relative to supplier on the map. I specified Greece and Macedonia in particular, because we have been able to obtain more data on cause of death in this region. The incidence of death is continuing to rise in this area," McLaren said, pointing to a specific area on the map.

"So, the red dots indicate deaths and the colors around the dot indicate the suppliers. The hot spots are important clues for us in trying to find out what might be creating the clustering," Sam said.

Maya stared down at the clusters of colored dots displaying instances of death following an isotope injection. "Is the same map available color-coded by cause of death?"

"Not yet. There is insufficient data available on cause of death. Initially we had difficulty obtaining data on cause of death but now we are getting more cooperation. We could use your help in looking at commonality in cause of death," McLaren said.

"Definitely," Maya replied.

Danny's eyes glazed over staring at the scatter dots on the map. She wondered about the choice of data identifiers for the umpteenth time.

Why do they forever use colors that you cannot differentiate?

Danny glanced away from the map to the wall where Maya had tacked photos. With malevolent curiosity she shifted her gaze back and forth from the photos to the map on the table. The change in perspective opened up a fresh idea, a new approach to seeing the mosaic from the House of Faun in Pompeii and the frieze from the tomb in Macedonia.

"Will you look at that? One would think that the painting on the frieze is supposed to depict the battle in which Alexander faced and attempted to capture or kill Darius, but does it?" Danny said.

"Not now Dan. Please focus. We are trying to get a handle on the isotope crisis," McLaren reminded his sister.

"Marc, I know, but this is important. Look at the colors, hues and lines on the photo of the frieze from the tomb. They almost resemble the outline of the coast of Greece and Macedonia. I don't know that I would have caught that if you didn't have the map spread out. Look, there is a definite distinction if you compare the photo of the mosaic from Pompeii and the photo of the older frieze that Maya's cousin found. They are not quite the same. The color hues are different. It's almost like the older frieze resembles a map," Danny said.

"It's understandable that they are different. They are not even from the same era. The mosaic is from a much later period. Based on what my aunt said, the fresco painting on the frieze that Christopher saw in the tomb would date back to the period around Alexander's death, 323 BC. On the other hand, the mosaic from Pompeii is thought to be a Roman copy of an earlier Hellenistic work Maya said.

"Yes, but they..." Danny's voice trailed off when she caught sight of her brother's glaring look.

Maya failed to notice the look and continued the conversation with Danny, "Precisely what were you saying about the Macedonian frieze and the later Roman mosaic? They seem very much alike to me. Granted the frieze found at the tomb has a different perspective and has more faded colors. It definitely seems like the same battle scene."

"Maya, the photo of the mosaic from Pompeii, the one the Curator gave you, does appear to have similar subject content, but to me your cousin's photo of the painting on the frieze has a different color rendition. I wouldn't just attribute this to lighting or fading. I think the selection of colors was intentional by the artist. You know, when I half-close my eyes and peer at your cousin's photo of the frieze, what I see looks much like the outline of a coast," Danny said.

"Outline of a coast? Whatever are you talking about Danny? They have basically the same subject, but one is just a lot older than the other," McLaren stated firmly, hoping to close the digression and return to the isotope problem.

"But, they aren't quite the same. The frieze has different hues and that makes sense because it is much older and more faded. The other point you should consider is that the aspect ratio is different," said Sam.

McLaren affixed his sister with a stare that clearly indicated that he wanted to curtail any further discussion about paintings and mosaics, "Dan, you know that you never see colors like the rest of us. Your color perception has always been askew. Face it, you are color-blind. Remember, in high school you had trouble in chemistry because you couldn't see color changes in the lab. Luckily, by the time you got to university you had found a cell phone app to use to identify color."

"That was a rather harsh statement bro," Sam said rushing to Danny's defense.

"My so-called disability, seeing color hues differently from you, might just be paying off this time. Watch this. It's a map I tell you!" Danny said, tracing the outline of what she perceived.

The others really did have trouble seeing it. However, when Danny used her index finger and slowly traced the outline for them, her friends began to make out what was quite clear to Danny. The scene on the frieze did in fact resemble the outline of a coast.

"Was your cousin Christopher color-blind, Maya?" Sam asked.

Maya nodded, "Yes, he did have a color vision deficiency."

"Well, landforms do change over time, but Danny might be on to something," Sam said.

The sudden heavy back-beat guitar rhythm of Bachman Turner Overdrive playing 'Taking Care of Business' on McLaren's cell phone cut the discussion. The intrusion demanded attention.

"Saved by the beat, instead of the bell," Sam chuckled.

****

"The call was from Dr. Shearwater. Pressure is being brought to bear on him about finding a solution to the isotope crisis. With the number of reported deaths on the upswing he's asking us to adjust the priorities. Number one is now examination of the nuclear production facility. Which has been pinpointed the potential source of isotope shipments correlating with higher mortality? Our orders are to proceed immediately to obtain a sample from this facility."

"So much for our discussion of visual deficiencies," Sam said.

"We need to get to the root of the problem. There's already stress world-wide because the Canadian facility is not yet up and running after repairs. The shortage is growing. It would be a really bad time to announce that alternative supplies are being linked to deaths," McLaren stated with a quick glance at the others.

"How do want to handle this phase?" Sam asked.

McLaren leaned against the table and outlined his thoughts, "One of us needs to go out to the Macedonian facility. Pack your bags, Danny. I might have been reluctant to send you out on your own, but, since you voiced that you'd like to be the one to conduct the inspection of the Macedonian operation, you're off. I'll give you a specific briefing about what we need you to look for in, say, twenty minutes? Sam, would you please arrange to get Dan flights and a car rental?"

Sam nodded, "I'm on it."

Swinging her hand up in a salute worthy of an army cadet, Danny smiled and said, "I'll be set to go in twenty."

"Sam, I'd also like you to use your network to find out more about the Russian recluse, the Macedonian and that female CIA operative," said McLaren.

Before leaving the room, Danny looked at Maya and asked, "Hey, Maya, do you think that you could ask the professor about the concept of the painting on the frieze being a map? I'm anxious to continue our archeological sojourn when I get back."

"Sure, no problem, I'll ask her," Maya smiled.

With his sister and Sam out of the room McLaren said, "If you've got a minute, Maya, there's a matter I'd like to discuss with you."

CHAPTER 29

No one seemed surprised when the departure of the half hour domestic flight from Athens to Thessalonica was delayed by a tire problem. When the plane finally got off the ground the flight was smooth. The landing, on the other hand, left much to be desired.

After stepping out of the plane onto the tarmac, Danny shouldered her backpack, and proceeded to the rental counter where she picked up a small vehicle to drive to the isotope production facility. Before long she was on the M-1 link driving north through Macedonia towards Karadavici in the southern Balkans.

On the route northward, the motorway narrowed from four lanes to two, passing hillsides covered in vineyards. Danny's destination was just north of the small village of Konopište, in the valley of both the Kozuf and Kozak mountains.

The car rental agent who had given Danny directions and landmarks to look for, indicated that she should look for a specific crossroads where she had to turn off. After that right turn there would be a gentle ascent marking the entrance to the remote isotope production facility.

Although Danny had given very short notice that she would be arriving at the facility to take samples, the security guard at the gate was expecting her. He notified the plant's CEO, Aleksander Petkovski of her arrival.

"Welcome Danielle. Even if your visit is for business reasons I take pleasure in seeing you. I am so glad you were able to find our facility. Like you say in Canada, it's off the beaten path."

The Macedonian took Danny's hand. With a confident subtlety, he leaned his head close to hers and said, "Say you'll stay and dine with me this evening?" His gold cufflinks came into view beyond the crisp white shirt sleeve which extended the appropriate length beyond the cuff of his dark, Italian made, pinstripe suit.

Danny smiled and nodded her acceptance. "How kind of you to offer. Yes, thank you."

"The pleasure is all mine."

"I'm sorry that my announcement that I was coming to your plant was rather hurried. Our task force felt that in view of the high instance of death after administration of isotopes, it was imperative that we commence our visits to each of the facilities supplying medical isotopes. A courier is on his way here to transport the samples that I will be taking," Danny said without giving any indication that this facility had been especially targeted.

"Come, allow me to show you into my office. You may write up your notes in here."

He guided her towards the office building. On the way he asked, "May I offer you a Turkish coffee?"

Danny thanked him but declined.

His private office was tastefully decorated with high end wooden furniture. On one wall was a pair of charcoal sketches of the ruins of a Greek styled temple. Its tall, slender, white columns were adorned with a graceful flower motif. On the adjacent wall hung a beautifully framed sketch of what looked like the Emerald Tablet. The artistry was so intricate that it took Danny's breath away.

"Oh, my, this is beautiful."

"It has caught your attention, yes? This precious piece is a depiction of an object that it is far more than beautiful. This is a sketch of the famed Emerald Tablet found by Alexander the Great during his famous expedition to India. He was so taken with the piece that he ordered that the Tablet be taken to Alexandria and studied. The text of the Tablet was said to reveal the secret of primordial substances and transmutations."

"The sketches are so detailed."

"Yes, it was the tradition of medieval alchemists to hang a copy of the Tablet. Like them, I have hung a copy of this Tablet, for there are many who would agree that the production of radioactive isotopes is modern alchemy."

A piercing ringtone announced a call on the Macedonian's cell phone. Petkovski looked down at the screen, then turned to Danny, "Please excuse me for a moment. I must take this call." He exited the room.

Danny knew that she would only have a moment or two. She snapped shots of the artwork and sent them to Maya. Her brief text accompanying the photos read, *Another piece of the puzzle. Can you get your aunt to do some research on the temple with floral designs?*

She put her cell phone away quickly before the Macedonian reappeared. She moved over to the broad expanse of window and looked out at the facility.

Aleksander Petkovski returned and apologized for the call. He walked over to stand beside her and waved his arm at the view below.

"Unlike the production in Canada, where you use a fission product, Uranium fuel, and irradiate it for eight days, then dissolve the fuel and recover the Molybdenum-99, our plant uses naturally-occurring Thallium and turns it in to Thallium-201."

"Isn't Thallium rare?"

"In general, it is a very rare element and cannot be produced in large quantities in a cyclotron, even if you have the world's largest cyclotron like you do in Vancouver. You just cannot do it because you do not have sufficient target material and you cannot obtain significant beam time. Nonetheless, Thallium-201 is an excellent replacement for Molybdenum-99 and here in Macedonia we have a huge mineral deposit, so we can do it. The plus is that we are not using highly enriched Uranium and incurring the wrath of America, like Canada is. So, because of the worldwide medical isotope shortage our production facility has come into its own. Are you ready to begin a tour of the facility?"

"Definitely."

Aleksander Petkovski ushered Danny to the security point that marked the entrance to plant operations. Here she exchanged her cell phone and passport for a visitor pass equipped with a dosimeter for radiation monitoring.

Danny felt uneasy leaving her cell phone. She considered it "her life" and was uncomfortable depositing it at the checkpoint but she understood that for security reasons cell phones were not permitted.

As they walked along inside the large facility Danny asked, "By any chance did you alter your production runs in any way? If your specs were at all off, there is a remote chance that the isotope produced might not have been pure Thallium-201."

"I can assure you that we take quality control most seriously. We work to the highest standards. Macedonia needs this industry and the public need to have confidence in our product."

"Well, let's get the sample off to the lab at the Institute. They'll assess whether the specific activity is right on. The sooner they do it, the better."

Danny carefully obtained the required number of samples, labeled them, and packaged them. She had them all set for shipping by the time the courier service arrived.

"Do I have your assurances that the results of the sample will be released to no one?"

"I understand, but unfortunately I'm in no position to make such a promise. It will not be up to me."

Danny noticed a vein on his neck quiver. She suspected that her response was not the answer he wanted. She was relieved when he refrained from arguing his position with her. No doubt he would take it up with someone higher up the ladder.

With the samples on their way Danny asked if she could see more of the facility and the Macedonian kindly obliged and gave her a full tour. He seemed very proud of the work accomplished at the facility.

Walking through the warehousing section of the plant Danny was astonished by the number of very large shipping containers.

They must be confident that they can retain a good share of the medical isotope market. Why in the world would they have so many large containers and why would they be laid out in a pattern?

Danny made a mental note to ask McLaren why the facility would arrange the shipping containers in this manner.

Although Danny had not been permitted to carry her cell phone, her host had not parted with his. Once again Aleksander Petkovski's cell phone rang. She saw worry lines on his forehead deepen when he looked down at the number.

"Please excuse me, again," he spun on his heel and darted into a nearby glass enclosed office.

Through the glass partition Danny could see the Macedonian's face turn beet red while he listened to the words of the caller.

****

"Your facility has been subject to too much scrutiny. In short order, they will realize. The isotope production facility must be erased and with it the nosy woman from CANDO. Get out immediately. I have commanded my men to destroy it."

Inside the small office Aleksander Petkovski was shocked by the words of his Russian benefactor. He implored the man, "There must be some other way.

I have put so much of my life into creating this facility for my country. I assure you your secret is safe here at the plant. There is no need to destroy it. The woman just came to take samples. She poses no threat to you. The isotope crisis will pass. Your secret is not at risk."

"I have spoken. All evidence must be destroyed, now!"

CHAPTER 30

McLaren was anxious to have an update on the progress from the newest member of his team. "Maya, do you have an update on the autopsy results?"

"Negative. There's not a great deal of hard data from autopsies because they weren't always performed following the use of an isotope."

"Is there anything to go on?"

"Well, in many cases, when an autopsy was performed, organ failure was identified as the cause of death. In those cases, the reports provide the symptoms prior to death and these include nausea, vomiting, retrosternal and abdominal pain, constipation, and pain in the limbs. In some cases, the hair came out in clumps. Reports also show effects on the central nervous system, cardiovascular and respiratory systems, depression, hallucination, lethargy, delirium, convulsions, and coma."

"Was there any commonality?"

"In all autopsies performed after use of the isotope, a toxin in the blood and tissue was present."

"And the toxin was?"

"Thallium, not just residual radioactive Thallium 201 as might be expected, but significant amounts of naturally occurring Thallium. Post-mortem examinations generally revealed damage to various organs. Haemorrhage in the mucosa of the intestine, lungs and heart, kidney damage, fatty infiltration of the liver and heart, degeneration of neurons, including ganglion cells and axons, with disintegration of myelin sheaths were common."

"Interesting," McLaren said cogitating on the matter. "Thallium is widely used in industry. It's extremely toxic and must be handled with the greatest of care. It has 25 isotopes, but the medical radioisotope needed for the patients was Thallium-201. If the specific activity of the product were too low, that might account for the deaths — straight up Thallium poisoning. The instant we have the results from the samples from the Konopiště facility, we'll have a better idea of what has been happening. Did you happen to hear anything from Danny?"

CHAPTER 31

Maya sat staring at the photos spread out in front of her. She thought back to the old days with Christopher, how they had played together as children and how he'd become a brilliant student at university, achieving a grade-point average that set him apart from other students.

What was he seeking? What had he discovered? What is the significance of the Roman mosaic, the ancient frieze, the temple and the Tablet?

Hoping that her aunt might have further information for her, Maya reached for her cell phone to call Switzerland. After what seemed like an eternity her aunt picked up.

"Maya, I was about to call you. I believe I've identified the temple in the etchings. The clue was in the distinctive design on the volutes at the top of the temple columns. Here is the conundrum: given the wealth of Macedonians and the abundance of materials available to built temples, why is there a striking lack of monumental temples in Macedonia?"

"I have no idea, Tante Hélène."

"Scholars have believed that the paucity of archaeological work in Northern Greece and Macedonia in the 20th century was to blame. However, the tempo of archaeological exploration has augmented in the recent times, so it seems logical that the lower than expected number of temples in Macedonia may be because in that area there were very few examples monumental religious architecture of the type common elsewhere in the Hellenistic world."

"Why would that be?"

"Priorities would be my guess. The relatively minimal investment in temple buildings contrasts with the enormous outlay on tombs. The great quantity and expensive nature of the goods placed in tombs attests to a desire by the Macedonians to ready their dead for the afterlife. This expectancy of the afterlife provides an explanation for the inconceivable wealth of possessions placed in Macedonian tombs and the corresponding paucity of temples, because there is a strong similarity between Macedonian tombs and temple facades."

"So, what did you find about the temple pictured in the etching? It's not Macedonian then?"

"Oh, but it is. That temple is quite unique. I believe it is an Ionic temple, commissioned by Olympias, Alexander the Great's mother, sometime after his death. I was led to this conclusion based on the flower design on the volute. Let me explain."

Maya could hear her aunt take a deep breath. She recognized the sign that her aunt was about to give a mini lecture.

"As I mentioned previously, in the photo of the temple you can see a star-like flower occupying the center of each volute. The volute is the spiral ornament, found in the base of the capital. The capital, which comes from the Latin *caput,* or 'head', is the top part of a column. The capital provides structural support between the column and the load thrusting down upon it, by broadening the area of the column's supporting surface."

"Yes, I can see that there is carving. It's like a snake, and on each side it terminates in a flower with two tendrils."

"Do you see the other marking resembling the Greek symbol phi carved in the center of each capital? Those particular design elements are rather distinctive and thus a signature point identifying this particular temple."

"I vaguely remember that Alexander's mother was not a Macedonian," Maya said.

"Yes, she was a foreigner, of Epirote religion. She had ties to the best known of Epirote sanctuaries, the oracle of Zeus at Dodana. Tradition called this the oldest of Greek Oracles. The original cult at Dodana honored a goddess, and the sacred myrtle flower was always central to the cult. Interestingly, Alexander's mother went by the name Myrtale until she changed her name to Olympias when she married Alexander's father, Philip Arrhidaeus.".

"When Olympias came to Macedonia she brought with her exotic habits including quasi-religious experiences, magic, and the use of snakes in rituals. The historian Plutarch said that Philip lost his erotic interest in Olympias because he saw a snake sleeping beside her."

"I can understand why that may have doused his fervor."

"Alexander always considered himself to be descended from deity. He claimed a god who had taken the form of a snake, had sexual relations with his mother, and that he was the product of this union."

"So, Alexander displayed signs of narcissism. Interesting."

"Without a doubt."

"Where is the location of the temple?"

"Good question. The exact location seems to have been lost over time, but I found a record of ruins of a temple bearing capitals and volutes with a unique flower design being found in southern Macedonia. I'll dig further."

CHAPTER 32

"Have you seen Danny?"

The question was posed by a tall, thin bespectacled technician who bore a strong resemblance to a computer geek. The young man was carrying a box over-flowing with computer read-out sheets under one arm and had a blue Puma soccer bag slung over the other shoulder.

McLaren turned to address the inquiry. He spotted the technician's embroidered name tag on the soccer bag.

"No, I haven't, but I suspect she'll be back soon. You're Lukas from her lab team, right? Can I help?"

"I've got the initial results from the sample Danny had couriered from the Macedonian facility. She wanted me to let her know these results right away." Lukas tried ineffectively to balance his load and not drop the pile of computer print-outs.

"Given her absence, you can discuss the results with me. What did you find?" McLaren asked. He wondered whether the lad would release the results to him or prefer to wait and give them to Danny.

The technician pulled off his thick glasses, looked directly at McLaren and announced, "The product is off. It contains contaminants. It is not pure Thallium-201. The sample also contained Thallium-205 and traces of Uranium-238."

"Any U-235?"

"I found none in the sample."

"Thank you. Impurity is the kind of finding I anticipated. We may be able to get a handle on this after all. Even a trace impurity level of non-radioactive Thallium-205 will lead to toxicity in the final product. Beyond that, Uranium-238 in the product would definitely lead to problems in toxicity."

"You'll let Danny know? I'd wait to discuss the results with her myself, but I have to head out now. I have a soccer match this evening," the technician said.

"Sure, no problem. Best of luck at the game."

"Anytime," the technician replied and headed out the doorway, oblivious to the fact that there would never be another time.

His luck ran out before the match.

****

The noise of the explosion was like a monstrous firecracker.

"What on earth was that?" Maya asked.

Sam and McLaren exchanged knowing glances. They were all too familiar with the deafening sound. They rushed to the front door. Maya dropped what she was doing and sprinted after them.

Pungent dark smoke billowed. Bright red-red orange flames flared up licking the wreckage of a Hyundi Santro. A meter-deep crater lay hollowed out of what had been the street. Windows everywhere were shattered. Metal and plastic were melted into the asphalt. Sidewalks were strewn with shards of glass and bits of twisted metal hung from the overhead power lines.

Maya made a dash to help a passerby who had been injured by the flying glass and was bleeding profusely.

McLaren ran back into the Institute, retrieved Maya's medical bag and grabbed a fire extinguisher. He delivered the bag to Maya and passed the extinguisher to Sam who had just completed a cell phone call to 112 to summon emergency crews.

McLaren dropped to his knees by Maya's side to help in her efforts. He did what she requested, placing pressure on the wound she was treating. Her patient, a heavy-set man, looked up at him in a white-eyed stare.

Several minutes later the piercing wail of sirens announced the arrival of police and emergency crews.

"Does anyone know where Danny is? She was on her way back," McLaren anxiously asked.

The police forensic experts, clad in white bunny contamination protection suits, began combing through the site. It had been a powerful car bomb. The force alone had launched the little Santros' windshield a block. Parts of the car had vaporized. Charred pieces of flesh were the only indication that there had been a driver.

The only clues left for police were a few pieces of flesh and a chunk of blue fabric on which was written Puma. The cloth appeared to have been part of a sports bag.

****

The sudden chirp from his cell phone diverted McLaren's attention from the forensic unit. He glanced down at the screen hoping to see Danny's name displayed.

Sam saw McLaren's jaw tense up. He recognized the signs that something was amiss. McLaren was knitting his brow in the way he did when he was dealing with his sister.

The voice McLaren heard at the end of his cell was muffled, but the message was clear, "If you want to see your sister again you will need to ensure that those lab results never get out to anyone or the same fate will befall her as the technician. Expect to be contacted about what you will be required to do next. No police involvement or you will never set eyes on your sister again. I'll be in touch."

The click he heard indicated that the caller had hung up.

McLaren looked stricken. The unsettling phrase echoed over and over again in his head. *Same fate will befall her.*

Sam looked at McLaren quizzically, "What's wrong?"

McLaren turned to face Sam, "The driver was Lukas. They killed him. They have Danny."

"No! We'll get her back," Sam seethed.

McLaren turned on his heel. He rushed past the debris and into the Institute lab. At this time of day, it was empty. He reached for the log to see who had entered the lab in the afternoon. He saw the time delivery of the sample was recorded. Other than Lukas who was working in the lab, only Maya and Sam had entered after the shipment arrived.

I wonder whether Lukas gave the results to anyone else besides me when he saw that Danny had not returned. He readily gave me the results but if he had greater concern for security he would have only released them to Danny. On the other hand, I am effectively the team leader, so he might have not been concerned about releasing it to me.

McLaren felt an increasing disquiet. He began to pace back and forth. He eyed the computer that Lukas had been using that afternoon and wondered.

Would Lukas have given the lab results to someone else? If so, who might that be?

Neglecting protocol, McLaren slid into the chair in front of Lukas's computer and tapped the computer keyboard. The dark screen suddenly lit up asking for a password. Drawing upon stealthy computer skills, he worked his magic to log into the technician's email account.

So, he crunched the data and then mailed out the results. Judging by the time, he emailed this out before he let me know that the product was off. I'm not the only one to whom Lukas gave the mass spec results.

CHAPTER 33

Aleksander Petkovski emerged from the room and clumsily inserted his cell phone in his breast pocket. The call had rocked him. His round face showed strain.

"Danielle, you admired the etchings in my office. By any chance would you like to visit the temple in the etching? It's not far from this facility. On the way, you can see some of the countryside. We'll pass through the village of Majden. It's a beautiful place, tucked away high in the Macedonian mountains. It is one of the most remote locations you will find in continental Europe."

"What a wonderful offer. Yes, by all means."

Even though her gut told her that his unexpected invitation was out of keeping with his demeanor, she was so enthralled with the idea of getting to see the temple that she threw caution to the wind.

Petkovski arranged for a driver and in short order they were in the countryside bumping along in an SUV up a steep serpentine road. His conversation was rapid-fire, hardly giving Danny a chance to ask questions. His manners had changed. He now appeared to be under a great deal of strain.

"The ancient temple that you will visit was commissioned by Alexander the Great's mother around the time of his death. It sits atop a mine said to have existed for over 5,000 years. The Ottomans who ruled this peninsula until the beginning of the 20th century, called the temple Majden, the Turkish word for mine."

Danny looked at Petkovski and smiled, "That's a very old mine."

"The mine has been closed for decades. Its western entrance lies beneath the temple. Under it is a network of corridors that extends about six kilometers. Each is paved with ancient cobblestones placed there by the Ottomans."

"Undoubtedly, we aren't the first to visit the temple," Danny laughed.

"Scientists from European universities have studied the mine since the beginning of the 20th century and they identified that it contains minerals that are found nowhere else on the planet, including the rarest of them all, Lorandite, a crystal containing Thallium. It is believed that Lorandite from this mine can register in a chemical and physical way the neutrino flux history from the Sun. In layman's terms, this Lorandite could help us understand the work of the sun."

Danny saw the stress lines on Petkovski's forehead begin to recede while he spoke about the mine.

"A few years ago, the eastern section of the mine was registered as a natural monument and made part of the Emerald Network of areas of special conservation interest created by the Council of Europe. The western section, where our isotope production facility lies, is a secure zone, off-limits to researchers exploring the mine. While their studies continue on the far side of the mine, our facility has been producing radioactive medical isotopes with the Thallium found in the mine. The proximity of a natural reactor to this ancient mine made this an obvious choice for locating our isotope facility."

"You don't have any problems with the area being a special conservation area?"

"No, Macedonians recognize that the production from my facility will help our economy and our bid to be part of the European Economic Community."

As they rounded a tight s-shaped corner Danny was awestruck when the ancient temple came into view. It was perched high. Shafts of sunbeams streamed through the openings between its slender columns, sparkling and glistening like a trail of diamonds trickling from the sky. An interplay of light and darkness danced on the centuries old carvings set above the columns creating a rhythm reminiscent of a sensual arabesque dance.

"History has it that after Alexander the Great's death, his mother, Olympias ordered this temple to be built far in the countryside on a hilltop considered sacred by the gods. The myrtle flower and the snake were symbolic. The flower was central to the Dodona cult to which she belonged. Look, you can still make out the floral design above the columns." He pointed up to the top of a column where a star-like flower with two tendrils that almost resembled snakes could just be seen.

"Wow!" Danny exclaimed. "It looks like time has caressed the temple."

Petkovski pointed to a narrow rock-strewn path that led up towards the temple. It was clear that they would have to climb through lose boulders on their ascent.

"We'll head up here in just a moment. I'll be right back."

Petkovski moved towards the driver's side to confer with his chauffeur. After a quick exchange, he went to the trunk of the car and removed a small backpack. Then he waved the vehicle off.

Danny glanced at her watch. *It's rather late in the afternoon to be sending the driver off.*

As if reading her mind, Petkovski said, "My driver will return for us after our excursion into times past."

Petkovski led the way up to the temple platform. The steep path made walking difficult. Pebbles underfoot rolled like marbles creating a tiny avalanche that give way and hindered traction.

Before they had even reached the temple, Petkovski's breathing was laborious. Perspiration dripped from his brow. On reaching the portico, he stopped, pulled several deep breaths and exhaled. He leaned against a column and gazed eastwards in an exalted ecstasy, like there was magic hovering on the horizon. He turned to Danny and nodded.

It was worth the climb. The view was impressive. The Kozuf and Kozak mountain range of southern Macedonia spread out below.

Petkovski led the way around the temple portico. On the far side, at the rear of the temple he paused. It looked like he was admiring the torus, the base of a column, except that there was nothing particularly special to be seen. His thick lips parted in a smile, "Now for a special treat. I have something precious to show you."

He turned his back to her to shield his actions.

CHAPTER 34

McLaren paced back and forth staring out the window at the yellow police tape cordoning off the bomb scene. Fire-ice burned in his cobalt blue eyes.

No police involvement or you will never set eyes on her. I'll be in touch. The words kept echoing in McLaren's ears.

"But why take Danny?" Maya asked.

McLaren didn't have an answer.

"What's salient here is that before the blast killed him, Lukas, Danny's lab technician, emailed the results of the sample taken at the plant to just one individual, Aleksander Petkovski. That plant was the last location where we had contact with Danny and now we can't reach her."

"We know she got there because she sent the sample back for processing. Aside from that she sent me a text with a photo of a temple," Maya said.

McLaren looked at her questioningly, "A temple?"

"Yes. Danny saw it in the CEO's office at the plant. She thought the print was similar to one in the etchings you photographed on the island," Maya replied.

McLaren and Sam exchanged glances.

"We've got to get up into the Kozuf mountains to the isotope production facility where we last had contact with Danny. Keep trying to reach her, Maya," McLaren said.

Sam tried in vain to reach Pescatori for helicopter transportation. McLaren pulled out all the stops, using all the resources available to him, and was finally able to arrange a lift. They were at a designated heliport in minutes.

The flight into the mountain range was quick and without incident. From the air, Sam and McLaren noted that the facility's security gate was up, and the guardhouse appeared empty.

The chopper pilot was anxious to get back; the flight was a favor and he was still under a time clock for his regular flight deliveries. He touched down at the isotope facility and the two men got out. He immediately lifted the whirlybird off and got underway back to Athens. Another pilot would return to pick them up when they requested.

Sam and McLaren were cautious entering the plant. A quick search at the front entrance revealed that the offices were all vacant.

"Keep a sharp lookout. Something is obviously amiss," McLaren warned.

The men walked through the empty control room where a schematic of the plant was affixed to the wall. Following it like a map, they proceeded further into the plant to the shipping and warehousing area where the din of the fans and diesel generators droned eerily in the hollow concrete space. A vast number of big, bulky, permanent shipping containers lay spread out across the warehouse floor, each one separated from the other in a specific pattern. They were bolted and locked to the floor.

"They are controlling criticality," McLaren announced. "This layout isn't what I usually see in a production facility of this nature. With shipping isotopes to hospitals, one would find smaller cardboard containers with lead pots inside. Given that the that lab results of the sample taken here showed the presence of Uranium, and given the size of these shipping containers, I would hazard a guess that this plant is not just producing Thallium-201 for medical use."

"You can surmise that from a sample and shipping containers?" Sam asked. He was impressed.

"Call it more than intuition. There are a number of indications that lead me to surmise this. This site is unique in that it has a naturally occurring reactor. The plant schematic shows a reprocessing area and there's ample evidence that this facility has been reprocessing when there is literally no need for them to have been reprocessing. There is also the fact that with Thallium-201 one would not expect such a quantity of large containers. There's no requirement for a large amount of shielding like you see with large containers. Beyond that, there's no need to have these large containers separated and arranged. It's an arrangement to control criticality."

"So, it's more than a hunch."

"The sample results from this facility showed that they were tainted with Uranium. The fact that no Uranium-235 was detected in the medical isotope is a signal. Natural Uranium found in the Earth's crust is a mixture largely of two isotopes: Uranium-238, and in far smaller quantities Uranium-235. U-235 is important because it is the only isotope existing in nature which is to any appreciable extent fissile. The fact that there was no U-235 detected in the sample indicates to me that the contaminant likely came from depleted Uranium left over after the fissionable U-235 had been removed in an enriching operation in this plant.

"Not good news."

"No, it's not. We both know, highly enriched Uranium is atomic bomb grade material. I strongly suspect that is what they've producing here. Depleted Uranium is the by-product produced during the process of forming enriched Uranium from natural Uranium and it is primarily composed of the isotope Uranium-238. U-238 was what was identified in the sample. The Thallium run must have been contaminated when they switched over."

"The background check on the Macedonian showed that his Russian friend was a financial backer of this isotope facility. Perhaps the Russian lent money to the Macedonian for the isotope facility and then wanted a bit more in return, like enriched Uranium," Sam suggested.

"Aleksander Petkovski is a very proud man. He's intent on making his country the shining star in production of medical isotopes. I can't see that he'd ever want his name associated with weapons of mass destruction," McLaren said.

Sam, who was still giving the matter some thought, replied, "It's not a good sign that this place is vacant. It shows they're finished with it. If that's the case, they'll want to completely destroy the evidence before they are found out. It's my hunch that they would use a bomb."

McLaren trusted Sam's instinct. His friend's experience gave him a leg up in these situations, "That's not a pleasant scenario. It might be effective, but the idea is crazy. An explosion would not only destroy the plant but would place dangerous levels of radiation in the area for years to come."

"For my money, if I were to use explosive devices to get rid of the evidence, I'd put the detonator close to the entrance to the facility and I'd place bombs at the entrance to the waste facility to seal it off. My best guess is the detonator's up in one of the front offices," Sam said darting out the door in a sprint.

McLaren quickly caught stride with Sam, "What exactly are you looking for?"

They dashed through the facility back towards the front offices.

"We may have given the front offices a cursory check when we arrived, but I think we missed something," Sam said.

Sam halted abruptly just outside the doorway of Aleksander Petkovski's modern, tastefully furnished office. He motioned McLaren to stop and listen. Closing his eyes and standing very still, Sam attempted to identify each sound and locate the potential ticking sound of a detonating device. When he did not hear it, Sam gave McLaren a signal to enter the room and conduct a sweep.

"Be alert for an action switch or command-activated devices. Look for trip wires, or pressure switches. If we find something, be wary because a secondary device may be present. Usually the secondary device is only a short distance from the primary," Sam warned.

Sam mentally divided the room into three horizontal sections and then moved his head and eyes from left to right, back and forth. He used the traditional sweep pattern. His first sweep was horizontal and covered floor to waist level, the area where IEDs are most commonly placed. On his sweep of the second horizontal layer, from waist to head, he hit pay dirt.

"Hidden in plain sight!" Sam announced.

He was looking at a long expanse of north facing windows covered with a thin metallic film on the interior surface. It looked a solar covering, but Sam dismissed this notion immediately because a similar covering of film was not apparent on the other glass panels, where one would expect to find the sun load much more oppressing. Sam recognized a very innovative way of detonating explosives.

"Clever! They're using a device to optically detonate insensitive high explosives," Sam said, pointing to the windows. "It's an explosive device formed by containing high explosive material in a transparent window. It's a technique that was developed in the seventies. Do you see that thin metallic film on the interior side? The film helps maintain the contact with the high explosive. It's designed for instantaneous detonation by a laser directed at the window. The laser pulse will vaporize the metallic film and create a shock wave that will detonate the high explosive and potentially other concurrently or sequentially individual explosive devices. My guess is that the laser pulse would be switched remotely and activated by a cell phone," Sam said.

"Okay mastermind. Now if ever is the time for you to put your years of military training into practice. We'll need you to work some magic here, so we can get on and search for Danny."

"I've got this. You'd better hurry. All I need to do is get the metallic film out from between the panes and dislodge the explosive material. Smashing the window and letting the explosive material drop to the floor will get it out of the specific target area. The mixture ought to contain insensitive high explosives. There's no way to tell how much time we have before detonation, so go. Find Danny. I'll deal with this," Sam ordered without a breath of indecision.

CHAPTER 35

It was a crapshoot. Sam had no idea when the laser pulse would be transmitted towards the window to induce detonation.

Bombs, bombs! I thought that I was going into civilian life to be a photographer, and artist, but no, I'm still dealing with bombs.

Sam's long fingers tugged at the transparent film trying to clear the window expanse of explosives. The task was proving more challenging than he had envisaged. It was almost impossible to dislodge the metallic film from inside the heavy window panes. He doggedly persevered until all of the film was removed. When he was finally able to see through the naked window, the scene beyond gave him an eerie sensation of déjà-vu.

An otherwise blue sky was almost obliterated by strange colored cloud formations in translucent rainbow hues rising up from billowing white clouds. The opalescent cloudscape resembled mystic lights. The sky was an abstract painting of pink and mauve at the pinnacle transcending through a white band into blue violet at the base.

The last time I saw an opalescent skyscape like that was on a hike on Mount Lushan in China. This sure looks like the sky I saw when the big quake unleashed its forces and put a spectacular end to our hike.

****

Further into the plant McLaren was desperately searching for a clue to Danny's whereabouts. It wasn't until he reached the Security office that his luck changed. Here he found a plastic tray containing his sister's personal belongings, including her cell phone. Quickly bypassing the security settings on his sister's phone, he checked for sent messages and incoming calls in the hope of identifying where she might be. In her last text Danny had sent photos of the etchings to Maya. He called Maya to ask if she had had any contact with Danny since then.

Maya replied in the negative.

McLaren's expression turned to one of deepening concern, "It just doesn't make sense."

"Maybe it does. My aunt reported that she has located the temple and it's in southern Macedonia."

McLaren raised an eyebrow, "That might explain why she's not here."

It still doesn't explain why the facility has been abandoned and why her phone is here.

"Tell me more about what your aunt said," McLaren urged.

A low rumbling roar broke the hollow quiet. McLaren instantly became aware of a vibration under his feet. At first the noise was like the rush and roar of stampeding cattle, then it morphed into an eerie, guttural rumbling noise that seemed to tear the modern building from its footings.

The terrazzo floor listed like the deck of a ship on a restless sea. McLaren fought to retain his balance. He dared not hazard a guess about the source of the ominous sound. It left him with an uneasy feeling.

That couldn't have been a bomb detonating. Sam has too much skill for that to happen.

The tremors hit in two distinct shocks, each lasting nearly a minute, with thirty seconds in between. The ground shook, windows rattled, and ceiling lights danced and chattered until they went out.

McLaren's phone call to Maya was lost in the mayhem.

Without a thought of trying to reconnect the call, McLaren hastily turned on his heel and dashed back towards Sam. He rounded the corner on the last corridor, opened his mouth to shout, but held back when he caught a glimpse of the scene up ahead.

****

The moment McLaren entered the room he zeroed in on the danger.

Sam had his back to the door and was bending over shattered glass on the floor. The ambient noise of the rumblings left him oblivious to the new danger.

A black garbed figure had stealthily entered the front office. In the bright light streaming through the now glassless window frames, there was little doubt about his murderous intentions. He raised his arms above his head to bring a heavy tool down on Sam's head.

Without a nanosecond to spare, McLaren hurled himself through the air at the assassin. The force of his impact knocked the man to the floor and forced the weapon out of his hands.

Alarm registered on the man's swarthy face. A vicious spattering of insults hissed from his mouth. In a lightning fast ninja move, he jumped to his feet and lunged with a vicious chop.

McLaren twisted in a corkscrew motion to deftly skirt the blow. It narrowly missed his head. He returned with a forceful strike that wickedly pitched the intruder off balance. The momentum propelled the assassin into the doorframe where he smacked his head with an audible crack.

He glared back at McLaren with murderous rage in his eyes.

As McLaren looked into his ghoulish black eyes he felt a sudden, soul-shattering chill. The features of something almost inhuman stared back at him. Was it a man? There were ornate tattoos on his head and part of his face – teeth on his cheek, an eyeball in the middle of his forehead. But even more dramatically, the whites of his eyes had been tattooed jet black, ample evidence that he had long ago decided that his life's mission was intimidation.

For a brief second, it seemed that the hatchet man would retaliate, but he unexpectedly bolted away, sprinting in the direction of the shipping area.

"If you're done here Sam, we have pressing matters. There's a good chance he knows where Danny is."

****

The assassin was lithe and fast. He seemed to know his way through the plant. He anticipated corners and easily slipped around obstructions, often knocking down everything around to impede the progress of his pursuers.

McLaren dashed through the obstacle course in hot pursuit, leaping over strewn equipment and barrels. For a brief moment, in the shipping area, he thought he'd been given the slip. He strained his ears. Breaking the quiet he heard a vehicle engine start up. He hadn't lost the scent. He raced off in the direction of the sound.

At the far end of the shipping lot he caught a glimpse of a white van peeling out. Luck was still with him. He looked around the maintenance area for transportation and spied two motorcycles used for security patrols. Keys and helmets were on wall hooks beside the bikes, at the ready for employees. The agile bikes were just what was needed to give chase.

Sam arrived to see McLaren mount one of the bikes, shift into gear and take off in the direction of a dust trail. In a heartbeat, he was on the other machine.

It was like old times. The rev of the engine was like music in McLaren's ears. Gripping the handlebars, he raced along the winding gravel road which climbed and curled like a rolled-out ribbon. Expertly, he negotiated the snaking corners with their tricky decreasing radius turns and negative camber. Adrenaline rushed through his veins.

For Sam, who was pulling up the rear, it felt for all the world like riding a motocross track. With accustomed skill, he made a point of coming down from speed before a turn, leaning in, and rolling on the gas after the apex, while keeping his eyes on the exit.

The van driver drove like a demon possessed, mashing the accelerator to the floor and pushing the van perilously to limits through the hilly terrain. He may have had the lead, but he was losing it. The bikes were definitely more agile on the tight curves. The van driver made a few mistakes in the corners, like braking too early or fast, or waiting too late to brake, and those errors lost him time.

As the road twisted and turned, climbing and dropping like a rollercoaster, the tremors increased. Under the seismic activity and intense dust, the ride became even more challenging. Every corner had ruts; downhill sections were off camber. The earth's forces thrust the bikers into narrow dry washes or onto sloping soft gravel banks, where the bikers narrowly dodged drop-offs and boulders. The swirling cloud of dust kicked up by the van made seeing the vehicle's red tail lights impossible.

Then it happened. A sudden thundering noise bombarded like a cannon firing at the enemy. The road pitched and heaved tumultuously. Confined in a deep rock cut that hugged the serpentine road, the bikers struggled to maintain their course. When the duo emerged from a tight blind corner in the rock cut, they came upon a huge hole yawning in the open road ahead. The van's tail lights were no longer visible, nor was the van. The gravel roadway had opened up like a trapdoor and swallowed the van.

Split-second reactions and agility saved Sam and McLaren from experiencing the same fate. Teeth clenched and hands squeezing the knurled handlebars in the firmest grip imaginable, each of the riders desperately jammed on their brakes. Tires smoking, hearts pounding, they dismounted and sprinted to the edge of the crevasse.

The tectonic plate movement during the powerful tremblor had moved the lithospheric slab plates. The gargantuan release of energy which ensued had ruptured the earth and opened a huge gaping crack. The van had been in the wrong place at the wrong time. It dropped at least one hundred feet into the chasm.

"What a fissure. My God, he didn't have a chance," McLaren gasped.

"Quite convenient for us," Sam replied. "No need to dig a grave for him."

McLaren's jaw tightened. He flashed Sam a silencing stare, "There's also no chance to question him about Danny!"

CHAPTER 36

Curious to see what was happening Danny stole a glance while Petkovski reached his pudgy hand down into a barely perceptible groove in the stonework of the temple. She heard an audible creaking noise. To her amazement a large slab of stone moved aside to reveal a narrow crumbling stairway descending from the temple platform.

"This way!" Petkovski encouraged.

Danny followed the Macedonian down the weathered stone steps. At the base of the stairway a heavy iron gate, with massive hinges, blocked their passage. The gate was similar to a defensive yett used in medieval castles.

Petkovski leaned heavily to push the yett open. Reeling in protest, the iron hinges groaned like a wounded animal. The blinding sunlight which bathed the temple at the top of the stairway, cast dark shadows below on the cobblestones in the stairwell. It was impossible to see what lay beyond the gate.

"Follow me. It's a bit of a walk. I'll take the lead."

Petkovski took down an old-fashioned torch hanging from the roughhewn stone wall and struck a match. The flame provided little relief from the darkness of the corridor.

Oh boy.... I really hope that I'm not making a mistake.

Danny glanced awkwardly back at the entrance. She turned her eyes forward to look down the serpentine, vault-ribbed passage. She squinted to see up ahead but the only time she could make anything out was when occasional streaks of torch light bounced off polished sections of the rock. *It was like* heading into black nothingness. Each step forward down the dark narrow passageway resonated a reverberating, funereal *sound.*

Without warning an alarming sound ploughed its way through Danny's body. The low, guttural, rumbling sounded like an angry fist pounding on the

197

wall. The clamor activated a neurological circuit from her ear to her spinal neurons. She jumped before her mind had time to process.

"Seismic activity," Aleksander Petkovski said calmly. He glanced around to look at Danny.

"A bit unnerving," Danny replied. The hair at the nape of her neck began to prickle. Dim lighting amplified the sense of dread she felt.

"This region is well known to be seismically active," his tone was congenial, meant to convey that rumblings of this sort were an everyday occurrence in this part of the country.

Leading their cortège, Petkovski lumbered on another few minutes until he stopped abruptly in front of heavy wooden door.

Danny could see nothing. She was following so closely that she stumbled into his back.

"Sorry."

In the uncomfortable silence she was suddenly aware of the jangling noise of keys. It was followed by a quick sharp scratch, then a soft hissing noise. She smelt sulphur and caught the spurt of a quick blue light.

He must be lighting another torch.

Another ominous rumble of thunder rippled through the air. The ground resonated like kettle drums. Danny shivered. She wished she could reconsider her decision to follow.

In the flickering light Petkovski withdrew a key from his backpack, unlocked the padlock and crossed the threshold. He motioned Danny to follow.

She froze, deterred by the tremble she felt beneath her feet.

"That noise is nothing for you to worry about. Think of it like subterranean demons fighting it out."

Danny smiled. She steeled herself and placed one foot before the other to cross the doorsill. She could hear her heart pounding in her ears. Gradually her eyes adjusted to the soft, low light level. She looked around. Although she could not say what she had imagined she would see in the subterranean room, it most certainly was nothing close to the scene in front of her.

The whitewashed room was almost a perfect dome cut away from the stone. Two marble sculpted caryatid pillars in the form of draped female statues stood on either side of the immense doorway through which she had entered. On the opposite wall were remnants of a frieze that had at one time stretched around the circumference of the room. Everywhere there was a glint of gold. The room literally seemed to sparkle and dance in the soft hue of the torchlight that bathed golden wreaths and statues, and silver and bronze vessels.

"What is this place?"

The Macedonian seemed too preoccupied to reply.

"All these golden pieces, golden daggers, pendants, and necklaces! Is this the tomb of a member of a royal family?"

"We are in a room that contains relics dating back to the time of my forefather, Alexander the Great."

Petkovski walked up a few steps onto a dais that held a huge altar decorated in dazzling gold. The bottom support panel of the altar, the predella, featured an intricate mosaic. It was one of the most impressive pieces in the room.

"This starburst" he said, pointing to the gold inlaid design on the altar, "is the emblem of the Macedonian royal family. The golden diadem, cuirass, iron helmet, and ceremonial shield once belonged to Alexander the Great."

Danny's cobalt colored eyes sparkled, and a shiver scurried down her back. She stifled a half-gasp.

It wasn't the golden starburst that caused her reaction; it was the predella. There, on the panel beneath the altar was an intricate mosaic. There was no denying that the artwork was exactly like the one in Christopher's photo.

The Macedonian bent down to kneel at the base of the altar. It was not out of reverence that he did so. He glanced around furtively to see where Danny's attention rested. Satisfied, he ran his right hand along the fret border of the mosaic. The pudgy fingers of his left hand fidgeted with the gold pendant that hung from chain around his neck. The unusual phi symbol emblazoned on the rectangular shaped pendant caught the light and shimmered.

Danny wasn't watching him. Her focus was elsewhere. She couldn't take her eyes from the mosaic depicting a headshot of Alexander the Great riding Bucephalus in battle.

"Listen. Do you hear something?"

Intrigued, she moved in closer to him, so close that she could smell the woody fragrance of his classic cologne. She listened and detected the trickle of water.

"One of the most profound artifacts from antiquity to have come down to mankind was placed in this room. The relic is considered the cryptic epitome of the alchemical opus, a formula that has been the inspiration of over 1,700 years of alchemy–"

A deep roaring sound like the clamor of a freight train charging through a concrete tunnel obliterated the sound of his words. The thunderous rumble from the depths of the earth grew more raucous, resonating throughout the room. The cobblestone floor began to vibrate intensely, shaking like a ship on rough seas.

The sound intensified. Danny felt more and more seasick. She clamped her eyes shut to banish the nausea. She felt powerless, swaying from side to side, in a futile effort to maintain her balance. After what seemed like an eternity the sturm und drang faded into a barely audible low frequency acoustic signature that dissipated leaving a hollow, heavy foreboding silence.

Danny opened her eyes. She looked up from where she lay on the floor and saw Petkovski. Cold fear spiraled through her. She knew that before deception comes out of the lips it is detected in the eyes. In the Macedonian's eyes she saw raging storm. Gone was the engaging silver fox. In his place was a demonic tormented soul whose freedom could only come if he destroyed her.

"Aleksander, what are you doing?" Danny shouted, trying to snap him out of his trance.

Oh my god! What's happening? He's holding that dagger like he's going to run me through.

Danny's imagination could conjure no set of circumstances that would explain why Aleksander Petkovski would suddenly want to attack her. She tried to find words that might calm him down. When that failed, Danny took quick action. She rolled onto her stomach, pushed herself onto her knees and lithely sprang to her feet.

Her abrupt move set him off. He charged at her fully intent on striking her with the hilt of the dagger.

"Get the hell away from me!" she screamed.

In the churning cauldron of darkness instinct took command. Danny swiftly jerked backwards to avoid the full impact of the blow. She lost her footing.

Fear rerouted her energy to survival, sharpening her eyesight and muscle response. She exhaled with difficulty. Her vision cleared somewhat. She struggled to her feet. Clenching her teeth in defiance, she drew back her knee and slammed it mercilessly into his groin.

Petkovski's face twisted in pain as his neck whiplashed back. Groaning, he stumbled backward.

Danny heard him curse.

Swiftly capitalizing on his misbalance, and ignoring the danger the dagger presented, Danny put her energy into her legs and charged full blast at him.

Her attempt to bulldoze him met with failure. He was too heavy for her to knock over.

With pupils so wide they obliterated the insipid gray of his iris, Petkovski glared at Danny in a grotesque grin, growling. He walked slowly towards her with a murderous look in his eyes, his intent clear.

Danny stood firm until the last possible second. Before he connected she sidestepped him. The moment he passed, she reached up, grabbed at the gold chain around his neck and pulled for all she was worth. Her maneuver met with a modicum of success. Her stranglehold forced the Macedonian to release the dagger. She frantically kicked it away into the dark.

Blind rage swept over the Macedonian like fire, in response to his searing pain. He bunched his shoulders and spun around quickly. Using his superior height and strength, he charged at Danny like a wounded bull.

The force of the blow rammed her backwards into the wall where her skull hit the stone with an ominous thunk. A starburst exploded and a myriad of colors flashed in her eyes. Her head twisted awkwardly to one side and blood trickled from the corner of her mouth. Limp like a wilted flower, Danny crumpled to the ground.

CHAPTER 37

Maya looked down at the caller ID. The call originated in Switzerland. It was Tante Hélène.

"Are you by any chance going to tell me that you have identified the location of the temple?" Maya asked.

"Yes. I have a more precise location for the temple ruins bearing capitals and volutes with a unique flower design. It is in the Kozuf and Kozak mountain range, quite near the village of Majdan, not far from Konopište."

"Did you say near Konopište?" Maya asked.

"Yes. This village is famous because it is close to the location of a mine which dates back to antiquity. It is said that the mine contains minerals that are found nowhere else on the planet. Fanciful rumors abound about the area. For example, just beside the mine is said to be a small hill where neither man nor livestock can set foot without being knocked down by a mysterious force capable of knocking down even a large cow. Word is that this hill contains Thallium, one of the most potent of poisons."

"Thallium? Tante Hélène you are a gem. Thank you so much for this information. I have to make a call. I'll be in touch later," Maya repeated.

The news made Maya spring in to action. She tried to contact McLaren, but her call did not go through.

Her next thought was Pescatori. Once Maya was finally able to reach him, it did not take much persuasion to convince the pilot to help her.

Pescatori suggested that they meet at a heliport in the heart of the Athens Riviera, at a hotel perched on a private peninsula overlooking the crystalline waters of the Sardonic Gulf. From there he would to fly her to the Kozuf Range to an ancient temple where her gut instinct told her she would find Danny.

True to his word, Maya found Pescatori waiting for her in the opulent hotel lobby. He walked with her over to the heliport.

"I've already filed our flight plan. I'll warm her up and we'll be off in no time. I'll swing out over the gulf towards the island of Aegina and then head north" he said smiling, his ivory colored teeth just visible through his salt and pepper moustache.

In a matter of minutes, the revs crept up. Pescatori applied the rotor load and the runners lifted off the tarmac. The Hummingbird leapt skyward to an altitude of more than three thousand feet.

Seated comfortably at the controls, Pescatori spoke affectionately about his passion, "She's nicknamed the Hummingbird. She's a single-engine bird built by Eurocopter, has a cruising speed of 138 mph and is built of composite materials. Her fenestron tail rotor makes her a particularly quiet helicopter."

"Come again?" Maya inquired, hoping that with more explanation she'd discover what he meant.

"Her fantail is essentially a ducted fan. The housing is integral with the tail skin and like the conventional rotor it replaced, it's intended to counteract the torque of the main rotor. She's ideal for light transport. Her useful load is just under 1600 pounds."

"How did you come to own the Hummingbird?" Maya asked.

Her question was a neat little segue that provided Maya with more background about Sam's effervescent friend. An American whose family roots were in Greece, he had decided to return to the Peloponnese after a stellar career in the US military. Pescatori had won the helicopter in a card game. He decided to use it to supplement his retirement income by shuttling well healed tourists. Since starting the flight-seeing charter business with one helicopter and filling the role of both pilot and maintenance engineer he had expanded his fleet to four whirlybirds.

"You won it in a card game? There must be more to that story," Maya said. "I know for a fact that you are ex-CIA. Sam let that slip when I was rescued from the island. I got the impression that you might still take the odd assignment."

"And you believe him?" he asked with a disarming smile.

Maya nodded.

He looked at her considering whether to provide any further information. He replied simply, "Well you could say that I occasionally keep my hand in."

"Oh, like for example doing some work with the female operative who McLaren met on the island," Maya asked.

"Whoa!" Pescatori gave her a questioning look. "What are you talking about?"

"I was in touch with Lazer in Ottawa about data for the isotope crisis and I asked if he would look into a few items on the periphery. He was able to uncover more about the woman who was on the island at the time I was being held there. His intelligence points to her being the companion of Petkovski at the state dinner McLaren's team attended on Lycabettus Hill. Lazer has been piecing things together and it looks like the woman is a CIA operative working undercover to delve into the affairs of a Russian who might well be involved in the sale of plutonium. For all intents and purposes, she appears to be the girlfriend of the Macedonian. You're on this, right?"

At first, she thought from his expression that he was displeased, but his look changed, and she was almost certain she detected a faint hint of a lopsided grin grow across his face.

"That is quite an interesting supposition, but somewhat farfetched, don't you think? Besides, it might place the young woman's life in jeopardy if information of that type got out. You've got quite the imagination."

"Your secret is safe with me," Maya said, looking at him in earnest.

Pescatori parted his lips to say something, but at that precise moment he was the recipient of an alert from the control tower.

"Ground Control warns that the Meteorological Station and Center for Seismic Activity has just issued a seismic alert. The Kozuf Range, where we're headed, is prone to seismic activity. Up here in the whirlybird you won't hear the sounds you'd hear on the ground during a quake. The rumbling sound doesn't come through when we're at altitude due to wave attenuation. Basically, we won't hear it and you won't feel it. The waves will lose intensity while they move through the air. We'll be safe up here until we land. I'll just need to watch where we put down. There may be aftershocks," Pescatori reported.

"Have you done this before, flown through while there was an earthquake?" Maya asked. She looked out at the landscape wondering how the aftershocks might affect them.

"Yes," he replied, his brows knit in concentration.

CHAPTER 38

Steep rocky sides embracing the roadbed foiled any attempt to circumvent the massive crevasse that yawned in the roadway ahead. The only way ahead was over.

McLaren leaned forward on the handle bars to get a better view of the terrain around the chasm that had unmercifully swallowed the van. Like a pro he pointed to the optimum take off point.

"Let's pray it doesn't lead to a dead end – no pun intended!"

McLaren rolled his eyes, "Thank you for your vote of confidence, Sam!"

"To Valhalla!" McLaren boomed out the ancient Norse battle cry while revving his engine. His eyes screamed defiance. He flung a raised arm forward beckoning Sam to follow him to the opposite side.

Sam had known McLaren long enough to realize that a major crevasse in the road would not hold his buddy back in searching for his sister. He also knew that it wasn't the jump that was the problem. There was no doubt that the dirt bikes they'd borrowed from the plant had sufficient power and agility to make the leap over the crevasse. The question was more about the landing. Did the duo still have the skills for such a long jump, after all these years away from dirt-biking?

The key was the approach. You didn't want to begin at an odd angle that might kick the rear out or send you off to the side. On a jump like this one acceleration had to be just right or you'd send the bike into an air-wheelie styled jump. On the other hand, if you backed off the throttle too much you'd send the bike into a nose dive which would be riskier than the air-wheelie.

Sam watched McLaren land the jump. "What if I said I wasn't up to it today?"

McLaren laughed. He and Sam had been through many adventures together since their high school days back in Lake Placid. Together they had come through scrapes, fights, and military engagements, and faced many a moment when disaster loomed and somehow, they had always pulled through.

"I'd tell you that you'll make the jump and you'll have fun doing it."

"Am I that predictable?"

Sam lined up for the jump. He assumed the attack position.

"Go for it!" McLaren shouted across the chasm to Sam.

Sam flashed a wide smile that showed his impossibly white teeth, revved the engine and launched off. Whatever he called out to McLaren on take-off was lost over the high-pitched whine. He remembered the trick – ramp up, front load, pull up the handlebar and keep the throttle steady at 85% so there was no loss of speed during launch.

McLaren watched Sam sail through the air like a circus performer. He knew that this wouldn't be the last time Sam followed him when the odds weren't good. He grinned when he saw Sam goose it just before landing and point the bike in a straight line to land like a pro that he was.

"Glad to see you haven't lost your skills!"

The exhilaration of landing the long jump quickly vanished. It was drowned out by a huge cannon-like noise much louder than thunder. The two men looked at each other.

"Let's get moving! That guy was hell-bent on heading this way. There's a chance that if we continue in this direction we may find Danny."

The two riders zipped along the tortuous narrow winding road, negotiating potholes and debris, never knowing what they'd find around the next corner. The roadway was so rough that the pair felt like their arms they were being wrenched from their sockets. Following a particularly bumpy uphill climb they pulled up to an astonishing view and stopped.

"Is that what I think it is?" McLaren said in disbelief. "It must have been spectacular!"

Ahead, perched way above on a rocky outcrop, stood the crumbling ruins of an ancient temple. It would have been a remarkable landmark in its time, offering an unrestricted view of the land below. Now many of the slender columns lay strewn about on the ground.

"Let's take a closer look," Sam turned off the engine.

McLaren nodded.

With the engine noise off an eerie quiet descended on the rolling landscape. Suddenly, breaking the silence, McLaren and Sam heard a wailing sound, like someone was calling for help.

McLaren looked left and right to determine the source, "I don't see anyone, but it might be coming from the base of the temple?"

From astride his bike, Sam cupped his left ear with his hand to try and differentiate the noise above the pulsating hum he continued to feel even after the whine of the engine had ceased.

They quickly dismounted and scrambled up the steep scrub covered slope towards the temple.

Although the ancient structure was just a hundred feet above them, the debris on the stony path's serpentine approach more than doubled the distance. Large chunks of marble and small irregular shaped pieces hindered their progress. Half way up they stopped, looked and listened.

"Help me!"

"Over there!" McLaren shouted pointing towards the portico.

✳✳✳✳✳✳✳✳

Aleksander Petkovski lay trapped under the heavy weight of a column. He was barely visible in the debris.

"What happened? Where's Danny?"

"She went to the village," he replied struggling for breath.

McLaren longed to ask more questions, but it was clear that Petkovski didn't have the strength.

"We've got to get this column off him. How heavy do you think it is?"

McLaren read Sam's thoughts, "Too heavy. Scout around. See if there's anything we can find to pry the column off him."

Their resourcefulness was truly put to the test. Sweat rolled down their faces; the two men tried relentlessly with a crudely improvised lever until at last they managed to relieve some of the weight the column was exerting. Getting the big man out from under the column was another challenge. Hope was beginning to fade when the pulsating beat of churning helicopter blades broke over head. A down rush of wind sent debris dancing.

Sam grinned. He knew that sound. He looked up and saw the unique fantail and bright red markings of a Eurocopter CE120.

The first person off the chopper was a petite, dark-haired woman. She crouched low to the ground to avoid the rotor wash from the Hummingbird, and headed up the stony path in the direction of McLaren and Sam.

"Maya! What are you doing here?" Surprise was evident in McLaren's voice.

"It's not a long story. After I spoke to you about the text message I received from Danny I grew more concerned. I really wanted to do more to help find her. When my aunt called with information about this temple, I put two and two together. I realized that the temple couldn't be far from the production facility. I couldn't get through to you, so I called Pescatori and asked him for a lift."

"Good thing you're here. Petkovski could use a doctor. He's down there."

"Where's Danny?" Maya asked. She looked in the direction McLaren was pointing.

"Not here apparently. Petkovski said she went to the village. He needs your help."

Maya moved quickly to get to the Macedonian.

"He's been complaining of nausea and abdominal pain" McLaren said.

Maya took his vitals, "We need to get him to a hospital quickly. Not only is he suffering from injuries from the column falling on him, he appears to be having a reaction to a poison. He shows signs of salivation. His nerves appear to be malfunctioning. He's starting to go into convulsions. There's little time to waste."

"Do you think you could use your helicopter to lift the column off him?" Sam asked Pescatori.

Pescatori, who had just made his way up the stony path to where the group was gathered, replied, "Yeah I've got some gear on board. I can give it a try."

"After we get the stretcher off the chopper, do you want me on board to help with the winch?" Sam asked.

"No need. With the set up I have I can operate the winch while flying. Just make sure you have your escape route because the weight of the column is going to push the chopper to her limits, even if she is called a little workhorse," Pescatori cautioned.

Pescatori got behind the controls of the Eurocopter and in no time lifted off. He circled about, came in low and hovered, creating a swirling cloud of dust. Once in position over the stone structure he activated a set of controls and lowered the cable for Sam and McLaren to attach to the column.

While the Hummingbird could carry a useful load of just under 1,600 pounds, lifting the column with the winch and cable proved challenging so close to the old temple. Somehow Pescatori managed to do it.

—

McLaren and Sam immediately rushed in with the stretcher. Painstakingly, they placed the injured Macedonian on it. They trudged down the stony slope to the roadway where Pescatori was in position for them to load the stretcher for transport to hospital.

Maya squeezed in beside the stretcher.

CHAPTER 39

Aleksander Petkovski lay ashen in the hospital bed. Minus his handsome gray wig, he seemed old and worn out.

The news the doctors had given was not promising. Along with the injuries he sustained when the column collapsed on him, he was suffering from a severe case of poisoning.

Maya hadn't left his side. While leaning over his bald head to swab his forehead, recognition began to dawn on her. She looked down at his bulbous nose and round eyes and wondered why it hadn't come to her sooner. Her heart faltered a beat. She felt the muscles in her chest tighten. The chilling memory came back to her and with it came a renewed sense of worry about Danny.

What has this lunatic done to Danny?

"Danny would have been excited to see the temple. She's so into archeology. I would have thought that she'd have wandered around the temple for hours. It seems out of character for her to just take a peak and leave," Maya manipulated the moment seeking out more information about the Macedonian's time with Danny.

"Danielle chose," he said and looked away.

Maya stared straight at him, her dark brown eyes penetrating his soul seeking further explanation.

Unexpectedly the Macedonian looked back at Maya and said, "You have your mother's eyes."

Maya drew a sharp breath, "Pardon, did you know my mother?" An icy shiver shot up her spine.

"Yes. I often saw her with your father," he replied. The dark circles and bags under his eyes made him look older than ever.

Maya tried hard to not to reveal her shock, "A man of your stature in the scientific community would have no doubt been present at some of the same conferences that my father attended."

Eager to know more, she surmised correctly that the best way to draw information from him was to play upon his ego. She baited the hook, aware that a narcist's need to express would lead him to confess. She would just use his narcissism against him.

Aleksander Petkovski gazed up at Maya. His pale eyes took on a luminous intensity. His ego stroked, he felt a pathological need to brag.

"For the last 1,000 years or more Macedonia has been under occupancy by those who robbed us of our lands and our culture. Alexander the Great ranks with the mythical heroes like Achilles and Odysseus, yet the greatness of my country and the legacy of Alexander the Great of Macedon have almost been lost, though the legacy of Alexander the Great lives on through me," he said.

Maya stared at him.

Although weak, he seemed anxious to tell his story, "Macedonia has only been a distinct state for some twenty plus years. Before that Yugoslavia and the countries that occupied Macedonia attempted to assimilate us. Do you think that Turks who occupied our lands would let us speak about our rights? Do you think that communistic Yugoslavia would leave any of their countries speak about their nationhood? The Serb-Croatian war arose because Croatia tried to speak."

Maya said nothing.

His voice was low and raspy. "Your father was a scourge who could have ruined my plans of raising Macedonia to be the leader in radioactive medical isotopes. He was a brilliant man and his research could have changed the medical isotope business, had I not stopped him. His nuclear expertise and capacity for innovation would have curtailed Macedonia's chances of becoming a leader in isotope production. He was so willing to share his findings and creativity with the nuclear world. Our edge would have been lost, but with his demise we could truly succeed."

Maya had trouble taking in what he was saying. It all seemed bizarre. His words, *had I not stopped him,* alarmed her. They made her wonder what role he had played in the horrific Nova Scotia plane crash which had killed her father and Christopher and everyone aboard the Swiss Air flight.

In a gravelly voice he continued, "As the isotope shortage burgeoned into a worldwide crisis, my expertise became needed more and more. Because Macedonia could supply much needed isotopes in the shortage, my country has gained international respect once again. In the nuclear industry, Macedonia's yellow sun of liberty is shining brilliantly."

Speechless and repulsed, Maya looked down at him in his hospital bed. Her mind flashed images of her father.

Petkovski's attitude was eerily serene, "It seemed impossible that your father could have survived that fateful plane crash, but apparently, he did. Nonetheless, he got my message and the tragedy of so many lives lost put the fear of god into him. After that crash, he went to ground and did not try to outshine me with fascinating ways to produce medical isotopes. With my rival out of the way, I took advantage of Macedonia's richness in resources. Ours is the only country with sizable resources in naturally occurring Thallium. From an old university friend, I obtained financial backing and began to implement my research in developing radioisotopes using Thallium."

Maya stood rigid, grappling with the startling admission the Macedonian had just made. She arrived at a disturbing conclusion. *This monster before me has admitted to having a role in taking the plane down. His actions killed my father and my cousin.*

Petkovski paused for a few seconds and took a deep breath, "My genius raised Macedonia to the forefront. Playing politics and getting the Americans to influence a long shutdown of the aging nuclear reactor in Canada was my added delight. Canada's old reactor had long outstretched its capacity. The isotope market was there for Macedonia's taking. I alone proved that our isotopes could address the need during this worldwide isotope shortage."

Maya worried that his verbosity was draining his remaining resources. She hoped he wouldn't expire before he divulged the details of his role in the deaths of her father, her uncle, and her cousin.

"Imagine my surprise when, out of nowhere, years after that fateful crash, your father re-emerged on the nuclear scene to help address the shortage using a cyclotron. This method would help supply isotopes, but it would never have the capacity to address overall need for medical isotopes. I was certain it would only be a matter of time before my arch enemy would resurrect and release his long-shelved work on producing radioisotopes without highly enriched Uranium. Thankfully, with some encouragement, he suffered a timely heart attack."

Maya sensed the blood course through her veins with fear and hatred. Horrified, she felt as though her feet might go out from under her.

He's completely unaware that dad had a twin brother. He killed both my dad and my uncle!

Before she had time to react to his story, a tall, olive skinned male nurse, who seemed barely out of his teens, entered the room and began to check the pumps and tubing attached to Petkovski. With syringe in hand he reached out to insert medication into a line.

"Wait! What are you inserting? There's no order for in-line meds for this patient," Maya said, her years of medical training kicking in. This was not a time to be adding meds.

"There must be some mistake madam. There is a written requisition for this patient to receive these meds."

"Let me check with the nursing station," Maya said, her tone hardened. She moved towards the doorway and walked down the hall to speak with the nurse in charge.

"There is no order for in-line meds," the nurse in charge confirmed after consulting a file.

When Maya returned to the room the nurse was gone and the Macedonian had lapsed into a coma.

CHAPTER 40

Sitting on a bench at the hospital heliport waiting for Pescatori to arrive, Maya tried to process what had happened. She found the notion that someone had deliberately killed the Macedonian almost impossible to believe. Facts were facts though and it was hardly likely that he would have succumbed to death when she left his hospital room.

The buzz of her cell phone broke her concentration. Her pulse quickened. She looked down at the caller ID with a sense of relief.

As usual Tante Hélène began her call mid way into the conversation, "Maya, I'm convinced that Danny's disability actually gives her an innate ability to take subtle cues and integrate features to find the unitary object."

Maya's experience with calls from her aunt had taught her to just listen and the call would eventually make sense.

"I searched and found an app that simulates how images appear through the eyes of a color-blind person. It's really been designed for web designers to determine how a website would appear to someone who is color-blind. Using the app, I took a look at Christopher's photo of the frieze to see what led Danny to believe it might be a map."

At the mention of Danny's name Maya withheld a gasp. She rubbed her forehead and tried to get her brain to focus on what her aunt was saying.

"Color-blindness is usually classed as a mild disability because those with it have a decreased ability to see or they perceive color in a different way. There are occasional circumstances where it can give an advantage. For instance, some studies conclude that color-blind people are better at discerning certain color camouflages." Professor Jullian said.

"Yes, I've read where during the war color-blind soldiers were an asset because they could see through the camouflage the enemy was using," Maya replied.

"I think that Danny was on to something. She saw through the ancient artwork and recognized that it camouflaged another purpose," Professor Jullian said.

Maya leaned forward on the bench and tucked a piece of hair behind her ear. Tante Hélène's words had caught her interest.

"The skill of hiding is aligned with to how human perception works. Human vision and perception work in two main phases: feature search and conjunction search. Allow me to explain. Feature search looks out for instantaneously recognizable characteristics like color, edge, and texture. On the other hand, conjunction search is a slower process where scattered clues from multiple features are integrated. Because your friend is color-blind, when she looked at the photos Christopher took of the frieze in the tomb she did not perceive some of the ordinarily identifiable entities and in consequence, she integrated in a different manner and thus may have seen a map."

Maya sensed Tante Hélène was getting close to something.

"I consulted an art history professor at the University of Bologna to find out more about camouflage painting. He told me that as an art form, historically, camouflage images have been mastered by only a few. The artist must strike a delicate balance between removing easily identifiable features while simultaneously leaving enough subtle cues for the objects to reveal themselves under a closer scrutiny."

Maya listened intently.

"There are profound examples of camouflage in art. For example, some say that Michelangelo embedded powerful and even dangerous messages in the frescoes of the Sistine Chapel, that he encoded these messages using his knowledge of mystic Jewish texts and that he intended some images to be insults to the pope. Another example is the Mona Lisa. History shows that Da Vinci used symbols. There are experts out there who contend that to the naked eye the symbols are not visible but with a magnifying glass they can clearly be seen."

"You definitely have my attention."

"I'm convinced that Christopher was on to something. The idea of a frieze being a camouflaged map is quite intriguing. I sought out the opinion of a very old friend who is now retired, Dr. Edward Pater. I piqued his curiosity."

Maya had heard her aunt mention Dr. Pater at other times. It made sense that she had contacted him. Influential academic work like the writings of Professor Jullian are increasingly done through collaboration, rather than sole authordom.

"You'll recall that I told you that much of what historians know of Apelles is drawn from the Roman historian, Pliny the Elder. Pliny wrote about Apelles and this artist's lost treatise on the art of painting. He praised Apelles for contributing a number of useful innovations to the art of painting. The recipe for several of these innovations, like his "black varnish", which served both to preserve his paintings and to soften their color, Apelles always kept secret. The secret of these techniques was lost when he died."

"Ah, so it's no mere coincidence that Christopher's flash drive contained several different photographs of the artworks of Alexander the Great in battle," Maya said, acknowledging what her aunt thought.

"I'm inclined to think that color-blind camouflage was another of Apelles' innovations. He was known to be a talented prankster, who did not get on with Alexander's general, Ptolemy Lagides. Pliny wrote that after Alexander's death Apelles secured employment in Alexandria in the court of Ptolemy I. Many of the anecdotes written about Apelles by ancient writers reveal a spirited, competitive, and at times impudent personality, who was always ready to spar with his critics. He was implicated in a conspiracy to overthrow Ptolemy but managed to clear himself and regain the King's favor. One ancient writer suggested that to achieve one-upmanship Apelles hid a map to the "treasure of treasures" within one of his paintings."

"Hidden in a painting, you say? But, weren't you theorizing that something might be hidden in the frieze?" Maya asked.

"Well yes. I am proposing this line of thought. Point number one — Prior to creating a frieze, an artist would usually do a full sketch. Because Apelles was so meticulous in his planning the stage, he might well have gone beyond sketching and created a painting before undertaking the frieze for the royal tombs. It would have been just like him to have amused himself by hiding clues right before the eyes of his audience. Point number two — There are very few examples of Greek wall art or panel paintings that have survived through the centuries, so there is not a lot of information about how they were crafted in Hellenistic times. Point number three — Historians have noted that Roman artwork was very often done by Greek artists and that these artists had a reputation for copying original Hellenistic paintings."

"I see where you're going. Apelles' original painting, which he used for the design of the frieze, must have somehow got to Pompeii," Maya said.

"Dr. Pater and I theorize that since the famous mosaic at Pompeii features Alexander at the battle of Issus, it was more than likely done by a Greek who based his artwork on the original painting done by Apelles. The artist who did the work on the mosaic at Pompeii would have replicated the subject matter of the long-lost painting, but as the color differences illustrate, this artist did not see the hidden clues that Apelles had set out years before for those who were gifted with color-blindness."

"Interesting theory."

"To put the theory to the litmus test Edward and I used the latest high-tech app for color blindness on the photos of the frieze. I am now more than ever convinced that Apelles meant to have his artwork camouflage a map," Dr. Jullian remarked.

"It is all beginning to fit together. When I met with the Brigadier, in Athens, the elderly man said that Christopher was certain he'd found a cipher. He said that Christopher had chosen the Tablet as the topic of his doctoral dissertation. He said it would mean more to Chris than if he'd located the remains of Alexander the Great, because identifying the location of his remains would have been terribly controversial," Maya said.

"Oh yes. That would have stirred up real controversy. It would have made it impossible for him to complete his doctorate in a reasonable timespan," her aunt replied.

"So, Danny's idea that the frieze is a map holds promise?" Maya asked.

"Why yes. Here is the reasoning. We used the color-blind app and we looked at how Apelles presented Alexander in battle. His breastplate depicts Medusa, the guardian, protectress. She was often portrayed as a gorgon with serpents wildly flowing where she once had golden locks. On his breastplate, she is an apotropaic symbol used to ward off evil. If you look there are strong diagonal lines across his shoulder. These make a trajectory that point to the handle of his knife, which is exactly where the line of vision of the eye on the head of his horse Bucephalus is directed. All the minor detailing on his cuirass points in the identical direction. They are all pointing to a tiny rectangle with something on it. With intense magnification a tiny rectangle with the Greek symbol phi, the symbol of the Golden Mean, can be seen on it."

Maya was accustomed to her aunt's dogged persistence.

"I am of the opinion that Christopher's background research led him to conclude that Apelles, who was well educated, chose to pinpoint the location of the Emerald Tablet using the Greek letter phi. It would have been his little joke. He knew that the famous Greek Philosopher, Plato, called the phi ratio the key to the physics of the cosmos," Dr. Jullian reported.

Maya had a mental picture of her aunt, open books piled high over her desk, ferreting out information, verifying Christopher's research and following up on tiny bits of seemingly inconsequential information to unravel the mystery.

"The Emerald Tablet is considered the oldest and most long-lived of alchemical documents and the most important work to have inspired alchemists. In thirteen pithy lines of enigmatic precepts of metaphorical and metaphysical symbology it provided insight into the fundamental structures of our physical, mental and metaphysical universe. Since the unity of all matter is a fundamental alchemical assumption, it seems appropriate for Apelles to have selected phi to identify the location of the Emerald Tablet.

"The Greek symbol phi, the twenty-first letter of the Greek alphabet looks somewhat like a zero bisected vertically by a line," Maya said.

"Yes, phi has long been used to represent the golden mean or golden ratio. This is the ratio used by visual artists for centuries as an aid to composition. Technically speaking, when two things are in the proportion of 1:1.618 (approximately 3/8 to 5/8), they are said to be in the golden mean. It is well recognized that dividing the parts of an image according to this proportion helps to create a pleasing, balanced composition," Professor Jullian said.

"Tante Hélène you certainly have been thorough!"

"Oh, there's more. Christopher's photos have evidence that he also saw a mosaic depicting Alexander at Issus. I think that my dear son followed that thread and when he unwound it, multiple strands of the story were revealed," Professor Jullian said. She proceeded to give Maya the highlights of her findings.

"That's a lot to take in. So, if the frieze is a map and phi pinpoints the location, where do you think the Tablet can be found?" Maya asked.

CHAPTER 41

Danny squinted in the darkness, rubbed her eyes, and desperately tried to think. Her head was throbbing to the point where she was having difficulty piecing together what had happened. It felt for all the world like trying to tune in a radio to a frequency so that there is no longer static.

Panicking isn't going to help you.

Whether it was her sense of fear acting as a stimulant and sharpening her memory, or her sense of touch when her outstretched hands felt the cold expanse of stone floor, something triggered her memory.

I'm lying on the stone floor in a room under the temple. The passageway to this room was so long that I must be in an area adjacent to the mine that he mentioned.

Danny had no idea how long she had been out. She wasn't in the habit of wearing a watch because she was never without her cell phone. She wished that she had it now.

Get a grip girl.

Danny sensed rather than knew she was alone; the Macedonian was gone. Something had triggered his irrational behavior. One moment he'd been the congenial host and the next his behavior was downright aggressive. In her wildest dreams, she had never anticipated he would behave that way.

Was it the thundering roar and the trembling floor that triggered his change?

Danny rose to her feet while massaging a lump on her head. She was not sure whether she had been struck by the Macedonian or by a falling rock. She felt moisture running along her face and reached up to touch her forehead. Her hand felt the sticky blood that dripped down the side of her face. She reached down to her shirt and tore off a strip to bind her wound.

Slowly, in the darkness, her pupils dilated so that she could see enough to make her way over to the door. She found it locked. A surging wave of panic

---

flowed over her. Desperately she ran her hands over the door trying in vain to find a latch or lever. She felt a bead of cold sweat trickle down her arm.

That's just adrenalin pumping. Breathe slowly. Signal the brain to slow the release of adrenalin. Don't let fear set in.

She had not checked in with her brother. By now he must be wondering about her whereabouts. She thought back to the game of mental telepathy that she and her brother used to play when they were children and happened to be apart. The idea was to think about the other person and try to transmit a message to them. She did her best to try a brain to brain communication with Marc.

She was annoyed with herself for getting into such a predicament. She had been taken in by the Macedonian's ruse.

If I hadn't been so excited to see the temple, I might have seen the potential danger.

Another tremor rolled through.

Adrenaline pumped through her body energizing her fear. A zap of instantaneous alarm set her brain on hyper alert. With her senses heightened, wound up to their maximum, she was suddenly aware of dust particles dancing in a beam of light. The narrow shaft of light was not enough for her to really see, but it did provide a bit of illumination. Her analytical mind went into gear.

When light beams interact with particles suspended in air, the energy can be scattered or absorbed.

She had air. Someone would figure out where she was. There was nothing to be gained by not preserving a positive attitude. A quote from Milton's Paradise Lost popped into her thoughts.

The mind is its own place, and in itself can make a heaven of Hell, a hell of Heaven.

****

The bike trip into the village of Konopište had been a bust. McLaren and Sam had not found Danny in the small village even after a search through the backstreets.

As the two riders bounced along the isolated stretch of road from the sparsely populated village back towards the temple, they were forced to make frequent detours to navigate around the debris. Chunks of rock and the occasional upturned tree littered the gravel roadway after the earthquake.

Up ahead, in the pastel sky a pair of golden eagles soared high above the ancient temple. It was now a silhouette against the last red-orange rays of sunlight. The temperature was beginning to drop. It would not be long before the sun fell on the horizon leaving the search party without daylight.

Going over a rise on a particularly bumpy section McLaren slowed to a stop.

"It just doesn't add up. We were so intent on getting the Macedonian out from under the column that we didn't ask enough questions. There's no reason Danny would have gone to the village. She didn't have a car. Her rental was still in the parking lot at the plant. How would she have gotten there? Dan wouldn't have set out on foot." McLaren asked.

"Highly unlikely."

The brevity with which Sam responded indicated his concern. He turned his focus towards to the pair of golden eagles soaring, their wings held in a slight, upturned V.

Up ahead the dirt road snaked through the low hills and up and over rises. Each section visible ended in a hairpin. At the furthermost switchback, where the eagles circled, like a mirage, a thin column of gray smoke rose from the grassland by to the road.

A tingling sixth sense gave Sam a renewed sense of hope. Pointing westward, he said, "Do you see that smoke?"

McLaren's eyes locked on the horizon. He thought he could distinguish a rhythm to the puffs of gray: three short puffs followed by three longer bursts of smoke, repeated by three short puffs. The intermittent puffs almost resembled a distress signal. It might just be a grass fire or air spewing from a vent hole in the earth, but it was worth investigating.

"Let's have a look."

McLaren took the lead heading cross-country along a faint game trail. Along the rock-strewn path, there were remnants of man-made stone formations, almost completely overgrown. He remained focused on the grassland where smoke seeped out. Soon he reached a pile of carbonate rocks where gray mist was being exhausting.

"Over here," he signaled to Sam.

McLaren dismounted and tramped over for closer look, waving for Sam to follow. He looked down at the volcanic-hydrothermal rock structure, bent his tall frame and knelt on the ground beside the vent hole. He cupped his hands over his mouth and called down between puffs of smoke.

A regular periodic emission of gray smoke continued but there was no re-ply.

Sam saw the moisture in his friend's eyes and couldn't tell if it was from the smoke or emotions. He did his best to remain positive.

"We found the Macedonian on the stairwell. Maybe he was on his way up from under the temple. Maybe there's a tunnel or chamber under the temple. Given the smoke signal maybe Danny or someone is under here," Sam offered.

"There's so much rock on that stairwell that it will take a long time to re-move enough to even get to the base of the stairway. It's time we don't have. We need to find a way to communicate with whoever is down there. Shouting down the hole doesn't seem to work. Got any bright ideas?"

Sam looked over at the little motor bikes. He remembered that two-way communication devices used by plant workers were clipped to the handle bars.

"How about those walkie-talkies? The plant workers must have used them on dedicated channels for on-site inspections. Cell phones would have been unreliable. We just need to find a way to lower one into the hole so that it reaches whoever is down there. We need a length of cord."

McLaren glanced around, "I think I see something we can use. Look at the electronic fence that borders the property. The top of the fence has a fine wire running the length of it. Maybe we can attach that wire to the walkie-talkies and lower one down the vent hole. We'll just need to cut the current so there's no risk of electrical shock when we borrow the filament."

McLaren sprinted back to the bikes, looked in the saddlebag and found pli-ers, wire-cutters and gloves. They were just the tools he needed. Always one to tackle jobs that involved working with his hands, he quickly short-circuited the electric fence and retrieved a long filament of wire suitable for his plan.

Sam checked that the batteries in the walkie-talkies were working. He care-fully attached the wire to one of the devices.

"Hold on to tightly to that walkie-talkie and the wire."

As Sam held on McLaren stretched out the length of wire and attached the second two-way radio to the far end of it. He laid the filament down on the earth with a rock over to keep it from unfurling. With his head down, he walked back towards Sam pacing off lengths and marking the wire in a number of spots.

"What are you doing?" Sam asked.

"I want to be able to know how far down the radio unit has descended. The markers will give us an indication. Don't let go."

McLaren climbed back up to where the smoke was emitting and crouched down beside the vent hole. He looked back at his friend who was holding the other end of the wire. "Okay, let's do this."

Methodically, foot by foot, McLaren began lowering the walkie-talkie into the vent. Suddenly there was a hitch. His hands felt the difference in tension. The wire began to curl back up. Time and again McLaren tried to lower the walkie-talkie, but the result was the same.

"Not good," muttered Sam.

****

Alone in the chamber far below, Danny tended to a small fire she had built on the altar under the ceiling vent. She debated about whether to keep the fire going or simply send out messages from time to time. She was all too aware that she did not have much left to fuel a fire.

That's odd. What's that sound? It almost sounds like metal scraping against rock.

She listened for a moment but heard nothing. Then she heard the faint sound again.

A dark object materialized from nowhere in the column of smoke above her small fire.

Good lord, I must be losing it.

She squinted at the ephemeral object suspended from nowhere. Its shape was now unmistakable. Amazed, she reached out over the fire to retrieve the walkie-talkie.

"Hello? Can you hear me?" Danny said into the speaker.

"Danny! Are you okay?"

The sound of her brother's voice was reassuring, "Physically yes, mentally no. I'm locked in. I want out of here. Please come down and get me."

"Why are you locked in? What happened?" McLaren asked hoping to get information to help get her out.

Danny sighed. She rapidly provided a condensed version of what had happened to her, ending with, "There was a huge rumble and Petkovski went nuts. That's the last I can remember. I was out cold. I awoke to find myself locked in this room, with a lump on my head."

McLaren murmured an expletive under his breath. He wondered what had possessed his sister to follow the Macedonian. He held his tongue. This was no time to express his views.

For a bright girl, my sister can make some dumb choices.

"What can I say? You went off with the wrong guy. We found the Macedonian injured on the stairwell. A stone column had fallen on him during the earthquake. He said you had gone to the village."

"So that's what that rumbling, and trembling was about. It was an earthquake."

"We need to get you out of there. Do you have any light down there?"

"There was an old torch on the wall, but it's gone out. A bit of light comes through down the vent holes. The ceiling is over 20 feet high. I don't see any way out of here other than how I came in. Please, help me."

"Sam's here with me. We'll go back to the stairwell and try to get through the rubble. Pescatori will be back with his helicopter and he'll help. We'll take the walkie-talkie with us, but it will have limited range. If we lose contact just remember that one of us will come back into range in the next half hour to touch base with you. In the meantime, hang in there, we're coming."

Sam mounted his bike for the ride back to the temple. Turning to McLaren, he commented, "It isn't going to be easy in that stairwell. There's a lot of debris in the way and remnants of the section of the stone column are blocking any entry to the area below. This is going to take a bit of time."

McLaren was well aware of the difficulties. Time was not on their side. Darkness would come on fast. He opened his mouth to comment, but the sound of his voice was obliterated by the loud noise of another aftershock rolling through.

****

Slowly, inch by inch McLaren and Sam carved a way down the stairwell. It was back-breaking work, but they were finally making progress.

I wonder if this is how the Egyptian slaves felt when they lifted the heavy rocks? McLaren mused.

"Can you help me down here on the yett? I'm hoping we can get enough purchase to bend it," Sam said.

Working with the pry bar they had previously used for Petkovski's evacuation, Sam was attempting to break apart the gate so that the two men could get past and enter the tunnel. He needed McLaren at his side to use the full force of their combined weight on his objective.

Sam's plan was working. The yett protested, squeaking loudly as they pushed and pulled on the lattice. Ever so slowly it began to yield to their torture; the old iron bars bent and the spacing between them grew marginally wider and wider until an old bar fractured.

Sam and McLaren were so intent on exerting pressure on the bars that they failed to notice the action taking place overhead.

In the sky above Pescatori was returning. He selected a landing spot and was about to set down when to his surprise his eyes caught sight of a dark colored helicopter coming over a rise. Its rocket pods were in clear sight. Years of combat experience came into play, triggering registration of a threat. Safety demanded that Pescatori alter his intended touchdown. In the blink of an eye he deftly maneuvered his helicopter sideways like a dragonfly in flight.

Sam was the first to hear the chopping sounds of the helicopter returning. Sensing another sound altogether, he looked up. It was like a flashback. On auto-pilot he shouted, "Gunship! Incoming!"

McLaren saw the flash from the right-hand rocket pod of the Russian-made chopper strafing a line of fire across the ground. A plume of smoke remained.

Sam pulled out a gun from a holster hidden at his ankle and commenced firing. Bullets peppered the Russian's helicopter's windscreen.

The cover spray had little effect. The Russian pilot held tight in a deafening hover just to one side of the plateau. Seconds later, it veered away and dropped out of sight.

On board Pescatori's helicopter Maya sat terrified, her eyes glued on the spot where the dark colored helicopter had disappeared. There was no way she expected the words that she heard next.

Above the thrum of the chopper blades, Pescatori shouted, "Maya, grab the Pelican Case – the large emergency pack. It's behind the seats. Get ready to hop out with it and run to the temple. Seek cover in the stairwell. That case should provide everything you need and then some. It's a might heavy. There's a military style walkie-talkie in there and I have one here to keep contact you. I'm going to position the bird at an angle so that you're not too exposed. On the count of three, jump out with the pack. Run for all you're worth. I'll cover you and so will the boys. Once you reach them, they can use the machine gun from the Pelican Case. I'll come back for you and the others once the Russians are out of here."

Maya opened her mouth to protest, "You can't be serious!"

"Deadly serious. I have to get the chopper out of here and the boys need what's in that case."

She looked back at him, dark eyes flashing, "What, I don't get a vote?"

Pescatori knew at that moment that she had what it takes. He brought the chopper around, put it in a low hover and looked at the petite young doctor beside him, "Ready on three?"

"Ready!" Maya jumped out in a hover exit.

She broke into a run, kept low, and sprinted across the open terrain to the temple, dragging the heavy case with her. Luck was on her side. No shots were fired. The Russians were still out of sight. Once she was well clear, Pescatori lifted off, banked, and accelerated away.

When Maya reached the portico, McLaren grabbed the Pelican Case from her. He gave her a hasty hug. He quickly released her and herded her down the stairs, almost shoving her through the new opening in the yet. In the safety of the underground tunnel, he passed the case to Sam.

The case held an excellent stash of emergency equipment but what was of most interest was the armory Pescatori kept on hand.

"Trust a decorated war vet to carry a machine gun in his emergency pack!" Sam laughed.

A gush of wind pebbled with grit from the dry plateau signaled the return of the Russian helicopter. It was followed by the rhythmic chop of the rotors. From the cover of stone entrance of the stairwell McLaren and Sam peeked out and saw a helicopter surge skyward over the ridge of the plateau.

The pilot of the Russian chopper banked, and the gunner's door came into view. Two vicious looking men in military fatigues popped into sight, uncoiling thick black ropes from the helicopter.

"Fast-rope descent!" McLaren shouted to Sam.

"They can forget that," Sam retorted. "Here's my pistol. If they try to descend, pick them off. I'm going to get the pilot."

"Are you kidding Sam? Hitting the pilot is a long shot."

"How much do you bet I can't do it?" Sam's impatience was evident.

"Why would I bet against you? I've known you long enough to have learned that if you say you can do it, you'll do it."

Sam clipped the fire selector to single shot, crouched and brought the machine gun to his shoulder, taking careful aim at the open gunner's door. He paused, then squeezed the trigger. His shot swiftly took out one of the men at the doorway. The others who were about to descend swiftly backed away from the doorway, affording Sam a clearer view of the interior.

Sam caught a glimpse the pilot's hands adjusting controls. Quickly switching the fire selector to the next round, he adjusted his aim towards the pilot, took a deep breath and pulled the trigger.

Maya's heart constricted. She looked on in horror.

The limp body of the pilot slumped over the controls and the now pilot-less helicopter shifted sideways dramatically. It began a nose spiral. Stuttering coughs emitted from the turbine. Fully out of control, it tumbled helplessly into the valley below the plateau.

Moments later Sam and McLaren saw the flash from a fiery explosion. It was accompanied by a deafening boom.

"It's a good thing that you didn't make the bet, McLaren," Sam said drily.

CHAPTER 42

We have to really move to find her. Time is of the essence. McLaren found it intolerable that they did not know where Danny was.

The incline of the cobblestone floor increasingly steepened while the low stone ceiling, supported by pillars and brick-vaulted archways, lost height. The tunnel snaked deeper and deeper into colder still air. The wall brackets that once held lighted torches all remained empty. McLaren held the flashlight steady while the three friends groped their way through the subterranean maze of rough-hewn walls. He was all too aware that more aftershocks could be expected. Countless tons of rock weighed over them.

"Watch your head. The ceiling was constructed for the height of the average human height more than a thousand years ago," McLaren warned.

"So far so good," Sam replied, his six-foot frame just avoiding a low-hanging protrusion.

"It's not a problem for me," Maya said, realizing that sometimes there are advantages to not being tall.

The passageway zigzagged, swallowing up the illumination. They were proceeding into a void. When they reached a fork, they had to make a choice, but both lengths of tunnel were pitch-black.

"Can you reach Danny on the walkie-talkie?" Sam asked.

"Negative," Maya replied.

McLaren ran the beam of his flashlight up and down the two corridors. It wasn't really obvious in which direction they should proceed. His senses probed the darkness like antennae. He reached out and placed his finger tips on the rough-hewn stone wall, feeling for some indication. Feeling nothing, he arbitrarily chose the right corridor.

A variation in resonance alerted him to a change. He no longer heard the scuff of their feet on the cobblestone. The right corridor must not be paved.

"Hold on, listen!" McLaren's emphatic words reverberated off the stone walls. The trio halted. When the echo stopped an eerie quiet descended. The haunting silence was broken by the dull sound of thuds that seemed to come from the path to the right.

"Sounds like we've found the right path!" Sam quipped.

"A good working theory. I'll accept it. Onward, this way!" McLaren called out waving his arm forward in a useless gesture that was lost in the darkness.

Several hundred steps through the soft shadows, the beam of the flashlight caught two figures from antiquity. Closer scrutiny by flashlight revealed they were stone sphinxes each guarding a side of an arched doorway. Their carved wings spread majestically in parallel to the vault, their muscular front legs emphasized the vertical lines of the entranceway.

"Wait! There it is again! I think it's coming from the other side of the door," Maya exclaimed.

McLaren stepped forward, bent over and with effort lifted the heavy iron stake that barred the heavy wooden door. He leaned in and gave the massive door a shove. It groaned open. For a half moment, he didn't breathe. A moment later, he stepped across the threshold. Adrenalin pumping, he beamed his flashlight into the chamber to probe the darkened room.

"Danny! Danny, are you in here?"

She's not here.

McLaren moved the beam farther into the room, sweeping it slowly to take another look around. His eyes were greeted by shimmers of light reflecting off golden pieces in the shadows of the subterranean room.

He stood, jaw clenched, gathering his thoughts, then turned to speak to his friends, "I don't..."

Before the words left his lips, he noticed movement in his peripherals. From less than fifteen feet away, in an area shrouded in darkness, he caught the glint of eyes looking out at him from the shadows.

Without warning a tall, slim shadow emerged from a dark nook and accelerated towards McLaren almost bowling him over.

McLaren felt arms tighten around his chest. He smelt the scent of his sister's silky hair the moment her ponytail swished the side of his face. He felt her sigh in relief when she snuggled up beside him.

"Marc, I knew you'd get my message and come for me!" Unseen in the darkness, tears of relief trickled down her cheek.

McLaren wrapped his arms around his younger sister, "Dan, you gave me quite a scare."

"Hey, me too!" Sam, eyes moist, strode forward to encircle Danny in an immense big bear hug. He planted a big kiss her cheek. "I think that was enough of a scare to last awhile, Dan. Please don't plan a replay."

Maya stepped up to embrace her friend, "Are you okay? I'm so relieved that we found you."

"Who in their right mind would just take off out here and go underground with a chap that was under investigation?" McLaren shook his head in a sign that Danny had once again tested the limits. Sensing her discomfort, he refrained from further upbraid.

Danny's head pounded. She lifted a hand to her temple and winced. She wished that she hadn't made the choice to follow the Macedonian.

Maya noticed Danny's reflex action, "Let me look at that cut on your forehead. I'd prefer to put a bandage on it before we walk out of here. Marc, can you get me some more light?"

Danny sighed, "I admit that I took a chance coming out to the facility, but I thought that Aleksander was a gentleman. In his office, I admired the etchings of this temple and he invited me to see the real thing. Of course, I jumped at the chance. I thought this was an opportunity to uncover a lead for us. He had a driver take us to the temple. He knew how to access a hidden stairwell and he led me down here."

"I would have been unnerved by the situation," Maya said, tending to Danny's wound.

"Aleksander said he would show me an artifact dating back to the time of Alexander the Great. He said it was one of the most profound relics from antiquity. He described it as the epitome of the alchemical opus."

"Didn't you have any reservations about going with him?" Sam asked.

"Not really. I wanted to see it," Danny replied sheepishly.

"A bit risky wouldn't you say?" McLaren said trying desperately not to launch into a tirade.

Ignoring McLaren, she said, "Aleksander was quite familiar with the passageway. I thought I had hit pay dirt when he lit the wall torches and the room took on an amber glow. My first impression was that the room contained an unfathomable wealth of antiquities."

McLaren simply shook his head.

"Then I saw it – the fretted mosaic – It's just like the one in photo on the flash drive. Will you look at this mosaic? Marc focus your flashlight on the predella, below the altar, over there."

The beam from McLaren's flashlight illuminated an intricate mosaic. It was a mesmerizing portrait of a warrior in battle. The Macedonian king and his black stead, Bucephalus, were portrayed in a pose that exposed the trauma of the battlefield. The artwork captured the implacable determination of Alexander the Great. The king's face was gaunt, his cheeks tautly shaped with deeply carved wrinkles, his luminous eyes widened in horror. Even the Gorgon's eyes on his breastplate were turned, horrified by what she saw. The artist had captured the warrior's mortality, vulnerability and mutability.

Maya let out a gasp. Danny was right. This mosaic looked like the one on Christopher's flash drive.

Danny's words tumbled along, "There was a sudden loud crack of thunder and the earth began to shake violently. Out of the blue, Petkovski turned on me. His eyes had the wildest look to them. When his big hands went for my throat, I thought he was going to strangle me. I realized that I had to do more than kick to fight back, so I reached up for the thick gold chain he always has around his neck. I pulled on it tightly, hoping to cut off his airway. I pummeled him for all I was worth."

Her friends exchanged looks of shocked dismay.

"Although I tried, Petkovski got the upper hand. I saw him charge at me. I felt his fists pounding my head the moment I yanked the chain of his gold pendant. Then, a shock ran through my spine, making its way to my chest. The next thing I remember is waking up on the cold cobblestone. Aleksander was gone, and the room was dark except for a bit of light from a torch on the wall. When I managed to stand and get to the door, I found it locked from the outside."

McLaren let out a deep sigh.

Danny unconsciously touched her bruised cheek. She hesitated before resuming her story, "I took the torch down to take a better look around. When I saw the dust sparkle in the thin shafts of light that fell on the golden pieces on the altar, I realized there must be air movement from ceiling vents. I knew you'd look for me, so I tried to get a message to you. I built a little fire to send out SOS signals from the large altar. The rest you know."

McLaren jaw tightened. He had feared the worst. "That was quite a predicament to find yourself in. You have no idea how relieved we are to find you."

In the torchlight Sam saw something glistening on the stone floor. He reached down to retrieve it.

"What did you find, Sam?" McLaren asked.

CHAPTER 43

"Let me see. Is it engraved?"

Sam passed the tiny rectangular piece to Danny.

"That's the gold pendant from the chain that Aleksander was wearing around his neck. I remember it. I was tugging on it when he was going for my throat. It's the last thing I saw before the lights went out."

Maya moved in closer to get a look at the pendant. Her eyes locked on the stylized Greek symbol phi, a zero bisected vertically by a line, engraved in the gold. She could scarcely believe it.

Could that be? She recalled what Tante Hélène had said about the artist Apelles and the symbol phi.

In the dim light McLaren caught the change of expression on Maya's face. "Maya," McLaren could almost see that she the wheels turning in her head, "What's going on?"

Maya took a moment to gather her thoughts, "My aunt related an interesting tale. It seems that Olympias clearly believed in her son Alexander's divine heritage and saw herself as custodian of his legacy. In a tribute to him, she had a temple built, the Temple of Eukleia, named after the goddess of glory. In this new temple she intended to lay his remains and personal treasures, including the famed Emerald Tablet. She commissioned his good friend Apelles to do artwork for the new temple. Always the joker, Apelles conceived the idea of recording the secret location of this temple. He hid a map pin-pointing the location when he painted a wall frieze over the door in the old royal tomb where Alexander's sarcophagus had been placed. According to the custom of the day, Apelles first created a painting to be the prototype for the frieze. The frieze can still be seen in the royal tombs. The prototype painting has long since disappeared, however there is reason to believe that it might have made its way to

Italy and been copied or adapted in a Roman mosaic in the House of Faun in Pompeii."

Danny listened with fascination, her eyes riveted on Maya, intent on hearing about the professor's findings. She moved closer to the mosaic. "So, I was correct when I said that I thought your cousin's photo of the wall frieze resembled a map. The mosaic here on the altar doesn't look like a map."

"Ladies, what's to say that this tale isn't a myth like so many other tales of treasures?"

"I'm inclined to believe my aunt, Marc. When I suggested to her that Danny, who is color-blind, discerned a map, my aunt used a state-of-the-art color-blind app to examine my cousin's photo of the wall frieze found above the door in the tomb that the Brigadier located. Tante Hélène is willing to bet that color-blind camouflage was one of Apelles's innovations and that the frieze was a map. He was such an impudent, spirited artist that the prank would have been just up his alley."

"So, did she say where she felt the map pointed?" Sam asked.

"Based on triangulation of the indicators, she believes it points to the Temple of Eukleia, in Macedonia," Maya replied.

"And you think that we are under the ruins of this Temple?" McLaren asked. There was incredulity in his voice.

"Yes. The floral temple markings are indicative," Maya replied.

There was a collective intake of breath. Sam let out a low whistle.

"The Roman historian Pliny, the Elder, who died during the eruption of Pompeii, wrote a Latin text about Alexander the Great and the Emerald Tablet. Pliny discussed an intricate map that identified where the Tablet was hidden. He also wrote that the Tablet would be revealed to the one who could decipher a riddle it posed."

"Did he know how the riddle went?" Danny asked inquisitively.

"Pliny postulated that the riddle might be derived from a stanza within the Tablet. The most likely stanza, my aunt thinks, would be: *What is below is like that which is above, and what is above is like that which is below.*"

McLaren tilted his head to one side, "That's quite the story, nonetheless we need to get out of here before more aftershocks hit."

"Oh, come on bro. It's not like we'll be down here again. Let's take a look around," Sam said, clearly having bought into the notion of a treasure hunt.

Maya looked directly at McLaren's eyes and made a request, "I realize the timing is not the best, but could we please take a look around?"

The question met with silence. McLaren wondered if his own sense of curiosity was threatening to override his judgment. Whether due to the contagious look in their eyes, or his desire to avoid an argument, he heaved a patient sigh, "Okay, I'm with you."

Maya smiled, "The use of that stanza is intriguing. It's a phrase that circulates throughout the occult and magical circles. It's been used by both writers and astrologers to explain why and how the world works, like the concept of the visible stars in the sky being linked to life on earth."

"Taken literally it could mean that what happens on any level can happen on the other, for example the macrocosm is as the microcosm, and vice versa," McLaren said.

"Alternatively, it might mean that the world displays structures on different levels. As above, so below is an artistic technique used in photography. I remember seeing a fantastic shot of a surfer dude at Teahupoo in Tahiti. The photographer used a special large underwater housing that gave a bubble effect which enabled him to capture the action both above and below the water. He photographed the over/under port and achieved a dual perspective. The photo was awesome," Sam said.

Sam's eyes were drawn to the ornamental design running around the outside of the mosaic on the predella of the altar. The border design consisted of repeated vertical and horizontal lines done in relief. Seeing his interest in the golden fret, Maya drew closer to him.

Maya stared at the fret and recalled that during her childhood she had often seen this type of design at Mayan ruins in Mexico. Her mother, who was trying to interest her daughter in archeology, had explained to her that it was called a fret or key and could be found in ruins worldwide, in Greece, Egypt, India, China, Scandinavia, and North and South America.

"If you think about what Sam said about the surfer photographed over and under port and we apply that notion to the fret in front of us, we might have our first clue here in the border of the mosaic. Some aspect of the rotation of the above and below about a central vortex, seems to have been the idea behind the use of that fret. The pattern and spacing is equal in spacing above and below," Danny said.

"That makes sense. Apelles would have completed this mosaic and he might have wanted to highlight a clue with this fret," Maya suggested.

Danny stared intently at the colorful mosaic, "Here are the indicators, right?" She drew her fingers along the diagonal lines made by the spears. "They're pointing to the hilt of Alexander's dagger. Strange, you'd have thought Apelles might have used gold here to match the design and highlight the head of the weapon, but he didn't."

McLaren ran his fingers across the ancient mosaic. The exquisite detailing was not quite even. He touched the hilt of Alexander's dagger and felt a small indentation, "It seems like something used to be in this depression."

Sam leaned in. He ran his index finger over the area McLaren had highlighted. In his other hand, he fingered the golden piece he had retrieved from the floor.

"Do you suppose it would be this?" Sam offered the golden piece engraved with a phi.

"Sam, I always knew you were more than a pretty face. Let me give it a try," Danny said excitedly.

Sam smiled and passed Danny the golden piece. Danny tried to insert it into the indentation. It was a match. In place, the tiny Greek symbol phi looked like it had always been part of the mosaic.

"My aunt said that the phi symbol was ascribed magical powers. It would make sense that Apelles selected it to be the x that marks the spot. The symbol phi itself plays on the theme of what is above is as below," Maya said.

"So, you're guessing that the phi symbol could be the keystone to the riddle," McLaren mused.

From the depths of his memory McLaren recalled a professor once lecturing that Adolf Zeising, the famous mathematician, had once stated that phi represented the golden ratio, a universal law of all formative striving for beauty and completeness.

Completeness, McLaren mused. He leaned over towards the mosaic and pushed his thumb against the golden piece.

To everyone's surprise the rock face on the left side of the predella moved. He pushed a little harder and something magical happened.

****

"I think we've found something!" McLaren shouted.

Sam pushed in closer to get a peek. "Talk about ancient meeting new, this is certainly the case. Ancient Macedonians definitely used stone pulleys, but they did not have polyester rope like this!"

"I thought that Archimedes invented the pulley and he came along well after Alexander. Didn't he study in Alexandria, the great city that Alexander commissioned?" Danny asked.

"You are partially correct Danny. Archimedes did come on the scene well after Alexander and he was a great inventor. He excelled in the design of war machines and his work on pulleys was a scientific landmark, but basic pulleys were around before him," McLaren said remembering a lesson taught during university.

"Well someone has updated the technology with modern polyester rope," Sam laughed.

"If the rope has been replaced, then someone has used it more recently. Let's see what happens when we pull the rope."

McLaren heaved on the pulley. To everyone's amazement a slab of rock shifted.

"Let me see!" Danny squeezed in beside McLaren.

McLaren hung onto the rope and stepped to one side for the others to see, "Take a look!"

Beneath the altar a little stream meandered under the rock face. Sitting on a rocky ledge in the stream basin was a gray-green tablet carved with unusual lettering. In the uppermost portion of the tablet a deep grass green stone with a slightly bluish cast sparkled.

"Good lord!" Danny peered at the tablet carved with ancient lettering.

Eager to have a closer view, Sam put one foot into the water and leaned to retrieve the Tablet.

"Don't touch it!" Maya shouted out with such vehemence that the trio half expected her to have a gun pointed at them.

"What?" Sam took his foot out of the water and glared at her, wondering what in the world was the matter.

"I thought you'd be thrilled to see this," Danny said looking at Maya in disbelief.

"It's not safe!" Maya said her tone firm. "Take photos of it if you like, but do not and I repeat, do not touch it!"

The three on-lookers had never heard Maya speak with such vehemence.

Holy cow, she's a real tiger when she takes charge! McLaren thought to himself.

"I know it's not safe. I suspect that the stone contains Thallium. That green hue on its face sets my alarm bells ringing. Aleksander Petkovski was in very bad shape and not just because a pillar fell on him. He showed symptoms consistent with Thallium poisoning. I wondered where he would have recently come into direct contact with Thallium. Seeing that Tablet, I think I know how. I am willing to wager that this relic from antiquity contains Thallium."

McLaren leaned in for a closer look. His expression was one of surprise and growing concern. Seeing the greenish color he said, "Okay, we should exercise caution. We'll need protective gear to handle that stone."

"Thallium is exceedingly toxic on contact with the skin. My guess is that Petkovski unwittingly touched it with his hands, without protection," Maya's eyes were locked on the glint of the Tablet lodged in the little stream.

"We came all this way to find it," frustration was clearly evident in Danny's voice.

"Aleksander Petkovski's hands showed signs that he had been in contact with a corrosive material. Because his symptoms resembled Thallium poisoning, I did some quick research at the hospital to find out more about it. The Allchar deposit here in Macedonia is the only area in the world were Thallium has ever been mined."

Despite hearing the conviction in her voice, Danny's reaction showed signs of disbelief. "Just by looking at it you are suspecting Thallium?"

"Thallium was at one time used in the "Clerci" solution, the standard for measuring the density of minerals. It was discontinued due to the high toxicity and corrosiveness of the solution," McLaren said.

"It's particularly dangerous because it is a compound that has high aqueous solubility and is readily absorbed through the skin. The initial acute symptoms of Thallium toxicity can include nausea, salivation, abdominal pain and gastrointestinal hemorrhage. It is so severe that death could occur within eight to ten hours. In cases where the Thallium disorders develop more slowly often the central nervous symptom is involved and the symptoms include: hallucinations, lethargy, delirium, convulsions, and coma. There are often circulatory problems that lead to cardiac failure," Maya reported.

"Are you saying that Aleksander Petkovski was displaying these symptoms?" Danny asked.

Maya nodded in the affirmative.

CHAPTER 44

Circling the plateau, Pescatori banked his five-seater Hummingbird and swept his dark eyes across the landscape. On the right side, in the valley below he could see the smoldering fuselage of the Russian helicopter that had almost taken out his chopper. Although no one was in sight, he was wary. He came around again, hovered and began to descend for landing.

He was edgy, and his expression reflected the apprehension he felt. Doggedly he checked the hands of his Nighthawk watch every few minutes. He felt like a sitting duck. Seismic activity was likely to continue. Daylight was waning and there was a good chance of another visit by the Russians. Worst of all he couldn't reach Maya.

Finally, staring grimly at the remains of the mangled Russian helicopter, he heard his walkie-talkie chirp.

"I take it you made it out unscathed. It's all good down here. We found Danny! What's more, we found something amazing! We have the Emerald Tablet in sight!" Maya exclaimed.

"That's incredible! I'm anxious to hear all about it. Don't stay down there too long. What with the seismic activity and the visit from our Russian friends, I would prefer that we get some distance from here," Pescatori cautioned.

He could hear Sam's voice now, "You don't happen to have protective gear on board, do you?"

Pescatori didn't even stop to wonder why Sam would ask the question, "Did you take a look in the upper section of the Pelican Case? You should find what you need in there."

The pilot knew that when Sam released the divider in the case he would find a hazmat suit, rubber boots, a mask, goggles and protective gloves.

"Should I ask how you come to be carrying these items?" Sam inquired.

"No, don't ask! It's for me to know and you to wonder!" Pescatori teasingly replied. "Keep in touch; I'll be up here waiting for you."

In the underground room Sam quickly donned the protective equipment and waded into the stream. It proved difficult for him to maintain his footing on the rocks. There were a few anxious moments. Finally, he was out of the water with his prize.

McLaren grinned. "Don't tempt the gods any further. Place it down on the altar so we can have a good look-see."

Sam laughed good naturedly. "You thought I was going to fall in."

The foursome peered down at the exquisite piece from antiquity. Still wet from coming out of the stream it appeared vibrant. Light reflected from the beautiful green crystal stone. The lustrous inner surface of the Tablet was carved in bas-relief. It held a mysterious message carried from the past.

"If it is Thallium it will lose its luster when it is exposed to air. It will appear to tarnish when it dries," McLaren warned.

****

Pescatori leaned back in the cockpit and pulled out his iPod. At first, he seemed relaxed; however, a sixth sense gnawed at him. It was like a feeling in his gut. He knew that he was not alone. He squinted into the distance, but could not make anything out. He reached for his binoculars and began to painstakingly observe the sky. He cursed himself for being careless and not taking sufficient precautions. The enemy was not gone.

It's probably a good thing I retired when I did. He reached for his walkie-talkie.

"I've got company! I just spotted a drone at one o'clock. That unique flying wing is telltale of a Russian Aero Zala 421-12, a micro-Unmanned Aerial Vehicle designed for surveillance and front-line reconnaissance," Pescatori reported.

"Either the Macedonian government is technologically right on top of things and is obtaining visual footage of the seismic action or someone is keeping an eye on the temple," Sam replied.

"Whatever. It's coming!" Pescatori snapped.

"That AUV is capable of two-hour flights within a forty-kilometer radius of its control station. It often carries a payload that includes a color video camera and a thermal surveillance device capable of viewing the lower hemisphere below the AUV," Sam reported.

Pescatori was reminded that Sam was always knowledgeable about flying machines, particularly when they had camera equipment.

The AUV was almost close enough for Pescatori to make out its markings in the dusk skylight when another one materialized.

"Guys, there's another one hot on its tail. The next one is larger. This last one appears to have a bigger payload capacity," Pescatori announced.

"What do you want to bet it's a Zala 421-16?" Sam said

"What would Russian drones be doing up there?" Danny asked.

For a moment her question was answered with dead silence. A second later came a staccato reply. "The predator's carrying a glide bomb. They're going to make another go!" Pescatori snapped.

It was the last communication they had from the chopper.

Pescatori knew he was vulnerable. With no time to get his whirlybird in the air, he burst out of the helicopter in a full run in the direction of the temple. The sprint made him short of breath. He dove for cover. He felt a huge rush of air whistle past his ear and a shell burst somewhere behind him.

There was no denying the hit. Pescatori felt the full impact. Woozy, he tried to use the walkie-talkie. It wasn't there. He realized he must have dropped it.

I'm losing my game.

Far below under the temple the sound of the rumble was muffled, but the floor shook with sufficient force to raise a cloud of dust. The four friends looked at each other with questioning glances.

"What just happened? Was that a seismic tremor? Was it a bomb?" Danny asked.

"Is Pescatori okay?" Maya asked, trying to keep her voice calm.

McLaren squeezed her hand. He could feel her body trembling.

"Come in old buddy. Can you read me?" Sam called out to Pescatori numerous times.

Each attempt to reach him failed.

Chapter 45

"We're pushing our luck. Quick, get the photographic shots you want of that Tablet and let's get out of here," McLaren ordered.

Maya longed to study the Tablet, but the stern expression on McLaren's face dictated that having further time with the artifact at this moment was not possible.

Danny sensed the tension in her brother's voice but nonetheless asked, "Why did Sam take it out of the water if we are just putting the Tablet back?"

"Danny, this treasure belongs to the people of Macedonia. We must not remove the Tablet or take anything from here. The people of Macedonia will want to protect and preserve this find. There is so much to study here, but now is not the time," Maya said.

Sam was anxious to get some artistic shots of the find, "Can you help me out on this Dan?" He hoped that by getting Danny fully involved in the photography would be able to head off any argument between the siblings.

Danny was more than willing to help. She held the torch at various angles so that Sam was able to take a full sequence of high-quality shots from different perspectives.

With the memory of Alexander's beautiful Tablet digitally preserved, Sam gowned up in the protective gear and picked up the Tablet. He climbed up onto the rock face that cradled the little stream and replaced the artifact in its secure hiding spot.

"Time to go," Sam picked up the Pelican Case and ushered the group out into the dark passage.

McLaren took the lead while they exited single file, trudging down the poorly lit tunnel back towards the entrance. Rounding the last corner, he felt a sense of relief when he caught sight of beams of light peeking through. Finally, the dark canvas before him had been punctured by a knife.

A heavy rumble rocked the tunnel. It was followed by several concussions in quick succession. The cobblestone floor began to tilt. The light ahead was lost and the space between the four friends became obscured by a cloud of thick dust.

When the cloud finally dissipated it was evident that they would not be leaving by this exit. It was blocked by a huge temple column that just had collapsed. Rubble around the column almost completely blocked the yett and the stairwell. Escape was impossible.

A cold sweat gripped Maya when she saw the way ahead blocked. She tried again, without luck, to reach Pescatori on the walkie-talkie.

This isn't good. Maya wondered what had happened to him.

"Wait a sec," McLaren said, looking through the iron bars of the yett.

Beyond the yett McLaren caught a glimpse of the ever-darkening sky. He focused on the heavy mass of broken columns blocking their way. The rope they had used with the lifting tackle to extricate the Macedonian lay on the steps amidst the rubble. His devious mind shifted into high gear. He would have preferred another way, but with the stairwell blocked there was really only one logical way out. He needed to retrieve the rope. He would have to get it through the grillwork.

Sam stepped forward and looked through the bars. He leaned towards McLaren and whispered, "This looks more like evidence of a dive bomb than seismic action."

McLaren nodded, "Not a cheery thought. Just help me get that rope. I've got an idea. I'm not sure what went on out there, but I think we'd better try to get the ladies out of here before anyone comes back."

Sam couldn't have agreed more. He flashed a pearly white smile in the direction of Maya and Danny to reassure them. Dutifully, he pulled on the rope, but to no avail.

The rope was tangled under the fallen columns, but by some miracle it was not directly under the weight of the massive stones. The four friends set up a brigade and passed rubble and rock segments through the yett. Finally, after moving what seemed a mountain of rock, they were able to get a clear shot at the rope and yank it through the bars.

McLaren looped the rope over his shoulder. "Okay, since this is no longer the way out, we'll head back to where we came from." He waved his arm over his head in a gesture that clearly meant follow me.

Shock registered on the faces of both women. Neither appeared pleased.

Sam did what was so characteristic of him and he made light of the affair, "Confucius say 'The pessimist complains about the wind. The optimist expects it to change. The leader adjusts the sails.' Our leader McLaren is adjusting our sails."

"You don't say?" Danny replied with more than a trace of annoyance.

Putting their trust in McLaren, they trudged back in a slow procession through the murky light. The monotonous passageway seemed to stretch to infinity. The sound of dragging footsteps made it obvious that the group was growing weary.

McLaren slowed at a fork in the tunnel, considering his alternatives.

Sam quipped, "You didn't think to sprinkle breadcrumbs, McLaren?"

McLaren knew spirits had not descended to an all time low when Danny spiritedly replied, "Sam, I would have eaten them. I'm starved."

After a good fifteen minutes, they arrived back at where they had started. The pair of ancient stone sphinxes guarding the entrance greeted them without a word. McLaren rubbed the right paw of the one on the right for good luck, then opened the heavy wooden door. He moved toward the center of the room, set down the Pelican Case he had been carrying and looked up at the 30-foot ceiling and the chimney vent hole that rose up another ten feet.

Danny moved over to his side and stared up at the ceiling, "I take it you have a plan, big brother?"

"Doesn't he always? He's spent a lifetime figuring out ways to beat the odds," Sam smiled remembering the creatives solutions McLaren had devised over the years for the scrapes the two friends had gotten into. His faith in McLaren went way back.

McLaren was listening and improvising at the same time. An idea had jumped into his head. He acknowledged to himself that this was another challenge where the chance of success was slim, but what the heck, he had to try something.

"The plan is for me to climb out of here through that vent and then pull each of you up using the rope that you're carrying," McLaren smiled.

"Oh, really," said Danny. Incredulity was obvious in her tone.

McLaren ignored her skepticism. He opened the Pelican Case, reached into the large lower compartment and removed a weapon like instrument that clearly resembled a crossbow.

"I caught a glimpse of these when we removed the hazmat suit. I think it will come in handy now," he said, removing a crossbow, a coil of thin Kevlar line, and a package of metal hardware.

From the package McLaren withdrew a collapsible titanium grappling hook. He attached it to the Kevlar line which he inserted into the crossbow mechanism. In doing so he noted the launching mechanism bore the insignia of the Ohio-based independent research organization that specializes in, among other things, national security innovations.

Sam wasn't surprised that Pescatori's Pelican Case held such a device. Predictably, his old buddy had contracts with a number of government agencies.

McLaren ran his fingers across the Kevlar line, no doubt selected for this application due to its high tensile strength. He recalled that it was rated five times stronger than steel. He removed a pair of metal Petzl Ascension ascenders from the package of hardware.

"Dan, can you make a foothold loop on the rope and a hand hold? They'll come in handy on the ride up," McLaren asked.

Sam looked on while McLaren assembled the device, "In Afghanistan we used grappling hooks something like that to breach tactical obstacles. We'd launch them in front of an obstacle and then drag it backwards to detonate the trip-wired land mines or set off the booby traps."

"Maybe that's why it's in the case. Today however, it's my ticket to ride," McLaren said.

"Mmm, there's a song about that," Sam chuckled.

After a quick series of checks, McLaren was set to go. He tied the rope securely on his waist, aimed and fired the crossbow up at the ceiling. The weapon emitted a soft swishing sound when it released the titanium grappling hook on the Kevlar line. The aim was true and the hook bit into the curved vent.

McLaren's risky plan was in full bloom now. He tugged on the line to test the resistance and found it taut. That was good news. It meant that the hook didn't have a flimsy hold. He didn't have a harness, but he had what he thought he needed. He secured the foot ascenders and attached the Petzl hand ascenders to the Kevlar.

Using his legs, upper body strength and grip strength honed from years of climbing, McLaren made his way up the line while the others looked on.

The ascenders slid up the rope easily. As McLaren drew closer to the ceiling another powerful vibration shook the cavern. Shale began to tumble from the ceiling. Like a heavy rainstorm, fine-grained clay and silt-sized sediment pelted down from above.

There were a few tense moments when it looked like the grappling hook might not have a firm bite. McLaren gripped the line tightly. Without the protection of a climbing helmet his only recourse was to look down at the floor far below him while attempting to shield his face from the falling stones. He wondered if the hook would hold.

Sam, Danny, and Maya stepped away from the cascading waterfall of stones. Hamstrung and lacking any means to offer assistance, they craned their necks and stared apprehensively while McLaren hung motionless twenty-five feet above them.

CHAPTER 46

Thankfully, the rock slide dissipated quickly.

McLaren could hear his own heart beating. He stared up at the cavern mouth gaping so many feet above. He waited for his breathing to calm down. Cautiously, he climbed a few more feet. His effort was rewarded. He now had a clear line of sight into the entrance way on the chimney style vent.

The rock surface was smooth but mottled, indicating perhaps that some kind chemical had leached out of the stone. He was forced to duck under the overhanging rock to climb into the last section of the chimney vent. The space proved to be tight, barely enough for him to wedge himself through. He tested the surface by kicking. Nothing crumbled.

Pressing himself against one side of the chimney, like an alligator he half crawled, half pulled himself, towards the soft light that crept through the openings between the loosely stacked rocks blocking the far end. A small wall of gravel had drifted up against the rocks. He scooped it away with his hands. Using the strength in his legs and feet, he thrust the rocks aside and heaved himself up and out.

The gentle wind felt cool on McLaren's face. It brought with it the smell of freedom. Overhead he could see the first evening star in the dusky skylight above. He took quick notice of his position relative to the temple. He was on a plateau. He slipped off his climbing equipment and set to work to pull the others out. He estimated the extra length of line he would need and attached the thicker rope to the Kevlar with a *carabineer*.

It had been agreed that McLaren would haul Danny up first. She was an experienced climber and would be able to model for Maya how to handle the ropes. She had also been down below the longest and McLaren was anxious for her to breathe some fresh air.

Maya was a quick study. She was so light that she was easily hauled up to the surface.

Pulling up the rear was Sam. He also chose to make the climb with the ascenders. With his customary panache, Sam enthusiastically climbed out of the chimney. He spread his arms spread high above him and stood like a colossus.

"I do like to make an entrance," Sam chuckled.

"Funny, I thought you were making an exit." McLaren grinned and, in a congratulatory gesture, high-fived Sam.

The moment of levity was very quickly replaced by seriousness. Off in the distance they could see the devastation that they had been lucky enough to miss while underground. On one side of them they saw the destruction of the temple which just a few hours earlier had stood timeless. On the ridge below the plateau lay the smoldering wreckage of a Russian helicopter. Tucked safely off to one side on a lip jutting from the plateau was Pescatori's helicopter. Not a soul was around.

Maya stared in bewilderment, "What happened?"

"Air strike," McLaren responded.

"Pescatori warned us that the drone he saw resembled a predator. His assumption looks to have been valid," Sam said, furtively glancing around and searching for clues.

Maya tried again to reach the pilot on the walkie-talkie.

McLaren let out a slow breath, his expression was grave. His mind whirred in puzzlement over Pescatori's fate. How was it that Pescatori's chopper was spared in the attack?

Sam's eyes were riveted on the shattered temple. The golden glow of the setting sun bathed the ruins in a dusky light illuminating the fallen columns. A good part of the beautiful stone structure was now just rubble. He could feel the hair on the nape of his neck prickle with concern and fear. Anyone buried under the collapsed pillars would have been crushed to death. If by some miracle they lay trapped inside a pocket, they would quickly succumb to suffocation.

"We have to find Pescatori. We need to conduct a thorough search right away. Darkness will be descending quickly," McLaren said.

He's an experienced operative, Sam thought. He sprinted over to use the communications equipment in the helicopter to radio for support. A sixth sense told him they were under surveillance.

Sam shepherded McLaren aside to confer, "Has it occurred to you that it's a trifle too peaceful?" In a whisper-quiet voice he traded conjectures with McLaren.

"So, this isn't random musing?" McLaren's brow line furrowed.

Sam gave him a nod that was off-set by a raised left eyebrow.

The men returned to where Danny and Maya were searching. The four of them thoroughly combed the ruins until they lost the light.

Sam was the first to indicate that for now continuing their search would be ineffective, "It's late. We'll have to call off our search for now."

McLaren agreed, "Maya, Danny, come on; we need to get out of here. Search and rescue is on the way. They'll have lights and equipment to conduct a more thorough look."

Despite being very anxious to continue the search, McLaren recognized that it had been a trying day. With the cool night air descending, it would be best to get everyone back to warmth and safety.

"We can't just leave," Danny pleaded.

"It's been a long day for everyone. The chances of us finding Pescatori in the dark are next to nil," McLaren replied.

Backup arrived soon. McLaren used his best psychology to convince the Danny and Maya that further search and rescue was best be left with the support teams. It was difficult to get them to agree.

In the end McLaren simply said, "I'm sorry. We gave it our best try. Right now, I'm going to speak with the search team."

"A lot of good our searching did," Danny replied. Strain was evident in her features.

The expression on Maya's face revealed the anguish she felt at not being able to find Pescatori.

Sam hugged Danny and kissed her on the top of her head. He could see that she was shivering. He put his arm around her and led her towards Pescatori's helicopter.

Maya trailed behind them, half-waiting for McLaren. She panned the scene desperately hoping to catch a glimpse of the chopper pilot who had so willingly given her a lift to this remote location. There was no sign of him.

McLaren provided the emergency support team with a statement about the circumstances surrounding Pescatori's disappearance. He supplied contact numbers and requested that he be contacted immediately if they had any news.

With a heavy heart, he walked over to the chopper. Common sense told him to leave the search up to the authorities, but he did not feel good about abandoning his friend.

With a sigh he looked back. *They are well equipped for the task.*

Like a seasoned pro, McLaren climbed into the cockpit and buckled in behind the controls. He lifted the Hummingbird off into the darkness.

Tears rolled down Maya's cheeks. Her petite body shook when she sobbed. Exhaustion had set in. She was so caught up in emotion that she was oblivious to the take off. It was not until they were up in the air that she realized that McLaren was at the controls.

Noticing her surprise, Sam flashed a comforting smile and said, "Chuck full of surprises, that's my buddy. McLaren's dad is a retired commercial pilot. He taught both his kids to fly when they were in their teens."

CHAPTER 47

The closed-door meeting at the Greek Center for Nuclear Scientific Research began at nine in the morning and was not over until dinner time. Representatives of the European Medicines Network who monitor the safety of medicines through a pharmacovigilance network sat side by side with scientists and contamination experts from the International Nuclear Safety Agency. They were collectively present to hear the results of the investigation into medical isotopes spear-headed by the Center for Nuclear Scientific research.

Dr. Dimitrios Souflias, Director General of the Nuclear Scientific Research Center, looking sophisticated in his tailored gray suit, made a short opening address in which he requested participants to continue to respect the secrecy of the proceedings. A news media blackout regarding the topics under discussion was still in effect. He announced that the CANDO task force had successfully rooted out the source of the problems. Manufacturing at that facility had been shut down. He introduced Dr. Patrick Shearwater, head of CANDO and Dr. Shearwater turned the meeting over to the project lead Marc McLaren.

The experts sat in rapt attention while McLaren delivered his presentation and explained the methodology, data, and findings. The high incidence of death in Southeastern Europe, following injection of the medical isotope was attributable to the specific activity of the product produced in a plant in northern Macedonia, being "off". When deployed, the resultant product was not pure Thallium-201 used in radioactive treatments. What was being produced at the plant in Macedonia was a product that contained non-radioactive Thallium, which was toxic when administered to patients. With greater vigilance, the proper product could be produced on spec and would be a viable alternative, helping to address the isotope shortage.

The question period that followed was lengthy and dynamic. McLaren fielded the questions with aplomb. He warned participants that due to the recent seismic activity in the area, the structural integrity of the Macedonian plant would have to be examined. If found whole, technical difficulties that led to an off-spec product could easily be rectified and the plant could produce much needed isotopes.

There was a round of applause from the participants. Dr. Souflias returned to the podium and announced that a written report on the findings would be forthcoming. He thanked the Canadians for their tireless work.

No mention was made of the Macedonian Aleksander Petkovski. Dr. Souflias had been shocked and saddened that an official with Aleksander's leadership capabilities would have been implicated in the illegal production of enriched Uranium. The less said the better until the entire case had been investigated and accusations confirmed.

Following the meeting Dr. Shearwater strode over to McLaren and pumped his hand vigorously.

"Terrific work, you and your team did a great job," Dr. Shearwater was in an unusually good mood. "Taking it from a statistical standpoint and examining the incidence of death following the administration of isotopes and correlating that to location and supplier of product was an excellent way to proceed. I particularly like that you added a medical doctor to your team to benefit from autopsy results. All in all, terrific," he repeated.

"Thank you. The team works very well together," McLaren said modestly.

"Just one little matter, the production plant in Macedonia," Dr. Shearwater left his sentence hanging.

"Yes, it was being used for the production of highly enriched Uranium," McLaren replied.

"Pity there'll be no conviction and sentencing of the CEO who ran the plant. However, from what I have heard he suffered a fitting conclusion for a villain who caused the poisoning and death of hundreds of innocent people in the name of power," Shearwater's tone was one of disgust. "I hear that the Russian benefactor for whom the CEO was producing enriched Uranium has vanished without a trace."

"We've seen the likes of him before. I'd estimate that it is only a matter of time before he resurfaces."

"You and the team have earned a well-deserved break. I've got another assignment for you. I'll brief you on it, but I recommend a few days R and R before you commence." Dr. Shearwater said with a smile.

****

Sam was waiting outside research center, in a little silver Porsche 911 when McLaren came down the steps.

"So how did your presentation go?"

"It was well received. You could have attended, if you wanted you know."

"Sitting inside has never been my cup of tea. I much prefer being on the open road and seeing the landscape change."

"I can see that!"

"Shearwater attended the meeting; I made the presentation. I'd venture to say that on the whole the INSA was relieved to have our findings."

"What about the Macedonian facility?"

"It's to be inspected for structural integrity, and then some," McLaren said alluding to the fact that the facility would be stripped of its enriched Uranium manufacturing capabilities.

"So, was the fact that the Macedonian was involved in nefarious activities even brought up?"

"No. It's a very complicated situation. The Greek and Macedonian officials were shocked by his death. They were horrified that he was involved in the illegal production of U-235. An INSA Security Force is looking into it. For that matter, members of the assembly were relieved that the plant was not destroyed and could be brought back on line to produce medical isotopes."

"So, our boss was pleased with the outcome?"

"Quite pleased," McLaren nodded and changed the subject. "Have investigators found any trace of Pescatori?" A somber expression revealed that he considered it a real possibility they had lost a friend in the skirmish.

For a moment Sam did not reply, "Well, a search and rescue team is still probing through the ruins."

There was something about Sam's tone that made McLaren stare intently at Sam's face. He had known him long enough to recognize that Sam was holding out on him. "What gives?"

"It's a mystery. It's as if he evaporated into thin air after he saw the drone."

McLaren looked straight at him and asked, "Did you try your international contacts?"

"Yup. I even tried that svelte chick that you had the hots for at that dinner, you know, the deep cover operative."

"I wouldn't say I had the hots for her. It was all in the line of duty," McLaren retorted.

McLaren was sure Sam was deflecting, "It's hard to believe that Pescatori would just disappear like that. Hopefully the authorities will find an answer."

"Do you want us to investigate?" Sam asked.

"Yes, because he's your friend, our friend; however, Dr. Shearwater and even the Americans have explicitly told us to leave it to state officials. But what about you? Are you content with leaving the search to them? I can see no reason not to look for him unless you're averse to disobeying those orders," McLaren asked.

McLaren watched Sam's expression carefully to assess his reply.

Sam appeared to mull the matter over. "Hmm," he answered, much to McLaren's surprise.

"Meaning, my friend?" McLaren pointedly asked.

Sam's response was not what McLaren had expected. He eyed Sam with such scrutiny that his friend fairly squirmed in his car seat. He was now certain Sam had more intel that he wasn't exactly sharing.

"Sam, I'm sure you are holding something back," McLaren snapped.

Sam grinned sheepishly.

"Interesting, that sheds a whole different light on the matter," McLaren said.

"Yup. I am quite confident that we can go back to Zermatt and resume our ski vacation," Sam chuckled.

CHAPTER 48

The evening was warm. The sky was filled with every shade of mauve and pink when the four friends strolled below the holy rock of the Acropolis toward the restaurant they had chosen for dinner on their last evening in Athens.

"The Strofi tavern is a fair hike from here but we can do it and then take a taxi back," Danny said.

"Is that the restaurant that overlooks the acropolis and serves traditional Greek food?" Sam asked.

"That it is," Danny said. She remembered that he had enjoyed the lamb stuffed with feta cheese on their last trip to Athens.

During the walk the four friends discussed the events of recent days. The Macedonian was the prime topic of conversation. Maya realized now that he had intentionally caused the deaths of three of her family members. There was little doubt that he had played a role in the crash of Swiss Air flight 111 off the coast of Nova Scotia that claimed the lives of her cousin Christopher and her father.

"Had my dad been able to present and share his research at that conference in Geneva, so many years ago, medical isotopes might now be produced with low enriched Uranium and the world-wide shortage might not have come about. But, the plane carrying him and his research went down, along with my cousin Christopher and his doctoral research on Alexander the Great and everyone on the UN Shuttle."

"I'd hazard a guess that Aleksander Petkovski felt that he had to take out the UN Shuttle. The NRU reactor at Chalk River was so old that he realized that, sooner or later, it would require a shut-down for repairs and that would lead to medical isotope shortages. Anyone with a capacity for strategic thinking could have predicted that scenario. He also knew that the Americans are highly opposed to production with highly enriched Uranium, particularly beyond their borders. Petkovski realized there would be a market for isotope production using Thallium. He positioned himself as a specialist in radiopharmaceuticals with the Americans. He lined up financial support from the Russian and he went for it. He anticipated the shortage and he sure didn't want your dad to be ahead of the game with a solution using low enriched Uranium produced and readily available using reactors in Canada."

"Petkovski was a narcissist in every sense of the word. He killed many innocent people. It's unthinkable what he did. All those people who died of Thallium poisoning when his plant produced off-spec product were victims of his narcissism. He was so intent on producing sufficient weapons-grade product that the quality control on the medical isotopes was all but forgotten," Maya said.

"There is now proof that he had a role in your uncle's death too," Sam said.

"He mistook my dad's twin, Matthew, for my dad. Dad and Uncle Matthew looked so much alike that it would have been easy to mistake them. It must have been a shock for Petkovski to see the likeness of my dad walking around at Chalk River when he thought he had died in the crash. He would have surmised erroneously that my dad had not been on that fateful flight," Maya said.

"From what we've gathered it appears that Petkovski poisoned your uncle at Chalk River with a drug that made it look like he'd suffered a heart attack," Sam said.

"What a waste of life. My uncle was a good man," Maya's eyes glistened with tears.

"Maya, Petkovski targeted you too – the accident on the highway, the break-in. He was after you because he was convinced that you had your father's research," McLaren said.

Maya felt a chill run down her spine. She remembered the death of the messenger at Pompeii. All that time she had not truly acknowledged that someone was out to get her.

"It's amazing to think that you discovered Petkovski's treachery by taking your cousin Christopher's Swiss knife flash drive to your aunt in Switzerland. It's curious that you found it on the dresser at the house your Uncle Matthew bequeathed to you," Danny said in an attempt to lighten the discussion when she saw Maya's pained expression.

"I think what must have happened was that my dad and my cousin were told that they couldn't go through airport security with their flash drives because they were knives. My cousin Christopher would have mailed his knife flash drive back to his dad, my Uncle Matthew, for safe keeping. Presumably he had his research on his computer and that would have ensured a backup. My dad opted to mail his knife flash drive to Tante Hélène, for a back-up, because he was planning on staying with her while he was in Switzerland, for the conference that he never got to attend."

"Petkovski's negligence in not ensuring that the product was on spec resulted in many deaths by Thallium poisoning. He thought so highly of himself that he felt he could use his position to gloss over the deaths his production facility had caused. He was intent on his reputation. He even tried to convince the community that there was no need to have CANDO conduct an investigation," McLaren said.

"When Petkovski took me to the temple, he told me proudly that he was a direct descendant of Alexander the Great. I think that from his standpoint possession of the Emerald Tablet was akin to custody of a ceremonial mace carried by a sovereign. When he began to tell me that he was descended from the Greek gods, that's when I began to think he was a megalomaniac," Danny said.

"Do you suppose Petkovski believed in the soothsayer's prophesy that whoever had Alexander's remains, would be invincible?" Maya asked.

McLaren nodded, "Maya, you put forward an interesting suggestion. How else would a man with his scientific training not realize that the Emerald Tablet contained Thallium? Exposure to Thallium by direct contact is most often lethal and yet he handled it."

"Well he wasn't exactly out for monetary gain for himself. He was financially indebted to his old Russian school friend," Sam said. "What's more, I'd say Petkovski had some ethical problems. He didn't see any harm in producing U-235 at the plant and shipping it off to his friend."

"He must have been elated when the NRU reactor was shut down. The opportunity he had been waiting for and working towards had arrived. There was a world-wide isotope shortage and he had the product to fill the need," McLaren said.

Maya stared thoughtfully, "Do you think that Petkovski knew my cousin had pinpointed the location of the Emerald Tablet?"

Danny was quick to reply, "That's a very strong possibility. With the security at the facility and at the mine, word might have gotten back to him that a young archeologist had been nosing around. Your cousin had photographs of the mosaic under the temple. Christopher must have been right in that very room."

"He was so close to the Tablet. I wonder if he actually got to see it?" tears glinted in Maya's eyes.

"I can't stop wondering about Aleksander Petovski's death at the hospital. Ultimately, he would have soon succumbed to death because of the Thallium poisoning, but I continue to have questions about the male nurse who was intent on putting meds in his line when there was no such order. Do you think someone was trying to hasten his demise?" Maya turned her head inquiringly.

"I doubt that we'll ever know," McLaren replied.

****

By five the following afternoon, McLaren and Sam had headed off for a briefing on a new assignment. Danny had remained in Athens with Maya to meet her aunt's flight. The two young women were now seated in the elegant Winter Garden in the Grande Bretagne hotel having high tea with Professor Jullian.

"So, will you be coming out of retirement to study the Emerald Tablet with the Macedonians?" Maya asked.

"Yes, I'm thrilled to be here in Athens and to have been asked to participate on this unusual collaborative project with the Greeks and Macedonians. It will be exciting to take up research on a project that my son initiated. Much has been written about the Emerald Tablet and it was believed that the artifact was lost forever. Now to have it in hand and have the privilege to be able to study it, this is not an opportunity to be missed," Professor Jullian said.

"You must be delighted with your son's research," Danny said.

"Yes, I really am proud of Christopher's work. He assembled the clues that led you to the Tablet. I know he wanted to discuss his work with me, but that never happened. I'm pleased that he had the presence of mind to back up his research on his flash drive and mail it back to his dad in Ottawa."

Professor Jullian avoided discussing his death. She always evaded the topic of the plane crash. It still pained her to think that she had lost her only son.

"All this was possible because your uncle left you our old home in Ottawa. I'm glad he did. You spent so much time there that it really is your home. Your uncle and I went through a rough period when I got tenure at the university in Switzerland. The distance meant that we couldn't hold our marriage together. Your uncle did a good job of ensuring that house was a home for you and Christopher," Professor Jullian smiled.

Maya thought she might have seen a tear form in the corner of her aunt's eye. "Yes he did. I used to love to go there after mom died. Dad was so caught up in his research. In contrast, Uncle Matthew always had time for kids."

"Well, I'm most appreciative that you found Christopher's Swiss Army flash drive and decided to give it to me in person," Professor Jullian smiled.

"It did make for quite an adventure," Danny said with a grin.

"The fact that you were able to discern a map within the photograph of the mosaic was quite amazing, Danielle. Most of us would have missed it, but then again, you and my son Christopher both are blessed with the genetic mutation of color-blindness. What a coincidence."

"I've never really heard anyone call it a blessing," Danny said with a laugh. "Speaking from the standpoint of a biochemist, it really is rather unusual. About eight percent of males, but only zero-point five percent of females are color-blind in some way or another. One would have expected my brother Marc to be color-blind, but no, he has great color perception and I have this 'blessing' instead."

"Well it certainly helped that you have this gift when it came to looking for clues," Professor Jullian replied.

Maya's face grew serious, "Researchers will need to be careful though. The Tablet contains Thallium. The Macedonian was not careful handling it. He must have carried it with his bare hands. You would have thought that he might have suspected that it contained Thallium since his own plant produced Thallium. His exposure in handling the Tablet caused Thallium intoxication that precipitated an attack on his central nervous system and that led to delirium, and eventually a coma. His death certificate reads cardiac arrest from Thallium poisoning. He definitely died a painful death," Maya said.

Professor Jullian's eyebrows rose in speculation, "My god, two Alexanders, each with similar reported symptoms at death and each having contact with the Emerald Tablet."

Maya tilted her head to one side considering, "It makes one wonder, doesn't it?"

"For years now, various theories have been put forward for Alexander the Great's mysterious death, including: intestinal bug; malaria; typhoid; and West Nile. There have been conspiracy theories too, but that assumption often comes to the forefront when a famous young person dies unexpectedly," Professor Jullian said.

"In medical school, we did a Cold Case team exercise where we had to put forward the cause of death of Alexander the Great. Using information garnered from detailed accounts recorded in history, we looked at whether his death might have been attributable to alcoholic liver disease or strychnine, but there was little data to support either. We considered that his wine might have been poisoned with a flowering shrub called white hellebore, which attacks the central nervous system. We ruled it out because it didn't fit all the symptoms," Maya said.

"Interesting, tell us more," Professor Jullian murmured.

"Historical accounts mention that in the week prior to his death, Alexander experienced chills, sweats, exhaustion and high fever, which are typical of infectious diseases including typhoid. Another diagnosis put forward was West Nile fever. Our group of medical students ruled that out because it normally tends to kill the elders or those with weakened immune systems. Besides, there was some evidence that West Nile Encephalitis could not have infected humans before the 8th century AD. It was first isolated in 1937 in Uganda. Also, assuming a similar climate to the present day, in temperate areas like Babylon, mosquito breeding may run from March through December, but reported cases of the disease in Israel have been from July through September, so the chances of Alexander dying from it in May are mitigated," Maya said.

"I thought that West Nile only concretely emerged globally recently," Danny said shaking her head.

"So, what did your team decide about the cause of death?" Professor Jullian asked.

"We concluded based on the historical information at hand, that Alexander's final illness was more characteristic of typhoid fever than West Nile. Typhoid can cause paralysis that spreads from the feet to the head. The shallow breathing that occurs would make a victim look dead. Our team suggested that this may have been why Alexander the Great's body did not seem to decompose," Maya said.

"Whoa. Are you telling me that the symptoms experienced by Alexander the Great are similar to those which you saw Aleksander Petkovski experience?" Danny asked.

Maya could almost see the wheels turning in Danny's head, "They are. Both had gastrointestinal troubles, nausea, vomiting, abdominal pain, headache, fatigue, hallucination, lethargy and delirium. The fact that Alexander the Great's body did not decompose probably related to a coma, which my team proposed at med school, but Thallium ingestion can also result in a coma."

"Are you speculating that Thallium poisoning might have been the cause of Alexander the Great's death? In all my years of study I have never heard of anyone ever considering it as a probable cause of his death," Professor Jullian said, her eyes widened in surprise.

"An autopsy would yield information, but for that you need a body. However, if it was death by poison it might be difficult to prove unless he was poisoned by heavy metal, which Thallium actually is. It's not clear how long other types of poisons would survive in bones for thousands of years," Maya said.

"Alexander the Great was known to treasure the Emerald Tablet. If he had handled it directly, and one might reasonably assume he did, then he could very well have died of Thallium poisoning," Professor Jullian hypothesized, a scholarly glint showing in her eyes.

CHAPTER 49

𝄢𝄢𝄢𝄢𝄢𝄢𝄢𝄢𝄢𝄢𝄢𝄢𝄢𝄢𝄢

A light mist hung over the water, extending to the edge of a bay where the shore rose up like an amphitheatre of lush Mediterranean vegetation into vineyards and woods.

Maya sat in the warmth of the sunlight on a bench in her aunt's garden, savoring the sweeping view of Lake Geneva. Below, the Swiss town of Montreux was nestled on the shore against a backdrop of snow-covered Alps. She inhaled the fresh mountain air, enjoying the serenity of the alpine scenery. So much had happened. She was glad she had made the decision to stay with her aunt a few days prior to returning to Canada.

The crunch of footsteps approaching on the crushed stone walkway interrupted her thoughts. She glanced in the direction of the sound and was astonished to catch sight of a familiar tall figure.

"Marc McLaren, what a surprise! I didn't expect to see you back here. I thought that you were off on another assignment," she tucked a strand of her dark hair behind her ear.

She looked up and smiled.

He grinned back. He thought Maya looked lovely in the simple white eyelet sundress. It accentuated her naturally tanned complexion.

"Work has been a bit crazy. I meant to contact you. I hope you'll forgive me," he looked for some indication that she accepted his work first approach to life. He was encouraged by the smile in her doe-like eyes.

"You're forgiven," Maya said stretching up on her tiptoes and planting a kiss on his cheek.

"Speaking of work, I really want to thank you for your contribution to our work on the isotope poisonings. Your help with the autopsy results really moved the project along. That's why I'm here. Our team is wondering whether you'd be willing to fit in some contract work with us when you are back in Canada and working at the hospital?"

Maya murmured her thanks but kept her eyes on the mist on the water. She was both elated to see him and yet somewhat disappointed by his invitation. She had quite enjoyed working with his team and now considered them close friends. At the same time, she was disappointed. She knew too well that long hours of work without someone to come home to can leave a void. McLaren was obviously devoted to his job, but she had been hoping that he might have a special place in his heart for her. Now it seemed obvious that he was just here her to recruit her.

"So that's the purpose of your visit today?" Maya said, looking directly at his handsome face. She paused before she gave her reply, "Yes, I think I would be able to fit in some contract work with CANDO." She was trying hard to mask her feelings for him.

"Great, so are you okay if we drive into town and complete the paperwork?" She nodded.

They got into the alpine white coupe which McLaren had rented and headed down the lane to the main road. To Maya's surprise they turned left, in the opposite direction to the town.

"I think you were supposed to take a right," Maya said.

"No, I think in this case the left seems really right," his deep blue eyes crinkling in mirth while the BMW M6 let out a mellifluous snarl through its four exhaust pipes.

"Please explain that one?" Maya asked, wondering what he was up to. She knew from Danny's stories that he could be a prankster.

"It will be clear soon. Just sit back and enjoy the ride," McLaren said, zipping the BMW M6 into fifth.

Maya turned her head and watched the trees fly by the windscreen. She wondered where he was taking her.

His left hand firmly grasped the leather steering wheel while his right hand ran the gearshift through its paces. McLaren was in his element, enjoying the feel of the road in the open road cruiser. He rounded a rise, pulled into a lookout point and parked. He extricated his tall body from the cockpit, walked around the vehicle, and opened the passenger door.

Her sense of surprise made the moment magical. In the still air the musical charm of cowbells tinkling echoed on the nearby slopes of snow-capped mountains.

McLaren leaned down, took her hand in his and helped her out of the roadster. He stared into her velvety brown eyes and intertwined his fingers in hers. Gently he pulled her towards him in an embrace. His lips hovered close to hers before he kissed her softly. "You know, I've wanted to do that for some time. Work kept getting in the way."

She kissed him back, snuggling in closer to him. She felt the roughness of his jaw.

"I don't suppose you would come with me on a little trip?" he whispered nuzzling his lips next to her ear.

Smiling up at him, she tilted her head to one side and responded, "That might depend where. I've noticed that some of the places you go hold an element of risk."

"Remember I said left seems right. Left takes us back to Zermatt. I'd like us to start over again and really get to know each other. There might even be some late season skiing left up there. Will you come with me? He put his arm around her waist, pulled her close and planted a long lingering kiss.

THE END

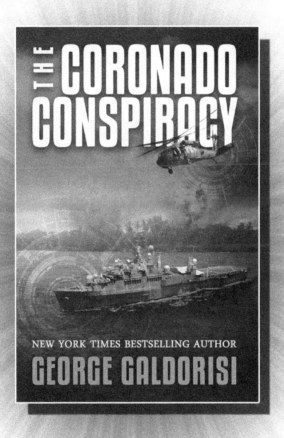

**THE THOUSAND YEAR REICH MAY BE
ONLY BEGINNING...**

ALLAN LEVERONE

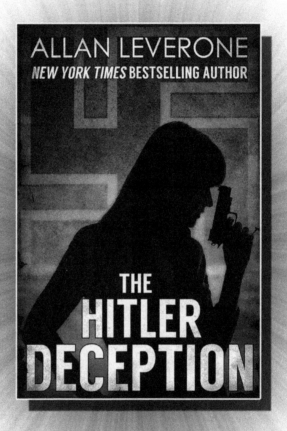

A Tracie Tanner Thriller

www.braveshipbooks.com

IT HAD ALL GONE TO HELL SO QUICKLY...

KEVIN MILLER

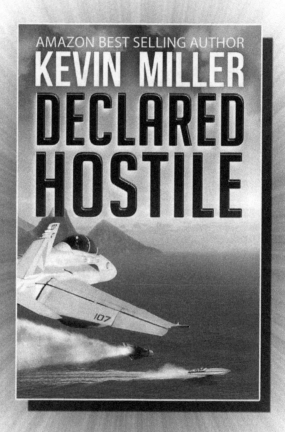

When does a covert mission become
an undeclared war?

www.braveshipbooks.com

THE HATE IS DEEP.
THE CAUSE IS SILENT.

JAMES MARSHALL SMITH

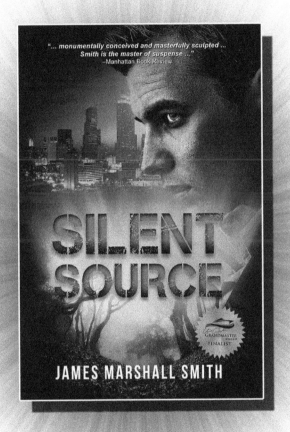

"... monumentally conceived and masterfully sculpted ... Smith is the master of suspense ..."
—Manhattan Book Review

SILENT SOURCE

GRANDMASTER AWARD FINALIST

JAMES MARSHALL SMITH

Time is running out...

9 781640 620735